About Th

Mark Yarwood has worked in animation, edited a small press magazine, written for television and the Plymouth Evening Herald. He was born in Enfield, North London and now lives in Plymouth, England with his wife and daughter.

His website is www.markyarwood.co.uk

Also by this author

SPIDER MOUTH
MURDERSON
LAST ALIVE
WELCOME TO KILLVILLE, USA
UGLY THINGS

THE AMOUNT OF EVIL

MARK YARWOOD

BiscuitBooks

This novel is entirely a work of fiction. The names, characters and incidents portrayed in it are the work of the author's imagination. Any resemblance to actual persons, living or dead, events or localities is entirely coincidental.

BiscuitBooksPublishers

A Paperback Original 2014

Copyright © Mark Yarwood 2014

The Author asserts the moral right to be identified as the author of this work

Printed and bound by Createspace.com

ISBN-13: 978-1499611083

All rights reserved. No part of this publication may be reproduced, stored, or transmitted in any form or by means, electronic, mechanical, photocopying, recording or otherwise, without the prior permission of the publishers.

Cover by Andy Hall of Frank Design Associates Limited

In memory of

Andy 'Wolves' Staunton

ACKNOWLEDGEMENTS

Once again I have many people to thank who helped me during the writing of *The Amount Of Evil*, but first I must mention my very supportive wife who has put up with my writing obsession, aswell as all the 'murders'.

Secondly, I must once again give thanks to John Hudspith, my editor, who has supported, advised, and repeatedly told me to 'Cut the fluff' throughout my writing process. His advice and suggestions have been invaluable as always.

I must thank fellow writer, Simon Dunn, for his technical advice, and continuing friendship.

Now I want and need to thank Maureen, John, and Alan Yarwood for their continuing love, encouragement and delicious sandwiches.

Andy Hall of Frank Design put the cover together with his usual skill and flare, and I thank him greatly for his hard work.

Issues dealing with police procedure were researched using the excellent book *The Crime Writer's Guide to Police Practice and Procedure* written by Michael O'Byrne. I also ascertained relevant material from PC Faye Webb. Thanks to Lizzie Fugeman for her proofreading skills.

Finally, I'm going to thank Maggie for everything she's done for me, my wife, and little Edie.

PART ONE
THE PUNISHMENT

CHAPTER 1

She thrust open the door, lurched forward, feeling the cold mud beneath her feet, the horizon rocking as she ran. Her chest pounded out a beat, a scream hovering in her throat, tears burning her cheeks and blurring her vision. Her legs fell away, slid behind, her hands shot out, sinking into the black mud as she fell to her knees. *Where? Where are they?*

She twisted her head round, gasped out a breath as she looked towards the open back door of the house. There was blackness inside the doorway- just shadows. She felt her heart again, racing, booming so loud. *Quiet. Must be quiet. Oh God, please.*

The darkness moved. The figure stepped out of the doorway, his eyes barely visible through the mask, the shotgun still in his hands. He took another step, then another, coming so slowly towards her. She scrambled to her feet, slipping as she sprinted towards the trees, seeing the dawn hiding beyond the hillside.

Please let me live! Please. Oh, please forgive me.

She looked back again. No. He was close, the gun lifted in his hands, pointing at her. She spun round and ran, feeling the scream pouring out of her mouth, vibrating her throat. She slipped and fell to her knees once more. Her tears poured down her cheeks, her hands shaking, lifting to pray to some higher force.

Please forgive me!

The masked man lifted the gun gently, so slow, and aimed. He took a deep breath as he saw his prey scramble and try and get away. He smiled as he found the trigger. Moving target, he whispered to himself, and took another deep breath. Now she would die. Now she would understand.

Watching her head turn, tears streaming down her white face, he squeezed the trigger.

The gun bucked in his hands, filling him full of power, sending the blood pounding through his head.

Blood burst from the back of her head and she slumped forward, her face sinking into the thick mud. He nodded, turned round and walked back to where his brother was still at work. He smiled as he stepped inside the house, knowing they were doing good work.

CHAPTER 2

Detective Inspector Jairus squeezed his bulky frame into the compact 60s style chair that Dr Sandra Ingham had plonked in the middle of her office. He tried to smooth down his new dark brown suit and sighed. Then he looked up and attempted to smile at Dr Ingham, to look relaxed, and suitably calm and at ease with the events of last June.

Almost one year ago.

He caught sight of himself in the mirror on the wall, saw his thick head, shaved brown hair. They were right, he did sometimes look like a Neanderthal.

'So, how've you been since the last time I saw you?' Ingham asked. She was dressed in her usual grey slacks and cream blouse. She was skinny, painfully so, Jairus thought. Her short, bobbed brown hair somehow made it worse, brought too much attention to her skeletal face.

'Great,' he said, 'I'm doing great. I'm back to work tomorrow and I'm looking forward to it.'

'You feel ready to return to work?'

'Yeah, definitely. I get bored sitting round.'

She smiled and wrote something down on her pad. 'That's good to hear. And what about the incident? Do you still think about what happened? Any nightmares? Flash backs?'

Jairus looked down and saw the knife in his hand.

Blood coating the blade, some on his white shirt. Carl Murphy lying on the floor, curled up in a ball, whimpering. 'No, none of that,' he said, avoiding her eyes. 'I don't think about it that much. It comes and goes.'

'And the guilt? You said, when you first came to these sessions, that you felt a great deal of guilt.'

After smoothing down his trousers, Jairus said, 'I was found innocent of any wrongdoing by the CPS. They concluded I'd acted in self-defence.'

'That doesn't stop you feeling guilt. You took another man's life. Naturally you'll carry the sense of guilt for a long time.'

'Carl Murphy was not a nice individual. I don't think evil is too strong a word.'

Dr Ingham went to open her mouth, but Jairus raised a finger when his mobile rang. He took it out, pulled himself out of the chair and turned away. 'Yeah, this is DI Jairus. What's that? Where? Yeah, I know where that is. I'll be half an hour.'

'Work?' Dr Ingham asked, frowning a little.

'Yeah, sorry, bit earlier than expected. Got to go.' He shrugged and opened the door.

'Remember, DI Jairus, guilt doesn't just go away. I recommend you come and back and see me soon. We've still got a lot to talk about.'

Jairus nodded, rushed out of the office and jogged to his car.

Jairus parked at the end of the long drive that snaked up the steep bank to the lonely house sitting on the edge of the field. It was obviously one of those postmodern constructions, but to Jairus it looked as if someone had dropped a gigantic greenhouse onto a plain brick building. He got out of the car and walked slowly across the drive and towards a pathway that went all the way up to the front door. He put his hands in his pockets and looked across the vista, taking in the hazy and very distant view of the City of London. He could barely make out Canary Wharf and the surrounding skyscrapers.

He looked round and saw Detective Sergeant Peter Moone striding towards him, his face blank. It had been months since they had seen each other, but Moone looked the same- short and lithe like a greyhound. Moone was just into his forties, but he looked younger until you got up close and saw the stress carved deeply under his blue eyes.

'Sorry to pull you back in like this, Jairus,' Moone began and swung round, pointing a thin finger at the house, 'but we've got two dead bodies, not enough manpower, and not a bloody clue.'

'Are the bodies inside?' Jairus nodded to the house.

'First one's round the back.'

Jairus followed Moone along a bricked pathway that led around to the back of the house. Moone stopped Jairus, pointed to the SOCOs' van, that was parked a few feet away, and said, 'They're still cleaning up inside, doing their bit and all that. Follow the duckboards and I'll show you the first victim.'

'What've we got?' Jairus slipped on some overshoes, then followed Moone along the duckboards and towards a white tent the SOCOs had set up at the back of the very muddy garden.

'Like I said, two DBs. One female, about mid-thirties, the other is a man in his late fifties. Father and daughter. Thomas and Marie Henry. Wait a minute.'

Jairus looked down at the bony, white hand that was gripping his sleeve, and looked up into Moone's watery eyes. 'What is it?'

'How's things?'

'Fine.'

'You OK to do this?'

Jairus shook his head and gave a brief laugh. 'I'm forty-five years old, Pete, so I don't need anybody to hold my hand. Yeah, I'm good, thanks for asking.'

'Anytime. I mean it. You can talk to me. Scout's honour.'

'Yeah, I know.'

With the tent opened by a passing SOCO, Jairus slipped inside, followed by Moone. He looked down, watching the white bodies of the SOCOs taking pictures and swabbing for clues. The woman was face down, her hands deep in the mud. Her long brown hair was sprayed out, matted with blood and brain matter. The mud around her head had a slightly red hue. Jairus knelt down, then looked up towards the back door of the house, along to the muddy footprints leading away from the doorway, each one marked by a small and numbered yellow plastic square.

'She was on her knees,' a voice said behind Jairus. He turned and saw Dr Jeremy Garrett, dressed in a green forensic outfit, stood in front of Moone.

'Wait.' Jairus held up a hand. 'Let me see if I can figure it out, just for old time's sake. You know, to clear away the rust.'

'Go ahead.' Garrett folded his arms.

With his feet stretched over two duckboards, Jairus looked down at the muddle of footprints, noting the ones made by size eleven boots and the others created by the woman's size six ballet pumps. He turned round and faced his audience. 'She was running for her life, but slipped over. The killer, who is tall, judging by his boot size and the length of his stride, walked slowly after her, taking his time. He wasn't in a hurry.'

'Well done,' Moone said, 'but you haven't seen what's inside. Wait until you get a load of that.'

Jairus followed Moone into the house, careful not to disturb anything, his hands buried into his pockets, his eyes scanning over every object in the large open-plan kitchen. It was certainly an expensive, generally well-designed abode, but not to Jairus' taste, as he liked something more traditional.

They stopped halfway across the tiled flooring, looking down at the sight that made Jairus take in a sudden breath. He kept calm, but his mind reeled backwards a year.

He saw Carl Murphy on the floor, his mouth gaping open, trying to suck in another breath. Pleading for mercy.

He shook his head and took in the body on the floor. Face down. Sprawled out in a star shape. Except his arms and legs were not attached anymore. Neither were his fingers. They had been sliced off and discarded across the floor. The blood was so bright red against the white tiles.

The head. He looked at the bloody stump of the neck, the spatters of blood spewing out from the open wound.

'What're you thinking, Jairus?' Moone asked.

'I'm thinking the cutting was done when he was alive, hence the amount of blood. The killer started with the fingers, then the arms. He wanted him to suffer.'

'We found another set of boot prints outside, coming from and to some tyre tracks. About size nine. The vehicle was parked on the left of the house.'

'Two of them, eh?'

'That's what the evidence suggests.' Moone swung round to Jairus, hands in pockets. 'You not going to ask me about the head? That's the best part.'

Jairus stared at him, flashed a smile, then looked again at where the head should have been. Souvenir? There had been so many famous killers that liked to keep their victims' heads that it was impossible to keep count. Jeffrey Dahmer for one, but that was about possessing a person, keeping them near. This was about suffering, punishment. And Moone looked actually stimulated, which meant he'd either stopped off for his morning double espresso or something very unusual was coming. 'OK, Moone, where's the head?'

Moone raised his eyes upwards, then pointed to the spiral staircase at the very end of the long kitchen. Jairus followed him. Moone took the stairs two at a time, then slid open the glass door that led to the roof. Jairus looked round at the rows of solar panels, something that would probably help reduce the heating bill, not that whoever owned the house would need it.

Moone pointed to back of the house, so Jairus looked up and focused far out across the metal roof to where his colleague was headed. At first, he saw the shape of it, like a weird kind of large matchstick, poking out of the centre of the roof. He walked closer, stopped and moved round and took it all in.

The metal pole had been hammered into the roof. He followed the pole all the way up until he was looking at the head in profile. Then he stood on the edge with his back to the drop behind him, just so he could see the face.

Thin face. Bony looking. Eyes shut, mouth slightly open. Skin white, hollow round the eyes. Blood around the neck. Lots of cuts. They didn't do it cleanly.

'So, what're you thinking?' Moone asked.

'He was obviously the main target, hence the

torture, mutilation and beheading. They took their time with him, and didn't hesitate when they found they had her as a witness. Bang. She's dead. They used to put traitors' heads on pikes, to deter others from committing the same act. Maybe they saw this man as a traitor.'

'Maybe they tortured him to find his money,' Moone said, shrugging.

'Found an open safe or anything?'

Moone shook his head, so Jairus strode back across the roof and through the sliding door and down to kitchen. The SOCOs were taking photographs of the body, so he moved round them, hearing Moone coming down the spiral stairs behind him. Jairus crouched, scanning the tiled floor, focusing on the pool of blood. It didn't seem to have spread out very far. He lurched forward and laid down on his front, closing one eye. Yes, the blood was seeping downwards, gathering between some of the tiles. He got up on his feet again and saw Dr Jeremy Garrett standing just outside the back door talking on his mobile phone.

'Excuse me, Doctor?' Jairus called out. 'Can we move the body yet?'

A SOCO came over and pulled off their white hood, revealing a middle-aged female face, rather bloated and red in the cheeks. 'Cate Benton, Crime Scene Manager. We're done with the body now. I'm curious, what have you seen?'

Jeremy Garrett walked in, putting away his phone. 'What's going on?'

'I need your people to move the body,' Jairus said, then he stepped back and joined Moone in the hallway where he was now holding an evidence bag.

'Look what I found,' Moone said, holding up the bag, a British passport clearly visible through it. 'The woman's passport.'

'Did you find his?'

'No, but hers was in a bag with some clothes, underwear, all that sort of thing.'

Jairus nodded. 'She was getting ready to do a runner. What's the timeline?'

'We're looking through CCTV and traffic cameras to see when they arrived. The tyre tracks suggest a four by four, Land Rover or something similar. We'll find them on one of the cameras. The woman's been dead about five hours. Not sure how long they worked on him.'

'They would've taken their time,' Jairus said and watched the man's body being bagged up by three SOCOs and lifted from the scene. He nodded to himself. He was right, the blood was seeping into the tiled floor and some of the tiles were crooked. 'Someone got some gloves for me?'

Dr Garrett passed him some gloves and he pulled them on, then crouched down, careful not the step in the blood. He took hold of the corner of a tile and lifted it, then another, until he was looking down at the door of a floor safe. When he reached in, he found the door was open. He opened the door all the way, then stood up and stepped back so everyone could get a good view.

'Bloody hell,' Moone said and gave a laugh. 'That's a lot of money.'

'Yes it is,' Garrett said and whistled.

'They allowed him to show them the money,' Jairus began, 'just so he'd think they were going to except his offering and leave. To add to his agony. This was about revenge.'

'Maybe we've just got a couple of psychos in town,' Moone said. 'It's happened before.'

'I don't think so,' Jairus said and walked through the house, finding a wide and winding staircase that led to the next floor. He was in the master bedroom looking at a white and clinical room. Everything was in its place. On the bedside table was a book about electronics. Nothing else stood out. He went to the pillow on the right side of the bed, an imprint of a head clearly visible. He looked at the other pillow and lifted it up, revealing a large kitchen knife.

'Thomas Henry was a self-made millionaire,' Moone said, from the end of the bed. 'Started a computer company in the nineties, then sold it and disappeared.'

'He knew they were coming for him.' Jairus lifted up the knife.

'Maybe. Or maybe he was just paranoid. He was rich and maybe feared being kidnapped or…'

'Then you hire some kind of bodyguard…but there isn't any sign of that, is there? Just a man and his daughter, and a knife under his pillow. Maybe it was something he didn't want anyone else to know about. Something he was ashamed of.'

Jairus passed the knife to Moone, then moved to the built-in wardrobe and slid it open. There were rows of tailored suits and shirts. Everything was neat, just like the rest of the house. He reached in and ran his gloved hand over the material, then stopped. He frowned and looked closer. It was a black and red dress, something a wealthy lady might wear to a party. What looked like diamonds ran along the hem of the dress in a strange pattern. Jairus pulled it out and laid it out on the bed. 'Why's he got an expensive dress in his wardrobe?'

'Cross-dresser? I don't know. I'll bag it up with the rest of the stuff. You still living at the house?'

'No, I sold it. I'm renting a flat in Southgate. Who

found him?'

'Guy who lives a few miles away. Said he'd popped over to visit. His name's Edgar Holzman.'

Jairus closed the wardrobe. 'Where is he?'

'At the station. You want to talk to him?'

'Yeah, of course I do.'

CHAPTER 3

With the flowers held tightly in his hand, Terence Marsland stood on the edge of St James cemetery. He stared down the narrow pathway that led all the way past the grey gothic looking church and down to the graves at the far end. He took in a deep breath, closed his eyes, pushed away the images that kept coming back, then walked along the path. For awhile he was doused in shadows until the sun swirled in his eyes and the shapes of graves formed in front of him. He stopped and took in the gigantic and ornate carving of an angel praying. He shook his head and moved on, heading for the smaller graves by the fence.

By the time he reached her headstone, she was with him. Her face was misty, sort of obscured, but she was there nonetheless. Never forget, he told himself and bent down to put the flowers in the urn.

Daisy Marsland, he read and stood up, feeling a twinge of pain in his back.

'I'm sorry,' he whispered and stepped back, feeling his eyes fill up.

There was someone to his right, a few yards away, hovering near another grave. He kept his eyes down, not wanting to intrude on someone else's privacy, but the shape moved, so he turned his head a little and was able to make out a feminine silhouette against the bright sunlight.

'Excuse me, I'm really sorry,' a slightly croaky woman's voice said.

Marsland turned and saw the woman smiling sadly at him. Her hair was blonde, long and wavy, obviously dyed. She was good-looking and probably in her late-forties. She looked like she had dolled herself up for something.

'I'm sorry,' she repeated, holding out her right arm that was in a cast. 'But I can't cut these flowers properly. Do you mind?'

He smiled, but kept his head down and took the flowers and scissors she held in her other hand. He cut the stems and handed them back, smiled briefly, smelling her perfume that was somehow familiar.

'Thanks,' she said and placed the flowers in front of a white headstone at her feet. 'I slipped in the bathroom a week back. Makes it a right pain to do anything.'

'I bet.'

'I'm sorry for your loss.' She pointed to Daisy's grave.

'Thank you.'

'Your wife?'

'No...my daughter. My wife died a few years ago.'

She lifted a hand to her mouth, her eyes wide. 'Oh, I'm sorry. That's awful. No parent should bury their child.'

He nodded. It was the first conversation he'd had with a real person in a long time. Yes, he'd chatted to ex-colleagues like Peter Moone, but that was about it. He looked at his watch and remembered he had an appointment in twenty minutes. 'I'm sorry, but I've got to be somewhere.'

'Oh, right, sorry. I shouldn't be nosy.'

'No, it's OK, I've just got to be somewhere. It's nice

to have met you.'

'My name's Jacqui,' she said and smiled.

'Terence,' he said and stepped away.

'Can I call you Terry?' she asked and laughed.

He grimaced inside and nodded and moved quickly back towards to entrance.

'I come every Monday,' she called out and waved.

Fifteen minutes later, Marsland pulled up outside some red brick council houses in Barton Close, his eyes scanning over the shabby front gardens, the rusty looking vehicles on the driveways, and the graffiti scrawled over the kids' playground to his left.

It was number 48 he wanted, so he got out and marched up to the black door and rang the bell. He could hear a female voice mumble something inside, then the door unlocking. A young girl, no more than twenty years old, opened the door. She had lank mousey hair and a china white face with a few light freckles scattered across her nose. She wore a pink cardigan and black leggings.

'Hello?' she said, squinting a little.

'I'm Terence Marsland,' he said and pushed a smile to his lips. 'I called you yesterday?'

The young woman laughed. 'Oh yeah, sorry. Haven't got much of a brain left.'

'That's OK. Still all right for a quick chat?'

She nodded and opened the door for him. 'Yeah, it's fine. I've just got my little'un off to sleep so we'll have to be quiet. You wanted to know about Ria?'

Marsland nodded and walked down the old-fashioned hallway. The young woman who had let him in was Sara Pitman, and DS Peter Moone had asked Marsland to pop in and talk to her, to see if there's anything she knew about a missing girl called

Ria Saunders that she wasn't telling the law.

Marsland stepped into the living room that was decorated the same as the rest of the house, like an old lady had been living there for the last hundred years. There was even a worn armchair next to the gas fire and a TV set that belonged in the 70s. A toddler lay asleep on a mat on the floor.

'Yes,' Marsland said and sat down on an equally outdated sofa. 'You were good friends with Ria, weren't you?'

'You from the police?' she asked, her eyes turning towards the kid.

'No, like I said yesterday, I'm just looking into her disappearance for a friend. Can you go over the last time you saw her?'

The girl sat down in the armchair and wrapped her arms around herself. 'All I know is that she meant to meet me at the George Pub in Enfield Town. We were going out for her birthday. Was going to be a great night but she never turned up. I was pissed off at first... then...'

'Of course.' Marsland looked round the room some more, past the dozing child, past the piles of unused nappies. His eyes stopped on a pair of Nike trainers, approximately size 9. 'It must be tough not knowing what happened to her. Do you live alone, Sara?'

'Yeah, apart from the little man over there. His father did a legger. Same old story.'

When she told the story her eyes didn't go up and to the left, which meant she wasn't recalling a true memory. Plus there was a shakiness about her voice; she was scared or nervous about something.

'Was Ria seeing anyone?' Marsland took out his notebook and pen.

Sara raised her skinny shoulders. 'I don't know. I

told the police that I didn't think so. She was in and out of my life really. We fell out a lot, cause most of the time she was slagging me off. Then we'd be thick as thieves again. But she didn't tell me if she was hooked up or anything.'

'Anyone in the past that she had been seeing?'

The girl's face changed. A knowing smile crept onto to her face as she said, 'Jamie Mills. She was seeing him a year before she went missing, but I'm sure the coppers had words with him.'

Marsland wrote his name down. 'I'm sure they have, but sometimes they don't ask the right questions. You got an address for him?'

'No, but I got his mobile number.' The girl pulled out a small white mobile phone, got the number up, then showed it to Marsland.

'Thanks.'

'Do you really think you'll find out what happened to her?'

'I hope so. You know she's not the only girl her age to go missing in the last year? There's a few who have disappeared that have a similar description to Ria.'

'Really? That's weird.'

'Yes, it is. Very weird.' Marsland got up, smiled and thanked her and told her to ring his mobile if she thought of anything. She said she would and saw him to the door. He walked across the street feeling the warm sun on his back, thinking about the girl and the things she had told him. There was something definitely off about her, a note in her voice and her manner that suggested something was overshadowing her life. Fear seemed to be the obvious thing to him.

He climbed into his car, started the engine, drove towards the end of the street and indicated to go right. He turned when the traffic was clear and drove towards the petrol station a few yards away, quickly turned round on the forecourt and headed back to Barton Close where he parked and watched Sara's house for a moment. It didn't take long at all.

The young man came across the street walking like a pit bull, with a similar build and facial features. He took out a key and opened the door and disappeared inside. Marsland smiled to himself then drove out of the road.

There was a monitor set up in the room next to interview room 1, and that's where DI Jairus watched Edgar Holzman from, taking note of his movements, which were minimal. He just sat in the interview room quietly in the paper suit they had given him to wear while his clothes were analysed. Holzman, who seemed to be in his early fifties, was sinewy, and there were definite signs of a daily fitness regime. He had a hawk-like nose and thick dark grey hair. Jairus kept watching him for a moment, then headed for the interview room.

He was about to pull open the door when he heard a familiar female voice call him from down the corridor. When he looked round he saw DI Ally Walker coming quickly towards him, a slight smile on her face. Her dark hair had been cut into a short bob. She looked good.

'Hello, Jay,' she said, smiling even more. 'It's been a while. What you doing?'

He let go of the door and leaned against the wall. 'Yeah, it's been a long time. What am I doing? I'm about to talk to the person who found two DBs this morning.'

'I see, well, after that you might want to head upstairs where Warren wants a word with you.'

Jairus kicked himself from the wall. 'Hang on. Warren? Commander Warren? What's he doing upstairs?'

'I don't know. When I went into the incident room this morning, there he was and he poked his head out to tell me that he wants to talk to you. Urgently.'

'Where's Queen Linsey?'

'God knows. Want any help?' Walker's eyes jumped to the door.

'In there? No, I'm fine. I'll be up in a moment.'

Jairus opened the door to the interview room, then heard Walker say his name again. 'Yeah?'

'It's good to see you.'

He nodded and entered the small cream room, which had a metal table at the far end. Edgar Holzman sat at the table, his head now raised and an expectant look on his face.

'I've been waiting quite some time,' Holzman said, a thin smile on his lips.

Jairus pulled out a chair and sat opposite him. 'I'm Detective Inspector Jairus, Mr Holzman. I'm sorry about the wait, but I was busy at the crime scene.'

'I can understand that. You're forgiven.' A bigger smile stretched Holzman's face wider.

'So, you found Henry and his daughter this morning?'

'I did.'

'What time was that?'

'Exactly 8 a.m. this morning. I happened to check my watch as I got out of my car.'

'And then what happened?'

Holzman sat forward. 'I went up to the front door and rang the bell, but there was no answer, which I thought was unusual.'

'Then what?'

'Then I went around to the back of the house and found his daughter lying there. It was quite a shock, as you can imagine.'

'I bet. Did you go into the house?'

'Yes, I wanted to see if Thomas was all right.'

'If I had seen a dead body outside a house, I think I'd go away and call the police.'

Holzman raised his shoulders. 'That's where you and I differ then. I wanted to know what had happened to my friend.'

'Did you touch anything?' Jairus watched Holzman smile, wondering how a man who had witnessed such devastation could be so calm. Never had he met someone who had found a dead body and remained so placid. Something began to itch in the back of his mind.

'I'm not stupid. So no is the answer.'

'Do you own a Land Rover?'

'No, and never have. I own a silver Volvo.'

'How long have you known the victims?' Jairus leaned back.

'About ten years. I met Thomas at a charity evening at Alexandra Palace, and subsequently met his daughter some time later.'

'Did Mr Henry have any enemies?'

Holzman smiled as if he'd known the question was coming. 'No, Thomas had only friends. He'd retired from the business world a long time ago. Any enemies he had would have been left behind.'

'If you don't mind me saying you seem very calm for a man who's just found his friends savagely murdered.'

There was a flicker across Holzman's face, a change in his demeanour. His smile completely faded and his eyes refrained from blinking as he said, 'I've never been an emotional man, DI Jairus. You can sue me if you would like. In my life I've seen a great deal of tragedy and I suppose it has hardened me to all the blood and guts.'

'Same as us coppers, I guess.' Jairus smiled and folded his arms.

'Am I a suspect? I mean, I was the person who found them at a remote house, so logically speaking...'

Jairus held up his palm. 'At this point you're not a suspect...but there may be more questions later.'

Holzman's smile returned as he pulled at the paper suit he was wearing. 'And when exactly do I get my clothes back?'

'When our team are done with them. Thank you, Mr Holzman, you've been very helpful. Someone will be in to take a formal statement, then you'll be able to go home.'

'Thank you, DI Jairus. And call me Edgar.'

Jairus took the stairs two at a time, then pushed the doors to the incident room open. DI Walker was behind her desk. 'There's something not quite right about him.'

Walker looked up from her computer screen. 'Who?'

'Edgar Holzman. There's something about him I don't like.'

'The old man in the interview room? I directed him there and he seemed very charming to me.'

'You would think that.'

DS Moone appeared in the doorway holding a couple of black and white photographs. He handed them over to Jairus and sat on a nearby desk. 'Take a look at them. Got a nice couple of shots of a Land Rover heading in the direction of our crime scene, and one of Edgar Holzman's Volvo heading towards the house just before 8 a.m. Guess we can rule him out.'

Jairus held up the shot of the Land Rover and tapped it.

'Stolen from a smallholding outside Cambridgeshire two days ago,' Moone said. 'Hopefully they'll be stupid and dump it without gutting it first.'

'No, not these two.' Jairus pinned the two photographs to the whiteboard, then took a real close look at the Land Rover shot. It was a grainy image, but he could make out two figures in the front seats. Their faces looked dark. 'Take a closer look.'

Both Walker and Moone got closer to the board.

'Too dark to see their faces,' Walker said.

'They're wearing masks,' Moone added. 'They weren't taking any chances on the drive over. They were careful.'

'Exactly,' Jairus said and turned around to find Commander Warren staring at him from the doorway.

'I need a word,' Warren said. 'Now.'

CHAPTER 4

It took no time at all to find Jamie Mills, Ria's ex-boyfriend. After a couple of phone calls to some ex-colleagues, Marsland was sat in his car staring at a building site just off Wood Green high street. Recently they had knocked down some derelict terraces houses and started building some plush-looking flats; it was all part of the regeneration of North London, but Marsland doubted it would decrease people's fear of the area at night.

It was getting towards lunchtime, so Marsland kept his eyes on the entrance, seeing the lorries making deliveries of sand and ballast. Then young men, some without their tops on, came out, chatting to each other and heading towards the cafes and nearby shops. One particular lad, who was stocky with a shaved round head, red T-shirt and jeans and a big Celtic tattoo on his right arm, looked familiar. Marsland got Jamie's photo up that he'd been emailed by Moone. He nodded. It was definitely her ex-boyfriend, and so he climbed out of his car and headed towards him. Marsland stopped dead in Jamie's way, his arms folded.

'Alright, mate, want to get out my way?' Jamie shook his head and went to move round the ex-copper.

'Jamie Mills?' Marsland pointed to the greasy spoon up the road. 'How about I buy you a terrible cup of tea?'

'Police I take it?'

'I used to be. I just want to ask you a few questions. Won't take long.'

'About Ria?'

'Yes.'

The labourer nodded and pointed behind Marsland where a more upmarket cafe with an Italian sounding name sat on the corner. 'I like coffee and they do a lovely and expensive Americano.'

'Fine.'

They sat at the back, near the toilets.

Marsland nursed a latte and took out his notebook. 'So?'

'This the part where you ask me when I last saw Ria?' Jamie said and relaxed in his chair, one hand round his Americano.

'That's right.'

'Fuck. What can I tell you now that I didn't tell the other lot back then?'

'Maybe something. Perhaps a little detail that you left out last time.'

'I didn't leave anything out!'

'OK, just calm yourself and think back.'

'Calm myself? Do you know what's it like when people look at you thinking you've done your ex-girlfriend in?'

Marsland nodded. 'I know you've been through a lot. Just think back and remember the places you used to go. People you met. Anything out of the ordinary that happened. You might have forgotten it and now...'

Jamie gave a strange sort laugh, then mumbled to himself. Marsland leaned forward and said, 'What was that?'

Jamie shrugged. 'Nothing. It was nothing.'

'What did you say?'

Jamie sighed. 'Do you know the big house at the other end of Enfield Town with the gardens all round it. The one on the way to Old Ridings' golf course?'

'Yes, Braxton House. Why?'

'Well, me and Ria went there the summer before she went missing. We got back together for a while and things weren't too bad. We ended up going to that house to sunbathe. But Ria wanted to go inside cause she'd heard there was a museum there. So we wander up to the front door, but some bloke in a suit comes out and tells us that it's not open to the public anymore. I go to walk off, but Ria's still going on to the bloke about the museum. He tells her he'll let her see it, but I wanted to go.'

'And then what happened?'

Jamie shrugged. 'He showed her the museum, which was pretty small apparently, and I waited outside sitting on the grass. When she came out she was laughing and stuff. Kept saying the bloke was charming and stuff. Seemed like a sleazy wanker to me.'

'Did you tell this to the police at the time?'

'No, cause it doesn't mean anything.'

Marsland sat back, knowing the lad was probably right and that it possibly meant nothing. But it was one thing the police didn't know about, that glimmering item among the dirt. 'Nothing else sticks out in your mind?'

Jamie shook his head. 'Nothing. Me and Ria split up shortly after that. She called it off. I tried to get back with her but she wasn't having any of it. You think it means something?'

Marsland stood up and put his notebook away. 'Not really sure. But it's worth looking into. You never know what might turn up.'

Commander Warren had sat down and made a quick phone call by the time Jairus had strolled into his office and taken a seat opposite him.

'No DCS Freeman?' Jairus said, his eyes fixed on a small photo frame on the desk- Warren and his wife and their teenage daughter and son.

'Sick leave,' Warren said, completely blank-faced. 'And DCI Webb is off at Scotland Yard. We are low on numbers, DI Jairus.'

'Which means?'

'Which means you're acting Detective Chief Inspector for a while, but don't get too comfortable.'

'You're kidding?' Jairus sat up straight. 'After all the bad publicity I've brought to the Met?'

Warren frowned a little. 'It's not ideal, I know, but I think your heart's in the right place, and more importantly you're a good detective. I had to fight for this though, Jairus. There's a lot of bodies upstairs that were against it, but I fought your corner.'

Jairus gave a laugh. 'Doesn't sound like there was much choice left.'

The Commander smiled. 'You were found innocent. That's that. They looked into the case and you were cleared. They tried to make it look like you took that knife along with the aim of killing Carl Murphy.'

'I went...'

Warren held up his hands. 'It's OK, they now know you wrestled the knife off him. It's over now. Let's forget it and look to the future. What's the story with this father and daughter getting tortured?'

Jairus leaned back in his chair. 'The father was tortured, the daughter was executed outright. Thomas Henry was cut to pieces and allowed to bleed to death.'

The Commander sighed. 'So a couple of psychos

wanted to have fun with a rich guy in a posh house.'

Jairus shook his head. 'No, this wasn't just a couple of crazy people out to have fun. They went there to make him suffer. They cut him to pieces. They allowed him to show them all the money he had in his safe, but they left it. Then, when he was dead, they cut off his head and put it on a metal pole and stuck it on the roof.'

'Why the bloody hell would they do that?'

'That's what they used to do to traitors years ago. They'd parade their heads on pikes. They wanted to make a point. This was about revenge and punishment.'

Warren began to smile a little. 'I knew you were the man for the job. Once you get your teeth into something, you don't let go.'

'I do my best.'

'But I'd like to be kept abreast of events. This Thomas Henry was apparently a very wealthy man and I've been informed he's done good things for charity. I'm already getting pressure to sort this out pretty fast.'

'I'm sure we'll be working on this as hard as we do any case,' Jairus said and stood up. He felt the bad taste in his mouth already, the same distasteful flavour he got every time he dealt with the top brass. He liked to keep his distance if he could, and, unlike some of the detectives he worked with, he didn't like to get on his knees and lick their arses. He wanted to do his job and go home and not have sleepless nights worrying about climbing the ladder. He had enough sleepless nights torturing himself with the past.

'I'm sure you will,' Warren said, stood up and stuck out his hand.

Jairus looked at his hand for a moment, wondering

if ambition was contagious, then shook it. 'I've got a request. I need DI Walker and DS Moone working with me on this.'

'It's two dead bodies, Jairus. You can handle that, surely?'

'Yeah, but the people who killed Henry and his daughter cut off his head and stuck it on the roof. It was a warning or message to someone, and not us. That means they're not finished.'

'OK, I'll give you Walker, but DS Moone is working on a missing person's case. Take it or leave it.'

'Fine,' Jairus said and left the office and walked straight up to Walker and Moone. 'Right, Walker, you're with me, and Moone, you can get lost.'

Moone frowned and said, 'Hey, I'm only working a missing person's case, so I'm always available. Any time, any place.'

'That's what I've heard about you, Moone,' Walker said, smirking. 'You're almost too available.'

'Ok, Pete, but keep a low profile.' Jairus squeezed Moone's shoulder.

'You know me, Jairus. Scout's honour and all that.'

'That's acting DCI Jairus to you.'

'Shit!' Walker's mouth fell open.

Moone said, 'What did Warren's arse taste like? Fuck.'

Jairus held up his hand. 'Let's get to business. I've been asking myself one question. How did our two killers get in? They had guns and masks and a bag of goodies. Thomas Henry slept with a kitchen knife under his pillow. He didn't just let them in.'

Moone nodded. 'I've taken a look round that place and it's a fortress. There's alarms all over the place.'

Jairus rubbed his hands together. 'Right then, Walker, you can look into who designed the place and find out who made it so secure. Now, both the father and daughter were up and dressed in the middle of the night. Looks like the daughter was about to do a runner. You find out where she was going, Pete.'

'What are you going to do?' Walker asked.

'I'm going to see a woman about a dress.'

After lifting out his sandwich tub from his satchel, Marsland opened it up, took out a ham and salad sandwich and took a bite. He chewed while watching the Victorian mansion house that sat in front of him. He was sitting on a bench a hundred yards away, right in the middle of the picturesque garden. Marsland didn't know the names of the flowers, but they were bright, all of various colours and types. Behind him, an elderly man sitting on a motorized lawn mower, roared up and down the lawn.

A few minutes earlier Marsland had taken out his mobile and dialled the office of Braxton House. A well-spoken woman answered, so Marsland had asked if he could talk to the new owner of the house, and was told that Mr Graham Burgess was currently out but would be returning momentarily. He said he would ring another time and hung up.

Now he waited, taking bites from his sandwich, sips from his flask of tea, and watching the lane that curled around the house, thinking what a ridiculous reason he had picked for turning up at Braxton House; he had the word of a not very bright labourer that some charming man had been coming on to his ex-girlfriend. It was thin at best, but it was all he had to go on. Marsland thought about the other girls who had gone missing in the last two years, then took out his notebook and looked at the list of names: Ria Saunders, Kelly Leigh, and Gina Colman. All with light brown hair. All quite thin and attractive. But he made a promise to himself and DS Moone. He swore that he would not get too involved this time, not like last time. He drifted his hand to his side and felt the scar through his shirt.

He looked up when he heard the rumble of an engine coming along the lane, and saw a red sporty Audi tearing along towards the house. The car swiftly took the bend and parked behind the house. Marsland quickly put away his picnic and hurried to the house. By the time he had reached the path to the large oak door, Graham Burgess was striding in the same direction. He wore dark jeans and a brown blazer jacket. He had short dark brown hair with a little grey at the temples.

'Mr Burgess?' Marsland called out.

Burgess stopped dead. 'Who wants to know?'

'Terence Marsland. I just wanted a quick word with you.'

Burgess waved his hand and began to stride towards the door again. 'I don't want what you're selling.'

'I'm looking into the disappearance of a young woman.'

The man stopped again, put his hands into his pockets and seemed to be grinding his jaw as he looked at Marsland. 'What are you talking about? And who are you exactly?'

'My name is Terence Marsland and I'm looking into the disappearance of a young woman called Ria Saunders. And you met her nearly a year ago.'

Burgess took a careful look at Marsland then stepped closer. 'Do you happen to have some identification? I take it you're from the police?'

Marsland shook his head. 'No, but I used to be.

Look, I thought you might be able to help me with this young woman. She's been missing nearly a year now.'

The man lifted his wrist and looked at his watch. 'I'm very busy today. But... So I'm supposed to have met her? Where?'

Marsland pointed to the house. 'Here in the museum.'

'There's no museum here now.'

'But there was then, when you first bought the place.'

The man turned and looked at the house for a moment, nodding to himself. 'Oh, yes, this place cost me quite a few pennies, but it was worth it.'

While Burgess had his back turned, Marsland brought up the photograph he had of Ria Saunders on his mobile, then held it out. When he looked round Burgess flinched a little, shocked at having the phone stuck in his face. He looked up, now a little annoyed.

'Look, if you're not a policeman, I don't see what business it is of yours chasing around after her. She's probably run off with some man. How should I know where she is?'

'You haven't looked at her,' Marsland said, raising the phone to Burgess' eye level, but still he didn't look at the photograph.

'You going to take a look or do I have to ram it down your throat?' Marsland kept his voice calm, but a ripple of anger travelled across his chest. His hand shook a little as Burgess finally switched his gaze to the phone, then quickly looked up again.

'She does look familiar but I can't be sure,' Burgess said, apologetically. 'I'm sorry I couldn't be of more help.'

There seemed to be nothing in Burgess' eyes, little giving away a lie or sign that he really did know her.

He put away the phone. 'That's OK, Mr Burgess, I'm sure you tried your best. I'll be back if I think of anything more I have to ask you.'

'Call me first though,' he said and straightened his tie. 'I'm a very busy man, so don't make it too soon.'

From Upper James Street Jairus turned left, then right into Carnaby Street and walked towards the end, where he knew there were shops that made custom clothes for all kinds of tastes. It was a street he'd always liked, with its lines of restaurants and cafes, independent clothes shops, and the general vibrancy of the place. Every kind of person could be found there so it was no wonder it was one of London's most popular streets.

Jairus looked up and saw the clouds drawing in, closing off the summer sun. A centipede of Chinese school kids, all wearing the same bright red rucksacks, cut him off just before he reached the shop he was after. In a carrier bag by his side was the dress they'd discovered at the crime scene, still folded inside the evidence bag. He'd been to several different shops in the last few hours hoping that someone might be able to give him some information on the dress.

He walked into the shop, ducking at the same time to avoid the chains and whips that were hanging from the ceiling. It was like a cave inside, with leather trench coats and basques lining the walls. Very little natural light streamed into the interior, so red light bulbs illuminated the room giving it a seedy feel. The customers were mostly goths, with a couple of relatively normal customers thrown in. He walked to the counter where a young man adorned in a leather trench coat, silver chains and bright red hair was sitting. He slapped the bag on the counter, making the man jump a little.

'Excuse me?' the young man said, looking through black eye make up. 'Was that necessary?'

'Know anything about dresses?' Jairus stuck his ID in his face and leaned on the counter.

'Do I look like I'd know anything about dresses?'

Jairus couldn't help smirk. 'Quite frankly, son, I'm not sure. There anyone here who designs dresses?'

The young man turned towards an archway behind and shouted, 'Trish? Trish, there's someone who wants to know about dresses.'

A young woman came slowly through the archway, her voluptuous body squeezed into a leather corset and long skirt. Jairus found it hard to keep his eyes from her milky-white cleavage.

'Hello, darling,' Trisha said and nodded for the young man to lose himself. 'What can I do for you?'

With his ID in his hand, Jairus said, 'I need an expert opinion on this dress.'

The girl looked down, then her dark, thin eyebrows rose dramatically. 'Oh.'

'What is it?'

'This dress...Winter made this. Looks like one she was working on a long time back. Maybe two years ago. Can I have a closer look?'

'Yeah.' Jairus carefully took the dress out and laid it on the counter. Trisha nodded, her black nails travelling down the material. 'Yes, this is definitely one of Winter's dresses. I remember going round her flat and she'd been working so hard on it. Weird thing is she wouldn't tell me much about them.'

'Them?' Jairus leaned forward. 'There was more than one?'

'Oh yes, I'm pretty sure there were six. It could be more but I doubt it. Hang on though...I don't remember the diamonds though.'

'What did she say about the person who ordered the dresses?'

'Nothing. All she said was that someone had ordered them and paid her quite a bit for them. And it all seemed hush-hush.'

'Can I talk to Winter?'

'No, because she died about two years ago.'

'I'm sorry to hear that. How did she die?'

'Slit her own wrists. She was quite a dark character, but I never saw it coming. She loved her job too much.'

There was now a scratching at the back of Jairus' mind and a swirl of suspicion in his stomach. 'Is there anyway I can see the stuff she left behind?'

Trisha shrugged, then licked her lips, giving Jairus a view of the silver stud through her tongue. 'I think all her stuff ended up at her parents' house. I'll write down their address.'

'Thanks.' Jairus took the scribbled address and put it in his pocket.

'Can I make another suggestion, darling?' Trish landed her eyes on the dress again.

'Go on.'

'I'd check those diamonds out. I'm no expert but I think they look pretty kosher.'

'Thanks. I know a man who'll tell me either way.'

CHAPTER 5

He didn't quite feel like going home yet, so Jairus took a turning off the Great Cambridge Road and headed left along towards Ponders End. He took another sharp left and carefully steered his Audi down the narrow back lane. On his left were the ends of people's gardens, but on his right were a row of ten lock-ups. He parked and sat there for a moment, listening to the engine quietening down. He looked at his watch. It was nearly ten at night. Tomorrow he would see Archie Hurvitz to find out about the diamonds when he got back from his holiday. The rest of Jairus' day was mostly filled with paperwork, the part he hated the most.

He took out his wallet, then slipped a finger inside and felt the key he kept there. After climbing out the car, he went up to the green lock-up and slipped the key into the lock and pulled up the door. It squeaked when he lifted the door, then he bent down and went into the darkness, and pushed it shut again. Feeling with his hand in the blackness, he found the cord and pulled it. A glow of light swirled in his eyes for a moment. He blinked, then focused on the filing cabinets and wooden furniture that lined the walls, all covered in dust. He'd boxed up most of Karine's stuff and put it here. He pulled over her old office chair and sat in it, staring at every stick of furniture that surrounded him.

What did it amount to? A person's life. The woman he was going to spend the rest of his life with.

Jairus rolled himself over to the 70s style sideboard she had bought for their house. He placed his hand gently on it, wiping away the dust a little. One day she was there, the next she wasn't. She never told him about her heart, never wanted him to know.

A tear slipped from his eye. He quickly wiped it away with the back of his hand, then turned round to look at the rest of her stuff, the piles of books and ornaments. His eyes stopped dead.

The safe.

Jairus took a deep breath and rolled himself over to the large dark metal safe he had bought a year ago. It sat in the corner of the lock-up staring back at him, its dials kind of making an emotionless face. He closed his eyes, found the dial with his hand and began turning it, feeling the numbers click into place. He heard the final clunk, then opened his eyes, feeling the pit of his stomach burn. He pulled open the door slowly and looked inside. He almost expected it to be gone, for it to have magically disappeared.

If I can't see it, it doesn't exist.

He slammed the door again, his heart now rattling in his chest, screaming out in his ears. He shook his head, his hands digging into his legs. With his jacket sleeve he wiped away another tear and stood up.

It doesn't exist.

Jairus pushed open the lock-up door, locked it behind him and jumped into his car. He turned to look at the garage, then drove in the direction of his flat.

It had been bothering Graham Burgess all day; why had the policeman turned up today? No, he wasn't a policeman at all, but some kind of private detective. So why now? He had driven back home with the thought crashing around his brain, trying to make sense of it. Perhaps, he thought, every now and then old cases get looked into, just as a sort of procedure. Yes, he liked the sound of that. Anyway, what could they possibly find out now that they couldn't then? Nothing, that's what. His worry lifted as he pressed on the remote control and watched the metal gates slowly open. He drove up and parked on his long drive, then strolled towards his large Georgian house. It was dissimilar enough to the other large houses that also lined the long road, but it also had the same feel of wealth. He opened the front door and stepped into the wide hall. He quickly turned off the alarm and looked down at the Evening Standard newspaper that was on the mat. He retrieved it and walked across the tiled flooring towards his kitchen. It was late, but he fancied a coffee. Anyway, he planned to stay up late and do some work on his laptop, so one coffee wouldn't really matter.

But why had the private detective turned up now?

He placed the newspaper on the kitchen table. He shook his head and went over to his coffee machine, filled it up and listened to it rumble to life. Then he sat at the kitchen table and unfolded the newspaper.

His eyes roared open, seeing the face staring up at him, the big photograph on the front page, and then the little image next to it.

No! What the bloody…

He calmed himself and began to read. Thomas Henry and his daughter, Marie, had been found dead in their home. Suspicious circumstances. Foul play, and all that police talk. They were appealing for witnesses.

Burgess looked up. His eyes sprang round the

room, his whole body alive with rushing blood, his ears now beating out a rhythm. The private detective had turned up, now Thomas Henry was dead. And his daughter.

Fuck.

He jumped up and ran over to the kitchen drawers and pulled the top one open. His lungs emptied. Nothing. He sifted through the forks and spoons. He opened the next drawer, but there was nothing. Where the hell were the kitchen knives?

Burgess shut the drawer, then shuddered, his eyes slowly moving towards the shape that was in the doorway, telling himself it was only his imagination, that nothing was really standing there.

The mouth smiled through the balaclava. The eyes widened.

Burgess backed himself against the kitchen work surface, his eyes jumping to the pistol that was in the man's hand. 'Please...'

'Please what?' the masked man asked and took another step closer.

'Please...just...I have money in the house.'

The man laughed, and there was deep anger in the voice. The eyes sharpened as he came closer, the lips pulling back and the teeth gritting. 'Money! You think money will save you? You will be judged now, Burgess. It's too late for you.'

'What do you want?' Burgess backed away, his eyes scanning the work surface for anything he could use as a weapon.

'Justice for those now gone.'

'I don't know what you mean. Please...'

'Is that what she said?' the man said, his voice shaking a little. 'Did she say please?'

'I don't know what you mean.'

Another figure emerged from the hallway. Another masked man, much taller. His gloved hands carried a shotgun in one hand and a large holdall in the other. He stepped in matter-of-factly and placed the bag on the kitchen table.

'Here?' the taller masked man asked.

The first man nodded. 'Yes, this'll do, brother.'

Burgess was thinking, trying to make his brain work, but the blood pounded in his chest too loud for any controlled thought. What exactly did these two men want? No, he was being naïve, stupid even. He knew what they wanted, why they had come for him. But how? How did they know what he had done? Who had betrayed him?

Only one course of action came to his mind and lips.

'I'm sorry,' Burgess pleaded, his hands up as if to pray. 'I'm sorry for what I did.'

'Are you?' the first man asked. 'Are you truly sorry? Are you asking for forgiveness?'

'Yes!' Burgess stepped forward. 'Yes, I'm truly sorry. Please, please forgive me. I didn't know what I was doing.'

The pistol shot out towards him, stopping an inch from his face, the barrel shaking. 'You did know! You enjoyed it!'

Burgess shook his head. 'I didn't. They made me do it.'

'Sit in the chair,' the first man said.

'Why? What are you going to do?'

'You'll find out,' the taller man said.

'Don't do this,' Burgess pleaded, gripping the work surface.

'Move! Or I blow your head off!'

He hurried over to the chair and sat down, his

hands gripping the wooden arms of the seat, icy sweat dripping down his armpits. What would they do? *Please! Please don't let them hurt me.* 'What are you going to do?'

A pair of gloves clamped down on his arms, forcing them to the chair. Then the tape was wrapped tightly around him, securing him to the back of the chair. Rope encircled his wrists. He tried to lift his arms, but he couldn't. His shirt was soaked through, sweat dripped down into his mouth, his whole frame violently shaking.

A masked face appeared in front of him. 'Don't bother struggling. It won't do any good.'

The taller man came to the table and opened the holdall. He seemed to look inside for a moment, then brought out a large hunting knife, his face turning to Burgess as he lifted it.

'Oh, no! Don't!' The chair rattled, smashed against the tiled floor. 'NO! PLEASE NO! Please…please, please, please! Listen to me. I'm so, so sorry!'

'Too late,' the taller man said. 'Brother?'

The other man appeared from the right, a syringe in his hand, which he placed on the table. Then he lurched towards Burgess and pulled down his trousers and threw them across the room. He took up the syringe again, knelt down and stuck it into his groin. Burgess jerked backwards, screaming.

'You wouldn't want to feel this.' The first man stood up, smiling.

Then the taller man came towards the chair, the knife in his hand, his eyes wide, his grin growing wider.

Burgess gripped the arms of the chair, his body jerking backwards. The chair wouldn't move.

He was screaming again, shouting for his

neighbours, pleading with God to do something. Pleading to be forgiven by anything or anyone listening.

The taller man stood up to his full height, the knife in his hand, his face all smiles. 'Now, that was painless, wasn't it?'

What had he done? Burgess suddenly felt lifeless, the blood draining out of him, his brain swimming off towards the ceiling. Then he lowered his head slowly, his heart rocking around his chest.

There was…Oh GOD! No! Please help me!

The taller man put the knife on the table and lifted up his other hand. Burgess' penis was lying in his gloved hand. It was pink and limp, but mostly bloody. 'You won't have any need for this any more.'

The first man walked round him and bent down, pushing his face close to Burgess. 'I suppose you want to die now, don't you? Well, you're not going to. Not for a long time. Brother, why don't you go and find a mirror, so Mr Burgess can watch?'

CHAPTER 6

Jairus had to park quite far from the centre of Hatton Garden and walk the rest of the way, his eyes flicking over the jewellery shops, the Gold exchanges and diamond centres; each establishment had a bright front, promising the cheapest prices for the best quality. He remembered the history of the quarter, which Archie Hurvitz had told him quite a few years ago now. Since medieval times the whole area had become a hub for the trade of precious metals and stones.

Ahead of Jairus, right on the corner of the next street, was the black and gold front shop of Archie's diamond business. He bought and sold and made a lot of money from it. Hurvitz Diamonds was emblazoned in gold across the front of the shop.

Inside, Jairus found suited young men standing over rows of glass cases that were filled with sparkling jewels. There were only a smattering of wealthy looking customers, while a couple of suited meaty-looking men seemed to stand guard at either end of the room.

'Hello, hello, Mr Jairus!' Archie came through the glass security door at the back and directed Jairus to his tiny office along the corridor. Archie was a small man with a round belly, smiling face, and black receding hair. His dark blue pinstripe suit was well-tailored and expensive as always.

Jairus sat in a chair opposite Archie's desk and smiled at him as he took a seat. 'Take a look at this, Archie.'

Archie frowned when Jairus placed the dress on the table. 'What, no pleasant chat like old times?'

'How are you, Archie?'

The diamond expert took out his eyeglass and gave a huge grin. 'Business is good, so I'm good. Now, talking of business...'

Eventually he looked up and removed the eyeglass. 'These are asscher cut diamonds. 3 carat. Asscher cut diamonds are very popular these days, Jairus, so you can pretty much get them anywhere. They're good quality though, nice clarity.'

'So there's nothing you can tell me about them, no way to find out who bought them?'

Archie sat back and raised his eyebrows. 'No, my friend, you know me better than that. Do I ever send you away empty-handed?'

Jairus smiled at him.

'Forget the diamonds. Yes, my friend, someone spent a great deal of money on this dress. That much is obvious. But look at the pattern the diamonds are laid out in. It's a symbol. An ancient symbol.'

'An ancient symbol? To do with what?'

'I'm afraid I don't know anymore. I read a lot these days. I've read so much I've forgotten most of it, my friend. But I remember that symbol from somewhere. I definitely remember that. And if someone went to the trouble to make an expensive dress with real diamonds on it, you can bet it means a great deal to that someone.'

'Yeah, you're probably right.' Jairus held up his hand as his mobile started ringing in his pocket. 'Yeah, It's me.'

'Hey, you might want to get yourself to Dulwich,' Moone said, sounding distracted. 'We've got another one. You're not going to believe your eyes. No word of a lie.'

'I'll be there as quick as I can.'

It was 10 a.m. by the time Jairus parked up the road from the crime scene, his collars pulled up round his neck now that it had started to rain. Already Moone had spread the cordon wide and sent uniforms door-to-door. He walked fast, passing the uniforms with clipboards in their hands, talking to neighbours on their door steps, then lifted the cordon and signed the crime scene log. Moone was standing on the driveway, his hands deep into his pockets. Even from a hundred yards away, Jairus could see the dark lines under his eyes, the scrunch of lines across his forehead.

'You look like shit,' Jairus said and pointed to the house.

'Owned by Graham Burgess,' Moone said, 'he's a businessman, 57 years old, owns a lot of property in Enfield and generally around Greater London. How's your stomach feeling today?'

'Fine,' Jairus said, and watched a couple of SOCOs enter the front door carrying large cases. 'That bad in there?'

'Pretty nasty. Get some overshoes on, and we can go in.'

The windows had been blacked out so nobody could see in, and spotlights had been set up in every corner. Nothing was hidden. Everything was bright, every detail was on display as the SOCOs did their gruesome work. Jairus kept walking, following the short body of Moone, and found himself on the edge of a long glowing kitchen. There were more lights, all glaring at him. He blinked and took in the shape before him. A chair. Just a chair. No, a man in a chair. He could see his arms strapped to the arms of the chair, the skin so very white. He stepped round the chair, his back to the kitchen table and surveyed the scene. He took in a deep breath.

A man strapped and tied to the wooden chair, his pale blue shirt sodden with dark blood. His hands are missing, severed at the wrist. He looked down and felt a little dizzy. They had cut off his feet at the ankles. Jesus, he whispered to himself or did he just think it? He was naked from the waist down. A rose of blood at the centre of his groin told Jairus all he needed to know.

Then he looked up, focusing on the shoulders.

No head.

Up the walls there was blood. It was the kind of blood spray made by a chainsaw or something similar. On the floor, just in front of the victim's absent feet were the kind of blood spatters caused by a blow from a blunt object.

Jairus looked up to Moone, who had turned away towards the kitchen units. 'Where have they put the head this time?'

Moone nodded towards the wall. 'The garden. Come on.'

Jairus followed him, moving out of the way to accommodate the white plastic suited SOCOs that hurried back and forth. Through the large French windows at the back of the house, Jairus could see the long stretch of lawn and the white tent at the centre of it. Again, the forensic team were coming and going, entering and leaving the tent.

They walked out through the French windows and out into the drizzle, then turned and entered the tent.

There it is. He stopped dead, allowing the object to form. Like before, the metal pole was hammered into the ground. On the other end, the head sat, its mouth open. He walked round and looked into the face. The eyes were closed, the skin slightly grey. The head was not facing directly forward, but slightly to the east.

'Has the head been moved at all?' Jairus asked, taking out his notebook.

'No, just as it was.' Moone shook his head.

'It's facing east.' Jairus noted it down. 'Get plenty of photos. Back to the kitchen.'

There seemed to be even more bodies crowding in, taking prints or swabbing blood or taking photographs. Jairus told most of them to leave. He watched their white plastic-wrapped bodies depart, then he looked at the victim, or what was left of him. 'Did you find the hands and feet?'

'In the bin along with his penis,' Moone said and raised his eyebrows. 'They've got real class these bastards.'

'Yeah, and two in two days,' Jairus murmured, then crouched down, looking towards the kitchen table. Something had caught his eye. He took off his jacket and laid it on the floor, then stretched out his body, his eyes a couple of inches from the tiled flooring.

Yes, there it was. There was a minute mark, perhaps blood. And about two feet to the right, exactly parallel with the first, was another mark. He turned round. 'Get a SOCO in here. Test this for blood.' Then he jumped back up, put his jacket back on and walked quickly from the kitchen, his eyes leaping over every object he saw on his way. He walked up the wide staircase, noting the paintings on the way up, mostly all modern art- splashes of various colours. All very grim looking.

He stopped halfway up the stairs when he saw

a mirror about the right size. He measured with his arms, nodded, then looked on either side and saw what he expected to see. Blood.

He put on a pair of gloves and lifted the mirror from the wall, then carried it carefully to the kitchen and nudged a SOCO, who had been testing the blood marks on the floor. He placed the mirror down and stood back.

'Jesus, bloody...' Moone said, his voice failing. 'They made him watch?'

Jairus nodded. 'Yeah, like I said before, this is about anger and revenge. They cut off his dick, so it's sexual too. We need to know everything there is to know about Burgess' history. Any previous criminal history.'

'I'll get on it.'

Jairus rubbed his face. 'Right, I want everything photographed in this place. I mean everything. And let's start by finding the connection between this victim and Thomas Henry.'

Moone looked round the flash kitchen. 'They're both wealthy businessmen. Maybe that's the connection.'

'No, you don't get this furious over money, and capitalism. No, you stand on street corners shouting about poverty or you join the Socialist Workers Party. There'll be a connection between these two of some kind. Get hold of Edgar Holzman too. I want to ask him about Burgess.'

'OK.'

'And I want a meeting of everyone today at lunchtime.' Jairus headed for the door.

'What are you going to do?' Mooned called out.

'Get some breakfast.'

Big red words printed on the glass frontage of the shop said: Roger's Fireplace. It was only a small business, squeezed between a launderette and a women's clothes shop not far from Cockfosters high street. Along the street were a few swanky looking restaurants that Marsland's always fancied trying but never got round to.

Inside the shop, the walls were lined with stylish and old-fashioned fireplaces. At the back of the shop a large bald man stood talking to a middle-aged couple. Marsland waited for nearly fifteen minutes before the couple left. He walked up to the counter, smiled and flicked his eyes over the shop. 'Nice place. Do you do good business?'

The owner nodded. 'Not bad. Things are a bit slow at the moment, but I'm hoping it'll pick up. Can I help you with something?'

'You are Philip Saunders?'

The man's eyes narrowed. 'Yes, why?'

'I'm sorry to bother you, Mr Saunders, I really am, but I need to ask you some questions about your daughter.'

'So you're from the police?'

'I used to be, now I'm looking into Ria's disappearance privately. I really want to get to the bottom of what happened. I can look into things more thoroughly than the police can. I can go places they can't.' Marsland looked the man in the eye and saw his confusion, then his sadness, all folding over him at once.

'There's not much I can say,' Saunders said and pulled up an office chair from near the till. 'One night she went out and then she never came back. It was totally out of character. She would never just up and vanish like that. Her and her mother were so close. There's no way she would just go without saying a word.'

'You think someone took her?'

Saunders looked at the counter, swallowed, then nodded. 'Someone must have. I just...don't want to think...'

'I know. I'm sorry. Ria was meant to meet her friend, Sara, that night, wasn't she?'

Saunders tutted and shook his head. 'Waste of space that girl. I've tried to get in touch with her so many times but I never hear from her. And she's a bleeding junkie.'

'Why do you say that?'

'I saw the silly cow down Tottenham High Road, saw her slipping money to some skinny bloke, then he passed her something.'

'I see. I'm sorry to ask, but do you think Ria...?'

With his face bright red, Saunders said, 'No way. Ria would never. She hated all that. That's why I think they fell out so much. She must've known what Sara was into. And I remember Ria telling me about some waster that Sara hung about with. Some kind of drug dealer.'

Marsland nodded, picturing the human version of a pit bull walking up to Sara's door. 'Do you think they might know something about Ria's disappearance?'

'It wouldn't surprise me. But wouldn't the police have looked into that? I told them all about this.'

'Sometimes things get overlooked, I'm afraid.' Marsland put his hand out to shake. 'I promise you, Mr Saunders, I'm going to keep looking into this and do my best to get the bottom of it.'

Marsland watched the man hesitate then take his hand, while his eyes watered a little. 'Thank you...I'm sorry, what's your name?'

'Terence Marsland.'

The man smiled. 'Thank you. Please let me know

what you find out.'

'I will.'

All the team were in the incident room when Jairus pushed open the door and walked across the floor. They were all munching on takeaway sandwiches and burgers that someone had bought and spread out on a table near the front of the room.

Jairus turned to the whiteboard and looked over the photos of the victims on the board. Three so far, he nodded to himself, but he had a feeling there would be more.

He picked up one of the slightly warm burgers and took a bite, then grimaced.

'Not enjoying that, sir?' Walker asked, sipping a coffee.

'It's rank. Did you look into the house? Who designed it and the security system?'

She nodded and put down her coffee. 'Yes, I did. Talked to the architect, Richard Dawson. Basically he designed it, got his massive wad of cash and never had anything to do with the victim again. Same with the security system people. Nothing dodgy I can see there. But somebody must have known how to get in.'

'Or maybe they knew their killers. Trusted them enough to let them in.'

Walker picked up her coffee again. 'It's possible.'

Moone walked over holding a half eaten sandwich. 'I checked the CCTV footage and we've got clear images of a car pulling up in the back lane. Looks like a dark blue Ford something. Two men, wearing masks, get out and walk up through the back garden and then somehow get inside. There's a blind spot at the back door. But Burgess wasn't home til later. Anyway, he's not going to let in two armed masked men.'

Jairus nodded. 'So, if the victims aren't letting them in, how are they getting inside?'

'Someone they all know?' Walker asked.

Jairus pointed at her. 'Yeah. Check who else knows the codes to the house. Both victims' houses in fact. Is Holzman here yet?'

Moone pointed a thumb at the door. 'I had a PC put him in room 2.'

'Ok, I'll find out what he knows about Burgess.'

There seemed to be little movement in Sara's house, but after a while Marsland could hear something. He lowered his car window and leaned his head out, trying to filter the noise of traffic from the sound coming from inside her house. Yes, there it was again, a baby crying, screaming for someone to come. He stepped out of the car and walked fast to the front door and hammered his fist on it. No noise from inside the house, so he walked round to the windows and got close to the glass.

He peered in, squinting, trying to focus on the shape on the sofa. The baby was still crying, the harsh sound cutting through his brain. The figure on the sofa was thin, and he could see blonde hair, he thought.

Marsland went quickly to the front door, and hammered at it again, then flapped the letterbox a few times.

'Sara?' he shouted, crouched down, looking through the slot.

He heard the sound of trainers scraping the path behind him before the shadow fell across him.

'What the fuck're you doing, mate?'

Marsland stood up and faced the pit bull man. He was probably early thirties, Marsland decided, then noted his stocky appearance, his beaten up and thick hands.

'There's a baby screaming in there,' Marsland said.

'So fucking what? What the fuck has it got to do with you? Why don't you sling yer hook?'

'I need to talk to Sara, then I'll sling my hook.'

The human pit bull sidled up closer, looking upwards, a dead-eye stare meeting Marsland's eyes. 'If you don't fuck off now, old man, I'm going to have to teach yer a fucking lesson. You got it?'

Marsland turned back to the door and battered it once more.

A meaty hand clamped down on his shoulder, spinning him round. Marsland threw out his fist, throwing his weight behind a punch to the pit bull's throat. The pit bull clasped his throat, coughing and staggering backwards. Marsland lifted his leg and kicked at the pit bull's ankle, making him cry out and collapse to the floor.

When Marsland faced the door, Sara was leaning against the frame, her lank hair half covering her face. She looked confused and her eyes were mere slits in her face. He grabbed her left arm, yanking her forward and ripping her cardigan's sleeve back. He saw the old and new needle marks, then looked in her swimming eyes and pushed past her, heading for the crying baby. He followed the sound up a short flight of brown patterned stairs. He found a red-faced baby lying in a cot, and gently picked him up. The baby kept screaming as Marsland carried him downstairs towards his mother.

Sara was now back on the couch, her eyes still blank.

'Here,' he said and put the child in her arms. 'Comfort him.'

He was pulled backwards, a bulbous arm clenched

round his neck. Then he was thrown across the room, smashing into the wall, sending a mirror shattering to the floor. The pit bull lurched at him, a huge fist held up, racing towards him. Marsland scrambled up as the fist caught him on the jaw knocking back down, then came another. He could only hold out his arms as the giant fists kept coming, kept smashing into his face and chest. It was never going to end.

The cry of agony and the swearing was painfully loud. Marsland looked and saw the pit bull man fall backwards, grasping for his back, shouting all the time.

'You fucking bitch!!' The pit bull man rolled over and got to his knees, his hand still clamped on his back.

When Marsland looked towards Sara, he could see the knife in her hand, her face completely empty.

Marsland picked up the child, hurried out the house, and began to dial for the police. He stopped and put away his phone when he saw an incident response car coming round the corner, heading right for him.

Edgar Holzman was sat calmly in interview room 2 when Jairus entered and placed a blank statement form on the metal desk. He sat down and folded his arms and smiled at Holzman.

'It's nice to see you again, DI Jairus.'

'Actually, it's DCI Jairus these days.'

Holzman raised his eyebrows. 'You are moving up in the world. Congratulations.'

'Thank you.' Jairus took out the photograph he had brought of Graham Burgess. 'Do you know this man?'

Holzman lowered his eyes, taking in the photograph Jairus passed to him. He stared at the image for a moment then raised his empty eyes. 'No, I'm sorry, I've never seen the man before. Has he committed some crime? Or is he your main suspect?'

Jairus slipped the photograph back towards himself. 'Neither. This man was brutally murdered last night. We believe there is a connection between this man's and your friend's murder. But you say you've never met him?'

'I can't honestly say that I've met the man or at least I don't recollect meeting him.' Holzman smiled.

'Maybe this was a friend of Thomas' who you knew nothing about.'

Holzman shrugged. 'It's quite possible. My relationship with poor Thomas was a fleeting one. He kept more and more to himself. I hardly ever saw him.'

Jairus leaned over the desk. 'Why that morning? Why did you go and see him?'

'I was driving by. I often get up early and go for a drive, get some breakfast... And I happened to think of Thomas and decided to check in on him.' The expression of the man suddenly changed. His smile faded and he looked suspiciously towards Jairus. 'Can I be totally honest with you, DCI?'

'It would be appreciated. We don't like it when people hold information back.'

Holzman nodded. 'You see, I didn't visit Thomas very much these days because...well, his behaviour was becoming increasingly strange. On some occasions I had turned up after phoning him to tell him I was on my way, but he would refuse to let me in.'

'Really? Did he seem upset?'

'Yes, he did. Sometimes very upset.'

After he stood up, Jairus leaned across the table and looked Holzman in the eye. 'The people who murdered Thomas and his daughter and Graham

Burgess, were extremely angry. They wanted to inflict pain and agony on their victims. So I'd suggest if you know something or might know someone who knows what this is all about, then tell them to come and see me, because they're going to keep on doing this until they finish the job.'

Holzman nodded. 'What makes you think they haven't finished?'

'Because they left a message, or a warning to someone.'

'Really? What sort of message?'

'I can't tell you that. Right, unless you've got anything else to tell me Mr Holzman, then you can go.'

CHAPTER 7

In interview room number 3, Terence Marsland was sitting waiting to be interviewed by whoever would turn up. Unknown to him, Peter Moone had been notified of what had happened and that Marsland was involved. All the way down the stairs from the incident room, Moone's stomach was turning. Shit. Shit. Shit. He'd been massively overworked and so very tired, what with the present caseloads, the new baby, and little Jack's screaming fits to contend with at bedtime. The only way he could think to relieve some of the burden was to get Marsland involved. He didn't really want to get him involved at all; he was quite aware of the stress and injuries caused to the old man by his last private investigation. But it was a simple missing person's case, or so he had thought.

He pushed open the interview room door and stared at the ex-copper. 'What the bloody hell happened?'

Marsland sighed. 'I had a bit of trouble with her boyfriend.'

Moone sat down and looked over the wounds and bruises on Marsland's face. The paramedics had taped up the worst, but there obviously hadn't been much they could do about his black-eye. 'So I can see. What did you tell the uniforms?'

'Don't worry. I didn't bring you into it. As far as they know, I just heard a baby crying and decided to poke my nose in.'

Moone let out a shaky breath. 'That's a blessed relief. So, Sara's a junkie and now her son's going to end up in care?'

Marsland nodded. 'Yes...I wish...'

Moone held up a hand. 'Don't worry yourself, he's better off without her. It's a shame, but perfectly true. What did you find out?'

'Not a great deal really. I talked to Ria Saunders' ex-boyfriend, Jamie, and he mentioned some rich charmer who she took a fancy to about a year before she disappeared.'

As he took out his notebook, Moone said, 'That's more than I found out. Nice one. Has this charmer got a name?'

'Graham Burgess.'

Moone froze and looked up. 'Tell me you're pulling my fucking leg.'

Marsland was blank-faced. Moone cringed, knowing that the ex-copper didn't have much of a sense of humour. 'Haven't you read the papers? No, of course you haven't. Oh bloody hell, Marsland. Graham Burgess was murdered last night.'

'How?'

After banging his head on the desk, Moone looked up. 'Cut to pieces. Penis, hands, feet. Head stuck on a great big bloody pole.'

'Is this part of a series?'

'Two separate events so far. Three dead. I have to go and try and dig myself out of a hole. You stay right here.'

Moone ran up the stairs, feeling as if he was heading to his doom, and found himself facing Jairus who was sipping a coffee in the incident room. 'Hey, you done with Holzman?'

'Yeah.'

Moone lowered his voice. 'Can I have a word, boss?'

Jairus put down his coffee and squinted at him. 'What's wrong? You never call me boss.'

'Can we step into the corridor?'

Outside, in the hallway, it seemed too quiet, and Moone thought his own voice sounded strange, sort of fading as he spoke. 'I'm sorry, Jairus, but I think there might be a connection between my missing girls and your murders.'

Jairus folded his arms. 'Yeah? Go on.'

'Well, I've been up to my neck in paperwork and the baby and Mandy and...'

'Just spit it out, Pete.'

'I've had Terence Marsland helping me on the quiet with the missing girls. You know what he's like. He's clever and being unofficial he can go places we can't.'

'For fu… who else knows about this?'

Moone rubbed his hair. 'Marsland, me and now you. That's all.'

'You sure? Think about it.'

'No one else. Scout's honour.'

'Good. Let's keep a lid on this. Where's Marsland now?'

Moone pointed to the stairs. 'Down in interview room 3. You want a word with him?'

'Yeah, or course I want a word with him.' Jairus shook his head and stormed towards the stairs, then stopped dead and swung round and came back. 'Did you send someone over to visit the parents of Winter Johnson, the girl who designed the dress we found?'

'Yes, a couple of uniforms, but they didn't find any dresses or designs or anything that could help us.'

Jairus nodded. 'They must have told her to destroy

the designs after she made the dresses. Do us a favour, find out what this is.' He took out a piece of folded paper and handed it to Moone.

With the paper unfolded, Moone could see it was a rough drawing of some kind of symbol. It looked like two triangles back to back, with a large letter 'z' going through the middle. 'What is it?'

'It was on the dress. Find out what it means. Oh, and any chance the SOCOs found a similar dress at Burgess' house?'

'No, nothing like that.'

'Burgess had a PA, apparently, so get her to come in. Oh, and where was Thomas Henry's daughter off to?'

'She had an E-ticket booked for New Zealand. She couldn't get far enough away.'

'Interesting.'

Marsland's head sprung up when the door opened and a tall and broad police officer appeared in the doorway. He looked down at him for a moment through his interrogator's eyes. His face was a solid block- deeply set eyes and thin mouth carved into skin-coloured granite.

'I'm DCI Jairus,' the officer said and pulled out a chair, then seemed to change his mind. 'I've heard a lot about you, Marsland. Can I call you Terence?'

'As long as you don't call me Terry.'

The large officer broke into a short-lived grin, then paced the room for a moment.

Marsland recognised Jairus from years back, in the time just before he left the force. They hadn't worked together, but he recalled hearing good things about him.

'You're a bit of a legend round here,' Jairus said,

turning to look at Marsland. 'They talk about you like you're Sherlock Holmes.'

'Hardly.'

'You met Graham Burgess, right? Just before our friends sliced him up.'

Marsland nodded, glad his appraisal was over. 'Yes.'

'What did you make of him?'

'Smug. Self-obsessed. Usual rich boy characteristics.'

Jairus nodded. 'Another rich boy died a few days before him. Same M.O. Cut to pieces. Whoever did it was angry. They wanted revenge, wanted to punish them.'

Marsland nodded again. 'What did they do to Burgess? Anything particular?'

'They cut off his penis.'

Marsland had a swirl of questions formulating in his brain alongside all the facts he knew about the missing girls. 'Was that the first thing they did?'

'Haven't had the post mortem results yet.'

'I'd check it out. Obviously sexual. Burgess met Ria Saunders and he tried to charm her. Perhaps they arranged to see each other again.'

Jairus eventually sat down. 'You think Burgess abducted her and the other girls?'

'It would make sense,' Marsland said. 'He chats them up, arranges a date, then abducts them. Maybe the first businessman they killed had another role in the girls' disappearance. Ria Saunders and the rest of the girls were the same age, had the same look. I'd bet money Burgess was involved in all the abductions.'

Jairus leaned back. 'Yeah, I think you're right. Burgess' killers left his head on a pole. I think they were sending a message to someone, which means they're not finished, which means there are a few conspirators involved.'

'A message that says we're coming for you.'

Jairus nodded. 'Yeah.'

'I'd check out Burgess' house.'

'Already are.'

'I mean Braxton House, at the end of Enfield Town. He bought it a year ago. It's far enough away from any other houses for the privacy he'd need. Must be plenty of dark dingy rooms inside.'

'Yeah, I think I'll look into it.' Jairus got up and leaned across the desk. 'And you...just leave this to us now. Got it? I mean it.'

'I will,' Marsland said, even though he knew he couldn't. He would never be able to leave it alone until he knew what had happened to all the girls. '

Then Jairus' face changed. 'I'm sorry about what happened to...'

Marsland held up his hand and shook his head. 'Don't. Just go and do your job.'

It seemed to take forever for Moone to get round the one-way system and reach the library. He preferred the old one up near the end of Enfield Town, with its stern and historic grey stone exterior. Now he parked up the road from the glass and steel face of the new library and walked towards it. He looked at his watch, wondering how long it would take to find the information on the symbol Jairus had scribbled down, and get back to the nick, half wondering if he had time to go home and see Mandy and the baby. He was hardly home these days and every time he did get home, he could see the coldness growing in his wife's eyes.

He was about to enter the automatic doors of the library, when his phone began ringing. He took it out and saw the unrecognised number. 'Hello?'

'Detective Sergeant Moone?' the voice asked.

'Yes, who's speaking?'

'Commander Warren. Where are you?'

Moone took the phone from his ear, mouthed a swear word, then placed it by his mouth again. 'Enfield Town. Outside the library, doing some important follow-ups.'

'I need a word. Stay there and I'll pick you up.'

The phone went dead, and Moone looked up, watching the traffic stream past, wondering what the bloody hell Warren wanted. Shit, he thought and realised it must be about Jairus.

It wasn't long before Commander Warren's chauffeur driven Mercedes pulled up outside the library. The door opened and Moone climbed in, finding himself sitting next to Warren, who was dressed in his sparkling uniform.

'What exactly has Jairus got you researching now?' Warren said, unscrewing a bottle of water.

'We found a dress at the first crime scene. It had a symbol at the bottom of it made out of expensive diamonds. It probably doesn't mean anything, but you know Jairus.'

Warren nodded. 'I do. That's why I put him on the case. He's about the best we have, but he can be a little... unconventional sometimes.'

'But he's got a good clearance rate, you've got to give him that.'

'Of course. How's the investigation into the second murder scene progressing?'

'We've got a few leads.'

'Such as?'

Moone turned away. He knew he had to refrain from mentioning the missing girls, or Marsland for that matter. 'Well, the fact that the killers are targeting local wealthy businessmen. And the fact that it all seems to be about revenge.'

'I see. That's exactly why I'm getting pressure from above. The victims were influential businessmen and they did a lot for charity.'

'We're all doing the best we can.'

'Do you think I was right to put him on this? Do you think it was too soon?'

Moone looked at Warren and thought he saw the stress deep in his tired eyes. 'Like I said, he's one of the best. And he's resilient.'

'But he's also prone to keeping things to himself and going above and beyond.'

'That's what's needed sometimes.'

Warren smiled. 'Sometimes, Moone, not all the time. That's why I want you to keep an eye on him.'

'Me? Spy on him and report back to you?'

'I need to keep him on a short leash. Just in case. He's been through a lot. And we don't want him creating any more bad publicity, do we?'

Moone felt his stomach flip over. 'He's my friend...'

'He's your boss. Don't get sentimental. He doesn't get sentimental over you. Don't make that mistake. Listen, all I want you to do is to keep me informed of how the investigation is going. That's not much to ask, is it?'

'I thought that's what we usually do.'

'Don't be sarcastic, Moone. You know what I'm getting at. Let me put it this way...you've been feeling the pinch lately, haven't you? What with the baby and your other little boy? I know, I've been there. Wouldn't a promotion help things? Bump up the wages a little?'

'Sounds a little like you're trying to buy me, sir.'

Warren sat back, a slight smile on his face. 'I

wouldn't put it quite that way. I just think a leg up to Detective Inspector is long overdue, don't you?'

Moone felt his gut twist, then tighten, and heard his wife's voice demanding him to take the promotion. To hell with Jairus, she'd say. But then he thought again, realising there were games to play, positions he could take up. Accepting the promotion and taking Warren's hand could lend a few cards to his deck. 'I'll see what I can find out.'

'You're a wise man, Moone. I'll put in a good word for you, as long as you keep me abreast of the investigation.'

'Like I said, I'll do my best.'

'Simon, pull over here, will you?' Warren shouted to the driver. The car slid to a halt and Moone climbed out and watched the Mercedes rejoin the traffic and rumble away.

'Bastard,' Moone said under his breath and walked back towards the library.

CHAPTER 8

He stood watching the grand house, his hands deep into his raincoat's pockets, looking up at the blackening sky, feeling the occasional spit of rain. Jairus' eyes turned towards the myriad flowers that surrounded him and found himself picturing Karine wearing a pale blue summer dress, her wavy black hair pulled back into a pony tail. It had been somewhere deep into the summer, perhaps around his birthday, and they'd spent the day sitting on the grass by the pond, or wandering through the grounds.

It was the day he'd fallen in love with her.

Jairus blinked away the thoughts and turned to look at the police constables standing round swapping stories, laughing, waiting for something to do. He focused on the house again, seeing the old stone work, the ivy clambering up one side, the large ornate windows. Did something bad happen inside that building? He turned and saw Walker heading towards him.

'Where is she?' Walker asked and looked at her watch.

'She's on her way.'

Walker joined him in his watch of the house. 'What you thinking?'

'That maybe Burgess and Henry had some very dark secrets.'

A red car pulled slowly along the lane to their right and stopped. The engine was running, while the female driver watched them with a mobile stuck to her face. Eventually the engine died and she climbed out. She was about forty, mousey hair cut into a sharp bob, and wore a dark grey jacket and matching skirt. She looked flustered as she reached Jairus and put on some glasses.

'Are you the policeman I talked to?' she asked, her eyes jumping to Walker every so often.

Jairus showed his ID. 'DCI Jairus. You're Kate Roberts, Mr Burgess' PA?'

She smiled awkwardly, and turned to look at the house. 'Yes... What are you looking for? I mean...'

'For any reason that those two men targeted your boss,' Walker said.

Roberts faced them both. 'I don't get it. Maybe they planned on robbing him and...'

'As far as we know, nothing was taken.' Jairus pointed to the house. 'We need to get in there.'

She walked with him to the door, and unlocked it. 'Perhaps I should look over his house, to see if anything is out of place. He has some very valuable items.'

'Yeah, OK, we've got some photographs that we can show you.' Jairus entered the large hallway. The smell inside was the same as his old school's assembly hall. The floor was the same too, polished wood. There were paintings on all the walls of stern looking men. To the right was a wooden set of stairs with a thick and ornate bannister.

'Where's Burgess' office?' Jairus pointed to the stairs with his eyebrows raised.

Roberts moved out of the way for the straggle of constables. 'Next floor, end of the corridor. I don't know what you expect to find.'

'Nor do we. But we need to examine his life, and his properties to find out why he was murdered. That way we can find the people who killed him. You want to help us with that?'

'Of course. I'll print up a list of the houses he owns.'

'Thanks. What sort of employer was Mr Burgess?'

Roberts pushed her glasses up her nose, her eyes watching the boots hammering up the wooden stairs. 'Like any other. He was a busy man, so he didn't have time for niceties.'

'I heard he was a charmer.'

'Oh, he was very charming when he wanted to be or when he needed something.'

Jairus started up the stairs with the PA following. 'What did he do in his spare time? Any hobbies?'

She frowned. 'Not really sure. He worked most of the time. I didn't really see him past seven at night.'

'Lady friends?' Jairus approached the last door at the end of the corridor.

'I think there was the occasional woman in his life, but nothing long-term.'

'This his office?'

'Yes.'

Jairus slipped on a glove and tried the door, but found it locked. 'You got a key?'

'Well, no. Mr Burgess is usually working in here by the time I arrive.'

He pointed down the corridor. 'Can you go and find my colleague, DI Walker?'

She looked confused for a moment, then sighed and walked away. Jairus waited until she had disappeared down the stairs, listening to the sound of her heels fading away, then faced the door again. He stepped backwards a little way and swiftly lifted his leg and smashed his foot against the door. He walked back even more, rested his back on the wall and kicked again. On his third attempt, the door flew open.

It was not a particularly large office, and the decor didn't seem to have changed since the Victorian owners had left. There were paintings of the English countryside on the walls, and at the back, sitting under a large window, was a heavy oak desk with a laptop on it.

Jairus walked round the desk and sat in the leather office chair, then flipped open the laptop. He turned it on, waited for it to boot up, then tried a few obvious passwords. No luck.

He sat back as he heard a pair of sensible shoes coming down the hall. Walker came in, her eyes examining the broken lock of the door.

'You kicked the door in?'

'Yeah, I didn't think Burgess would mind. Can you get the IT boys down here to take this away?'

'You think you're going to find incriminating photos on there or something?' Walker leaned on the desk.

'You never know. The uniforms found anything?'

'They've only just started looking.'

Jairus huffed, stood up, then looked around the room, really taking it all in for the first time. Everything was old-fashioned, nothing had been touched. Little suggested that Burgess liked spending a lot of time in his office. He walked quickly past Walker, who was calling the IT boys, and hurried round the building until he found Kate Roberts. She was resting her backside on her car and talking to someone on her mobile. She ended the call quickly and smiled expectantly at Jairus. 'Yes?'

'What was so special about this building?'

Roberts shrugged. 'I don't know. I think he just liked the look of the place. He was going to restore it.'

'Any of his other properties have historical relevance?'

She looked confused. 'No. He owns apartment buildings, some factories and places like that.'

'Places he earns money from?'

'Yes. All investments.'

He nodded and turned to the building. 'How much did he buy it for?'

'Three million, four hundred.'

'Jesus,' Jairus said. 'Have you got anything on the history of the house?'

'We've got some leaflets that we keep because people come back asking about the house's history.'

Jairus followed her into the hallway, then off to a small office near the back. Roberts took a leaflet from a pile and handed it to him.

There was a photo of the house on the front, then smaller pictures of the interior. It was built in the Jacobean period. His eyes scanned down quickly. He stopped when he read the word PRISON. He looked up at Roberts. 'It says here it was used as a prison during the Second World War. Where were the cells?'

'Cells? I don't know. I've never really read the leaflet before.'

More than likely, he thought, the cells would be below, dug deep into the ground. 'What about under the building? Anything down there?'

'No, I don't think so. There's some stairs, but they just lead to a storage cupboard.'

'Show me.'

She went ahead, walking slowly through the ground floor, turning occasionally to look at him questioningly. Finally they came to a flight of stone steps that led to a large cupboard. She opened it and let him see the piles of toilet rolls, cleaning fluids, mops and kitchen equipment. Jairus stepped forward.

'Is this stuff moved often?'

'I don't think so.'

'Well, the dust's been disturbed.' He crouched down, inspecting the floor. There was a scrape mark forming a perfect arch. Jairus jumped to his feet and climbed halfway back up the stairs. 'Walker! Get down here!'

The PA stared down at the floor of the cupboard. 'What've you found?'

'I think you should go and wait upstairs. Now, please.'

Roberts slowly stepped away, then hurried up the stairs as Walker came down. She stopped, her hands her on her hips. 'What is it?'

'Get hold of the SOCOs. And seal this whole place off.'

If there was a connection between the missing girls and Graham Burgess, Marsland had decided he would be the one to find it. He looked in the rear view mirror and saw the state of his face, grimaced, but was quite aware time was ticking by. A thought had occurred to him on several occasions; what if the person who had taken the girls liked to enjoy their time with them? What if he liked to stretch it out, to put them through a living hell?

Then Marsland's thoughts returned to the house he'd parked across from; it was home to the parents of the latest missing girl, Gina Colman. There was a link between Ria Saunders and Burgess, but there was nothing as yet concrete suggesting the other two girls were taken by the same person. It was only their look that had inspired his gut to ignite. Moone had admitted the same. All three girls had almost the same hair colour, style and facial features, so much so they could be related.

Marsland touched his face and winced. This would be tricky, he decided, and climbed out of his car and headed over the road to the small terraced house with the gleaming white door. He rang the bell, and waited, then saw a large figure through the frosted glass in the door.

A balding man with square glasses opened the door and looked questioningly at Marsland. 'Hello?'

'Mr Colman?'

'Yeah?'

'I'm sorry to bother you, but I'd like to talk to you about your missing daughter, Gina.'

Mr Colman frowned. 'Have you found something out? I mean, are you from the police?'

Marsland shook his head. 'I'm afraid not, but I believe I can help in finding out what happened.'

'If you're from the papers...' Colman began to shut the door.

'Mr Colman, I've had many years experience of working in the police force. And I can find things out that the police can't.'

'What happened to your face?'

Marsland touched his wounds. 'Car accident.'

'Why should we listen to...'

'Who is it, Derek?' a short, plump woman asked from inside the house. Then Marsland could see her carrying a basket of washing. She had shoulder length straight blonde hair. Her eyes had deep dark trenches beneath them.

'No one, darling,' Derek said and smiled at her. 'He was just going.'

'Who are you, luv?' Mrs Colman came closer, examining Marsland carefully. 'You look familiar.'

'I think I can help find out what happened to your daughter, Mrs Colman.'

Mr Colman ran a hand down his face as Mrs Colman pushed him out of the way. 'Who are you?'

'My name's Terence Marsland. I used to be a...'

'You're the one that saved that girl, aren't you?'

Marsland inwardly cringed. 'Time is of the essence, Mrs Colman. If I can be of...'

Mrs Colman pushed her husband to one side. 'Derek, go put the kettle on. You want a cup of tea, luv?'

Marsland smiled and stepped inside.

'Go through to the kitchen,' Mrs Colman said and gently steered him forward.

Mr Colman was filling the kettle and setting out the mugs while Mrs Colman pulled out the chairs round the kitchen table.

'That was wonderful what you did for that girl,' Mrs Colman said, her voice breaking a little, her hand clutching the gold crucifix round her neck.

'Thank you,' he said and looked through the window towards the garden.

'Do you think Gina's alright?'

Marsland turned to face her. 'I'll do my best to find out what happened to her.'

'You promise you'll tell us the moment you find out?'

Mr Colman leaned against the work surface. 'He can't make promises like that, Sue.'

'You can, can't you, Mr Marsland? He found that girl, Derek, didn't you? You found her.'

Marsland no longer wanted to be there, the mother's eyes seemed to be growing with desperate hope. He looked at the father and saw that all his positivity had already deserted him.

'Do you mind if I look at her room?'

'How do we know you are who you say you are?' Mr Colman straightened.

'Derek!' his wife barked.

'What if he's one of those bloody journalists?'

Marsland stood up. 'Perhaps I should come back another time.'

'No, please.' The wife rushed round the table, blocking his exit. 'Take a look in her room. Maybe you can see something that the police missed.'

Marsland smiled and noticed her hand tightening around the crucifix again. 'OK, I'll do my best.'

'Wait.' Mr Colman came towards him holding a mug. 'Here's your tea. You know that Mrs Downs said she saw Gina getting in a dark-coloured sports car that day? She's wasn't very reliable, you know she was getting a bit scatty in the head and all that, but it's the only thing we've had to go on.'

'I take it she's no longer around?'

Colman shook his head. 'Died a few months back.'

'Did Gina keep a diary?'

Mr Colman shrugged, but Mrs Colman said, 'Yes, she did, luv, but I've never been able to find it. You should talk to Jenny, her best friend. Works at Pearsons in the town.'

Marsland took a sip of the tea and placed the mug on the table. 'OK if I go up to her room?'

'Upstairs, last door on the right,' Mrs Colman said, smiling. 'You go and do your thing.'

Marsland went down the hallway, then up the thickly-carpeted stairs, feeling a sickness filling his stomach.

Jairus knew it would not be too much longer until he could enter the room they had found. It had taken all his strength to pull away and wait for the SOCOs to do their magic. He'd tried sitting in his car, but his hand kept drumming on the steering wheel and his legs would jitter. He was driving himself crazy, so he knew he was probably getting on Walker's nerves too.

He walked away from the crime scene, down one of the paths that led to the giant pond. Swans nestled in the reeds at the far end and there were ducks following each other across water. He picked up a stone and lobbed it as hard as he could. The water gushed upwards, then folded in on itself. He crouched down, gripping his head, his eyes still seeing the blackness that had been beyond the door. He had opened the door, looked in and smelt the grime and stale air. It had tried to pull him in, but he'd resisted and run up the stairs and taken giant panicked breaths once in the garden.

He saw Karine lying in the bathroom, so thin and white. Carl Murphy in a ball, pleading.

Jairus turned on his heel and marched towards the crime scene once again, his eyes fixed on the beautiful house, the pretty flowers that seemed to crawl from under its belly.

Two SOCOs were coming out when he reached the house. One put away a camera in a case, the other was carrying a UV light.

'Can I go in yet?' he asked them both.

'Grab an outfit and help yourself,' one of them said, but he didn't notice which. He went to the SOCO van, grabbed a suit, put it on and strode to the house. It seemed much darker inside, now he was out of the bright sun, and blobs of light swirled in his vision. He walked down the stone steps and towards the glaring artificial light that made the SOCOs' shadows stretch out the door and along the wall.

With his hood firmly on his head, his gloved hands clenched into fists, Jairus took a deep breath as he stepped down onto the concrete floor. The air was cool, but damp. He stood in the small room, looking across the bodies that were already going about their business, while he tried not to focus on what would have gone on inside the small cell when the door was locked. He moved on, carefully edging round the evidence markers scattered across the floor. His eyes diverted to the left, only partially taking in the two objects attached the wall. They came into focus, forming into two manacles that were screwed into the stonework. Below them on the floor was a stain, and the stench of urine burnt into his nostrils.

'DCI Jairus, sir?' a young male voice said.

He turned and came face-to-face with a boyish looking SOCO. 'What is it?'

'Next room. Well, next two rooms actually.'

His eyes followed the SOCO's thumb and found a secure looking door. It was the only new-looking thing in the place. Reinforced glass. Bolts. Padlock. The whole works. Jairus walked through and found himself in another narrow room. He shook his head. He closed his eyes, then opened them and took it all in. There were four seats, all fixed to the floor, facing a partitioning wall. There was a large window in the wall. He looked through the glass to the next room through where he saw a metal bed with restraints on each corner. When he swept his eyes to the floor behind the chairs, he noticed something. Marks on the floor. Something with three tiny feet had stood there at one time.

He swept back out of the room, up the stairs,

ignoring a call from one of the SOCOs, and stepped out into the sunshine. He pulled off his hood and coughed out a breath, then wrestled the forensic outfit from his body.

'You alright?' Walker said, rushing up to him.

'Yeah, I'm...' He saw the concern in her eyes. 'No, I'm not alright. I'm really fucking not.'

'It's OK to get upset. Just means you're still human.'

He rubbed his eyes. 'Sometimes I wish I wasn't. But then I'd be like the animals that did...'

'How bad is it down there?'

Jairus folded up the forensic outfit and gave it to Walker. 'Three rooms. One where it looks like the victims were chained up, a second where they were chained to a bed and abused, and a third...'

Walker waited. 'What? What about the third room?'

'Four chairs bolted to the ground, facing a window through to the room with the bed.'

'Bloody...they watched?'

Jairus rubbed his eyes, trying to remove the flashes of torture, of blood, the girls screaming. 'Four chairs, which means four watched while one of them...and one set of chains, so they would've had one girl at a time.'

'So, they really abducted all the missing girls? That's what you're thinking?'

'Come on, Walker, what do you think? All the girls were the same age, had the same hair colour. They looked like sisters. Yeah, they took them alright.'

'What now?'

'We have to wait for the forensic report on that place,' Jairus said and started walking away. He stopped and faced Walker again. 'Talk to the PA, find out anything you can about Burgess. We need to know everything. Tear his properties apart, find the film.'

'Film?'

He nodded. 'There are marks on the floor, looks like a tripod was set up for photographs or for filming it all. My money's on a video camera. They'd want to be able to watch it over. The PA needs to see Burgess' other house, to tell us if there's anything missing or out of place. And get the IT people to take his laptop.'

'Already done. Where you going?'

'Post mortem results.'

CHAPTER 9

Jairus found Dr Jeremy Garrett in his small office, writing up some reports and listening to Johnny Cash very loudly on his CD player. He knocked on the open door, but the doctor didn't look up, so he walked in and leaned against the wall, listening to Cash grinding out 'Own Personal Jesus'.

'Oh, hello, DCI Jairus,' Garrett said, smiling and turning the music down.

'I prefer his older stuff,' Jairus said.

'You a Cash fan?'

'Yeah, isn't everybody?'

Garrett got up and rolled his eyes. 'Not everyone appreciates him. Haven't seen you in a while.'

With Garrett leading the way to the autopsy room, Jairus followed with his hands deep into his pockets. 'Yeah, been away a while.'

'Sometimes it does you good to get away,' Garrett said once inside the autopsy room. He washed his hands thoroughly, then put on some gloves.

'Sometimes.' Jairus rested his back against the tiled wall, feeling the coolness of it through his shirt. 'So, did the deceased tell you anything?'

'They always tell me everything,' Garrett said and pulled back a sheet from a table in the middle of the room. On the table was a circular saw, which Garrett picked up and held out to Jairus. 'The tool used to cut off Henry's limbs, and also Burgess' wrists and feet. The fingers of both victims' hands were removed using a pair of small shears. Oh, and it was probably the same tool used to cut off Burgess' penis. Which was found along with his hands and feet in the bin. And Burgess' toes were all smashed by something like a hammer.'

'Thank you.'

'My pleasure.' Garrett put the saw on the table.

'Was the penis removed first?'

Garrett nodded. 'Yes, it was, and I found a needle mark in his groin. They injected him with a local anaesthetic before removing it.'

Jairus nodded. 'They wanted him more composed, not to be in too much pain when they removed it and showed it to him.'

'Indeed. It was a regional anaesthetic. I'd check for recent theft in local hospitals if I was you.'

'Will do.'

'You've got a particularly sick pair of individuals on your hands, DCI.'

Jairus kicked himself away from the wall. 'Yeah, and they're angry, and they want revenge.'

'Well, if there's anything else I can tell you...'

'The woman. Henry's daughter. Marie.'

'Oh yes, she died, as you know, from a single gunshot to the head. Took apart her brain. She would have died instantly. Compared to her father, she hardly suffered.'

'They just couldn't let her live.' Jairus nodded to Garrett then headed out through the door and along the corridor. It was quiet. Too quiet. He tried to concentrate on the sound of his shoes tapping at the floor, and not on the whimpering. The pleading was growing louder, until it was a scream piercing his skull. He saw the sign for the gents' toilet and hurried towards it, shunted open the door and looked round the lime green walls. The gleaming urinals stared back at him. He opened a cubicle door, and shut it behind him. He stood there, facing the door, breathing hard, the whimpering growing louder in his ears. His mouth opened, stretched wide, his fist hammered against the toilet door, his shout echoed round the room.

Marsland saw DS Moone sitting in his car with the windows open, his mouth wrapped round a baguette. He walked over and climbed in the passenger seat. Moone raised his eyebrows, removed the roll from his mouth and wiped sauce from his chin.

'Bloody hell, Marsland,' Moone said, picking up his takeaway coffee. 'Why did you want to meet me in a supermarket car park?'

'Gina Colman,' Marsland said. 'The last girl to go missing.'

'Hang on, you're not supposed to be looking into that anymore. What do you think you're playing at?'

'You know as well as I do, that you lot need my help. You haven't got the manpower. We can keep it just between you and me.'

Moone huffed out a laugh. 'What is it with people and secrets at the moment? Look, Jairus is in charge of this, not me. Talk to...'

'Gina Colman had a dark secret, or at least she had a secret she thought her parents wouldn't like.'

Moone turned to face him. 'How do you know that?'

'I talked to Mr and Mrs Colman.'

'Jesus...'

'Listen, Gina kept a diary, I know because her mother saw her writing in it, but I couldn't find it in her bedroom. She kept it well hidden. Plus, Mrs Colman is very religious. The whole time I was there she kept clutching a crucifix round her neck. And the father's an angry and judgemental man.'

'So?' Moone sipped his coffee.

'So it must have been a very serious secret. Something her parents couldn't ever find out.'

'And what is it?'

Marsland shrugged. 'I have a theory. I need you to check something out.'

'What?'

'Take a look at Burgess' cars. See if he owns a dark sporty-looking car. Gina was seen getting into one the day she vanished.'

Moone sighed, then took out his notebook. 'Ok. I'll check it out. And what're you going to do?'

'I'm going to go and see her best friend. If anyone would know her secret, it would be her best friend.'

'OK, but please don't get beaten up and arrested again.'

Marsland climbed out and leaned his head into the window. 'Just find out about the car.'

Jairus opened the door of the interview room with his elbow, careful not to spill the two cups of tea he carried. He placed them on the table and smiled at Burgess' PA, Kate Roberts, then pulled out a chair and sat down. Detective Constable Tobey Balewa had already taken a statement and was now sitting with his arms folded facing Roberts. Jairus pushed a mug of tea towards Roberts then sat back and stretched out his legs.

'I hope it's not too milky for you,' Jairus said and smiled. 'I like mine milky. How do you like your tea, Tobey?'

'Black, sir, two sugars,' Tobey said, looking a little confused.

Jairus nodded. 'I'm sorry for all this, Kate. Do you mind if I call you Kate?'

Roberts shook her head, then sat forward. 'What did you find down there? I mean...if it was something... well, bad, I can assure you it had nothing...'

Jairus held up a hand, smiling. 'Yeah, I know, Kate. It's alright, we know you didn't know anything about what went on down there. I mean, if you knew, you'd tell us, wouldn't you?'

Roberts nodded, clutched her chest. 'Of course. I didn't know...I mean, what did go on down there? Is it bad? Is it really bad?'

'We'd like you to look at some photographs, Kate.'

She swallowed and nodded her head. 'OK, but it's nothing...I mean, it's not..?'

'It's nothing gruesome,' Jairus said, then signalled to DC Balewa to give him the envelope. He then opened it and took out the shots of Burgess' house. 'These were taken of Burgess' house. I take it you're familiar with his home?'

'Yes, I've been there a lot. That's where he'd tell me to come when he wanted to discuss any issues that had arisen.'

Jairus put a hand on the photographs and pushed them towards Roberts. 'Take a look. Tell me if you spot anything out of place or anything missing.'

Her long thin hand pulled the photographs towards her. She turned them over slowly, as if she expected to see one of a dead body. She swallowed again, then looked at the first shot, then the second, and she went through the whole set.

'Nothing out of the ordinary?' Jairus leaned across the desk.

Roberts shrugged. 'Not really. I'm not sure what I'm looking for.'

'Anything missing?'

The PA carried on through the photographs again, then stopped. She frowned, her forehead crinkling up a little. 'This one…it's from the hallway.'

Jairus took it. 'Yeah, and?'

'Well, I suppose Mr Burgess could have moved it, but it seems to me that a rare mug is missing. It had an Arcadian design, it was bought from Bonhams for about four thousand pounds.'

'And that's the only thing you think is missing?' Jairus stood up.

She nodded. 'That's the only thing I can see.'

Jairus picked up her mug of tea, then his own and nodded for Tobey to open the door for him. He walked out and along the corridor and awkwardly entered the next interview room. A plump woman with thick curly brown hair sat at another metal desk. She wore an ill-fitting blue cardigan and white blouse. She looked up expectantly and smiled a little when Jairus placed the milky tea for her, next to a pile of photographs.

'Milky, two sugars,' Jairus said and sat down. 'That OK? Might be a bit cold.'

Valerie Gartrell felt the cup and smiled. 'It's fine. I looked through the photographs like you asked.'

'Yeah, and did you see anything that's out of place?' Jairus leaned back in his chair, waiting.

She shook her head. 'I don't think so. I don't really take much notice of his stuff.'

'You've been cleaning for Mr Henry for quite a while, yeah?'

She nodded and lifted the tea to her lips. 'About three years.'

'And what sort person do you think he was?'

She sipped the tea, her eyes jumping down to the photographs, and up again to Jairus. 'He's...sorry, he was...well, a very private person. When he first interviewed me for the job, he made sure I wouldn't bring anyone with me. Not even one of my family.'

Jairus felt his heart jolt a little. 'Why do you think that was?'

She shrugged. 'I don't know. I suppose he really didn't trust people. Probably thought he was going to get robbed.'

'Maybe. Can you look through the photographs one more time? Just to be sure. Really look at them.'

Valerie shrugged and picked up the photographs and started looking through them.

Jairus leaned over, watching her eyes. 'This time imagine you're there, walking through the house... cleaning and...'

She looked up at him, frowning.

'Please, can you try? I know it sounds stupid.'

'Alright.' She started going through the photographs again, but this time very slowly. Jairus sat back, his arms folded across his chest, waiting. Then Mrs Gartrell stopped on one photograph, then went back to another, her forehead creased up. She looked up at Jairus, half smiling with embarrassment, he felt. She held a photograph of the living room- the mantelpiece to be precise.

'I can't believe I didn't notice the first time.'

'What is it?' He took the photo.

'There was a painting above there. I must have dusted it a million times. I can't believe I totally missed it.'

'What was the painting like?'

'Sort of weird looking. Looked gruesome to me, but I couldn't be sure what it was, but there was something disturbing about it.'

Jairus got up and smiled down at her. 'Thank you, Valerie, you've been a great help. One more question. Did Mr Henry's daughter ever come over?'

'That's funny you should say that...she did come over once. It was only a little while ago. She came in and said she needed to find something she'd left there...she went upstairs, then left.'

'How did she seem to you?'

'A bit flustered. In a hurry. Is that any help?'

'Yeah. Thank you again.'

Walker pulled up outside Graham Burgess' house and looked at the exterior, the size of the windows, the large driveway, wondering how much it cost.

'About three mil,' DS Moone said, poking his head through the passenger window, making her jump. 'You were wondering how much it cost, right? Come on.'

Walker climbed out, locked the car and followed Moone towards the house. A WPC was standing on the driveway waiting, her face official and blank.

'Need to pop round the back and take a look in the garage,' Moone said to the WPC.

'Yes, sir,' the WPC replied. 'Need to sign the log.'

Moone took the clipboard the WPC held out to him, signed it and handed it to Walker. She scribbled her name and handed it back.

Moone took the garage keys off the WPC then led Walker right round the back.

Halfway down the long pathway, Walker tapped Moone on the shoulder. He turned and faced her. 'What?'

'How come you got me to meet you? You could've done this on your own.'

Moone shrugged and smiled. 'I wanted an extra set of eyes.'

'You're not trying to get me on your own so you can tell me you fancy me, are you?'

Moone laughed, stuck up his middle finger and began walking towards the garages. 'Why would I do that? I'm a married man. And besides, I know there's only one copper you have eyes for.'

'Shut up,' Walker said sharply and overtook Moone. 'What are we expecting to find?'

'Gina Colman was picked up in a dark car. Something sporty.'

'She was the third girl to go missing, wasn't she?'

'Yes, only went missing a couple of months ago.' Moone stopped as he reached the wide brick building, which was cut into three garages.

'What do you make of Jairus these days?' Walker asked, watching Moone pull out three sets of keys from his pocket.

He looked up, a little quizzical. 'I thought you didn't want to talk about him?'

She raised an eyebrow. 'I mean, do you think he's OK? After what happened?'

'If you're asking me if I think he's OK up there, then the answers no.' Moone tapped his temple, then approached the first white garage door.

'You think he's fucked up?' Walker joined him.

'Of course he is. He killed a man. That tends to mess with your mind.'

Walker snatched some keys off Moone and walked to the next door. 'Then why is he back working?'

'Because we've not got enough detectives. And Jairus is good at what he does.' Moone tried a key in the first lock but it didn't open.

'You should've seen him at the crime scene today.'

Moone faced her. 'Why, what happened?'

'He came running out, and his face was white. Looked like he was going to have a heart attack.'

Moone sighed. 'I'm not surprised, Walker. He's been through hell and back, what with Karine and then Carl Murphy. Personally, I wouldn't waste any tears over Carl Murphy, but that's me. I mean, he tortured and murdered an eleven year old kid, just because of his skin colour.'

Walker nodded, tried the last garage door. It opened and she lifted the door. 'I got lucky. Looks like a dark sports car to me.'

Moone joined her and looked down at the sleek bodywork of the Audi R8. Dark metallic blue. 'Well done. Now all we have to do is get the SOCOs to give it the once over, but I bet Burgess gave it a good clean.'

'Yes, you're probably right.' Walker turned to Moone, narrowing her eyes at him. 'So why did you bring me here?'

There was a strange look in Moone's eyes as he turned to her, his hands in his pockets. 'I've been offered a promotion.'

'DI?'

He nodded.

'That's great. Yet, you look troubled.'

Moone kicked a stone away from him. 'The promotion is in exchange for keeping a close eye on Jairus, reporting back on the case. The Commander doesn't trust Jairus to be very forthcoming.'

'You're bloody joking? He's trying to buy you?'

'Scout's honour.'

Walker sighed, then took out a pair of gloves and pulled them on. 'You got the keys for this passion wagon?'

Moone threw them at her. She caught them and

opened the door carefully, making sure not to disturb any fingerprints that might be on the handle. She stared down at the car seat, a sudden buzzing coming from the back of her mind. She smiled to herself, then looked over at the expectant DS Moone. 'How tall was Burgess?'

Moone shrugged. 'Hard to say. Last time I saw him he was minus head and feet. Hang on.' Moone took out his mobile and seemed to call the incident room, trying to find someone who could dig out the relevant information. Eventually, he put his phone away and said, 'Five-eleven, thereabouts.'

'Hmm...' Walker crouched down. 'Now, I'm five-eight, and I'd have trouble driving this car at the moment. Look, whoever was driving this car last was pretty short. They've pulled the seat forward really far.'

Moone rushed over. 'Bloody hell, Walker, you're right. Hang on, what about the PA?'

'She's about my height.'

Moone nodded. 'Right then, let's get this to the SOCOs.'

CHAPTER 10

Marsland walked slowly through Pearsons Department Store, his eyes flickering over the young and old faces that ambled past him, the heavy carrier bags in their hands. He sniffed and smelt the place, the memories flashing back at him. Christmases melt into one. The desperate rush to buy a present, any present that might satisfy his wife.

He stopped by the relatively new section of the store that was aimed at young women. He scanned over the payment desk in the corner, seeing a tall, skinny brunette and a shorter, slightly overweight, but pretty young woman next to her. Both of them were wearing black blouses with the shop's emblem above the right breast.

He walked over to the desk, but only the tall skinny one lifted her head, an automatic and severely fake smile appearing on her lips.

'Can I help?' she asked.

Marsland looked at the other girl. Her name tag read: Jenny. 'Can I ask your co-worker to take a look at a dress? She's about my niece's size.' After getting a nod from the skinny boss, Jenny followed Marsland over to some rather short dresses in bright colours.

'What sort of thing was you after?' Jenny asked, smiling a little.

'I'm sorry, Jenny, but I'm here to talk to you about

Gina Colman. She was your best friend, wasn't she?'

'I'm sorry, but what's this about?'

'I've been asked to investigate her disappearance. I've talked to her parents, now I wanted to ask you about her.'

'There's not much I can say, really.' Her eyes dropped, while Marsland noticed she started tapping her leg.

'Can I just ask you a few questions?'

Jenny looked over to her skinny boss. 'I've got a break in twenty minutes. I usually go up to the restaurant on the top floor.'

'OK, I'll see you up there in twenty minutes?'

Jenny smiled awkwardly. 'Alright. I better go.'

Jenny stuck to her word. Marsland watched her, now wrapped in a dark green hoody, coming up the escalators and entering the canteen. He held up a hand, she nodded and walked over to his table and sat down, her pale blue eyes jumping onto the single mothers and old ladies surrounding them. Marsland pushed a baguette towards her, then a pot of tea and a cup.

'I bought a tuna mayo roll, if you want it?'

'Thanks, but I'm not very hungry.' She looked down and examined her short nails.

'Tell me about Gina.'

She sighed. 'What do you want to know?'

'Anything. What was she like?'

Jenny raised her shoulders, then swallowed hard. 'Nice. Kind. She was a good friend.'

'Did you spend much time at her parents' house?'

Jenny shook her head. 'No. She always came round mine.'

'You moved out of your parents'?'

'When I was seventeen. Couldn't stand it anymore.'

'Parents can be overbearing.'

'Yeah, tell me about it.'

He smiled and pushed the pot of tea further towards her. 'Have some tea. You've got to stay hydrated.'

She smiled and reluctantly picked up the pot, poured herself a cup, put in some milk and stirred it. Marsland watched her do all of it, but he wasn't there, not really. He was standing in front of a giant wall covered in barbwire, wondering how he was ever going to climb over it.

He took a deep breath as he watched Jenny blow on the tea. 'Gina had a secret, didn't she?'

Her eyes jumped up. A change in them. Suspicion. 'What do you mean?'

'I mean she kept something from her parents. Something she didn't think they'd understand, or approve of.'

Jenny put down the tea. 'I don't know.'

'You were best friends, so she wouldn't have kept it from you.'

Jenny shrugged.

Marsland decided to change tact. 'The day Gina went missing, one of your parents' neighbours said she got into a sports car. I think it was a man driving. If I'm right, it was a very good-looking and charming man.'

Jenny's eyes remained downwards, but she shook her head.

'Yes,' Marsland continued, 'I think that's the secret she was keeping from her parents. I think she was having an affair with this man.'

'No,' Jenny said, her eyes now filled with tears.

'No? Why not?'

'She wouldn't get into a car with some strange

man.'

'Why not?' Marsland put his hand across the table. 'It's OK, Jenny. You can tell me. Her parents wouldn't understand, but I do. You were more than friends, weren't you?'

The tears came harder then, and Marsland could only sit back and watch, occasionally passing her a tissue from the pack in his pocket. Eventually, Jenny managed to tidy her face, blink back the rest of the tears and blow her nose.

'You won't tell her parents, will you?'

Marsland shook his head. 'No, I won't. I just needed to know. I'm sorry I put you through that.'

'It's alright.'

'Who would Gina accept a lift from? I mean, did she know anyone with a flash sports car?'

Jenny shook her head. 'No, I don't think so.'

Marsland nodded. 'When's your break over?'

She looked over at the large clock on the wall. 'Just about now. What do you think happened to Gina?'

Marsland sealed off the horrific images in the back of his mind. 'I don't know. I really don't know.'

Downwards, deep into the bowels of the Edmonton Fortress, Jairus travelled with his hands in his pockets. He turned left at the entrance of the cells, and into a long grotty corridor that delivered him to a deeper part of the building. Paint was peeling from the walls, the carpet was marked by a million boot prints. As he approached the last door on the right, he could already hear the deep base and angry electric guitar. He knocked and opened the door.

It was a small dark room, illuminated only by the glow of the horde of computer screens dotted around the room. There were only two bodies, both wearing black jeans, black T-shirts, huddled over keyboards. It was the man closest to Jairus that blinked round at him, then nodded and pulled back his long brown hair and tied it back. His skin was incredibly white, almost translucent. He swung round in his chair, turned the music down, and nodded to Jairus.

He was Rich Vincent, head of the IT department, catcher of many a paedophile, and lead guitarist in a band called Ravenfire.

'Hey, Jairus, what can I do for you?'

'That your band playing?' Jairus pointed to the stereo in the corner.

'Yep, that's Ravenfire in all our majestic glory. Did you come to our last gig?'

Jairus nodded. 'Yeah, I did, and my ears are still ringing. So, Rich, what can you tell me about Mr Burgess' laptop?'

Rich rolled his chair down towards the silver laptop, then flipped it open. 'Well, my friend, I can tell you that your Mr Burgess was either a very boring man or very, very careful about what he used his laptop for.'

'Yeah, why's that?'

'Because, there's bugger all on it that's of the slightest interest to anyone. He's looked at sites to do with antiques, cars, business, and so on. And do you know the weirdest thing?'

Jairus walked over and leaned against the desk. 'What's that?'

'No porn. Nothing. Not even lingerie sites.'

'So, maybe it's just his business computer and he likes to keep it clean.'

Rich laughed, and the other black T-shirt at the back joined in. When Rich stopped chuckling, he shook his head. 'I don't care who you are, or what job you do... I mean, you could be envoy to the Queen of England, or whatever, at some point you're going to get bored and end up surfing looking for shemales or whatever gets you off. But there's not even any that he's tried to erase from his hard drive. Never ever trust a man who doesn't have porn on his computer. That's my motto.'

Jairus laughed and patted Rich's back. 'Yeah, and it's a great motto. So, apart from the lack of porn, anything at all interesting?'

The IT geek held up a finger that had quite a long black painted fingernail. 'About three years ago, your man was very interested in the Freemasons. He spent a long time researching them, then tried really hard to delete it all. But he couldn't get it past me. I printed it all up for you.'

Jairus found himself being handed a folder full of printouts. It was basically a book's worth of information on one of the world's most clandestine groups. His stomach turned over. The thought of digging into the world of secret societies filled him with unease. Some of the highest ranking police officers were Freemasons, and it was a world that none of them seemed to want to talk very much about. And there was only one person he could think to ask that might tell him something about the whole organisation. If there was a chance that Burgess, or even perhaps Thomas Henry, were both Masons, then Commander Warren might be able to give him an introduction to their mysterious world.

'Thanks.' Jairus lifted the folder, then turned towards the door.

'I take it you've delved into the murky waters?'

Jairus turned to see Rich Vincent smiling with his eyebrows raised.

'What?'

'The international database of porn that we call the Internet. I take it you've downloaded your fare share of dodgy jpegs?'

'I couldn't possibly comment.'

'Well, if you ever need a porn buddy, I'm your man.' Rich rolled away on his chair and faced a large monitor.

Jairus froze. 'A what? What did you say?'

'I was offering my services as a porn buddy. You know, the person you give your house keys to so they can go to your home and destroy all your pornographic material in case something should happen to you. What if you get killed crossing the road, and then your mum ends up going through your stuff...?'

'Thank you, Rich.' Jairus headed out the door with the folder tucked under his arm.

'Did you see the way he looked at me?' the taller of the two men said as he stood by the kitchen. He'd just boiled the kettle and turned to face the man he called brother, who was sat on the sofa.

The man on the worn red sofa nodded, sat hunched over, trying to focus on the soap opera on the TV. Anything to blot out what they'd done. Just noise to kill the time between deaths. He doubled over. He wanted to let his mouth open, to pour out the scream.

Then SHE flashed into his mind.

She was sat in the corner of her bedroom. In his mind, her bedroom was pink and fluffy, but now he couldn't recall if it was or not. It was just him and her, and a couple of people he cannot even picture.

'I said, did you see his face?' The taller one walked from the kitchen and collapsed next to him on the sofa, his stubble-covered face grinning, his dark eyes vacant of any true emotion, but glee.

Her face faded, jerked back through time. 'Yes, I saw his face, alright?'

The taller one smiled and sipped his tea. 'And how did he look to you?'

'I don't know.'

'To me he looked like he was facing the Devil himself. Or God! Yeah, God himself.'

'Yes, he looked shit-scared.' The shorter one laid down a little, pulling his knees up to his chest.

The taller one looked at him quizzically, then prodded his back. 'You don't seem to be enjoying yourself. You should be revelling in it all.'

'Should I? Why's that?'

The taller one jumped up, his arms flailing about as if he was about to conduct some monstrous orchestra. 'Because we have power! We decide who lives and dies. Those fuckers will die. And they will repent their sins.'

The shorter one turned to him, seeing his grinning mouth. 'You don't care about that. You just want to kill.'

The taller one's arms came down, his face full of disappointment. 'Yes, I want to kill, but now I feel as if I'm serving a greater good, like a kind of mystical power is burning in me. Don't you feel that?'

The puke rose in him, he shut his eyes. It was all worth it, he told himself. And he needed the man he called brother. He had to have him by his side to complete his horrific, but just task.

'You're not talking to me. I hate it when you ignore me!'

'Alright, yes! Alright? Yes, I feel the power.'

The taller one stood for a moment, staring silently. 'Have you got the name yet?'

The man on the sofa shook his head. 'No, not yet.'

'When will you get it?'

'Soon.'

The taller one crouched down beside the sofa, looking him in the eye. 'I need to do it again. I really need to...'

'You've only just done it!'

'I know. But...I just need to again. You need it too.'

'We'll find the next one and we'll punish him. I promise.'

'And I get to do what I want?'

'Yes.'

He saw her again as he closed his eyes. She was back in the pink fluffy room, smiling, so happy with life.

The shadows moved, forming into men, coming towards her, their eyes wide with evil desire.

The first bodies that rushed from the room were all suits, each well-kempt, but all tired-looking. They had folders under theirs arms as they left the conference room, some of them discussing another case in hushed tones.

Jairus was leant against the wall, waiting, seeing the Commander still talking to a silver haired suit in the conference room. When the Commander came out, he spotted Jairus and gave a brief smile.

'Just the man I wanted to see.' The Commander nodded for Jairus to follow him back along the corridor and into another office. The Commander shut the door and indicated to a chair. Jairus sat down and waited as the Commander seated himself.

'Two businessmen savagely murdered now, Jairus.' The Commander sat back. 'People are concerned that this is going to become a series. You think they're right, don't you?'

'Depends on who THEY are, sir.'

'The papers. Haven't you read the headlines?'

'Haven't had time. I expect the press office have a load of clippings for me.'

Warren nodded. 'I think it's time for a press conference.'

Jairus couldn't help sigh aloud. He knew it was on the horizon, a wavering image of him sitting in a crowded room full of sweaty eager journalists. He hated the attention. Other detectives liked the limelight, but he dreaded it. Always had. When Murphy died, it was bad. The press hounded him for months, hammering at his door of his home in Hertfordshire, swarming round. He shuddered remembering it all.

'I don't want to hold it, sir.'

The Commander lost his slight smile. 'You need to do this, Jairus. After what happened, you need to face the press. You need to get back on the horse...'

'Yeah, but I'm not someone who enjoys...'

'I don't care what you enjoy. You're doing it. It's your bloody job.'

Jairus sat up. 'Sir, I need to ask you a favour.'

Warren looked quizzical. 'By the look on your face, I don't think I'm going to like what you're going to ask.'

'Maybe not. On Burgess' laptop we found some information on the Freemasons. It was from a couple of years back, but it's something to go on.'

Warren leaned forward. 'Hang on a minute, are you going to start dragging the Masons into this whole mess, just because one of the victims happened to Google them? Bloody hell, Jairus.'

'Sir, with all due respect, info on the Masons was all we found on his laptop that was slightly out of the ordinary, plus he'd tried to make bloody sure he'd wiped it off. Which makes me wonder why. What if he was a Mason? What if Thomas Henry was a Mason?

That could be the link.'

Warren lowered his voice. 'And what about the dungeon you found? I hope you're not going to try and link...'

Jairus held up a hand. 'None of this is going to find its way out in the open. All we need is to find out if Graham Burgess or Thomas Henry were in the Masons. End of story.'

Warren sat back for a moment, his eyes never moving from Jairus. 'OK, let's not bullshit each other any longer. I'll call some people and find out. You wait here.'

Jairus watched Warren slip out of the office and along the corridor as he took out his mobile phone. There was no need to question the Commander, to ascertain whether he was a member or not; Jairus was very aware of the fact that most of the officers above him had long since been drafted into the group. He himself had never been approached, but neither did he expect to be. He wasn't wanted. His face didn't fit, and he was glad for once that he was who he was.

After only a few minutes, Warren came back into the office and shut the door. He looked blank for a moment as he put away his phone.

'The answer is yes, both Burgess and Henry were Masons at one time.'

'What does that mean? They left?'

Warren sat down. 'That's correct. Burgess was a Mason for nearly a year, then obviously decided he didn't fit in, or whatever. Same story with Henry, but he only lasted a few months.'

Jairus had a pulse of uneasiness pass through him. 'So that means it's likely that our two victims met at that time. Maybe they found they had other common interests.'

'Good riddance,' Warren said and stood up sharply. 'I hope that is an end to that part of the inquiry.'

When they were both at eye level, Jairus looked down for a moment. 'I'm afraid not, sir. I respect the privacy of your membership and all that goes with it, but this is a murder investigation. The killers of Henry and Burgess left a message, the head on a pole. They're going to kill again. What if another member of the Masons is next? Are you going to watch that happen?'

Warren's face reddened just before he turned to face the window. 'What do you expect me to do?'

'I'm going to need a list of other members of the same lodge that might've left around the same time.'

'Fine. You'll get it. But let me warn you, Jairus, that if the Freemasons of Enfield find themselves hassled by you or any of your colleagues, then it won't be just me they've got to worry about. The boot will come from high on up. So you'd all better tread very carefully.'

CHAPTER 11

It was raining hard when Marsland walked towards St. James cemetery, his eyes blurry from all the grimy water cascading over his face. He'd never ever bothered with umbrellas, and that had bothered his wife so much. After a heavy shower he'd see the discarded metal skeletons in the gutters and point them out. More evidence for his case, she would say and sigh.

He stood at the gate, seeing the God Is Great sign, the sharp, grey church in the background, the black cloud closing in on everything.

His eyes scanned over the graves in front, the ones sinking into the ground, long forgotten. Charles Winston, In Loving Memory, 1901-1976, a particularly decrepit tombstone. Everyone gets forgotten, he said to himself.

He thought he heard something, perhaps a voice between the traffic ripping through the wet streets. He turned and saw a woman watching him from across the other side of the road, a beige umbrella in her hand, smiling a little sadly.

Jacqui. The woman he had met previously in the graveyard with the cast on her hand. Even though he wanted to turn away and keep walking through the rain, he stood frozen and smiled. She held up a finger, looked both ways and then ran across the road towards him. She stood close and lifted the umbrella for him too.

'You're soaking wet,' she said, looking concerned.

'I'm Ok.'

'And what happened to your face?'

'It's a long story.'

'I see. Do you visit every day?' She looked towards the church.

He shook his head. 'I was just out walking.'

'In the rain?' She laughed. 'Fancy a drink in the pub? Doesn't have to be a proper drink. Tea if you want?'

There was no fight in him anymore, a lack of will to say no and drift off by himself. He raised his shoulders and suddenly he was walking with her and heading to the Rose and Crown on the other side of the road.

There were a few young men gathered round the bar, most of them dressed in clothes daubed with paint or dry mortar. Jacqui directed him to a table near the entrance to the beer garden. He sat and watched her order two teas from a young dark-haired girl behind the bar.

Jacqui sat down and smiled. 'You're having one of the bad days, I can tell.'

'That obvious?'

'I know what it's like. The bad days and the good days.'

He smiled. 'You've lost someone too?'

'Yes, a year ago. My younger son.' She looked down at the table, her hand smoothing the surface.

'I'm sorry to hear that. How old was he?'

'Nineteen.'

The barmaid brought over their teas and they sat there for a moment, listening to the rain hammering at the windows, and the young lads at the bar chattering away.

'I hope you don't mind,' she began, stirring her tea, 'but I looked you up. I thought I recognised you that day in the graveyard. You're Terence Marsland. You saved that girl and the policewoman.'

Marsland looked down at his tea and the rainwater dripping from his hair. Once again, the limelight had found him. There seemed nowhere left to hide, not even among the dead. 'It just sort of happened. It was actually the police officer that saved the day.'

'But you're a hero. Your family must be proud.'

'It's only me and my son now, but I don't hear much from him anymore.'

Jacqui looked startled. 'Why not?'

'I don't think he's very happy with me. And I can't blame him.'

'That's not the way it should be. It said in the paper that you're a private detective, so you must keep busy.'

He laughed at hearing the label she used. He remembered reading it too, during his last dabble into the media's unpleasant spotlight. 'They made a mistake. I'm not a private detective.'

'Oh, so why did you end up involved in all that business?' She sipped her tea.

He shrugged. He'd asked himself the same question many times, and had nightmares where he's not the one strangling a killer, but the other way round. Then there were the flashes of Daisy...

He shook the images away. 'I guess I was just sticking my nose in where it didn't belong.'

'But you did good. You saved them.'

'Yes,' he said, recalling the price he had paid for the good he'd done.

'So, tell me,' she said smiling a little, 'are you still poking your nose in?'

He nodded. 'I'm afraid so. I'm looking into something for a friend. Which means, I suppose, I haven't learnt my lesson.'

'Which means you still want to do some good.'

He hadn't looked at it that way before. For him he'd simply been doing a favour for a former colleague, harmlessly poking his snout in to help out. But hadn't there been a deep need in him to do something with the time he had left? He smiled. 'Maybe you're right.'

'I am right. Now, I'm going to ask you something, and I've got a feeling you're going to say no, but hear me out.'

'Go on,' he said, feeling his stomach tighten.

'I go to a club on Thursday nights. It's held at the old Ritzy cinema, the one in Enfield Wash. Why don't you come along?'

'I don't think it's my kind of thing, but thanks.'

'I'm not accepting that. You can't spend the rest of your life shut up in your house.'

Marsland found his mouth opening, another excuse teetering on his tongue. Then something strange happened. He didn't believe in fate, or signs from the so-called Gods, but he held his words back as a van came into view through the window. It was the van from the florists next door. He'd never taken much notice of the shop before, but now he read the words printed decoratively on the side of the van: Daisy Flowers.

He nodded, and smiled at Jacqui. 'OK, I'm sure it won't kill me to come along.'

'I'm sure it won't. The other members don't bite. Or carry knives. You'll be perfectly safe.'

There was bustle in the incident room as Jairus entered the next morning. All along the corridor, he'd been massaging his neck, trying to get out the knot that had tied itself up during the night. That's what you get for trying to sleep on a hard sofa in the family room, he thought. He couldn't face going home; he knew it was going to be a night of constant electric pulses in his brain, bringing image after image. If he had been trying to sleep at home, even in his new flat, the old ghosts would visit.

In the middle of the night, after staring out the window, watching the black rain streak down the glass, he'd got up and headed for the incident room and picked up a marker pen. After an hour, he'd found that he'd drawn patterns and lines and names on the whiteboard. Everyone was there, every photograph, every crime scene. Even the missing girls' photographs.

It was then 8.30a.m. when he pushed open the incident room door and slapped his hands together, making everyone turn to face him. DS Moone and DI Walker were there surrounded by a couple of detective constables and four uniforms. They'd all got his message about the morning briefing. He pointed at the whiteboard and saw the now senseless ramblings of a madman. 'Listen up, everyone, because we're going to need you all on the ball. We're going to have to cover a lot of ground in the next couple of days. Time is running out. We've now got a list of businessmen who were once members of the mysterious Freemasons, but have since left. Now, I don't care if you're in the Masons or not, because we've got a job to do. I'm pairing you up and you're going to check all the names out. Also, we're going to have to talk to the relatives and friends of the missing girls. If these are revenge killings, then you can bet the killers are among them somewhere. We're working with the assumption that all three girls were taken by Burgess and perhaps some accomplices.'

Moone stepped forward. 'Sir, Walker and I checked out Burgess' dark blue Audi, which fits the description of the sports car that apparently stopped to pick up Gina Colman the day she disappeared.'

'Yeah, and?'

'The car looks like it hasn't been used in months, plus the driver's seat had been adjusted for a very short person. Burgess was about five foot-eleven.'

Jairus smiled at Moone. 'Nice. Good one, Moone.'

'Walker spotted the car's seat.'

Jairus looked at her and saw her smile awkwardly. 'Well done, Walker. Have the SOCOs come up with anything useful in the car?'

'Nothing so far,' Walker said. 'Looks like Burgess or someone gave it a good clean. Hardly any usable prints so far. They'll let us know what they find.'

'Good,' Jairus said and dug his hands firmly in his pockets, while stifling a giant yawn. 'Now, there's folders on the table with your action lists inside. Get it done and let me know what you find. I've also given some of you a list of robberies from local hospitals. We need to find out where our killers got the anaesthetic they used on Burgess. Now get out there.'

After grabbing a takeaway coffee and a bacon bap from the pile on a nearby desk, Jairus sat in a chair and watched the uniforms and detectives grab a folder and head out. He covered his mouth when he yawned again. He was on the edge of exhaustion and he knew it. Walker wandered over.

'You look knackered,' she said, grabbing a coffee.

'Yeah, thanks for that.'

'That's the same suit you were wearing yesterday. And the day before. You slept in that, didn't you?'

He looked down at his crumpled suit. 'It's all part

of my style.'

'Did you get any sleep last night?'

He stood up and gulped down the coffee. 'Some. Look, we need to get out there and find out who's next on our killers' list.'

'OK, who do we go and see?'

Jairus picked up the sheet he'd left for himself. 'Raymond Crow. Head of Crow and Co Private Bank. You want to drive?'

'Alright,' Walker said and headed for the door, then turned to look back at Jairus. 'Probably best I do, actually, as you'd probably fall asleep at the wheel.'

Jairus tried to sit back and relax as Walker drove them across London, heading east towards the warrens of London, the thin and wormy and grimy streets of the East End. He knows the areas of deprivation are punctuated by the occasional redevelopments. Like his grandfather's old stomping ground in Bethnal Green, the few streets lined with cottages, the same old pub on the corner that he drank in after the war. Nothing much had changed, except the people; now the residents were high flyers prepared to pay extortionate amounts of money for milk, bread, pasta and booze, as well as their homes.

And hovering in the distance, surging upwards like some rocket waiting to be ignited, the hazy image of 1, Canada Square, Canary Wharf. The financial hub sits around it, smaller skyscrapers all crosslegged and praying at their master's feet.

Somewhere between his eyes closing and springing open again, his head nodding forward, the streets spread themselves wide and shiny glass and steel grew out of the urban sprawl.

Walker steered towards a car park, then they walked

the rest of the way to 1, Canada Square. Inside, Jairus pointed to a map on the wall. Crow and Co Private Bank was on the 46th floor.

As they got out the lift, they found a long lilac carpet leading off to various departments and a central reception in the middle of it all. Jairus showed his ID to one of the young women sitting behind the star-shaped desk. 'I'm DCI Jairus. I need to talk to Raymond Crow.'

The girl's deeply-tanned face rose briefly to his ID. 'Do you have an appointment?'

'No, but we need to talk to him urgently.'

'I'm not sure he'll...'

Jairus leaned over. 'Yeah, I know, just call him now and tell him it's a matter of life and death.'

The girl blinked, then began speaking to someone on her headset.

'You know that quite a few of the names on that Masonic list are based in this area?' Walker said.

Jairus nodded as he leaned on the desk. 'Yeah, I know. It's because so many of these high flying business types work out here, but live in the outskirts where there's better schools, cleaner streets. So they settle in places like Enfield or Hertfordshire.'

The girl behind the desk suddenly stood up. 'Mr Crow will see you now.'

Walker began following the girl. Jairus stayed back, turning to look beyond the glass-walled offices filled with cubicles and figures sat in front of myriad computer screens. London hung hazily in the distance, and beyond it was the suburbs where the killers were probably waiting and planning.

Raymond Crow's monstrous and clinical office was at the far end of the building, allowing him a vista that took in the city skyline. There were only two large paintings, one on either side of the office, both splurges and streaks of deep dark blacks and reds.

Raymond Crow was sitting at the large glass desk at the centre of the room, facing two thin monitors. He turned his chair, stood up and smoothed down his suit. He then carefully walked round the desk and put out a hand for Jairus to shake.

Raymond Crow was forty-seven years old, but looked much younger, with only streaks of silver hair just above his ears. Women would consider him quite good-looking, Jairus decided, and watched Crow smile and nod to Walker.

'I was told you wanted to see me because it's a matter of life and death.' Crow smiled, then sat down at his desk.

Jairus sat down in a chair opposite. 'You've read about the recent murders in Enfield?'

'Hardly get time to read the papers these days,' Crow began, 'although I do catch the evening news. But yes, I have heard something about it. They were businessmen, weren't they? So that means you're here because you think I might be next?'

Jairus cleared his throat. 'Mr Crow, we have to ask you some questions.'

'Go ahead. I have nothing to hide, but I do have a briefing and call to make in half an hour.'

'This won't take long, but it might save your life. Have you ever been a member of the Freemasons?'

Crow leaned back. 'I've got a funny feeling you already know the answer to that question.'

Jairus nodded. 'We do. We believe you joined a Masonic lodge in Enfield. But you left only two months later.'

'That's correct.'

'Why did you quit?' Walker asked.

Crow's eyes jumped to her. 'Frankly, I got bored. It's not quite what you think it's going to be. And apparently it takes a long time to rise through the ranks and I just don't have the time for that.'

'Yeah, I know what you mean,' Jairus said. 'Why did you join in the first place?'

'Why does anyone join? To rise in the world, to make money, to make deals.'

Jairus looked round the room. 'Looks like you're pretty much set up here. You must make quite an obscene amount of money.'

Crow laughed for a moment. 'Yes, but there's an elite world out there that I still want to get in on. The big boys try and keep some of us out.'

'How dare they,' Jairus said and pulled out the photographs he had brought along. 'You ever met this man?'

Crow took the photograph of Graham Burgess. 'No...no I definitely don't recall his face. And I have a very good memory. Who is he?'

'Graham Burgess. He was murdered on Monday 20th May. And he was a member of the same Masonic lodge that you belonged to. But you've never met him?'

'Maybe he just wasn't there when I was.'

Jairus pushed another photograph across the desk. This time it was a passport photograph of Thomas Henry. 'Thomas Henry. Also a member of the same Masonic Lodge, also murdered.'

'Oh my God,' Crow said, raising his eyebrows. 'But again, I don't know him. I'm sorry.'

Jairus stood up. 'Let me warn you, Mr Crow, that two men are killing for some kind of revenge. I believe they plan on killing again. If you do know something, and if you're fearing for your life, then we can protect you.'

Crow stood up and laughed. 'Thank you, DCI...?'

'Jairus.'

'Thank you, but I'm not in fear of my life. And if I was I'm sure I can afford my own protection. I hope you capture the people who murdered those men.'

Outside, when they reached the car, Jairus leaned on the roof and watched Walker open the driver's side. 'What do you think?'

She looked up at him. 'About Crow? Do I think he's involved? Well, if he is, and he thinks some psychopathic killers are gunning for him, he seems pretty calm about it.'

'Yeah, he does. But then again, he is high up there in his ivory tower.'

'Maybe the dead businessmen were rivals of Crow and he had both men killed.'

Jairus climbed in. 'No, I don't want to sound like a cliché, but the killings were personal. We've got nothing tying Raymond to the two victims. We need to check where all the men on that list were when the girls were taken.'

CHAPTER 12

The address DS Moone had for Ahsan Nazir seemed to be some rather worn-looking offices above a intercontinental supermarket, a barber's and a café in Poplar. Moone had DC Michelle Carr tagging behind, walking slowly, her dark eyes lifted towards the offices. He turned and faced her, realising he'd never worked closely with her before. She was taller than him, which always made him feel a little self-conscious. She was from an Afro-Caribbean background. She was also one of the most attractive officers he'd ever met, which made him always self-aware in her presence, the way he had been with his wife all those many years ago.

'Shall I do the talking, or do you want to?' he asked, a smile on his face.

'Why, because I'm black and he might open up to me?' She raised her eyebrows.

He stepped back. 'No! I mean, I just thought...'

'I'm winding you up,' Carr said, beamed a smile, then entered through the glass door that led to a threadbare carpeted staircase. They went up and found Ahsan's business on the top floor.

The door was ajar and Moone could see a fan whirring round and a thick-bodied Asian gentlemen sat at a large scratched desk with a laptop in front of him. He was sweating profusely, and, when he looked up, he sighed and rubbed his face.

'If you think you're going to take anything, you've got another thing coming.' He stood up and folded his arms.

Carr flashed her ID. 'Don't panic, Mr Nazir, we're the police.'

Nazir sat down carefully and wiped his forehead. 'Police? I haven't done anything.'

'I'm DS Moone, this is Detective Constable Carr. We'd like to ask you a few questions about the Freemasons.'

The businessman's eyebrows perked up and he wiped more sweat from his brow. 'The Freemasons? What about them? What are they saying about me?'

'They haven't said anything about you,' Moone said.

'Mr Nazir,' DC Carr said, soothingly. 'We just need to know if you joined the Freemasons awhile back or not. You're not in any trouble.'

He frowned, but then nodded. 'Yes, I did. I met a businessman that was going to join and he said that I should also join. But it wasn't my cup of tea. If I'm truthful, I don't believe I fitted in there. If you know what I'm saying?'

'What exactly are you suggesting?' Moone said.

The man shook his head. 'I don't know really, I just got the feeling they didn't respect my business. I own properties I rent out and a couple of shops. I buy and sell stuff. I got the feeling they were looking down on me.'

Carr smiled. 'Could you possibly look at some photographs for us? Just to see if you recognise anyone?'

Nazir raised his shoulders. 'All right, I don't mind.'

Carr took out the two photographs of Burgess and Henry and placed them on the desk. Nazir looked down at both photographs, but his eyes stayed on Burgess' for quite some time before he looked up and said, 'That man. I remember him. I talked to him quite a bit. There was a meal we all went to. I chatted to him in the bar afterwards.'

Carr pointed to Burgess' photograph. 'This man? You're positive that it was this man?'

'I'm sure. Because he said some very strange things later on.'

Moone raised his eyebrows. 'What sort of strange things?'

'About girls.'

Carr sat forward. 'What did he say exactly?'

'There was a couple of girls serving drinks and he said some very rude things about them. He'd had too much to drink by then I think.'

'Do you remember what sort of thing he was saying?' Carr asked.

Nazir frowned. 'I don't remember really, just rude stuff that he wanted to do to them. It was very disgusting.'

'Did anything else happen?' Moone asked.

'I only remember that man being taken away by another man. He sat him down and was obviously telling him off. After that, when I went back they both seemed very friendly with each other.'

Moone raised his eyebrows at Carr. 'What was he called, this other man?'

'I don't remember. Actually, I don't think I knew his name. Names don't seem important to them. It's all about having faith in something bigger than you.'

'I see.' Moone sat back. 'And would you recognise this man again?'

Nazir smiled a little. 'Yes. Show me a picture and I'll tell you if it's him.'

Moone smiled as he stood up. 'Thank you, Mr Nazir. You've been a great help. We'll try and get some photographs over to you. We may have to get you in to make a full statement too.'

Nazir raised his shoulders. 'Alright. I'll do what I can to help.'

Carr got up. 'And maybe you should stay somewhere else for a while. Just for your own protection.'

'Alright. I have a cousin I can stay with for a while. But I have a business to take care of.'

Moone stepped towards the door. 'Just be vigilant, Mr Nazir. We'll be in touch.'

Jairus briefly stopped off at the station to pick up a few preliminary reports that had eventually come through. As always, budgets were involved and the cogs moved slowly. So far, the blood taken from the dungeon under Braxton House suggested that three different girls had been kept there. Bleach had been used around and on the bed, removing any evidence of the sexual assaults that had almost certainly taken place there. Also, the SOCOs had confirmed the marks on the floor were made by some kind of tripod.

Jairus leaned on the desk, his head spinning a little. He felt puke rise in his throat, but swallowed it back down. He went over to the windows that looked on to the darkening streets. It had been a long day of making inquiries, of talking to business people who didn't seem to care that anyone had been, or might yet, be murdered. He kept his anger in check when he faced them and their apathy, but felt the blood boiling and raging around his body. He'd also phoned round a few antique shops to see if the missing items from the victims' homes had been sold. No luck so far.

He opened the window, letting the warm air pass over him. The traffic still rumbled past, the occasional car horn honking, voices shouting, a double-decker bus droning by. Life was carrying on.

Carl Murphy was lying on the floor, blood oozing from him, pooling round his body.

Jairus clasped his face and closed his eyes.

It was time to go home and try and get some sleep. He had sleeping pills that had been prescribed for him that he had hardly ever taken. They were little blue pills that promised they would knock him out. He picked up some reports and headed down to his car.

On the way home he saw the turning for Ponders End, then suddenly swerved the car, narrowly escaping a collision with another car. He drove down the back lane behind Hertford Road where his lock-up was situated. He got out and unlocked the garage door and slipped inside. The musty smell gripped his nostrils as he found the cord and turned the light on. As he stood in the centre of the lock-up, he surveyed the furniture and boxes and papers and the shelves of Karine's books. Mostly they were factual stories or history books. She was never one for fiction.

He had a flash of memory as he walked over to the box that contained all their old photographs. His plan was to sift through them and submerge himself in the memory of her. Instead, a front cover of an old book floated up through the darkness of his mind. It was a Victorian image of Enfield, with horse-drawn carriages and trams filling the roads. His hands dragged across the spines of all the books, his eyes picking out the various titles.

There it was, the thick book with grey cover and red titles. The book was called SECRET ENFIELD. He wanted to learn more about the prison that was under

Braxton House. He didn't really understand why he wanted to know more about the cold dark place where the girls had probably met their end. Perhaps, he thought, if he could see it as an actual place of crime and punishment, of something used officially and for good, then it would lose its grotesque aura. There was no doubt he would be entering the place again, so he needed to be able to separate himself from what had taken place in there. Yeah, right, he thought, just the way he'd been able to separate himself from what had happened in their old home.

He grabbed the book and swiftly headed for the door, trying to keep his eyes off the large iron box in the corner with its judgemental eyes and mouth. He stopped, breathed in, tried to remain calm and turned to the safe. As always, it stared blankly back at him.

He turned away and slipped under the lock-up door and back to his car.

Then Jairus headed home, and, not for the first time, he almost headed automatically for the house they had shared in Hertfordshire, with the small conservatory and the even smaller office that Karine had claimed as her own.

Jairus redirected his journey and parked his car in the private car park underneath the grubby-looking block of flats that were tucked behind the tube station in Southgate. Even as he walked across the dry and warm car park, he could hear drunken voices outside the kebab shop, commuters exiting the tube station, buses groaning past. He headed up the stone stairwell that was wedged between a florist and a sports shop, which led to his new place.

He opened the door, switched on the light and put down the book and reports on the table by the door. It's open-plan, just like a spacious studio flat, except there's a separate bedroom with ensuite bathroom. All there is keeping the wood floor from being completely empty is a cumbersome leather sofa and a small glass coffee table. His TV sits on one of the yet to be unpacked boxes across the other side of the room.

He made a cup of tea, then scrambled around in the bathroom cabinet looking for the sleeping pills. He couldn't find them there, so found his dark blue suit jacket, and retrieved the pills from the inside pocket.

He took one out and rolled it in his hand, now sat on the sofa, sinking down into it. With some tea in his mouth, he threw the pill between his lips and tasted its bitterness. He swallowed. Too late now, he thought, unless he stuck his fingers down his throat.

He leaned back, trying to relax, his eyes jumping all over the flat and finding the history book by the door. He jumped up and walked over and grabbed the book. Back on the sofa, he opened it up and began to read, but after a while he realised he hadn't taken in a word of it. His fingers traced the pages, then flicked through, finding the text about Braxton House, and the old black and white photograph of its exterior. There it was, so rigid, so self-important. Nothing bad could happen there.

His eyes flicked open. His head bobbed up. How long had he been asleep? He looked at his watch. Maybe a couple of minutes. Then he turned the page of the book, trying to read the next paragraph, trying to stop the jumble of words from fading into blackness.

Jairus' eyes opened. He took in the fact that he was leaning to one side, his neck bent at an awkward angle. He tried to move, but a spasm of pain jabbed into his spine. He pushed himself up, saw the book was now on the floor, and put it on the sofa as he decided to take a shower. Chances were he'd wake up early and want to hurry to work, maybe grab a black coffee on the way. He'd have to make sure he was ready to go.

He scrubbed himself red raw, dried himself and threw on his dressing gown and walked into the lounge, his feet slapping against the wood floor. He began to read the book again, then took a brief look at his watch. It was just after 9 p.m.

His eyes read another line, but it seemed a few seconds later that his brain registered the meaning. He read it again, this time aloud.

'So concerned were the Victorian residents that rebellion was a mere week away, they decided to construct an escape tunnel beneath the house.'

He looked up and saw the lights of the streets and bodies walking along.

A tunnel. He swallowed, then put down the book. What if there was a tunnel down there, a part of the building they haven't discovered?

He ran towards the bedroom for his suit jacket and found it lying across the bed. With his mobile in his hand, he dialled Walker, his heart now punching into his ribs, waiting and praying for her to pick up.

'Jay? What's happened?' Her voice was tired, distracted.

'We need to get over to the crime scene at Braxton House as soon as possible.'

'Why, what's happened?'

'Just get what we need to get in there. Some gloves and stuff. Better bring a torch. Meet me as soon as you can. Ok?'

'Alright. I'll...'

He hung up and looked down at the book again, rereading the words about the tunnel, then hurried to get dressed.

Jacqui didn't really drink anymore, so had suggested picking Marsland up from his house, which she did. They had drove for a while in silence towards the building where the club was held. Beyond it, just a few hundred yards away, Marsland had noticed his old Comprehensive School, now renamed something ridiculous. He couldn't remember exactly what it was called, but was pretty sure it ended with the word Academy. It was one of those little annoying new labels that they put on things these days, just to be more American.

There was scaffolding on one side of the former cinema and bingo hall, showing the council were desperately trying to preserve it. It was listed and that prevented it from being turned into another block of flats. These days it was a place for old people to hang out and try to grip onto the past, yet to find some kind of continuity with the present.

Marsland felt he was being sucked into a world he'd done his best to avoid since he'd turned fifty. And the blonde woman by his side, while the radio blasted out Dolly Parton, was driving him there.

Two hours later, a little time after there had been a line dancing class that Marsland had refused to take part in, he found himself sitting in one of the ancient remains of old Enfield, looking around at the middle-aged men and women, the last of a dying civilisation. He was sitting at a worn table, lots of scratches and ring marks from a million pint glasses, staring across the long hall. The ceilings were high above him, with dusty chandeliers hanging above the room.

There were two bars along either side of the hall, but only one was open with two young men serving the elderly customers.

Jacqui was at the bar chatting to her much older friends, most of which were elderly ladies. Marsland looked at his watch. It was 9.45 p.m.

Jacqui came back with a glass of wine for herself and placed a pint of bitter in front of Marsland. He noticed her smile had grown larger, more animated.

'They're a nice crowd, these lot,' she said, her eyes sweeping the room.

'They seem it.' He sipped his pint, while delving into his brain and trying to bring back any kind of conversation.

She nodded, smiled awkwardly and took a drink of her wine.

'You been coming here long?' he asked.

'A while. Let's see... Well, it must have been ages ago.'

'But it's good to have somewhere to go.'

She smiled, then her eyes lit up. 'Oh, how's the case going?'

He stopped mid-sip. 'It's going OK, I think. I've found out some stuff, but it needs to be put together in some kind of order...but...'

'But?'

'But I'm starting to wonder if I should be poking my nose in. I'm sure the police can handle it from here.'

Jacqui reached out a hand and placed it over Marsland's. 'But you won't be able to leave it alone, because you're a good man.'

'I don't know about that.'

Jacqui let go of his hand, her head turning to stare across the hall. 'Oh, there's Carol. I need to have a word with her. I'll have to go over there. You see, her legs are pretty useless these days. I'll be back in a mo, OK?'

Marsland nodded, and watched her hurry across the room to a table near the stage.

'Hi,' a voice said to Marsland's right.

A scrawny woman with a long wrinkled face and tightly-permed hair was smiling brightly at him. 'I'm Sandra. Sandra Tarrant. I'm a friend of Jacqui. I used to live next door to her, actually. Now I only ever see her here.'

'Nice to meet you,' Marsland said and watched Sandra sit down.

She said, 'I shouldn't even be talking to you.'

'You shouldn't? Why not?'

'Well, don't tell her I told you this, but she gave me orders not to tell you too much about her.'

'Really?' Marsland turned and saw Jacqui chatting to her friend. 'Why do you think she didn't want you to talk to me about her?'

Sandra laughed. 'I suppose I'm a bit of a blabbermouth usually. I guess she wants to keep a bit of mystery.'

'I guess.' His curiosity was sparked. 'She had a son who died, didn't she? Her younger son?'

'She told you about that, eh?'

He nodded. 'A little. He was nineteen, wasn't he?'

Sandra suddenly became rigid, her eyes jumping over to where Jacqui had gone. 'Oh dear, I've been spotted. I better go. I'll talk to you later. Bye.'

Marsland turned to see Jacqui coming towards him, her face sullen, full of concern. The smile she put on as she sat down opposite him hardly hid the worry that filled her eyes.

'I see you were chatting to Sandra. What did she have to say?'

'Nothing really. Just came over to say hello. She said she used to live next door to you.'

Jacqui nodded, her fingers tapping at the table. 'That's right. About a million years ago.'

'You've never mentioned your husband.'

'Haven't I? Oh well, not much to say really. We met, had a couple of kids together, then he buggered off with the barmaid from the local. Hardly heard from him since.'

'That's a shame.'

'What about your wife?'

He felt himself tighten, the wall having come down automatically. 'Not much to say either. She died a few years ago.'

'But I bet you were close?'

He nodded.

'And at least she didn't do the dirty on you.'

He smiled. Suddenly he was back in the hospital room, his wife's mouth moving, the words of betrayal crumbling out. He looked up at Jacqui, her face had swapped from sad to smiling brightly. 'She was a good woman.'

'I'm sorry, but you must be bored here.' She finished her glass of wine.

'Oh, no, I'm fine,' he lied, looking at his watch again. 'But I do have a lot of stuff to do tomorrow. You know, poking my nose in and all that.'

She got up, grabbed her handbag and her cardigan. 'Come on, I'll drive you back home. I could do with an early night too.'

Although he felt guilty at dragging her away from her friends, he happily went, feeling a weight lift from him as he followed her plump body towards the exit. Some of her friends waved as they crossed the hall, but all Marsland noticed was the way some of the ladies whispered to each other in hushed voices, while their eyes followed them as they walked.

'I've just got to pop to the loo,' Jacqui said and disappeared into the toilet near the exit.

Marsland put his hands in his pockets and read the notice board. Most of the notices were to do with various classes, like knitting and line dancing and cooking. He felt a breeze spread across his back and a door creak open behind him. Marsland turned to face the gent's toilet where a tall, balding man with a red face came ambling towards him.

'You're Terry, that right?' the man said and stuck out his hand.

'That's right,' Marsland said and shook his hand.

'Don. You came with Jacqui? Yes, she's an interesting lady. We had a few dates at one time.'

'Really?' Marsland turned to make sure she hadn't walked out yet.

'Oh yeah, long time back. She told you about her sons?'

'Not a lot. You know something about them?'

'Just about everything. It's tragic what happened to her youngest. No one saw that coming. Now, the other one...'

The ladies' toilet door opened and Jacqui stepped out, her eyes widening when she saw Don talking to Marsland. 'What you two been talking about?'

'Nothing, darling,' Don said and winked at Marsland, then sauntered off towards the bar.

Jacqui was far too quiet when she drove him home, and this made Marsland wonder if she had in fact heard something of what he and Don had been discussing. Dolly Parton was yodelling from the stereo again and Jacqui was humming along, but she didn't even seem to look at him or really notice him sitting next to her. All Marsland wanted to do was get into his house, have a cup of tea and forget the whole night had happened.

When she pulled up, Marsland almost jumped out and ran to his door. But he stopped as he opened the door and got ready to step out. He thought he'd heard her saying something and turned to face her. 'Sorry?'

'What did you say to Don?' Her face was drawn, her eyes almost wet with tears.

'Nothing. He was…well, he was talking about you…'

'I thought you were different,' she said, sniffing a little. 'I thought…I know you're a police…well, that you were a policeman, but…'

'You know I'm nosey. I can't help it.'

'Please, just let the past be left where it is.' It seemed to be her last words on the subject, so he climbed out, unsure of exactly what crime he had committed. Almost immediately she drove off and he watched her brake lights flash on, then the car turning right.

CHAPTER 13

There were only a few lights that beamed up the exterior of the old house. Jairus stood back among the flowers, past the incident car that was parked up, lights flashing on the gravel driveway. Walker was moving round the outside of the house. He could see her torchlight bouncing round occasionally. He had his hands in his pockets, his eyes digging round the base of the building, wondering where the tunnel might be. It was probably all just nothing, just his imagination running wild. His suspicions were taking over, making every innocent new piece of information into something sinister.

The female constable who had entered the house a few moments ago, came out followed by a tall and broad male uniform. He was an inspector, and he looked quizzical as he walked towards Jairus.

'DCI Jairus?' The inspector stood in front of him, blocking his view of the house. 'Inspector Portman. We've had a look inside and we can't see where there might be another room.'

Jairus nodded and walked round him, then breathed in deeply and headed into the house. The spotlights that the SOCOs had left behind illuminated the place. He kept walking, his eyes always forward, his shoes tapping away at the stone steps that led him all the way down to the store cupboard. He walked through, careful not to disturb the yellow evidence markers, his eyes examining the floor and the manacles on the wall. He stopped and looked around, scanning everything about him, calculating, adding it all up. Then he turned his head, a slight buzzing somewhere in his brain, directing him towards the glass security door. He pushed it open, while his stomach turned over. A hand seemed to have grabbed and squeezed his heart. He stopped dead, his eyes once again searching everything. He crouched down by the metal chairs, focusing on the point where the metal struts were bolted to the floor. There was a thin line in the ground. Almost invisible. He leaned in further, putting his face close to the minute gap.

Yes. It was easily missed. The SOCOs were looking for blood, fingerprints, and other evidence, but not trapdoors. He pushed his fingernails into the gap and dug into it, trying to pull it upwards. Then he grabbed the leg of a chair and heaved it, pulling it back. There was a clanking sound and the hidden door opened.

He was looking into a hole in the ground, about four feet square. A ladder led down into the darkness. He poked his head down, sniffing the damp air.

Jairus heard Walker calling somewhere inside the building, echoing out to him. He looked down again into the darkness, trying to hear any sound that might drift up to him. Then Walker's footsteps came into the room. He turned to look at her, to try and read her face. He saw her eyes burn open, her mouth part.

'Shit,' she said and came forward, her torch in her hand.

'I'm going down there,' he said.

'Hang on. You can't go down there on your own.'

'I've got to. Go and get some forensic equipment from the incident car outside. It'll be in the boot.'

'Wait here.' Walker jogged outside and soon came back carrying some gloves and overshoes.

Jairus slipped them on, keeping his eyes towards the black hole, avoiding Walker's questioning stare, then he began lowering himself to the ladder.

'Why don't we wait until the SOCOs get here?' Walker asked, as she crouched down and handed him the torch.

'I'm not waiting. I need to see what's down here.'

'Do you think it's wise you going down there? You don't know what's waiting for you.'

'Then get another torch and follow me down, but hurry up.' Jairus found the first rung with his foot and turned on the torch. The light hovered about the dusty concrete floor. He swept the light round, illuminating the brick walls. Someone had carefully crafted a tunnel that seemed to stretch on for at least a hundred yards. He turned and climbed down until he hit the concrete floor. With the torchlight in front of him, he moved on slowly, taking careful steps, trying to see down the tunnel, the blood crashing about his ears. He felt something deep inside him as he walked, some sense of the darkness that had started in this underground place. Evil was somewhere in the tunnel with him, perhaps watching. No.

That was ridiculous. There was nothing down here. Then the torchlight hit something. It was metal. It was a large metal cupboard with a padlock. He felt the lock in his hand, then the thin metal bolt it was attached to. He lifted the heavy torch and smashed it down on the lock. It seemed to loosen, so he smashed the torch down a few more times until the padlock clattered to the floor. He took a deep breath before pulling open the doors. There were shelves, but most of them were empty. Only one shelf had anything on it. DVD boxes labelled 1 to 3.

He swept round, hearing footsteps far behind, and another torchlight bouncing round. Walker was coming.

He turned back and pointed the torch towards the darkness. The tunnel ended in another fifty yards or so. He walked towards the bricked wall that signified the end of his search. He saw something on his right. An opening or archway. Yes, an archway and a metal door. It was bolted, but not padlocked. He took in a long, hard breath and grasped the first bolt and pulled it across. Then he reached up to the second bolt and did the same. Now his heart was racing, gushing blood beating about his head. He took hold of the metal door and slowly pulled it open. The door squeaked a little. He stopped and faced the blackness inside. He thought he heard something, some distant whisper or breath. Then the smell, a foul and stale stench clawing at his face. He clenched his left hand and pointed the torch into the room. He saw the brick wall at the far end of the small room. Then he moved the light downwards to the floor.

He jerked back a little. His heart was beating hard, chest rising and falling. There was something on the floor. He pointed the light again, dragging it across the shape.

Jesus... He halted the light on the mattress. He let his eyes take in the skeletal shape that lay diagonally across it. It was a bruised and naked female, her hair wild and matted. He crouched, stretching out a hand, reaching out for a bony dirty foot. He grasped, and fell back, the skeletal form flipping over, her eyes burning wide. Screaming! Screaming.

Jairus lurched forward and grasped her to him. She did not fight back, just moaned and cried into his shoulder.

Walker stood at the door, her eyes wide and full of tears.

Sitting on the bench just in front of the house, Jairus put his head in hands, closed his palms over his face. He felt a single tear and wiped it away. He was still shaking. He looked at his hands as they trembled, his heart still thumping. If he stood up he doubted he would be steady.

He'd carried the girl in his arms towards the square of light. It was as if he carried nothing. Walker was before him, her torchlight showing the way, her eyes glancing back at him. So much concern in her face for the girl and him. When he asked her name, she gave him only an empty stare, a little dribble hanging from her chin. He felt her arms and the bone digging into his palms.

The paramedics swarmed him, taking her from his grasp and delivering her to the nearby ambulance. Then she was gone.

He ordered two uniforms to make sure she was secure.

Then he sat down on the bench while he watched the white bodies of the SOCOs disappear into the house one by one.

Walker came away from the house, dark rings under eyes. She stepped up to Jairus and looked down at him.

'You OK?' she asked.

He raised his eyebrows.

'I know, stupid question. Let's get you out of here.'

'I need to carry on...'

Walker sat on the bench next to him. 'But there isn't anything more for us to do right now.'

He nodded. 'Maybe I should go and wait for the girl to say something.'

Walker sighed. 'You saw the state of her. God knows what she's been through. I think it's going to be a while before she talks. If ever.'

Jairus gripped his face and groaned into his hands. 'She has to talk so we can get to the bottom of this mess.'

'Come on, I'll take you home.'

'I've got my car.'

'But you're too wound up to drive. You're shaking for one thing.'

He looked at his hands and saw that she was right, then lifted his heavy body and followed her to her car.

Jairus could feel her eyes jumping from the road and landing on him. He could also feel the questions queuing up in her throat. He ignored it all and looked out at the streets of Southgate, seeing the lights of the pubs and restaurants reflecting in the damp streets. The rain was hard and figures ran from it towards the tube station that was more like a huge carousel dumped in the middle of the town.

'I don't feel like going home,' Walker said, cutting through his thoughts.

'I can't say that I relish the prospect.'

'Then why don't we stop off and get a drink?'

He looked over and saw her raised eyebrows and her cheeky smile. He nodded and she drove them back around the town centre and along to the White Hart Pub, where she parked round the back.

Inside the pub, with its hard wood floors, long bar and pool table, they sat near the back in a quiet corner. There was hardly anyone in the pub and Jairus was glad. He wanted some peace and quiet, time to think.

He travelled back from the bar with his bottle of lager and a large glass of red for Walker.

'Thanks,' she said and sipped her drink.

He sat and watched her, remembering how much he used to fancy her- how much he still did. She reminded him of Karine a little. Something about her hair and mouth. They both also had honeyed skin.

'There's something you want to ask me, isn't there?' he said.

She laughed and put down her drink. 'Is it that obvious?'

He nodded and sipped his beer.

'I suppose, I just wanted to know how you're feeling...after...you know?'

He sighed and leaned back. 'After I killed Murphy?'

'You make it sound like you went there that night to deliberately stab him.'

Jairus gave a dry empty laugh. 'Yeah? And isn't that what everyone thinks?'

'No, it's not. Most people are thanking God that he's done with. He made people's lives hell.'

'That's no excuse for taking someone's life, is it?'

'I just think you're being too hard on yourself.'

It's punishment, he thought, that he was inflicting on himself, just as their two killers were measuring out to their victims. If he was right, and the two killers did indeed see themselves as avenging angels, getting revenge on the men who had abducted and tortured the girls, then he knew he wouldn't be able to totally condemn them. But he had a job to do.

He looked at Walker and felt the guilt flow over him again, the wave of it rising and beating against his chest and throat. There was so much he wanted to tell her, but couldn't. He reached into himself and grabbed something, anything to tell her about the night he had met Murphy.

'I held him.'

Her brow crinkled. 'Held who?'

'Murphy. He was lying on the ground, his blood leaving his body. At first I just watched him dying. I was thinking, like everybody else, that he was worthless, evil and better off dead. Then he starts pleading, then... he says something... I couldn't hear what he was saying at first, so I knelt down and I realised what he was saying.'

Jairus clenched his teeth as it came back to him. The image is bright. Murphy whispering, holding himself, curled up in a ball. Jairus looked into Walker's eyes. 'It's funny, but I remember my granddad telling me about all the men he saw on the beach at Normandy, all lying there curled up in the foetal position. It was a little while before he realised that they were dying. That's what Murphy was like. Lying there...curled up...praying.'

'Jesus...' Walker gripped his hand. 'Let's get out of here. Maybe get a bottle of wine...and go to your place?'

He nodded.

The lift was silent, the red numbers counting the floors, while Sir Robert Garter leaned his back against the mirrored back wall. He stretched out his arms and yawned. It had been a long flight back from New York and his meeting with the board of Fernham Industries had been somewhat disappointing. Only the meal he'd enjoyed with Karen Holman in the Kuruma Zushi had been memorable, but far too short.

Sir Robert turned and faced the mirrored walls. The bags under his eyes seemed more puffy than usual, and he was quite sure his suit was bulging in all the wrong places.

The doors opened and he walked the short hallway, up the steps and let himself into his penthouse apartment. The glass that spread right across the apartment allowed him a perfect view of the Thames. It slithered beneath him, a luminous green snake slipping through the city.

He pressed his brow to the glass and watched the lights on the bridges, the tiny cars, the houseboats moored on the riverbank. He'd missed this view. There was nothing quite like it in New York, he decided.

There was a change of light, a shadow of movement in the glass. He spun round, but saw nothing. Only the moonlight beamed in, soaking the floor with its blue light. The long sofa and its shadow stretched back towards the rest of the apartment. He was too tired, that was the problem, and he was meant to be up early again the next day.

He went to his shower room and turned on the water, and watched the gush of it, the steam rising to his face. He undressed quickly, then stepped into the shower, and washed away the remnants of New York from his body.

When he felt suitably cleansed, and dry, he pulled his robe tightly round his wide body and opened the bathroom door.

The barrel of the gun wavered for a moment, the arm and head behind out of focus. Then the eyes become clearer. Sharp. Angry.

'You will be punished,' the mask said, and pressed the gun into Sir Robert's forehead.

'If you're here to rob me...' he began to say, but a sickness filled him. It was the eyes. The hatred in them.

'Out.' The gunman stepped backwards, allowing Sir Robert to step out into the hallway.

'I don't have a lot of cash about the place, but there are quite a few works...'

'Shut up! Stop talking!' The gun shook, the mouth snarled.

Then a second figure appeared at the end of the corridor, a silhouette against the skyline. When the gunman directed him towards the newcomer, Sir Robert made out the shotgun in his hands, then saw the large bag at his feet. He began to hope and pray that they were here only to rob him.

Then a strange thought entered his head. It was a hollow thought, but it stung so sharply. His wife; if he was dead, killed in a robbery gone wrong... No, that wasn't possible. Perhaps a rival businessman? Perhaps they were here to kidnap him, he thought.

'Put your hands in front of you,' the second, taller figure said.

Sir Robert put out his hands, clasped together as if he was about to pray. The plastic strap went round his wrists. The masked man jerked it, tightening it.

'Please.' The word left his mouth, but he hadn't expected it to.

'Please?' The second figure looked over Sir Robert's head. 'Did you hear that, brother?'

'Yes, I heard what he said.'

The gun tapped against back of his head. He flinched against the hard coldness of it.

'Sit down.'

'If you're here to get some kind of ransom, then I can arrange...'

'Just sit the...fuck...down!'

Sir Robert lowered himself to the sofa behind him, feeling the icy sweat dripping down his back. 'What do you want?'

The taller man came forward, pointing the shotgun

at him. 'Same old questions. What do we want? What do we want, brother?'

The other one walked round. His eyes fixed on Sir Robert. They seemed empty then, and he stared for a moment, his hand clenched.

'I want you to beg for forgiveness.'

'What do you think I've done?!'

It was the one with pistol that dug into his pocket and brought out a small photograph of a smiling young woman. It was the kind of photo taken in one of those photo booths. He looked away from the picture of the girl. 'I'm sorry, but I've never seen her before. Please, listen...'

'Are you going to beg now?' the taller one said and walked over to the bag. He looked inside for a while, his head turning to look at Sir Robert, a grin on his mouth.

When he saw the tool, Sir Robert jumped up, scrambling backwards over the sofa. The taller one had produced a hammer and walked slowly towards him.

'Wait!' the other one said, and pointed the gun at Sir Robert's head. 'You're telling me that you don't remember a young girl... a young beautiful, innocent girl that you destroyed?!'

He shook his head, feeling the sweat covering his sides and back. He could almost feel the hate emanating from the one still gripping the photograph. The other, taller one, was smiling.

'Please, don't do this.'

The man holding the photograph walked round, disappearing from his sight. He turned to see the man with the hammer, still grinning.

The noose fell over his head. It tightened, making him choke. He could still breathe. Again it tightened.

The rope was being pulled back, forcing him upright, pressed against the back of the hard sofa.

'I beg you! Please!'

The shorter one's face appeared again, but calmer, his voice softer. 'Then do you want forgiveness?'

'I don't know what I'm supposed to have done.' He felt the tears run down his face.

The shorter one moved away as he nodded to his partner, who grinned and came forward, the hammer lifted high into the air.

'No! Please! I'll do anything! Please! Please! Don't...'

The hammer came down. He screamed, his body writhing against the rope. The pain roared up through his hand. He clenched his eyes shut, feeling the urine leaving his bladder.

He looked up and the hammer flashed down again, the scream barely forming in his throat.

'You're all alone up here,' the man with hammer said, examining the tool and wiping the blood off. 'That'll teach you for buying somewhere so high up. Won't it?'

He felt the bubbles of spit and tears meeting on his face. Snot ran into his mouth, while he panted hard. He looked up, his vision seeming to blur and rock side to side. The whole world wasn't even around him anymore. Not one he recognised.

He sniffed and looked at the shorter man. 'Please. Please, I don't know what you're talking about. I don't know...I don't know who she is.'

'You do know, you...fucking...fucking liar!'

He jerked back, the gun barrel digging into his cheek. There must be some way out of this, he thought. *Oh, God please, save me.* 'Are you...please...are you going to kill me?'

'That depends.'

'Please don't. I have a wife and children.'

The shorter one laughed hollowly, his head turning to exchange disbelief with the taller man with the hammer. 'A family? Say you want to be forgiven and I'll let you go.'

The words stuck on his tongue for a moment. He could hardly form the words his mouth was so dry. He cleared his throat, then spoke, half in a kind of prayer, half in pleading. The man with the photograph nodded and paced, listening all the time.

'So you admit your guilt in this?' the shorter one asked.

'Yes, anything. Please just don't kill me.'

The photograph was placed back in his pocket, then he looked at Sir Robert blankly as he said, 'Do what you want with him.'

'The pleasure will be all mine.' The hammer was lifted again.

He walked into the bathroom and shut the door behind him. He pulled off the mask. He looked into the steamed up bathroom mirror and saw his damp hair covering his forehead. Then the weeping started as he dropped to the floor and gripped himself. The screaming was coming to him, even through the door. He clamped his hands on his ears, but still it came. It was not just the screaming that came from the fat businessman in the other room that his partner battered to death. No, it was every one of them. The men they had killed, and the girls who their victims had destroyed.

He dried his eyes. There were more of them out there, or so he had been told. He could not stop now.

CHAPTER 14

The glow of red light passed through him and into his dreams. Marsland's eyes opened, but all he saw was blood for a few seconds. Then it faded back into the light from his alarm clock. It was the baby that haunted his sleep; the young innocent boy who was now in the care of social services.

The red numbers on his alarm clock came into focus, and he sat up, rubbing his eyes. It was nearly 5 a.m. He pulled back the covers and put his feet on the floor.

His mind returned to the dream that was fading into the blackness. Soon it would be lost. He grabbed for it, but it was no use, all he had was a sense of loss.

Then he thought of the girl, Sara, who was now in detention, waiting for her court appearance. She wouldn't serve any serious time, and perhaps with some help she might actually be reunited with her child. Marsland ignored his own doubt and put on his slippers.

He'd helped put her in prison, the least he could do was help her. What good was poking his nose into police investigations going to do him or anyone else? This would be his last time, he decided, as he went downstairs and filled the kettle. As soon as he had helped Sara with a character reference, and paid for her rehab, he would return to his quiet life.

With his mug of tea in his hand, he sat down at the

kitchen table. He would go and visit Sara and tell her what he had resolved to do.

The street seemed so wide in the early morning quiet of London. Pieces of litter rolled towards him, a sheet from a newspaper wrapped itself around his leg. Jairus kicked it away and looked ahead, towards the skyscrapers of the city. He turned north, then back to the east. He looked beyond the small forensic tent that had been set up in the middle of the cordoned-off street. Two squad cars sat with lights flashing at the easterly end. There was another just behind Jairus, with a few uniforms guarding the area.

There were more and more figures appearing along the street, some stopping to stare at the scene, to wonder what had happened. Then they would carry on towards their work.

Moone was walking towards him, notebook in his hand, tapping it against his leg.

'This is bad,' Moone said, looking towards the tent.

'Yeah. What are we looking at?'

'A severed head. Looks like it was dumped in the middle of the street.'

'So why are we here?'

'Anonymous tip-off called into the station. The caller said it was connected to our murdered businessmen. We've sealed the area off, no traffic coming through.'

Jairus nodded and looked round at the buildings. 'That's what they wanted. They wanted a fuss. They wanted disruption. The city loses money. We sit up and take notice. Do we know whose head it is?'

Moone shook his head. 'Not right now. I'm sure we'll soon find out. So, apart from causing a disruption, why here?'

'They're here. They have to be.'

Moone looked round him. 'Who?'

'The person they're sending this message to. They cut off the head and dumped it in the middle of the street.'

'And they did it in full view,' Moone said, pointing to the traffic camera staring down at them like a vulture. 'Come and have a look. I've already had the footage downloaded and sent over.'

'You're getting efficient.' Jairus followed Moone over to his car and they both slipped inside. Moone took out a tablet device and loaded up the footage, then pressed play.

Jairus watched the grainy colour images, dated only a couple of hours earlier, of the empty street. It was quite dark, but suddenly a blue car drove up the street and stopped, seeming to hesitate for a moment. Then the car came closer to the camera, stopping in the middle of the street, and, after a few moments, the passenger got out carrying a rucksack. His hand went in. When he pulled his hand out of the rucksack, he had the head by the hair. He stared at the camera, lifted the head in the air, then suddenly released it. The head rolled along the tarmac. The passenger climbed back in and the car roared off out of view.

'Have we identified the car?' Jairus asked and climbed out.

'Yeah. Stolen. It turned up burnt out. Little chance of any evidence.'

'Yeah, but better be sure.' Jairus pointed to a figure coming across the street. It was a tall and wiry suit. He flashed a badge at one of the uniforms on the cordon, then slipped under the tape.

'What do you think you're doing?' the wiry detective asked Moone. Jairus stepped between them. 'Ask me the questions.'

'Who are you?'

'DCI Jairus. Who are you?'

'DCS John Millar. City Police. I'll be taking over this now. Your lot can be moving on.'

Jairus pointed to the SOCOs' tent. 'Head. Dumped in the middle of the street. It's our case. Let's not piss on each other's shoes. Alright?'

'Who's head?'

'Sir?' A stocky uniform, with a shaved head, came striding over, his hand still clamped over his radio. He looked round at all of them, so Jairus pointed a thumb at himself.

'They've just found a headless body in an apartment not far from here,' the uniform said. 'The place is owned by Sir Robert Garter.'

DCS Millar rubbed his face and sighed. 'You know anything about this?'

Jairus nodded. 'Yeah, like I said. It's our killers. This is their MO. We're in charge here.'

'Ok, fine. Whatever. But this is our city. Tread very carefully.' Millar turned and headed back to his car, while Jairus faced Moone. 'That's the second time I've been told that recently. It's starting to piss me off.'

Moone laughed, a little tiredly.

As they headed back to their cars Jairus saw Moone grinding his jaw. 'What is it?'

'You haven't asked about what they found in that cupboard last night.'

Jairus stopped dead. 'Yeah, because I saw. DVDs. I'm half hoping it's not what I think it is.'

'Films of the girls, labelled, one, two and three.'

'One for each girl?'

Moone nodded. 'Looks like it. Some of the discs were missing though. You going to view them?'

'Yeah. Any news on the girl we found?'

Moone unlocked his car. 'She's not in a good way. Malnutrition. Dehydration. Luckily she had water to drink, but not a lot. They've got her on drips and all that. They'll be giving her a physical examination soon. As for her mental health...'

'I know,' Jairus said and slipped inside his car. 'Meet you at the scene.'

Jairus sighed when he saw the uniforms lined up outside the base of Sir Robert's building, their brass badges, the tell-tale sign that they were made up of City of London Police. It was about to get messy. They were out of their jurisdiction, which meant the City Of London Commissioner would be flexing his muscles already.

Not only was the presence of another constabulary bothering Jairus, but he had also spotted an army of journalists and TV camera crews being held back by the police. He held his ID out the window and was allowed to enter the site. He drove down the ramp and into the underground car park. A few squad cars were parked by the lifts, while a large control unit lorry has been set up alongside the SOCOs' van.

He got out and was approached by a uniform who signed him into the crime scene log. Moone was standing talking to DCS Millar in a parking bay near the back, in the shadows.

'Hello again, DCI Jairus,' Millar said, folding his arms across his chest.

'What the bloody hell's going on?' Jairus pointed his thumb behind him towards the police lorry.

'Like I said earlier, this is our jurisdiction, therefore our crime scene. The Commissioner called me fifteen minutes ago and told me to secure the scene. I believe he'll be on the phone to your boss right now.'

'Yeah? Well, I don't give a shit. I'm going up there.'

Millar smiled. 'Fine by me. Just grab an outfit from the SOCOs. And don't put your grubby hands on anything.'

Jairus turned to Moone. 'Do us a favour, Pete, go and grab a couple of forensic outfits, would you?'

After looking the two of them over, Moone left.

'Wish I had my people so well trained,' Millar said and laughed.

Jairus stepped closer to him and lowered his voice. 'It makes me suspicious when I'm suddenly being sidestepped. You and your Commissioner seem intent on keeping this under wraps. Want to know what I think?'

'This should be interesting.'

'Sir Robert Garter. Rich businessman. Bound to be a Freemason. You and your boss Freemasons too?'

The DCS' expression changed. The laughter in his eyes was replaced by simmering fury. 'Listen to me, Jairus, you better watch yourself. If I hear you've repeated that to anyone else, then we'll make your life hell. You got that? We can destroy you quite easily.'

'Who's we?'

'Just piss off and have a look at the crime scene.' Millar stormed away and entered the control unit.

Moone came back wrapped in a white plastic outfit and held one out to Jairus. 'What was that about?'

'Trouble. That's what.' Jairus pulled on the outfit, while scoping the scene at the entrance of the car park. Up the top of the ramp he could see the uniforms holding back the squabble of journalists. Closest to the line of officers was a man in his late thirties, with a mop of greying brown hair. He wore a brown leather jacket and jeans, and held a Dictaphone in his hand.

'Isn't that Ian Pritchard up there?'

Moone faced the entrance. 'Er...yes, I believe it is. Why?'

'Do us a favour and tell him to get lost, but also tell him to meet me down the street in an hour. There's a takeaway food van down the road when you turn left out of here.'

'What you up to?'

Jairus put a finger to his lips. 'Just do it.'

Moone walked up the ramp, while Jairus pulled on the hood and mask and entered the lift. He travelled up to the penthouse, where the doors opened and he was confronted with a long corridor that was crowded with white-suited SOCOs. Each one was stepping along the metal platforms that had been laid all the way to the living area, some taking photographs and others swabbing for blood. He stood for a moment taking it all in, noticing that far in the distance was the silhouette of an overweight man sitting on a sofa. No head, just a bloody stump.

Another female SOCO, a set of dark eyes over a white mask, approached him with her arms folded. 'I'm Anna Ford. I'm the Crime Scene Manager. If you want to take a look, please keep to the steps.'

He nodded and followed her advice, keeping his eyes on the man on the sofa and the rope that was still attached to the stump. The killers had obviously tied him back, keeping him upright while they tortured him.

When Jairus entered the living area, noticing the expanse of the Thames below the windows, he found more SOCOs working the scene. One was stood to the right of the body snapping away. Another was kneeling at DB's feet, looking upwards. The SOCO on the floor looked at Jairus for a moment.

'Just about the worst I've seen.'

Jairus came round and took it all in. He examined the lack of hands, feet and then the several stab wounds in the chest. They looked wild, uncontrolled.

'I've seen two others just like this.' There was blood sprayed along the floor on either side of the body.

The man who was kneeling stood up. 'Dr David Berriman. I'm the pathologist.'

'DCI Jairus. What do you think?'

'What do I think? They really went to town on this gentleman. They tied his hands and feet, roped him to the post over there, then began to cut him to pieces. They probably started with his fingers, then his hands, then smashed his toes. Cut off his feet and at some point started stabbing him. From the lack of blood in some of the wounds I'd say that his heart stopped pumping during the attack. Lastly, they cut off his head. The fingers, hands and feet are in the bathroom. God knows where the head is.'

'We found it in a street about five minutes from here.'

The pathologist's eyes widened. 'Really? This is all very interesting. I mean, whoever tortured and killed this man was very patient and deliberate. He enjoyed his time with him without a doubt. Yet, later on, he came back in a rage and stabbed him wildly until he was quite dead.'

'There are two killers.'

'That makes sense. I'd say one of them is torturing and killing purely for pleasure, the other is doing it for other reasons.'

Jairus looked at the wounds in the chest. 'Like revenge?'

'More than likely. It's the usual motive.'

Jairus nodded. Taking careful steps across the metal plates that the SOCOs had put down, Jairus went to the bathroom. Again, there was a SOCO taking photographs of the limbs that had been carefully placed at the tap end of the large bathtub. There was a spattering of blood round the hands and feet.

He blinked, feeling a little dizzy, stifled by the forensic outfit. It was suddenly burning hot in the apartment. Too many bodies. He took slow, calming breaths.

Murphy was lying in the bathtub. Glassy dead eyes looking up at him.

Jairus walked quickly from the bathroom, pulling at the zipper. Then something caught his eye. A little way up the hallway there were a few doors. At the last door, a tall and broad uniform stood guard with his hands resting on his stab vest. Unlike everyone else, he was without a white outfit, just gloves and overshoes.

As he wondered what the uniform was guarding, Jairus walked towards him and removed his hood. 'What's in there, sergeant?'

The uniform remained blank-faced. 'I don't know, sir.'

'Then why are you standing guard?'

'Mine's not to reason why.'

Jairus nodded. 'Yeah, I suppose not. Who told you to guard this room?'

The uniform looked thoughtful for a moment, his eyes darting back down the hall. 'Not sure I can say.'

'Just me and you here chatting.'

'I suppose. DCS Millar, by way of the Commissioner. No one's to go in.'

'Well, you can let me in. I'm DCI Jairus.'

'I'm especially not allowed to let you in, sir.'

Jairus nodded, showed his empty palms, and made to move away.

He swept round and threw himself into the

uniform, sweeping his foot round and knocking him off balance. The large copper toppled backwards to the floor, while Jairus headed into the room.

Everything was pretty much white. Big paintings on the walls. Massive bed at the centre of the room. He stepped closer to the bed, focusing on what was lying on top of it.

A dress. A black and red dress with a diamond pattern at the centre of it.

'Sir, what the...' The uniform came in, his eyes also jumping to the bed.

Jairus took out his phone and took some snaps, then walked back along the plates and left the apartment.

When Marsland made a few inquiries through another of his old colleagues, he found out that the likelihood of Sara Billings getting off with a reduced sentence or something even less was very slim. Apparently, a thorough search of her house produced a large quantity of heroin, so the charges had gone up from assault with a deadly weapon to possession with intent to supply. Her boyfriend had done a runner leaving her to face it alone.

His stomach knotted as he walked up to the gates of Holloway Prison. He pressed the buzzer and waited. A voice asked who he was.

'Terence Marsland, here to visit Sara Billings.'

The door opened and a tall and bearded prison officer let him through and walked him down a long corridor towards the reception area to sign in. Then he was escorted by another prison officer towards a metal detector. He went through and then walked towards the metal gates at the other end where a female prison officer was waiting. She told him the rules, all the stuff about passing objects and all the other details, then let him into a long cream-painted room filled with desks. He seated himself in the back corner and waited.

Soon a door opened on the other side of the room and a plump and sour-faced female guard escorted Sara Billings towards him. She looked slimmer and paler than he remembered, dressed in jeans and a blue sweatshirt, with an orange vest over the top of it. Her face was gaunt and grey.

She sat down and faced him, blankly. 'Yeah?'

'Hello, Sara,' he said and smiled.

Her eyes seemed large in her withered face.

'Do I know you?' Her hands folded other one another.

'I'm Terence Marsland. I was at your house the other day, remember? I came around asking about Ria? Ria Saunders.'

'I know Ria. I know who fucking Ria is. Why's it always Ria? Ria! Ria!'

'I'm here to see you. I wanted to see how you're doing.'

Her eyes zipped round the room, her skinny hands pulling at her hair. 'I'm great. I'm just fucking great. I think I'm going to pretty much die in here.'

He leaned across the desk. 'You're not going to die in here, Sara. Did you tell them about your boyfriend? The one you were hiding the drugs for? He got you to hide them there, didn't he?'

'I will die in here and what'll happen to him?'

'Your baby?'

She nodded, while tears poured over her cheeks.

'He'll be looked after. What's his name?'

'Dylan.' She started scratching at her arm furiously.

'Dylan's going to be OK.'

'He's better off without me. I know. I know. Some nice people will adopt him. Yeah, I know.'

'You need to tell them about your boyfriend, what he got you to do.'

'He'll kill me.'

'I'm not going to let that happen.' He reached out his hand across the table, but stopped when he saw the prison officer watching.

'I'm a bad person.' She rubbed her arm, her eyes staring at the table.

'You're not. You've just...well, you've...'

'I've done some terrible, evil things. All I wanted was to get away from things, to escape, know what I mean? I just wanted to lose myself. So I've pretty much said yes all my life.'

'That doesn't make you a bad person.'

She looked up, her swollen eyes staring across at him. 'Tell that to that girl. What happened to her? Where did they take her?'

Marsland's brain scrambled for a moment, then fell back into place. 'What girl?'

'I didn't know what he wanted her for. I just needed the cash.'

Marsland tried to engage her eyes. 'Sara? Sara? Look at me. What are you talking about?'

'The girl! The girl! He wanted me to pick her up! I thought why not? He promised money and good times. All I cared about was getting out of my head. I'll do anything when I'm like that.'

'Sara, what are you getting at? Who wanted you to pick up who?'

'The girl. The girl. He got me to drive his car and offer her a lift. All I had to do was say I knew her friend, and get her to get in the car.'

'Gina Colman? You're talking about Gina Colman?'

Sara shrugged. 'I don't know! She was young, light brown hair. Pretty. I don't know who she was.'

Marsland could feel his body tightening. He wanted to grab her and shake the words out. With a deep breath, and a soft voice, he said, 'Sara, what happened then? Where did you take her?'

'I don't know!'

'Please, Sara. Try and think. Her family need to know what happened to her.'

Sara covered her face for a moment, then nodded. 'Near Brimsdown. There's a road behind those tower blocks on the other side of Durants Park. You know it?'

'The industrial part?'

'Yeah. I was told to take her there and tell her I had to make a phone call. I ran up the road to the phone box. When I came back she was gone, and he gave me the money. He told me if I ever told anyone they'd kill me and take away my baby. They said they were rich and powerful and could easily do it.'

'Who was he, this man?'

She shook her head and sniffed. 'I don't know.'

'What did he look like?'

She began crying again, and wiping her nose with her sleeve.

Marsland got out his mobile phone and found a photograph of Graham Burgess. He held it out to her. 'Sara? Sara, is this the man who paid you?'

She stared at the image for a moment. Then the tears began again. 'Yeah. It's him. I'm so sorry. Tell her family I'm so sorry.'

He put away his phone. 'Where did you meet him?'

She shrugged again. 'He just pulled up one day in his car. He said he wanted to talk and he'd pay me. I got in and he took me to his house. It was massive. I couldn't believe the size of the place. He told me to sit down. Then he got some money and threw it at me. Then he...he got me to do stuff to him. He said he knew about my habit and said he could give me money. Said I just had to pick this girl up. He needed to talk to her, that's all. I didn't care. I just needed the money.'

'What happened then?'

'Someone rang the front doorbell and he shouted at me to go upstairs. I went into a bedroom and waited. I could hear him talking to someone downstairs.'

'What were they talking about?'

'I don't know. I couldn't hear. All I wanted was my money. I just wanted to get out of there.'

'Did you see the person who visited?'

She shook her head. 'No. He came upstairs and said the man had left. I'd picked up this little vase thing off the side and was looking at it. I'd been thinking about nicking it. See how much it was worth. He must've known what I was thinking and said I could have it. Said the man that had just been downstairs had given it to him and he didn't like it anyway.'

'So, you left with it?'

'Yeah.'

'Where is it now?'

'I don't know. In my house somewhere. In amongst the crap. I should've sold it. I don't know why I didn't.'

Marsland got to his feet. 'Thank you, Sara. You've been a great help.'

CHAPTER 15

Jairus pulled up at the entrance to the building, where the journalists still picked around for crumbs. He watched for Ian Pritchard, but, as expected, he was absent. He steered the car left and carried on towards the next corner where a food van had been set up. A dark-skinned woman and a young man served up gourmet takeaway meals. There were quite a few customers queuing up, but Jairus spotted the brown leather jacket of Ian Pritchard as he stood nearby sipping a cup of coffee. He tipped away his drink and came over to Jairus' car and climbed in.

As he drove off, Jairus looked over at the journalist as he rifled through his satchel bag for something.

'So, did you find out anything juicy today? Anything you can add your lies to?'

Pritchard stopped rifling and raised his eyebrows. 'Lies? Come on, you know I'm a well-respected and honest journalist. I'm not one of the scum.'

'Yeah, of course you're not.'

Pritchard pulled out a Dictaphone, but Jairus glared at it. 'Don't you even think about turning that on.'

'Oh come on, you can't expect me to go empty-handed?'

Jairus took a turning and parked in a corner, in the shadow of a new apartment building. He turned in his seat and faced the journalist. 'What do you know about Sir Robert Garter?'

'I'm presuming he's been found dead in his apartment.'

'Yeah, but you didn't hear that from me. Apart from being rich and greedy, what do you know about him?'

'Married. Two kids at boarding school. Usual rich man's life.'

'Do you know if he was a Freemason?'

The journalist's eyes widen. 'You're joking, right? Freemasons? This is to do with Masonic rituals and all that?'

'Again, you didn't hear that from me. What about it? Was he a Freemason?'

Pritchard coughed out a laugh. 'He was a very wealthy, influential businessman. Of course he was a Mason. You don't rise up through the ranks if you're not a Mason, do you? Although you're doing pretty well.'

'Have you ever seen this before?' Jairus took out his mobile and showed him a close-up shot of the symbol on the dress.

'Not really. Doesn't look Masonic. Are you trying to tie in Garter's death to Masonic rituals and all that rubbish? The Freemasons are just a big boys' club, and they can close ranks when they need to.'

'You in the Masons?'

'Fuck off!'

'Then how do you know? Look, give me your number and I'll text you that symbol. Look into it and tell me what you find out. And it doesn't find its way into the papers.'

'How do you know you can trust me?'

Jairus grinned. 'Because, you came very close to being dragged into a very damning inquiry last year. You don't need any more trouble on your back. And

I'm trouble. I'll make your life hell. Find out what you can about the symbol and anything Garter was involved in, then you'll get the scoop. There'll be a press conference tomorrow, so I'd be there if I was you. Now, why don't you get lost?'

Pritchard put away his tape recorder and laughed. 'What?'

'You can't be very bright, Jairus.'

'Can't I?'

'Well, you can't be if you haven't been asking yourself how you got to walk back into the limelight after you killed a suspect. And you have to wonder how you got promoted and made SIO on this case. Anyway, you mull it over.'

Jairus watched him climb out and reversed the car and swung it round. He'd done everything he could to keep his own questions about the promotion in the dark. Now the lights were glowing.

With a sandwich in one hand, and a cup of tea in the other, Marsland sat watching Sara's house. From information he'd picked up from Moone, he knew that the front door wouldn't be very secure. It was a basic front door lock. It was also highly unlikely that her boyfriend would be on guard either; undoubtedly he would be off on the run somewhere.

Marsland finished his sandwich and his tea, then climbed out and walked quickly to the front door. A dog barked somewhere, and there was the distant sound of children shouting.

The door was scratched and battered, and definitely not secure. From a long history of turning up to suspects' doors unannounced, he knew how easy it was to gain access. He turned to his side, stepped back a little, then rammed his body against the door.

The lock shunted but the door remained in place. He stepped back and slammed into it again.

The door opened, and the house yawned at him. There was a smell of stale cigarettes. In silence, he stood in the hall for a moment, listening for signs of life, or for more meatheads come for a confrontation. Nothing happened.

First, Marsland walked into the living room that was in a state, with bags of nappies ripped open and scattered across the room. DVDs and clothes had been thrown onto the armchair. Cushions from the sofa were also in the middle of the floor.

He stepped over the detritus and looked about the rest of the room. There was a kitsch unit in the corner with a few ornaments on it, but nothing that would have come from Burgess' home.

Marsland continued the hunt. He went upstairs and into the first bedroom he found. There was a worn old double bed, the duvet half hanging off. The wallpaper was peeling from the walls and clothes were scattered and discarded over the floor. There was signs of drug use. The sort of box junkies keep their paraphernalia in was sitting open on a bedside table, but it was empty. He pulled everything out from the drawers, threw the clothes and underwear on the bed, but couldn't see any vase. He tried the next room. It was a single bedroom, but this one looked untouched.

There was not much in the room, so he abandoned the search and went to the bathroom which was in the same sort of state as the downstairs.

The bath looked as if it hadn't ever been cleaned. The sink had lumps of dried toothpaste dotted about it. Long brown hairs covered everything. He was about to walk out again, when he caught sight of an object sitting next to the basin taps. He smiled as he walked over to a small white and blue vase that had oriental designs on the outside. There was a toothbrush stuck in it, which Marsland took out and left in the sink.

Back in the smaller bedroom, he sat down and took out his mobile phone. He photographed the vase and began to look online at antique auction sites, focusing on the London area. He gathered a few email addresses and sent out the photograph of the vase and prepared to leave the house. On the way out, he noticed he had already received one reply to his message.

He waited until he was inside his car, then opened the email. It was from a man called Art Collins, an auctioneer at a small auction house in West London.

'Mr Marsland,

I was very interested to read the email you sent me, especially when I viewed the jpeg you enclosed. I'm no expert on Chinese vases, but it's my opinion that the vase is a replica of one made for the Qianlong Emperor. The original was made in 1730. The one you possess was probably made in the 19th century but still worth at least £50,000 at auction. I suggest taking the vase to Highman auctioneers for authentication and valuation as they handle such items. I hope I've been of some help.

Art Collins'

Marsland picked up the vase from the passenger seat and stared at it. He couldn't help wonder why Graham Burgess had given away the expensive vase on a whim, especially to someone like Sara, who he undoubtedly looked down on. Marsland could only think that it was either his sick sense of humour or some kind of subtle slight to the person who had given it to him in the first place. Whoever the person had been, Marsland was going to track them down and find out exactly what they knew of Burgess' private activities.

The incident room was busy, so Jairus took a DVD player and headphones to one of the interview rooms and set it up. He sat down with some of the tapes in front of him. A couple of the uniforms had already been through Burgess' collection of homemade videos, so he already knew that so far they had only evidence of him raping and torturing Gina Colman. Some of the cases had been empty. Someone had already been there and taken the DVDs out. Jairus had a sinking feeling inside him, and it wasn't just from the fact that he was about to view one of the films; there was another darker emotion and an idea that was surfacing little by little. All the facts were adding together and building something macabre and sinister, and the fact that the Freemasons were now painted into the picture was setting him on edge. He would undoubtedly start butting heads with his commanding officers, but he couldn't ignore the fact that everything in the investigation was steering him towards some kind of secret organisation.

He was about to press play on the DVD player, when there was a knock on the door and Walker poked her head in.

'Hey, where've you been? I thought you would've text me or something.'

He smiled. 'Yeah, sorry about that. We've had another body turn up. Things have been manic.'

Walker shut the door. 'It's OK. We're not engaged or anything. I had fun though.'

'Yeah, me too.'

She glanced at the DVDs. 'You going to watch those?'

'That was my plan.'

'You think that's wise? It's not long ago you were suffering with post trauma and all that. Do you really think you should...'

'I have to,' he said, cutting her off.

Another knock at the door and DS Moone entered. He looked at Walker as he said, 'What's happening? Is he sitting in or what?'

'Sitting in on what?' Jairus asked.

Moone looked at him. 'We looked into all the girls' family and friends and ex-boyfriends, and guess what? We got ourselves a suspect. Chris Jenkins. Been in and out of prison since he was knee high, right little troublemaker. Angry, lots of assaults on his record. Apparently, he went out with our second missing girl, Kelly Leigh, for a little while. We're about to interview him. You want to sit in?'

Jairus shook his head. 'You two have fun.'

Moone stepped over. 'Come on, Jairus, I thought you'd love to give a suspect a grilling. He's probably our guy.'

'Good. I hope he is. But there's something else going on here.'

Walker moved closer. 'What do you mean?'

'At the crime scene this morning the City of London Police had a sergeant guarding a bedroom in Garter's apartment. I managed to sweet talk the uniform and take a look inside. There was a dress on Garter's bed, just like the one we found at the first crime scene. So, why were they trying to make sure I didn't see it?'

Moone dragged a hand down his face. 'Oh shit. Do you think they're closing ranks because of the Freemason thing?'

Jairus nodded. 'Of course. All the victims were either in the Masons or had been in the Masons at one time. Whatever their motives are, they're going to try and make all this go away.'

'And what the bloody hell do we do?' Walker said.

'Nothing. You two stay out of it.'

Moone shook his head. 'So you're going to go headfirst right at them, I suppose? And what then? Lose your job?'

Jairus shrugged. 'Yeah, well, they've made me the sacrificial lamb in all this anyway. One minute I'm a pariah, then I'm SIO on this. Someone knew this investigation was on the horizon and pulled some strings to get me to lead it. To them I'm expendable.'

'Well, fuck them then,' Moone said. 'Let's get on and do our job and sod them.'

'Just go and interview your suspect. I'll watch the video of it later. Both of you, just go on and do your jobs.'

They looked at each other, then Jairus, and left in silence.

Chris Jenkins was sitting in a relaxed fashion when Walker and Moone entered the interview room. He had his hands behind his head and watched the two detectives sit down with a slight smirk on his face.

His solicitor, Rick Ashton, sat back a little, his legs crossed with a notebook in his lap. He smiled briefly when Moone caught his eye.

Walker went through the procedure with the tapes, saying who was present and the date and time, while Moone made sure the video recorder was going.

Walker sat forward, her arms neatly crossed, and said, 'Christopher Jenkins, you were nineteen years old when in 2002 you were charged with ABH when you head-butted a man, then kicked him in the face several times, because you said he was trying to push into the queue in your local bank.' She looked up at him and saw he was still smirking and looking off towards the wall.

'Then, during a friend's twenty-first birthday party at a club on Tottenham High Road, you got into an altercation with one of the club's bouncers. Again, you head-butted him, punched him, then, when he was on the ground, you kicked him several times in the face. Then, you took out a large knife and cut off two of his fingers. You took them and threw them into the River Lea so they couldn't be reattached. You were charged with GBH with a deadly weapon. You served six months.'

Walker paused, waiting for Jenkins to look at her. 'Then, a year later, you again assaulted a young man in a pub because he was looking at your girlfriend, Kelly Leigh, and you took out your knife intending to cut off his fingers or worse.'

Ashton cleared his throat. 'My client was never found to have a knife in his possession on that particular occasion.'

Walker nodded. 'No, he got rid of it that time. So, Christopher, would you agree that you're an angry young man?'

Jenkins laughed. 'I'm young. I'm fit. Full of life, darling.'

'Let's go back to Kelly Leigh,' Moone said, sitting forward. 'You went out with her for nearly a year, didn't you?'

'My client's former relationships...' Ashton began, but stopped when Jenkins held up a hand. He leaned forward and said, 'What's Kelly got to do with all this? She went and fucked off on me, and that was it.'

'But that wasn't quite it, was it, Christopher?' Walker smiled a little. 'You followed her everywhere and apparently frightened off a few potential boyfriends.'

Ashton sat up. 'If you're trying to imply that my client had some kind of involvement in Kelly Leigh's disappearance, I must remind you that this was looked into at the time.'

Moone nodded. 'Yes, it was, Mr Ashton. No, we're not trying to suggest your client had anything to do with her disappearance. We're just building up a sketch of his personality. I mean, you are an angry young man, aren't you? And you didn't take Kelly's rejection of you very well, did you?'

'Who does take getting the elbow very easily?' Jenkins relaxed and stretched out his legs.

'Where were you last Sunday?' Moone asked. 'That's the 19th of May.'

Again, Ashton cleared his throat. 'My client does not…'

'Depends what time,' Jenkins said, smiling.

'Late Sunday night to the early hours of Monday morning.'

Jenkins looked upwards, seeming to try and remember. 'Hmm…let me see, I believe I went out for a few drinks at the Coach and Horses in Enfield Town, then went home and…yeah, that was all.'

'Did you go to the pub with anyone?' Walker asked.

'No, darling. Just went on my own. I enjoy my own company. I saw a few birds in there, but none of them were my type.'

'None of them as pretty as Kelly?' Walker smiled.

Jenkins looked at his solicitor for a moment, and shook his head. 'What is it that you two have with her? Fuck me, she disappeared ages ago and you never found her. You did a shit job back then, now I'm sitting here again and what? You think I had something to do with it?'

Moone shook his head. 'No, Christopher, we don't think that. But we believe we do know what happened to Kelly.'

Jenkins' face changed. 'Go on. What happened to her?'

'We believe she must have been abducted on her way home from her job in Boots. She left work that evening, but never got home. CCTV footage showed her walking through the shopping centre…then she vanishes. Unfortunately we found her blood at a recent crime scene. Looks like she was killed there.'

'You're having…fuck. Who the fuck took her?'

Walker shook her head. 'We can't go into details at the moment, Christopher. Look, Chris, where were you on Monday night through to the early hours of Tuesday?'

He frowned again. 'Monday night? I was at home.'

'You live in a bedsit, yes? Priory Road? Off the Great Cambridge Road?'

'Yeah. I was there. Went home. Surfed the net for some porn, watched TV and went to bed.'

'Can anyone confirm that?' Moone asked.

'My client's doing his best to answer your questions, DI Walker,' Ashton said, sounding rather bored. 'Why don't you get to the point?'

Moone smiled apologetically. 'Yes, you're quite right, Mr Ashton. Chris, we think that maybe you found out what had happened to Kelly Leigh. We, of course, don't know how you came by that information, but we believe you sought revenge. Your temper got the better of you, and you and an accomplice went round to the house of the person you believed abducted and killed her. Then you tortured them, then killed them.'

'What the fuck?' Jenkins' head jumped up, his eyes wide. 'Fuck off. You're having me fucking on. I did not...I don't fucking know what fucking happened to her. How the hell do I know what happened to her?'

'It's quite understandable really,' Moone began. 'I mean, I don't know how I'd react if I found out that the woman I loved had been abducted and tortured and raped and killed. I don't blame you...'

'I did not...I didn't have anything to do with that. Fuck off. Yeah, If I found out someone had done something like that I'd cut off their balls and...'

'Don't say anything more, Chris,' Ashton said, sitting up. 'My client won't be answering anymore questions. Do you have DNA evidence to implicate my client? Any witnesses?'

Walker shook her head. 'No.'

'Then you won't be charging my client?'

Moone said, 'No, we won't. Not at the moment.'

Ashton turned to Jenkins. 'Come on, Chris, you're free to go.'

When Chris Jenkins and his solicitor had left the interview room, Moone turned to Walker. 'I don't bloody believe it. That's why Jairus didn't want to sit in on the interview. He somehow knew that Chris Jenkins wasn't our man.'

'You don't think he is either?' Walker asked and picked up Jenkins' file from the table.

Moone stood up. 'No, and I'm willing to bet on the fact you don't.'

She sighed and opened the door. 'No, you're right. He's an angry and violent young man, but I don't think he killed all those men. So now what?'

'We keep on interviewing friends, family and all that crap. It's all we can do at this stage.'

Walker looked thoughtful for a moment. 'You know

Jay is up there looking at the DVDs we found?'

'So?'

'I'm not sure he's up to it. I'm worried about his state of mind.'

Moone squeezed her shoulder. 'I worry about the state of mind of anyone who does this job. Don't worry about Jairus, he can take care of himself.'

CHAPTER 16

Jairus was staring at the blank screen in front of him, the third of the films having ended. Tears on his cheeks, he felt the anger burn up through him, the urge to grab the monitor and hurl it at the wall.

The door to the room opened and Commander Warren stood there with a strange expression on his face. He seemed to look about the room for a moment then fixed his eyes on Jairus.

'You've been watching the films, I understand?'

Jairus wiped his face and nodded. 'Yeah, thought I should.'

The Commander nodded. 'And what did you find?'

'Burgess. And Gina Colman. The sadistic bastard put her through hell. I'll be surprised if she ever mentally recovers from what she's been through.'

'Oh God, that poor girl.' Warren shut the door behind him. 'Didn't you find any other films with the other victims in?'

'Victims? That's an interesting word. You talking about the young girls or the dead businessmen?'

'I was referring to the businessmen. That's what they were, DCI, victims. That's why you're investigating, to find and arrest the people who murdered them. Don't forget that.'

Jairus stood up and folded his arms. 'I won't. But my job is made very much harder if other officers try and slip evidence past me.'

'What does that mean? Are you referring to the City Of London Police and their investigation into Sir Robert Garter's murder?'

'Yeah. Do you know that they had a sergeant guarding his bedroom, trying to keep me from seeing a crucial piece of evidence?'

'The officer in question was simply securing the evidence. Look, I've had the Commissioner on the phone. He was very upset to have his crime scene interfered with.'

'He was upset? It's our bloody case!'

The Commander held up a finger. 'But there's procedure and the crime was committed on their territory.'

Jairus walked away for a moment, trying to suck down his anger. 'Sir...with all due respect, I feel like someone's trying to tie my hands in this. They tried to stop me seeing a dress that was on Garter's bed. It was the same as the dress we found at Thomas Henry's house. All these murders are linked, all the victims were either Freemasons or were at one time. I know the lads upstairs want to brush that little fact under the carpet, but I can't. I won't.'

Warren stepped closer. 'Listen to me, DCI Jairus. No one is trying to cover anything up. I won't stand for those kinds of allegation. All the evidence will be looked at, and examined for their relevance to the case. Sir Robert Garter was an influential man. He had friends in high places. So, therefore, this whole case needs to be handled very carefully. You're giving a press conference this afternoon, and there is to be no mention of the Freemasons. It has no relevance.'

'No relevance?!' Jairus heard the sickening laughter in his own voice. 'And what about the three girls they took, and tortured and raped and murdered?'

The Commander was red-faced, but his expression was blank. 'You said you only found films of one of the girls, and that only Burgess was in the film.'

Jairus nodded, but the sickness crept into his stomach.

'Then you haven't got anything tying Sir Robert to the kidnapping of those girls?'

'No, sir, nothing at the moment.'

'Then when you give the press conference this afternoon, you will not link the disappearance of those girls, or the films you found, with the murder of those three businessmen, when you give over the details of the case. Three businessmen have been murdered, as well as Thomas Henry's daughter, Marie. There is to be no link to be made between the Freemasons and their murders. Do you understand, Jairus?'

Jairus looked down for a moment, but said, 'Yes, sir. I understand. I won't make a link between them.'

'Good. I'm glad to hear you say that. I want us to be able to trust one another. Let me remind you that I fought for you to be put on this case. It wasn't an easy decision and I don't want to regret it.'

'I understand.'

The Commander nodded, then looked at the DVDs. 'You better get those back into evidence. And start preparing for the press conference.'

Jairus heard the door shut and the footsteps of Warren trailing off down the corridor. He sat down again and stared at the monitor's blank screen, while the films began to play again in his mind.

Highman's auction house was situated a little way from Mayfair, and the building was a little less grand than Sotheby's, but it was nonetheless impressive.

Marsland managed to park a few streets away at an extortionate rate, then walked all the way to the enormous stone archway and the large wooden double doors. He carried the vase in a small box he'd found and stuffed it with newspaper. When he'd looked online at past auctions on Highman's site, he'd seen that indeed a reproduction of a similar Chinese vase had been sold quite recently. Of course, the identity of who had bought the vase was private.

It was easy enough to ring and get an appointment with their chief valuer; all Marsland had to do was say he believed he was in possession of an original Qianlong Emperor's vase. Frederick Davey could not have implored him more to come and let him view the object. Then Marsland realised he had a secondary problem, and that was how to get Mr Davey to leave his office long enough so he could look through his computer records.

Marsland entered through the large wooden doors and found himself in a pristine white-washed corridor that led onto more doors, glass this time. Beyond that was a large reception area. A few statues were positioned around the corners of the room, most of which were adorned in items of jewellery or famous pieces of clothing. Massive canvases were hung at each end of the room. Each with splashes of random colours- the sort of modern art that Marsland hated.

An Arabic-looking young woman stood up from behind a desk and approached Marsland.

'Good afternoon, sir, and welcome to Highman's auction house. Can I help you?'

'I've come to see Mr Davey about an item he was interested in viewing.' Marsland held up the box.

The young woman smiled, then produced a small tablet device which she zipped her finger over. A second later she smiled again, and pointed to another pair of doors to the right of Marsland.

'This way, sir. I hope your journey was not too bad. Did you find us OK?'

'Yes, I did.' Marsland followed the woman along a corridor lined with glass walls in which more jewellery was encased. At the end of their walk, Marsland found himself approaching another smaller doorway. But this time a metal detector separated him from the door, and a large man in a suit stood with arms folded nearby. Marsland was frisked, then put through the detector and allowed to enter the next room carrying his box.

As he was placed into the company of another young woman, almost interchangeable with the first, Marsland began to wonder if his plan of surreptitiously sneaking a look at Davey's files was feasible.

The young woman took him to another door, where she smiled brightly and left him and walked away. Marsland saw a buzzer on the door and pressed it. The door opened automatically and he found himself standing inside a long barren room. The room was white like everything else in the building and the walls lined with artwork. There were also a scattering of black and white photographs that seemed to have been taken in the auction house.

Mr Davey was small, with thick brown wavy hair. He wore an expensive-looking suit and bright pink tie. He got up from behind a large expanse of oak desk and put out a hand to Marsland, while his other hand pointed at the box.

'Welcome to Highman's, Mr Marsland. I take it that is the object you mentioned?'

Marsland nodded and raised the box. 'That's right.'

'Good. Good.' Mr Davey went round his desk and

sat down after pointing to the chair opposite him. 'So, Mr Marsland, I believe you think you have a vase made for the Qianlong Emperor?'

Marsland smiled. 'I think we both know that is highly unlikely.'

Davey smiled. 'Of course. Perhaps a reproduction. 19th century?'

'I'll let you be the judge of that. I believe you might have sold a similar vase not too long ago.'

Davey looked towards the ceiling for a moment, then swivelled his chair round to his computer screen. 'Hmm... Yes, I think you're right. It should be on my records. We get so many items pass through our hands, it becomes difficult to keep them all in your head.' Davey tapped slowly at the computer screen for a moment, squinting a little. 'Yes. 19th century reproduction of a Chinese vase. Went for £50,000.'

'Do you mind me asking who you sold that to? I mean, if they're a collector...?'

Davey laughed a little. 'I'm afraid I'm not allowed to give out that information. Don't worry though, I'm sure the person in question will learn of your item, should you decide to auction it.'

'That's good to know.'

'So, Mr Marsland, can I see the vase? It helps with the valuation.'

'Of course.' Marsland smiled outwardly, but his mind raced, wondering if Mr Davey would actually be able to recognise the vase as the same one they had previously sold. Even so, he knew he couldn't stall much longer and began to unwrap the box, then produced the delicate vase.

The eagerness in Davey's face was unmistakable as he stood up and came round the desk. He took the vase gently and turned it in his hands, while squinting. He then turned it upside down and smiled. 'I think we might be in business.'

'Really? That's good. I don't suppose there's a toilet I can use nearby?'

Davey hardly looked up from the vase when he pointed towards the door. 'Yes, it's left out the door and near end of the corridor. I'll let you out, just buzz when you want to come back in. Sorry about all the security, but we used to get robbed quite a lot in the old days.'

Marsland walked out the door once Davey had pressed a button under the desk. He turned left, found the toilets, then made sure no one else was in there with him as he took out his phone and dialled DS Moone.

'Hello, Marsland,' Moone said, sounding tired.

'I need you to phone the number I'm going to text to you. Call the number in exactly ten minutes.'

'What? Why? Where are you?'

'I'm looking into something for a friend. Please, Moone, do me this one favour. I'll never ask you for another favour again.'

There was a sigh on the other end. 'Well, that's a lie for starters. And what am I supposed to say when I ring this number?'

'Ask if Mr Davey is there. When they say he's in a meeting, say that you're from the police and you need to him to urgently come outside. I'd use a landline if I were you.'

'OK, Sherlock. Bloody hell, Marsland... Right, OK, I'm phoning in exactly ten minutes.'

The phone went dead and Marsland spent a little time washing and drying his hands before heading back along the corridor to Davey's office. He buzzed the door, noting that he had about five minutes before

Moone would call.

'Did you find it OK?' Davey asked, now back behind his desk, the vase sitting in front of him.

'Yes, thanks. So, what do you think of the vase?'

Davey's eyes fell to the object. He traced a finger carefully down one side. 'I think it's very beautiful. I do believe it's a 19th century reproduction, but nonetheless, it is still a much sought-after piece of antiquity. If we make sure our usual collectors are aware of its sale, it should get a great deal of interest.'

There were a few minutes of talk about the vase's history and the period the original vase would have been from. Through all Davey's speech, Marsland thought he did a great job of feigning interest. But all the time he listened, he was thinking about his task of getting into Davey's computer files.

Then the phone was ringing, and Davey looked up with apologetic eyes as he lifted the receiver and began listening.

'I'm sorry, Dana, say that again. Yes? Where are they? Why do they want to speak to me? Ok. Well, OK I'll be down in a minute. Get Stuart to meet me by the exit. OK.'

Marsland watched Davey put down the phone, his forehead deeply creased. 'I'm sorry, Mr Marsland, but I have to go downstairs for a few minutes. Would you like to come down with me? Dana will get you a tea or coffee or even a glass of wine if you wish?'

'Could I possibly wait here. I'll guard my vase.'

Davey shrugged. 'OK, but you'll be locked in. I'll be back in a couple of minutes.'

Marsland smiled and nodded as he watched the antique expert head out the door, then heard the buzzer go and the electronic sound of it locking. He looked at his watch, then looked round the room for any cameras. If there were any, they were well-hidden. He went round the desk and sat in front of Davey's computer. Marsland gave a sigh of relief when he saw that Davey had neglected to log out of the system. He began clicking on different files, searching through the various menus, but it took a few minutes before he got to the previous sales history.

He was just about to open the files, when his ears pricked up. A sound like high heels tapping at the floor outside had reached his ears, but the sound seemed to fade away. He looked back at the computer screen, so close to finding out who had bought the vase originally. His pulse had begun to beat in his neck and ears.

His head shot up towards the door. The buzz sounded. No, not right now. The door was clicking open. Marsland grabbed the vase and swung round to face the window, calming himself.

'Is everything OK, Mr Marsland?'

He turned round to see the second young woman staring at him, a big smile on her face. 'Yes, I'm fine. Thanks.'

'Mr Davey sent me up to see if you'd like a tea or coffee. Or we even have a house wine?'

'No, I'm fine thanks.'

'OK. Mr Davey won't be long.'

'That's great.'

The door clicked shut again. Marsland put down the vase and sat back in front of the computer, then double-clicked on the sales history. Yet more information filled the screen, and it seemed endless. He kept turning his head as he moved the mouse, convinced he could hear someone coming, or imagining that Davey was on his way back up.

Now he was looking at piles of information. Then

he noticed the date section and, knowing that the vase was sold nearly a year and half ago, he put in a rough date. More information flooded the screen, and his heart was pulsating in his chest, his hands shaking, his breath starting to come fast. What the hell did he think he was playing at? This would be his last case. He promised himself that much. A nice quiet life, because he had nothing to prove to anyone.

He sifted through the files before him, feeling that the search was probably endless. Then he felt relief flood through him when he spied a search panel halfway down the page. He entered the information he had on the vase and waited, watching the egg timer doing its thing, his eyes jumping to the door every now and again.

Suddenly an image of the vase appeared on the screen. It was a paragraph of information on the sale, then next to it was a link to the purchaser's information. He clicked on it.

He was looking at a name and address. He quickly got his notebook out and began to scribble the information down. He looked towards the door, definitely hearing the sound of shoes coming this time. Then he heard the door buzzer go as he closed the files. With only seconds to spare, Marsland jumped up from the desk, strode round the desk and sat down. He was breathing hard when Davey entered the office, gave his apologies, and said someone had been wasting his time.

Marsland controlled his breathing and smiled. All the time they chatted, he kept looking down at the scribbled name in his hand.

Mr Harold Jones, I'm coming to see you, he thought.

Jairus sat down at the table set up for the press

conference and looked about the room at the swarm of journalists. The seats were crammed and all he could see was a myriad of eyes staring back at him. This was a part of the job he loathed. He had a skill of twisting his way out of appearing in front of the cameras, but this time Commander Warren had pretty much made sure he was delivered to the press room.

He looked down at the statement that the press liaison officer had given to him minutes before he sat down. Now Commander Warren was on his right, and DI Walker on his left.

Jairus carefully looked over the journalists, scanning the crowd, searching for one particular face among the horde of the curious. He stopped. Near the front he caught sight of Ian Pritchard, Dictaphone in hand. He gave Jairus a subtle nod, but he ignored it and began to read the statement before him.

'As you all probably know, three businessmen were recently murdered by an as yet unknown assailant or assailants. The first murder was committed last Monday. Thomas Henry and his daughter, Marie Henry, were killed in their home. That night Graham Burgess was also killed in his home. This morning Sir Robert Garter was found dead in his apartment that overlooks the Thames. We are working carefully with the City of London Police to try and solve these murders. We can now announce that we believe the three murders are connected.'

Jairus swallowed down his anger. 'We beg the killers of these men to come forward and hand themselves in. We know that you feel anger towards businessmen like the ones you have taken out your rage on, but now is the time to stop.'

Jairus looked round the room for a moment, ignoring the TV cameras and flashes. 'We also make a plea for anyone who has information about the killings to come forward. You might be married to, or have some kind of relationship with the killers. Please, come forward if you suspect that you know someone involved. You'll be helping them in the long run, not betraying them. Thank you for coming today. We won't be taking any questions.'

Jairus raised himself slowly, waiting, holding back. Commander Warren was already heading down the steps and towards the door.

'DCI Jairus, is it true you're investigating a possible connection between the murders and the Freemasons?'

Jairus watched Commander Warren jerk his head toward the audience of journalists, then hurry from the room. When he looked round, the asker of the question, Ian Pritchard, was smiling at him.

Commander Warren slammed the door to his office and swung round to face Jairus, his eyes blazing. 'Jesus Christ, Jairus, how the bloody hell do they know about that?'

Jairus had rested against the desk, waiting for the rebuke. He made his face empty, free of any sign of guilt. 'Search me. You know what the press are like.'

Warren breathed hard then stepped forward. 'It's very fishy how they just happened to have pulled that information out of the air like that, don't you think?'

'Yeah, but there are some journalists who are just as cunning and just as good as detecting as some of us. It doesn't take much to put it all together. It's the one thing the victims have in common. They never had any business dealings, they didn't mix in their private lives, apart from when they were Freemasons.'

Warren looked away, his eyes turning towards the window and the light rain that had begun. 'I guess the damage has been done now, although I'll get it in the neck. My job is hanging by a thread, Jairus. And so is yours.'

'Yeah, I've been there before.'

Warren nodded. 'Anyway, is there any news on a suspect yet? I hear Walker and Moone interviewed someone?'

'Yeah, but we let him go. He wasn't our man.'

'You sure?'

'I watched the video of the interview. I'm sure. We'll keep an eye on him though.'

'Well, you'd better get back to work.'

As he headed for the door, his boss called out to him. 'Yes, sir?'

'A message was left for you a little while ago. Raymond Crow phoned and asked for you. He said he had some information that might be relevant to your investigation. Said he'd be at the Gold Street Brasserie until 4 p.m. Go and see him, Jairus. He might actually have some useful information. Oh, and if I find out that any of my people have been talking to the press, then God fucking help them.'

Jairus smiled and left his office.

It was getting well into the afternoon when Marsland escaped the hordes of London pedestrians and the blare of traffic noises. He had a headache when he had left Davey's office after telling the auctioneer that he would bring the vase back for a full valuation at a later date. The man looked disappointed, but nonetheless he said goodbye and gave Marsland his card.

Now the wider roads and green fields passed him by. He had the window down and his arm stuck out, even though there was a light rain coming down. In the last few hours, he'd had an unusual feeling come over him, and the only way he could describe it was as a kind of release. He was in the process of helping solve the mystery of what exactly had happened to the three young girls who had disappeared. In a moment of clarity, he knew this would be his last case. The intangible guilt he felt over the death of his daughter would somehow be repaid, or balanced against the light he would shine into the last moments of the three girls' lives. He was in no doubt that the two missing girls had perished, but he wanted some kind of peace for their families.

Then his mind turned to Jacqui. He felt guilt at the thought of her. The woman had obviously been reaching out to him in some way, perhaps out of loneliness, but he had repaid her kindness with suspicion and nosiness. When he found her, he would make it up to her in some way, he just didn't know how yet.

Marsland was pulled from his thoughts by his satnav telling him to turn left at the next roundabout, which he did and found himself driving down a long tree-lined road. The houses were set back, with long driveways. The houses themselves would probably be worth a fair amount, but they didn't seem to be the homes of people with expensive tastes in antiques.

He found number 153 and pulled up outside the four bedroom home. It was painted white with a black door, and there was a silver Volvo parked neatly on the driveway.

He took out his mobile and rang the number that he had found along with the address. After a few rings, a slightly croaky voice seemed to whisper into his ear.

'Hello, who is this?'

'Is this Mr Harold Jones?'

There was a pause on the other end, and Marsland

heard no signs of life for a while. Then the voice came back. 'Yes, that's correct.'

'I'm Terence Marsland and I believe I have something that belongs to you.'

There was then a little laughter on the phone line. 'Really? What is it?'

'A Chinese vase. It's small and beautiful.'

'Really? Well, I'm not sure if it belongs to me, but I'd quite like to view it. I'm a collector, you see?'

'OK, well, I'm very close to you, so do you mind if I come round with it?'

'Not at all. You have my address then?'

'Yes. I'll be there soon.' Marsland ended the call, playing back the voice in his head. The man seemed friendly and not at all surprised Marsland had phoned him.

Marsland waited a few minutes, then climbed out of the car, taking his time and fetching the box with the vase inside. He walked up the drive and pressed the doorbell.

It was at least two minutes before Marsland saw signs of movement through the small window in the door. A man was coming slowly to the door, then he was opening it, revealing a worn face and silvery grey hair. The man smiled brightly, his energetic eyes jumping to the box in Marsland's hands.

'Hello, Terence Marsland,' he said and shook Mr Jones' hand.

Jones opened the door wider and pointed along the hall. 'Come through to the kitchen, Mr Marsland.'

'Thank you.' Marsland walked along a dimly lit hallway and into a spacious kitchen. It was modern, with tiled flooring and gleaming worktops. He turned round and placed the box on the kitchen table, moving a small pile of letters as he did so.

Mr Jones entered the kitchen, his eyes jumping to the box. 'Can I see the vase that you think belongs to me?'

Marsland smiled, and unpacked the vase and placed it on the kitchen table. Mr Jones raised his eyebrows and looked at Marsland.

'Where did you say you came across this vase?'

'A young woman had it.'

'Really?' Mr Jones scratched his head. 'Well, I bought it for a friend. I can't quite understand how this young woman came by it. Wait a moment and I'll fetch my glasses.'

Marsland watched him walk slowly away, noticing that he limped a little. He seemed quite fragile, but there was something in his eyes that sparkled.

Marsland reached out for the vase, his eyes falling on the mail on the kitchen table. He read the address. He frowned, noticing a different name on the letters than the one he had noted down from Davey's computer. He read the name again: Edgar Holzman.

There was movement in front of him. Marsland spun round to see that the man had returned. His eyes were staring.

Marsland felt the iron grip clasp onto his right wrist, jerking him forward, towards the man. He tried to pull himself away, but the man was strong. His eyes were wide, burning through Marsland. Then he felt it- the cold burn down below. He looked down and saw that somehow a blade was sticking into his stomach. The man had stabbed him. Marsland suddenly felt cold. He was shaking.

When he looked up into the calm face opposite his, the man lifted a finger to his lips and said, 'Shhh. Be quiet now.'

Marsland grasped out, trying to grab the man's

face.

The knife pierced him again, and the man let go, releasing him to the floor. Marsland fell backwards, tripping back over the table and landing flat on the floor. He automatically touched his stomach and saw the blood covering his hands, then looked up at the figure standing over him holding the knife.

'Thank you for returning my vase, Mr Marsland. Very kind of you. I'm afraid though I cannot have you die in my house and leave a mess. Don't worry it won't take long for you to die now. Just lie down and let it happen. Now I have to go and prepare my car for your body.'

Marsland shuddered with the icy coldness flooding over him and realised he was going into shock. He watched the man step over him casually, carrying the bloody knife off with him. He clamped his hand down on his wounds, feeling the warm blood oozing from him. He didn't have long left. He looked round and saw the washing machine and the wall behind it. Hidden. Marsland gritted his teeth and rolled himself over, careful not to drag his bloody stomach over the floor. He pulled himself along, trying to ignore the pain and dizziness. He reached out his bloody hand towards the wall. Not near enough. He dragged himself closer and pressed his index finger against the wall hidden by the washing machine. Exhausted, and cold, he moved round and collapsed to the floor, the darkness creeping in all around him.

CHAPTER 17

In among the wide streets and the overshadowing skyscrapers of Canary Wharf, Jairus found a narrower thoroughfare that led to a few pubs and restaurants. This was Goldstreet, aptly named after the one asset that all the suited men and women of the area worshipped at the feet of.

Jairus walked into the large and brightly decorated interior of the Goldstreet Brasserie and was approached by a young woman in a black and white trouser suit. He showed his ID, asked for Raymond Crow, and was directed to a private alcove near the back of the restaurant where the businessman was nursing a coffee. Crow got up and put his hand out.

Jairus took the firm handshake and sat down, taking the time to look round the place.

'Must cost quite a bit to eat in a place like this.'

'It's quite pricey, but you get what you pay for.' Crow smiled and lifted his coffee. 'Would you like something to eat or drink?'

'No, thanks. I prefer good old fish and chips or a takeaway curry to all this showy rubbish.'

'Me too. But it looks good to wine and dine clients here.'

'You left a message saying you had some information for me.'

Crow put down his coffee. 'That's right. I'm afraid

I have a confession to make. I lied before.'

'About what?'

'About not knowing Graham Burgess.'

Jairus leaned back. 'How do you know him?'

'I think you probably know that already. You're a clever man.'

'Seems so sometimes. Depends what company I'm in.'

'I know what you mean. I'm always finding myself surrounded by idiots.'

'So, you met Burgess when you joined the Freemasons?'

Crow turned his coffee cup in its saucer. 'That's correct. I joined because, as I said before, I thought I might join the ranks of the rich and influential.'

'Like Sir Robert Garter?'

'I read about his murder. Do you really think he was killed because he was in the Freemasons?'

'I can't answer that. How well did you know Burgess?'

'Not very well, but well enough to know there was something off about him.'

'What do you mean?'

'Well, let's just say that quite a few of the female staff at the hotels we had frequented had plenty to complain about.'

'Sexual assaults?'

Crow nodded.

'Have any of them made an official complaint?'

Crow laughed. 'The high-up members of the Freemasons don't have complaints made against them. And if they do, they make them go away.'

'Can you name one of the hotels where one of these incidents happened?'

Crow sat back. 'Hmm...I'm not sure I want to risk

my reputation by going up against the Freemasons. Do you know how influential they are in the business world and the media? They can, and have, destroyed men on a whim. Do you remember that MP a few years back, the one who was secretly filmed with a young woman while he was wearing a football kit?'

'I remember something about it.'

'Well, I happen to know that the girl in the film had formerly been in the employment of a businessman who also happened to be an influential Freemason. The MP had upset the businessman a year earlier. They paid her a lot of money to get the MP into bed and destroy his marriage and reputation.'

'Interesting. So, aren't you scared that the people who murdered Burgess will come for you?'

'Well, number one, I have security.' Crow pointed over to the entrance, where Jairus observed a broad man who was packed tightly into a dark suit. The bodyguard was sitting in a booth near the door, his eyes scanning everybody who came and went.

Jairus turned back to Crow. 'And number two?'

'If they are targeting Freemasons, I'm sure it won't be for the reason that they're merely Freemasons. There must some other motivation. And seeing as I've done nothing that would warrant two killers tracking me down, I feel perfectly safe.'

'Good.' Jairus sat back, watching the self-important man in the suit, feeling that Crow had other motives for making him cross London other than the useless information he had provided. He better have something, he thought, as he couldn't stand time wasters.

'So, is that all you had to tell me? You could have told me that over the phone.'

There came a smile from Crow as he sat forward.

'Guilty as charged. The real reason I got you here is to offer you a job.'

Jairus huffed and stood up. 'I have to go. Thanks for wasting my time.'

'Wait. It would be a highly-paid security job. Very highly-paid. In fact, you could name your own price. I mean, how long do you policemen have in your careers before you're burnt out?'

'Enjoy the rest of your day.' Jairus fought the urge to grab the smug businessman by the collars and shout into his face. With his fists clenched, he stormed from the building, eyeing the bodyguard as he left. He had a scar down the side of his left cheek and shaved blonde hair. The guard stared back at Jairus through deep slits either side of his nose. Jairus carried on and headed back towards his car. He stopped when his phone rang in his pocket. 'Yeah?'

'Guess what?' Moone said, excitedly. 'Remember that regional anaesthetic they found in Burgess' body? Well, turns out a batch was pinched from Chase Farm Hospital six months ago. I talked to someone at the hospital and they told me they had their eye on one particular nurse. Her name's Jenny Howes. Want to talk to her? I've got her in the station.'

'Yeah, I do.' Jairus ended the call.

With a file tucked under his arm and a coffee in his hand, Jairus backed himself into the interview room and nodded to the youngish, skinny girl sitting at the battered desk. She twitched a little, her brown eyes opening wide, while her hands tugged at her dark brown hair. She tried to smile, but Jairus could see that she was nervous.

He sat down in the chair opposite and pushed the file halfway across the desk, noticing her eyes jump to it, her hand tugging at her hair again. She was dressed in a pink T-shirt and black leggings and Ugg boots. Jairus smiled and sat back.

'I'm sorry about dragging you in like this, Jenny,' he said and pushed the coffee towards her.

'No thanks. I'm fine.' She nodded a bit madly. 'What's this about? Have I done something?'

'Jenny, you're a nurse? That right?'

'Yeah, that's right. I work in the casualty department. It's bleeding manic.'

'I can imagine. I don't think I could do your job. I mean, it must be pretty tough looking after the sick day after day, and seeing people dying all round you.'

Jenny shrugged. 'It's not that bad. Yeah, there are tough days, but there are good days too, when you get to help people. Yeah, people die, but what about your job. I mean, I couldn't deal with all those murders and robberies.'

'My job? It's different, because the people are already dead when I meet them.' Jairus watched her as she smiled a little. Her eyes looked a little wild. She was definitely a little high on something. 'If I did your job, I think I'd need something to keep me going. Especially on the night shifts.'

'Coffee. That's all we have. Like everybody else.' She looked away at the walls and up to the thin windows.

Jairus sat forward. 'Yeah, but that's not all, is it, Jenny? I hear about doctors taking stuff all the time. It goes with the job.'

'Not me.'

'Not you?' Jairus stood up. 'There's a new test we can do. I can go and get it, and if you prove positive, then I'll have to tell the hospital. And then that'll be the end of your nursing career. Won't it? They tipped us off about you.'

Jenny sunk her head into her hands, her dark hair covering her face. 'Shit. Shit. I can't lose my job…'

'I can make it go away, Jenny.'

She looked up, wiped away her hair. 'How?'

'I can tell them I investigated and you were clean. Must have been someone else.'

'Really? Why would you do that?'

Jairus sat back down. 'Because, I need information from you.'

Her eyes narrowed. 'Alright. What info?'

'You stole some drugs and a couple of bottles of anaesthetic from the hospital, right?'

She shrugged. 'Don't think I should actually admit guilt.'

'I'm not recording this, Jenny. No one's listening. I need to know who you passed it on to. I'm guessing some sleazy, skinny drug dealing type, right?'

'I'm not going to grass anyone up, am I?'

'Aren't you? Well, it's either that or lose your job.'

She stared at him for a moment, then tutted and shook her head. 'Shit. You better not let on it was me. I sold it to Adrian Wells.'

'Did he ask you to get some anaesthetic?'

'Yeah, told me what drugs he wanted and asked for the anaesthetic too. God knows why he wanted it.'

He pushed a pen and paper towards her. 'I need an address.'

She scribbled the address down.

'Thanks, Jenny. Now, if I hear you've been nicking stuff from the hospital again, I won't be so nice. Got it?'

'Yeah, yeah,' she sighed and looked away.

Jairus drove through the belching traffic towards the

address that Jenny had given him. He shook his head when he read it. The estate where Wells was now living was one of the worst in Enfield. It had always been trouble, and lived up to its reputation as a home to Enfield's habitual criminals.

Jairus got off the Great Cambridge Road and drove over Carterhatch Lane Hill and swung a left into the Holmwood estate. He parked and bent his head, looking up to the depressing concrete tower block that overshadowed the whole place, then the graffiti-scrawled children's playground that sat at the centre of it all.

That was where he found Moone, resting his back against the climbing frame, his hands deep into his pockets. A teenage kid riding a child's bike went by, giving them the dead-eye.

'Lovely meeting place this,' Moone said, straightening up.

'Yeah, lovely. Where does Adrian Wells live?'

Moone's eyes travelled round the grotty grey houses opposite, then to the six-storey block of flats behind them. 'In Hell, apparently. Which is probably the best place for him.'

'We need to hurry up. Did you see that kid on the bike? He's the eyes and ears. They know we're here.'

'The flats behind us. Number eight.'

Jairus walked as fast as he could towards the flats, then took the concrete steps two at a time. He made his way to number eight and found the door wide open, the acrid sweet smell of marijuana hitting his nostrils. 'Shit. Pete, he's done a runner!'

Moone ran up the other end of the balcony, while Jairus stopped dead. He sniffed the air, then looked out of the corner of his right eye. The front door had been slightly swinging when he reached it. To his right was a narrow passageway that led to a much narrower balcony at the back of the building. It was where the pigeons liked to sit and shit on passing pedestrians. Jairus edged his way along the passageway, trying not to scrape his suit on the brickwork. He could just about squeeze through if he breathed in hard. As he reached the end, he heard heavy, desperate breaths and the sucking sound that meant someone was smoking to his right, just round the corner.

Jairus rushed round and saw the skinny body of Adrian Wells sitting on the wall in among the bird mess, his legs dangling over the drop. He wore dirty looking shorts and a grey T-shirt, a cigarette limp between his bony fingers.

'Don't do it, Adrian, don't jump,' Jairus said, sarcastically.

'I ain't fucking done it,' Wells said and sucked on his cigarette.

'Good to know.' Jairus gripped him by his shorts and yanked him backwards, sending him sprawling to floor.

'Fuck! I could've gone over!' Wells moved towards Jairus, squaring up to him.

'Get back!' Jairus stood firm.

'Yeah, what yer going to do?'

Jairus jabbed his fist, cracking Wells on the nose, sending him crashing back to the wall.

Wells yelped, and clamped his hand on his bloody nose, while Jairus hurried back down towards his flat. He passed Moone and went inside, then swept into Wells' bedroom where he found a grimy mattress in the corner surrounded by drugs equipment sprawled across the floor. He picked up his stained pillow and grabbed a small knife he found under it. He marched back round to where Wells was holding his bloody nose, grabbed his hand, and pushed his thumb inwards. Wells yelped again, and Jairus jammed the knife into his hand and stood back.

'What the fuck...? You can't fucking punch me.'

Jairus pointed to the knife. 'I can when I think I'm in trouble.'

Wells dropped the knife. It clattered on the floor.

Jairus grabbed Wells' arm, yanked it behind his back, and frogmarched him back towards the flat where he saw Moone. 'Pete, be kind enough to go and get the knife that's lying on the floor back there.'

'Will do.' Moone headed off, while Jairus pushed Wells into his flat and made him sit on his grubby mattress.

'So, Adrian, you've got yourself in a bit of a tight spot.'

'You fucker. I'll get a lawyer and tell them that you punched me in the fucking nose.'

'Yeah, and I'll tell them you came at me with a fucking knife. Who do you think they'll believe? Listen to me very carefully, Adrian, because we can both profit from this situation. I need information.'

Wells pulled up his T-shirt and wiped the blood from his nose. 'What information?'

'You got a nurse to nick some drugs and anaesthetic from Chase Farm Hospital six months ago.'

Wells looked up sharply. 'I didn't. You got nothing tying me to that.'

'I've got a nurse who will say otherwise. But I just want to know what happened to the anaesthetic. Apparently you got her to pinch the drugs and a couple of bottles of anaesthetic. Why?'

Wells shrugged. 'I guess she just grabbed whatever she could.'

'Just two bottles? Come on, Adrian, talk to me or

you go inside again. I will do you for pulling a knife on me. Plus, I'll put a rumour around that you fiddled with some young girls.'

'You fucking...you shit-bag wanker.'

'Yeah, I know. Terrible, isn't it? So who put you up to stealing the anaesthetic?'

'I can't fucking say, can I?'

'Yes you can fucking say, because you don't have any fucking choice.'

'No, I can't say cause I'll get me bleeding throat cut.'

'So, they're a mean bastard then?'

'Psychotic is more like it.'

'They been inside a lot?'

'They got life, but they had it away.'

'Really? Give me a name, Adrian, and I'll make sure they don't slit your throat.'

Moone walked in with the knife in an evidence bag and looked at Jairus, then Wells. 'Any luck?'

'Adrian was about to give me a name.'

'Fuck sake. Jesus... John Ashmore.'

Moone looked round at Jairus, his eyebrows raised. 'John bloody Ashmore? The Belham Butcher?'

'You sure, Adrian?' Jairus stepped over to him. 'You're not telling me pork pies?'

'No. I nicked the stuff for John. You better get him before he guts me.'

'We will,' Moone said. 'You really think John Ashmore is our killer?'

'One of them,' Jairus said, nodding. 'I remember reading about him. He liked to torture his victims. Liked to cut them up while they were still alive. And when he was done, he'd take something for a souvenir.'

'It's bloody well him then.'

Jairus nodded. 'Yeah, it's him.'

Edgar Holzman had managed to find a quiet and secluded spot to dump Marsland's body. He was in no doubt that it would be soon discovered and probably by a dog walker, but he was quite satisfied that the police would take a fair while to connect him to the victim. It would give him enough time to resolve a few complications, and finish what he had started. He was under no illusion that he would get away free.

He looked at his watch as he drove towards Palmers Green and estimated that he probably had a window of forty-eight hours to complete his tasks. It would be tight, but he would make it.

When Holzman rolled Marsland's body into the shallow ditch he thought he heard something like a rasping breath, so knelt down by him and leaned in. There was a faint sound. He took his wrist and waited. Yes, a slightly detectable pulse. Holzman put his hand over Marsland's face, covering his mouth and nostrils and pressed down. Then Holzman heard an engine coming towards him, taking the dirt track that would bring the vehicle close to him. It would not matter if Marsland was now discovered, he decided. He was nearly all the way gone. Holzman got to his feet and threw a few broken branches over him and headed back to his car.

He drove carefully along Green Lanes, then parked his Volvo, which he knew he should soon dump as well. He walked quickly to the gate on the side of the kebab house. The gate led to an iron staircase that would take him to the flat above the Turkish eatery. He so hated the smells that drifted up from the establishment, the stench of scorched flesh, but the visit was important.

He tapped the letterbox five times, waited a few seconds then gave one more tap. The door was opened by the tall man with shoulder length hair and puppy dog eyes. As always, his mouth hung open.

'Come in. Welcome.' The tall man, otherwise known as John Ashmore, walked back inside and sat at the table in the living room. The TV was on and the BBC news bleated about some unimportant business.

'Where is he?' Holzman walked round the room, his eyes tripping on the discarded items lying on the stained sofa.

John was halfway through a bowl of cereal, the milk dripping down his stubbly face. 'He went out.'

'Where did he go exactly? He's supposed be careful.'

John turned round briefly, wiping milk from his mouth. 'He said it was important. He looked pretty upset.'

'He's weakening.'

John nodded. 'That's right. He almost threw up during the last one. Almost ruined my pleasure.'

'You enjoy it all very much, don't you, John?'

John nodded. 'Of course. I never would've stopped if those bloody pigs hadn't got so lucky.'

'I'm sure you wouldn't.' Holzman stepped round and stood behind John as he carried on scooping up the soggy cereal. 'Why don't you eat cereal like a normal person? In the morning, like everyone else does?'

'Well, I'm certainly not normal, am I?'

'No, you're not.' As he looked around the room one more time, Holzman slipped the semi-automatic pistol from his waistband and screwed on the silencer he took from his jacket pocket. Then he pointed the weapon at the back of John's head. 'Do you think he's the weak link in all of this?'

'Yes, but I'll keep him in line. It was the same on the inside. I'll protect him.'

'I'm sure you will, John.'

The gun puffed out a bullet. John jerked, the spoon rattling against the bowl, his head butting forward, his skull exploding up towards the wall.

Holzman lowered the gun to his side. 'That's the end of you, you imbecile,' he said, then examined the room for a moment. He then walked into their bedrooms and gathered any written evidence of their crimes so he could incinerate it later on.

When he was ready, he stood by the door and carefully drifted his watchful eyes over everything, even John who was bent over the table, his blood and brains spattered across the wall. He smiled and shut the door after him.

By the time Jairus had turned up and parked outside the Red Dragon pub, the uniforms had already cordoned off either end of the street. He looked down and saw the silhouette of the PCs and other officers patrolling and keeping vehicles away. It was the same to his left. He looked forwards as he walked, noting that Moone was standing near the kebab shop, a plastic cup of something in his hand. One of the Armed Response Unit vans was parked along the street and two of the men were getting out, now with their vests on and Heckler and Koch submachine guns resting in their hands.

Jairus reached Moone and pointed towards the flat above the kebab shop. 'Are they up there?'

Moone sipped his tea and nodded. 'Kebab shop owner says two men, one short, one very tall have been living there. He said he saw the shorter one go out a few hours ago. He hasn't been back since.'

'What? Then what the bloody hell are all the uniforms doing? Get them out of sight. Do it now.'

Moone lifted his radio and began giving orders. As soon as he was finished, he looked at Jairus. 'Sorry, but they were set up like this when I got here.'

'He might come back. We need to be here waiting. Preferably inside.'

Moone looked upwards. 'So we're going in?'

'Yeah, John Ashmore's too dangerous to let go. Get two of the Armed Response Unit to follow me up.' Jairus entered through the side door and up the iron staircase, coming face to face with the front door. Behind him, he heard the boots of the Armed Response Unit hammering at the staircase. He let them go in front, while he knocked on the door. There was no sound from inside, so he slapped the letterbox a couple of times, but there was still no answer. He turned and saw Moone halfway down the stairs, police radio in his hand. 'Pete, go round that side. I think there's a window leading to a flat roof.'

Moone nodded and took one of the Armed Response Unit across towards the roof.

Jairus hammered his fist on the door as he raised his voice. 'John! John Ashmore! It's over, John. Come out and face us. We need to talk.'

There was still nothing from inside. The only sound was the passing traffic, a jumbo jet flying overhead. He hammered the door again, but still nothing. 'Right, we're coming in.' Jairus nodded towards one of the armed officers. He put away his submachine gun and produced a compact battering ram, which he swung backwards, then heaved towards the door. The wood splintered, jarring the frame. On the second swing, the door crashed open.

Jairus stepped away and let the two armed officers move cautiously inside, sweeping their weapons round the interior, shouting to one another as they searched the flat. Jairus heard the word 'clear', then followed them inside. He stopped halfway across the living room carpet, his eyes fixing on the body at the table and the blood that had caked the wall and dripped downwards. He stepped a little closer and saw that pieces of skull and brain had also stuck to the light green wallpaper.

'Which one is that?' Moone said, coming into the room.

Jairus bent over the table, trying to get a good look at the dead man's face. 'John Ashmore. And the world sighs with relief. Question is, where's his partner? And who is his partner?'

'Maybe he'll come back.'

Jairus shook his head. 'I don't think so. Something tells me that he's had it away on his toes.'

Moone walked towards the bedrooms and looked into both of them. 'All their stuff seems to be here. What do you think happened? The partner decided to off John? Maybe they had a disagreement or something?'

Jairus frowned. 'I don't know. Whoever it was, he obviously knew him. He was relaxed, still eating his cereal, leaving the killer to walk behind him and bang.'

'Why would he leave his stuff behind?'

Jairus looked towards the bedroom. 'Exactly, if his partner offed him, then he would've taken his stuff. Go through his belongings. Try and find an ID. And get a doctor down here and the SOCOs. Better hurry up about it.' Jairus took a pair of latex gloves from his pocket and pulled them on. He stepped round to the body, trying to get a better look. Clumps of brain and skull sat among the cereal, the milk now pink. He turned it all over in his mind, imagining the events. John eating his cereal, his friend apparently having gone out somewhere. The kebab shop owner didn't see him return. Perhaps he came back another way. It was entirely possible. Or... Jairus turned to the door. Or someone had come round to see them, and John answered the door and let them in. He knew them, and was relaxed enough around them to carry on eating.

Jairus spun round, looking towards Moone. A phone was ringing faintly. 'That you, Pete?'

Moone shook his head, so Jairus turned to the body. He crouched down and listened, hearing the faint ringing emanating from the body. He carefully put his hand under the table where he could see a rectangular shape in John's jeans. He slipped out the phone and looked at the number calling. No name. He looked at Moone, who shrugged.

Jairus accepted the call, but said nothing.

There was breathing on the other end for a few seconds. Then someone cleared their throat.

'That's not John, is it?' The voice was shaky.

'No, it's not. John's dead.'

'You're lying.'

'I promise you I'm not. I'm looking at him now. He was halfway through a bowl of cereal when someone shot him in the back of the head. He must have let his killer in.'

'The fucker! The fucking bastard.'

'Who was it?'

'Fucking... I'll deal with him.'

'Will you? You're not a killer, are you? It was John who did the killing, wasn't it? You're not a bad man. Just furious. Angry.'

'What the fuck do you know?'

'I know about anger. Trust me.' Jairus walked into the first bedroom as a PC entered the flat. 'Talk to me. I know you're suffering. Tell me why you're killing them.'

'You're a pig, right?'

'Yeah, I'm DCI Pig.'

There was a sickening laugh on the other end. 'If you're doing your job properly, you'd know by now.'

'The girls. You knew one of the girls. I don't know which one, but I soon will. You found out what they did to her. How they raped her, tortured her...'

There was whimpering on the other end, the sniffling snotty breaths of someone crying.

'I'm sorry,' Jairus said. 'But that's what happened. Come in and talk to me about it.'

'Fuck you. You don't know. I loved her. I fucking loved her.'

'It's over. John's dead.'

'You think I can't do the next one by myself? Fuck you. I will. I'll prove you wrong.'

The line went dead. Jairus turned and found the PC and Moone staring at him. 'What?'

'That didn't sound like it went very well,' Moone said. 'Do you think he'll go after the next one?'

'That's the plan. And we'll be waiting.'

CHAPTER 18

Jairus stopped his car as he was about to drive down the ramp into the car park beneath the station. Two patrol cars came out, their sirens beginning to scream as they roared away. He carried on, the light disappearing, the shadow of the concrete ceiling and posts swallowing him. He was thinking about the flat in Palmers Green; so small and grimy, and ordinary, but also the home to two savage killers. No, he corrected himself. Just one savage, maniac killer. Dead now, but not forgotten.

The SOCOs were now taking the place apart, collecting the fingerprints, the fibres, the hairs. It would not be long until they knew who the second killer was, especially since John Ashmore's prison files were on their way. Jairus had an inkling that the second killer had met him there and struck up a friendship of a kind. The question still remained how the killers knew the victims.

As he parked up, Jairus saw DI Walker hurrying down the stairs from inside the station. He climbed out and called to her.

'It's Marsland!' she shouted. 'He's been stabbed.'

'How is he?'

'They've rushed him into surgery. He's in a bad way.'

'Get in, I'll drive us.'

Bryan Macintyre walked across the park, the sun shining brightly through a gap in the clouds. He passed through the shadow of the two tower blocks, and recalled playing football in the park after school with his friends. He looked right and could barely make out his old junior school, then stared across Green Street to the small terraces houses opposite. He walked on and sat on one of the three benches over the street from her house, staring at the windows and the door, now painted black instead of green.

Then he sobbed, his face in his hands, his body shuddering. He let out a howl, and a woman pushing a pram looked at him strangely then went on her way.

He rocked for a while, hugging himself, knowing he was alone, that John had now gone on before him to Hell. It was where he belonged. And so would he end up there in limbo, forever burning. But he would not repent his sins. They would scorch and torture his soul, but he would never repent for the deaths he had caused, for he was just. They had taken her from him, and he had had his justice.

He took out the sheet of paper from his wallet and stared at it. There were three more names on the list, each of them belonging to the demonic order of the Freemasons. He was in no doubt what they had done to her and why; they had offered her up to Satan and he had taken her eagerly.

Another tear ran down his cheek and entered his mouth.

His mind went back to a vile man he had met long ago. Edgar Holzman. He'd been a familiar face to him, like a haunting dream.

Bryan was told he had a visitor and then he'd been taken to the room that smelt of sweat and desperation. The other inmates were huddled over the tables, staring longingly towards the door, waiting for their visitors.

There he was, a man who looked much older than he actually was, a frail-looking shell that hid so many secrets. The man shuffled in, his sharp eyes taking in Bryan.

He had sat down opposite and introduced himself as Edgar Holzman, and told him he had some bad news. Holzman talked in a soothing voice, informing Bryan that he knew how much he was suffering, how much his rage was building. They were the same, he told Bryan, shared the same loss and anger. Then he left, telling him he would come back to see him, and he would bring him some information about what had happened to Leigh, and the men who had tortured and murdered her.

Bryan got used to the old man and his smile, his gentle voice. He smuggled him gifts, cigarettes and other items for him to trade with. Eventually Holzman told him what happened to Leigh and how she'd been seduced by a man called Graham Burgess. This made Bryan want to scream and punch and kick, to grab a blade and stick it into someone. But Holzman taught him to remain calm, to use the power of his anger to focus. He would have to wait until he was released to exact his revenge, Holzman said, and promised he would be there to help him on the outside.

In his cell, he'd lain facing the cream wall, imagining the revenge he would take out on the men, seeing himself cutting them to ribbons, the blood pouring out of them while they begged for mercy. Then it came to Bryan one night - the one terrible fact he was trying to ignore. But the truth burrowed into him like a parasite; he would not be able to torture them, or even kill them. He needed someone who had tasted death and enjoyed it, and he knew only one man in the prison who fitted the bill perfectly.

It did not take long to gain the trust of the tall and bearded Belham Butcher. His searching blue eyes took him in with suspicion at first, obviously knowing that the other inmates usually gave him a wide birth. He instilled fear in them. He was capable of great physical and mental cruelty- it was what he fed off. But Bryan gave him the gifts that Holzman smuggled in, and soon a strange kind of friendship began.

Then one day, as they sat eating opposite one another, Bryan asked John Ashmore if he would like to kill again. On the outside, he added. Ashmore smiled and nodded and kept eating his shepherd's pie.

Bryan began to cry again as he rocked on the bench, knowing he had been betrayed by Holzman, that he had walked in and killed his only friend. He looked at the list of names again. He could do it, he whispered in his mind, he was capable of killing the last of the men himself. He would prove the policeman wrong.

It was too loud in the corridor as they stormed along it. Doctors and nurses and the echo of people talking or weeping. Jairus disliked being in hospitals. North Middlesex hospital was worse than most, with its crumbling façade, the tired faces of nurses and the endless stream of patients. Walker hurried on before him, pushing through doors and heading for the ITU. Jairus stopped on the way, looking at everything going on around him. Life. Somewhere in the maternity unit life would be beginning, the tearful faces of new parents. He swallowed it all in, knowing that death was here too, all around him, closing in. It was hiding in the light and dark, waiting. He could almost smell it.

Carl Murphy. The dead businessmen. The three missing girls. They were there too, deep inside him, almost whispering to him. He turned off the volume and walked towards Walker, who had stopped to see where he was.

They reached the Intensive Care Unit and Jairus showed his ID to a nurse, and soon they were taken to a room filled with people in scrubs. They crowded round a shape on a bed, wires and tubes twisting out of it. Jairus went to step into the room, but an Indian doctor touched his shoulder and shook her head.

'Does he stand a chance?' Jairus asked.

'He's lost quite a lot of blood...' the doctor said, but Jairus quietened everything down around him. He stared at the unconscious and pale face on the bed, then turned and walked back along the corridor and found a seat.

Walker followed him. 'He might be alright.'

'Maybe. Where did they find him?'

'Out near Loughton, in a ditch. Someone walking their dog found him. I can't believe he didn't die right there.'

'Yeah, but people have survived worse. The women who survived the Yorkshire ripper, they had their skulls caved in with a hammer.'

Walker nodded. 'Who the bloody hell would do it?'

Jairus looked to his left when he heard shoes tapping along the corridor. Moone was coming towards them, his head bowed, a frown cut deep into his face.

'Do you know anything?' Jairus asked.

Moone looked edgy, his eyes avoiding Jairus. 'I think I might.'

'Tell us.' Walker prodded him.

Moone looked at her. 'He rang me and asked me to call an auction house near Mayfair. He wanted me to get some antique expert to go outside.'

'Outside?'

'A diversion of some sort.'

Jairus huffed. 'We need to get hold of his mobile and track where he's been,' he said. 'Go to the auction house and find out who he saw and what they talked about. Pete, has this got to do with the missing girls?'

Moone shrugged. 'Maybe. I don't know. You know Marsland, he doesn't let go of something easily. It probably was. But why the auction house?'

Jairus got to his feet. 'Items were taken from the victims' houses. Maybe he was trying to track them down, and maybe he found something out that lead him to getting knifed. Whatever it was, we need to trace his movements and find out. You two get on it now.'

Moone nodded and walked back up the corridor, taking out his mobile as he went.

Jairus turned and saw Walker giving him a questioning look. 'What?'

She smiled. 'Sorry. I was just wondering what's going on in that thick head of yours.'

'I wish I knew.'

'You OK?'

He nodded. 'Yeah, of course I am…No, that's a lie. I'm far from OK. I've messed up. I've basically challenged that man to kill again. We need to find out who might be next. You got that list of the men who used to be in the Freemasons but left?'

'I have the list on my phone,' she said and took out her mobile. 'So how do we know who might be next?'

'Well, they got Wells to steal the drugs about six months back, so why wait all this time?'

'Maybe they had someone on the list, but weren't able to get to them?'

'Could be,' Jairus said. 'Check through the names and see who's been away abroad or unreachable for whatever reason, then text me the results. I'll see you later.'

'Where you going?'

Jairus didn't answer, just strode down the corridor and headed back to the reception where he showed his ID again and asked for Gina Coleman. He was directed to a room far along the ward. A uniform was sitting outside. He got up quickly when he saw Jairus walking towards him.

'How's she doing?' Jairus poked his head in the door.

'She's stable, sir,' the uniform said. 'They've got her on a drip. They said she'll be alright. Well, physically anyway.'

'Yeah, she's been through hell and back.' He looked her over. Her face looked serene, even though she had yellowed bruises about her face and shoulders. He could see where she had been held down. He let the door shut. 'What's your name?'

'PC Lloyd Douglas, sir.'

'You keep a close eye on her, Lloyd. I'm counting on you. Anyone comes sniffing around here asking about her, then you call me. You got it?'

PC Douglas took the card that Jairus held out to him. 'I won't let her out of my sight.'

'Good man.'

DS Moone was close to home when his mobile rang and the worried voice filled the end of the line. He pulled over, the glittering traffic flashing past as he heard the Commander's voice on the other end. There was stuttering and slurring in that voice. Come and find me, he said and hung up.

And so, feeling very pissed off, knowing his promotion was slipping away, Moone turned round and headed for the White Webb's golf club. He broke the law, by sending a text to his wife while steering. She didn't answer, which let him know where he stood.

Moone flashed his ID and carried on through the lobby of the golf club and into the enormous clubhouse, where the Commander was at the end of the bar. Two other men in ridiculous trousers sat on either side of him. They laughed at his absurd stories, but soon made off when Moone came over.

'Ah, Moone, good man,' Warren said and signalled for the barman.

'I'm here to take you home.' Moone folded his arms.

'You'll sit down and have a drink.'

'I'm driving.' Moone sat down on the stool next to him.

Warren shrugged and picked up his drink and sipped it. 'Suit yourself. You know something, Moone? I feel like I can trust you.'

'Really? That's nice to know.' Moone caught the barman's eye and they exchanged tired looks.

'I mean it. You're not like Jairus at all. He just won't let go of things.'

'Why's that a bad thing?'

'Just... Well, sometimes you're meant to toe the line, do what your boss...your bloody boss, for God's sake, tells you to do!'

'You brought him back from the dead. You made him SIO.'

'You don't have the rank to be SIO, if that's what's bothering you.'

Moone shook his head. 'No, that's not bothering

me. I've got too much going on to worry about being SIO.'

'Good, because it's a risky place to be. You put your neck on the line and chop! They cut off your head!'

'Is that why you brought Jairus back?' Moone felt safe enough to touch on the subject, enough of an alcohol barrier to stop any future recoil.

'What do you think? I had to. I didn't have any bloody choice. Jesus Christ, Moone. One minute you're doing your job, the next... Bloody hell, how did things get so messed up?'

For a moment Moone got a terrible feeling that Warren was about to cry, but the cloud passed and the Commander swallowed the rest of his drink.

Good news is the best medicine, Moone thought and said, 'At least one of our killers is out of action.'

'Are they? Was it really John Ashmore? And he's dead?'

Moone smiled. 'Yes, and he's dead alright.'

'Thank God. That sick bastard.'

'But the other one's out there still. And he's got an agenda.'

'But Ashmore was the scary one. He was an utter psychopath. We've got nothing to worry about now.'

Now for the bad news, Moone thought. 'Marsland's been found stabbed twice. He's in a bad way.'

The Commander stared at him. 'Marsland? Stabbed? How did that happen?'

'We don't know at this stage. I'm going to talk to an antique dealer tomorrow who he went to see before it happened. Strange thing is, he also went to see one of the victim's friends in prison. Sara Billings. I think Jairus will go and have a word with her tomorrow.'

'Jesus...' Warren rubbed his face, then slammed his fist on the bar.

'Easy, sir.'

Warren looked at him, thunder crossing his face. 'It's getting too much, Moone! Too bloody much!'

'What do you mean? You're starting to worry me. Look, why don't I take you home?'

'Who's next?'

'I'm sorry?'

Warren fought to get to his feet, holding himself up on the bar. 'The businessmen! Who's next? Does Jairus know? He must bloody well know.'

'He knows as much as anyone,' Moone said as he followed Warren out into the street where a warm breeze wrapped around them.

'No, he knows more than anyone else, he just won't help. He won't play the bloody game. The ironic thing is...he could've been...oh well, what will be will be. Right, Moone?'

Moone nodded, then shook his head when Warren lurched off awkwardly towards the car park.

Jairus had been through the door a matter of minutes before the buzzer echoed in his flat. He was tired and it took him all his willpower to get up from the sofa and walk the few feet to the door. He pressed the intercom and heard Walker say hello. He pressed the button, pushed the door open and listened out for the sound of her heels hitting the concrete steps.

She looked tired too when she came into view, but she smiled as she walked inside. She pulled her arm from behind her back, revealing a bottle of vodka. He nodded and got a couple of shot glasses.

'How you feeling, or is that a stupid question?' She sat down on the sofa and unscrewed the bottle top.

'I feel like shit,' he said and put the glasses on the coffee table. 'I've basically challenged him to go out and kill. His first actual kill, in all likelihood. So it'll be my fault if he does. Do we know if any of the businessmen on the list was away in the last six months?'

Walker took out her phone. 'Unfortunately, we've got three. Daniel Mason was in the States for two months. Kenneth Shearman was in a car accident and was in hospital for nearly a month. Sergio Luna was also abroad for a while.'

'So, we need officers at all of their homes. You better call the station and get them over there.'

Jairus poured the vodka, half listening to her talking to someone back at the station. All the time she talked, he was wondering what she expected from him. Why had she come over? The exhaustion hit him like an articulated lorry. All he wanted to do was fall into the blackness, to face the wall and pull the covers over his head.

'It's done,' she said and put down her mobile.
'Good.' He picked up his vodka and necked it.
She did the same. 'You want to get drunk?'
'I thought that was the plan?'
'Depends.' She smiled and raised her eyebrow.
'I see. Listen, Ally…'
'Ah…' She sat back. 'I don't think I'm going to like this.'
'I haven't said anything.'

Walker poured herself another. 'It's in those caveman eyes of yours though.'

'All I was going to say is that I'm tired. I'm so very tired.'

'You don't sleep.'
'That's right.'
'Because you won't let yourself. You keep beating yourself up over Carl Murphy and you'll keep doing

it.'

'That's right.' He necked another vodka and got to his feet and paced the room.

'What is it? What is it really? What's really eating away at you? I knew you must've been bad in those months you were away, because you never once contacted anyone at the station. Not even me. And that hurt.'

Jairus gripped his face and groaned. It was all too much. His brain was suddenly on fire, every inch of his body aching. 'I couldn't. I couldn't be around anyone. I needed to be alone. I felt like…like I was infected.'

Walker got up and put her arms around him. 'But you weren't. We wanted to see you. I wanted to see you.'

'I wanted to see you too, but not like that. And I can't be with you right now.'

She let go of him. 'Why?'

'Because I need to be able to think, to breathe. I need to find him, and I need to find out who the other men were that took those girls.'

'And then?'

He shrugged.

Walker huffed out a laugh and grabbed her jacket and walked out the door.

Jairus sat back down on the sofa, staring at the door for a while, then at the bottle of vodka. He poured himself another, took it down his throat quickly, then took out his phone, bringing up the photograph of the dress that was found at Garter's place. Something about it was sitting uneasy with him. The two killers had their reasons for being there. One for the pleasure of the kill, one for justice; an eye for an eye and all that crap.

There was that voice whispering to him, telling him

something wasn't the way that it seemed. He had a sense that someone else's hand was involved. Then who? His mind rushed backwards to the killing of John Ashmore. He had let his killer in.

That's who John Ashmore's killer had been. The person bridging the gap between the killers of the businessmen and the young girls they abducted. Something Rich Vincent had said had stayed with Jairus. Porn buddy. The killers somehow knew how to gain access to their victims' homes. Someone must have arranged it, someone with inside knowledge. Whoever he was, Jairus would find him and get the answers he needed.

CHAPTER 19

Jairus parked at the home of the last name on their list, the one DI Walker had been assigned to. No one had gone inside yet, just stayed on the outskirts, watching the house. It was still early and there were small signs of life inside, like the occasional light coming on.

Jairus walked past the two uniforms sitting in their patrol car, and carried on to Walker's car. He climbed in, and kept his head turned towards the grandiose houses. They were all similar - each one large with lots of ornate windows, long driveways and expensive cars.

'Morning,' Walker said, and he heard her take the lid off a takeaway coffee. 'They're just getting up.'

He looked at his watch. 'Yeah, it's still bloody early.'

'No sign of anyone stalking them, you'll be glad to hear.'

He nodded. 'He probably doesn't have the bottle, but... Well, he might turn up to find out either way. I'm sorry about last night.'

'You don't have to be sorry.'

He turned to face her, to see her sad face. 'Don't I?'

'No. I misread it all.'

'You didn't. I just... can't at the moment...'

Walker pointed to the house. 'The door's opening.'

Jairus jumped out as a suited figure stepped out onto the driveway. There was a woman behind him, and a young child standing at her legs. Jairus saw the man look at him, his face suddenly breaking open, his eyes widening. Then Jairus took out his ID, making sure the man could see it.

The man nodded his head, his body visibly relaxing. 'Go into the kitchen, Fiona.'

'What's going on?' the thin attractive woman asked, ushering her child back inside.

'Just go into the kitchen.' The man turned to Jairus and seemed to take in a large breath.

'Kenneth Shearman?' Jairus asked.

'Yes. Perhaps we can talk in the living room.'

'Yeah, Ok,' Jairus said and stepped into the wide wood floor of the hallway. He could hear the sounds of kids playing somewhere and a distant TV. Childish drawings were pinned to the walls. He turned to see Walker coming towards him. 'Can you get one of the uniforms to look after the family?'

She nodded and went back out onto the drive, while Jairus walked into the living room. It was massive, with large bright windows. Kids' toys filled one corner of the room.

Shearman sunk into a large leather armchair and clasped his hands together, his eyes falling to the floor. Jairus could smell the guilt from across the room.

'You know why we're here, Mr Shearman?'

He nodded and looked up briefly. 'To arrest me.'

'Ok. But before that why don't you talk to me.'

Shearman nodded again, then swallowed. 'It's all really quite...it's not what it was supposed to be.'

'And why don't you tell me what it was supposed to be?'

'I joined the Freemasons, because it seemed that's what you do. Everyone I know seems to be a Freemason. I was told that sooner or later they come to you and they invite you in.'

'And did they?'

Shearman swallowed. 'I thought they had. I joined and went to dinners and seemed to be getting on very well. Then I was invited to a meeting. Well, it was more like a meal. It was at Braxton House. There were several men there who were supposed to be important businessmen. But I only recognised Graham Burgess who had been the man I mostly dealt with. It was him who invited me there.'

'Do you remember the names of the other people there?'

'Not really. I might recognise some of them again. It's hard to recall...because, well, we had a meal, then wine, lots of wine. But I started to feel strange. Sort of very happy and excited. Looking back on it now, I know I must have been drugged.'

'Do you remember what happened?'

He shook his head. 'No, just flashes...strange... But not really. But about two days later I got a phone call and was told to meet someone in the car park outside my work. I went down and a car pulled up with a man inside.'

'What did he look like?'

'He was about sixty, perhaps older. He looked... Well, nasty really. There was something not right about him.'

'And what happened next?' Jairus saw Walker enter the room from the corner of his eye.

'He showed me a film...oh, God, I mean, it's not my fault... I didn't even remember any of it.'

'What happened? Just tell me, and we can sort this out.'

Jairus saw the man grimace, his hands grasping and scratching at each other. Then he looked up as he said, 'There was a girl...she was chained to a bed... And I was...I was... I mean, I don't remember...'

'We'll need you to look at some photographs. To try and identify the girl and the men...'

'She was trying to scream and she was crying! Oh God, please... Please help me! Please don't...'

Jairus reached out and put his hand on the man's shoulder for a moment. He looked at Walker then. 'We need to get Mr Shearman to the station. To make a full statement.'

'What will happen to me?' Shearman asked as Walker helped him up.

'I'm not sure at this stage,' Jairus said. 'Somehow the other victims' houses were entered without any sign of forced entry. Does anyone else have access to your home?'

Shearman looked up quickly. 'Well, I had an arrangement with Mr Burgess. Look, I have rather valuable items in my home that... Well, I bought and I haven't claimed...well...'

'I understand. I'm not interested in that. What did Burgess arrange with you?'

'He promised that if the Inland Revenue or the police raided my home, he would be notified of it through his contacts beforehand and could remove certain items. Apparently he had a similar arrangement with other members.'

'And you trusted him?'

'He was a highly regarded Freemason.'

'I see. One more question. Do you remember what the young girl on the bed was wearing?'

'I'm not sure. Maybe a dress...yes, a black dress.'

'And the man who came by your work, what did he say when he showed you the film? What did he want?'

'He said he wanted me to keep quiet about it or he'd send it to the police. But that he might have something for me to do one day.'

Jairus nodded to Walker, then watched her escort the man from the room.

Hugo Mortimer was halfway through fixing his tie when he heard the hammering at his front door. Then he heard Eve calling out to him, tiredly moaning that someone was at the door. He shouted back, telling her he could hear it quite as well as she could. Then he put on his suit jacket and walked down the stairs. Sunlight was streaming through the glass at the top of the bleached door. And he could see movement outside. He pulled open the door and saw a young man staring at him.

'I need to come in, I'm from the police,' the young man said, his eyes jumping over Hugo's shoulder then back round the street.

Instinctively, Hugo knew something was wrong. He began to shut the door quickly. 'Go away. I'll call the police.'

The door smashed back at him. Hugo skidded back along the floor, his back slamming against the banister. He tried to get up, but the young man slammed the door behind him and leaned over Hugo. A large knife was in his hand, his eyes wide, his teeth gritted.

'Get up!' the man grasped Hugo by his jacket and pulled him to his feet.

'I'll get my wallet. I've got money in there. And I can get more.'

The man kept pushing him towards the kitchen, pressing a hand against his back.

Then there was Eve's voice from high above them, echoing down the hall. Her voice straining out, to know what was happening. Hugo looked up, then at the man.

The young man pointed upstairs. 'That your wife?'

'Girlfriend. Please, just take whatever you want and go.'

'My name's Bryan.' He sat down after pulling out a kitchen chair, the knife still firmly gripped in his hand. 'Does she know what you've been up to?'

Hugo, full of confusion, looked about the kitchen for anything he could use as a weapon. 'I don't know what you mean.'

'Yes you do...you...fucking liar!' Bryan stood up, the knife in front of him. 'Do you ever think about her? About the things you did to her?'

'Listen, I really don't understand who you're talking about. Please...please leave my house.'

'You're Hugo Mortimer?'

He nodded automatically, then swore inwardly. He should have lied. 'Yes, but you must have the wrong Hugo Mortimer.'

'You're in that satanic cult, the Freemasons?'

'No...I mean, yes, I joined a little while ago...it's just a club.'

'You fucking liar! You fucking...!' Bryan lurched forward, jabbing the air with the knife, his mouth wide, spit leaping from his teeth.

Bryan's head spun round to the stairs, the knife wobbling in his hand. There was the sound of soft footsteps padding down the steps. 'Tell her to come down!'

'No! Listen...'

The knife was suddenly closer to Hugo, so much so he couldn't focus on it. But the face behind was wild, the eyes wet and wide open. The mouth snarling.

'Please don't hurt her.'

'I'll cut her open if you don't get her in here!'
'Eve! Come here.'

Eve hurried the rest of the way down, then froze. Her hands clamped her mouth, the freckles of nervous blood crawling up her neck and chest.

Hugo put his hand out, his eyes begging her to come to him, his fingers snapping together.

'Eve, come here!'

'Get in here!' Bryan waved the knife at her, then she rushed past him and grasped Hugo.

'Now tie him up! Do it or I'll cut his throat!' Bryan pulled out some plastic ties from his pocket, and threw them on the floor.

Eve scrambled across the floor, tears in her eyes, half watching the crazy man with the knife.

'We need a chair!' Bryan jabbed the air, pointing to the dining area to his left. 'I have to do this right. He won't be laughing at me then.'

'No one's laughing at you...' Hugo said, trying to engage with Bryan. 'Can I call you Bryan?' Hugo suddenly recalled a film or TV programme, where some psychologist said it was important for the victim to make themselves as real as possible, to illustrate their lives. 'I'm Hugo. This is Eve. We're going to be engaged soon. Then we're...'

'Shut up! Shut up! Shut fucking up!' Bryan grasped his own head. 'You didn't think about that when you did those things to her! When you did those terrible things to her.'

Eve sniffed, her eyes turned to Hugo. 'What does he mean?'

'I don't know. I don't know what he's talking about.'

'You're a Freemason!' Bryan screamed, then pulled out a gun from inside his jacket. 'You're one of them.

And you worship the Devil.'

Hugo and Eve grasped each other, trying to get away from the gun he kept waving around, staring at the darkness of the barrel.

'Please,' Hugo said, his voice breaking up. 'Please don't kill us. We haven't done anything. I swear to God that I don't know what you're talking about.'

Bryan stopped, his eyes fixed on Hugo. 'You swear?'

Hugo nodded. 'I do. I swear.'

'Would you swear on the bible?'

'Yes, anything.'

'But you're a Satanist, you don't believe in God.' Bryan put the knife on the kitchen work surface, then grasped the table.

'I'm going to go for him,' Hugo whispered to Eve.

Her eyes blazed. 'No, Hugo.'

'You grab the knife.'

'He's got a gun.'

'Shut up!' Bryan bellowed, grabbed up the gun and pointed it at the chair. 'You sit in the chair, and she'll tie you to it.'

Hugo got up, giving one last fleeting look at Eve. She shook her head, but he hurried on toward Bryan, moving quicker. Then he lurched, grasping Bryan's gun hand, wrestling with him, pushing him round the kitchen. He could hear Bryan's crazy, angry words in his ears, and smelt the stale breath too. Then the gun was falling from both their hands, smashing against the floor, and Eve was screaming.

Hugo saw the sliver of light, the sun catching the blade. Then he felt the deep burn, then coldness. He fell back to the cooker, his hand touching his bloody stomach. Bryan's eyes were white and wild above him, his skin so green.

Then Bryan lurched over to the sink and noisily vomited.

Eve's face appeared in front of Hugo, so close, her face all red and wet with tears. Bryan ran from the house, his boot's thuds fading.

With the family liaison officer dealing with the wife and kids, Jairus sneaked away, ready to talk to the guilty businessman across an old table in a plain cream-coloured room. He was so close to the end now, he couldn't fail to grasp it. It would soon be over and he could rest for a while.

Then his mobile was ringing.

He took it out, saw that Moone was ringing him, then answered and heard the sound of a car engine in the background. 'Pete?'

'There's been an attack! A guy broke into a house and tried to tie a man to a chair. He had a gun and knife. The man's been stabbed. It's near you. Ten minutes away. Ferndown Street.'

Jairus hung up and ran for his car, jumped in and took off, roaring down the street, taking the turns wildly, making cars skid away from him. The sound of protests far behind him as he gripped the steering wheel, picturing Bryan laughing, the bloody knife in his hand. No! Please no. Don't let him die. Please. Please. No.

Carl Murphy lying on the ground.

Jairus shook his head, concentrating on the road again. Shit! Where was he going? He'd overshot the turning. He put the car in reverse and went back a little way, then hit the accelerator, spinning the steering wheel.

It must have been five minutes, but could've been five hours to Jairus. He parked half up the kerb and ran into the open door of the house, hearing the half screams, half whimpers of a woman. In the kitchen, a young woman was covered in blood, a man curled up, his face almost translucent. Jairus pushed her away and pulled the man towards him, clamping his hand on the bloody wound.

'Bandages! Now! A shirt will do. And a credit card!'

The woman looked blankly at him for a moment.

'Go!'

The woman scrambled to her feet, while Jairus bent over the man. His eyes were fluttering. 'Hey! What's your name? Hey! Come on. Talk to me!'

The woman came back with a shirt and a credit card. Jairus grabbed the credit card and pushed it against the wound. 'Hold this! Keep pushing it against the wound. Got it?'

She nodded and did as she was commanded. Jairus began ripping the shirt to pieces. Then he sat up a little, trying to listen out. Yes, there it was, the faint cry of the ambulance.

Jairus was bent over, sat on a plastic chair in the corridor of the Accident and Emergency department. He'd turned his ruined suit jacket inside out because of the bloodstains. Hugo's blood, not Carl Murphy's this time. He looked down to his white shirt and the red handprints.

Then Walker came towards him carrying two plastic cups of coffee. She stood for a moment, watching him. 'You look terrible.'

'Yeah, and I feel it too. One of those for me?'

She looked at the two cups. 'I'm not sure you need more coffee. Look at your leg.'

He looked down, saw his leg jittering madly and pressed his hand down on his knee. 'I'll be OK.'

'If you say so,' she said, passed him a coffee and sat down next to him. 'I don't know why you're looking so distraught. You saved Hugo's life. If you had got there any later, he wouldn't have made it.'

Jairus gave a haunted laugh. 'Yeah and he wouldn't have been in that situation if I hadn't challenged the killer.'

'I just talked to the girl. From what she said, I don't think he really meant to kill Hugo. He grabbed the knife and struck out. She said he seemed terrified.'

Jairus nodded. 'How long before he does kill? After talking to Eve, do you think Hugo's one of the abductors of the girls?'

'No, I don't.' Walker took the lid from her coffee and blew on it. 'He just doesn't fit into that world. He likes to go out clubbing and drinking and playing football at the weekends. It just doesn't fit.'

Jairus sipped his coffee. 'It doesn't at all. I want you to find out Garter's movements around the time the girls were taken.'

'What you thinking?'

'I'm thinking that whoever's been feeding Hugo's attacker his info has been doing it for other reasons.'

'The girlfriend said he called himself Bryan. I checked with the prison files sent over from Dartmoor and it seems Ashmore was chummy with a Bryan Macintyre. He was inside for armed robbery.'

Jairus put his coffee down by his foot. 'We need to know Bryan's movements. How he's involved.'

'He was in prison until six months ago.'

'So did he know one of the girls before he went away? Was she a pen pal, or what? I want to know all about Bryan. Where he lived, his favourite colour.... Everything.'

'You got it.'

He looked at her and gave a brief smile. 'I'm sorry by the way.'

'I know you are. So am I. I just want you to know that I'm here if you want to talk. About anything at all. No judgements. I feel like you want to talk to me, to get things off your chest... But then you close up again.'

He stood up and stretched. 'You really don't want to hear what I've got to say.'

'Yes I do. Don't you trust me?'

He dragged a hand down his face. 'You know I trust you more than anyone.'

'So talk to me.'

'I will. Soon. But not right now. I need to get back to work.'

There was a muffled ringing and Jairus pulled out his mobile. Moone was calling. 'Yeah?'

'I'm at the auction house. Just talked to the bloke who Marsland went to see. Turns out they talked about some Chinese vase. The bloke says Marsland wanted to know who had sold one recently. Seemed real interested in that information. Do you think it's to do with the items Ashmore took as souvenirs?'

'Not sure. You find out who sold the vase?'

'Yeah. Got an address. Checked it out and guess what? Turns out Edgar Holzman bought the vase.'

'Shit.'

CHAPTER 20

A light rain was falling on Jairus as he strode towards the house, his hands deep in his pockets. The house was unremarkable, like Holzman himself. Still, Jairus scolded himself for not listening to that whispering voice inside his skull. He'd known there was something not quite right about Holzman.

Officers somewhere back at the station were running up information on his past as Jairus walked up the path and past the uniform officer with the crime scene log. He signed in, then moved round the scattering of SOCOs. The focus of the attention was the kitchen. One particular white suit was spraying something round the kitchen floor while Moone watched on.

'What we found?' Jairus leaned against the counter.

A ruddy and freckled face looked up from the white hood. 'Someone used bleach to clean this area. I'd say there was probably blood here. It was done not that long ago.'

Jairus nodded. 'Marsland came here. He must've confronted Holzman about the vase, for whatever reason. Then Holzman stabbed him, and took him to the woods to die.'

Moone rubbed his chin. 'Marsland went to see Sara Billings before seeing about the vase. She might know what's going on.'

'Let's talk to her.'

'So what's Holzman's connection to all this?'

'We know he supposedly found Henry and his daughter. My guess he was there to make sure they were dead. I think maybe he's cleaning up. He knows all the victims somehow. Shearman told me he had an arrangement with Burgess. Burgess would go to his house and hide valuable items that the Inland Revenue didn't know about, just in case they decided to investigate him. What if the other victims had similar stuff to hide? Maybe Burgess had the keys to all their houses.'

'And that's how our killers got inside. Makes sense. Where does Holzman come in?'

'I'm not sure. But he was in contact with Bryan and Ashmore. Somehow Holzman met Bryan and realised he could direct his anger, focus it on their businessmen victims. The description Shearman gave of his blackmailer fits Holzman. So I think Holzman was working for Burgess.'

Moone sighed. 'So Holzman helps Burgess blackmail several businessmen, then manipulates Bryan and Ashmore into killing them all. Why? It doesn't make sense.'

'It makes sense to somebody somewhere. I'll need to talk to Hugo when he's back with us. And we need to talk to anyone who knows Bryan.'

'Got someone on it now.'

Jairus crouched down, his eyes searching the floor.

'You might want to change your clothing,' Moone said, looking at his chest.

Jairus looked down at the bloodstains. 'Yeah, I will. So, Marsland gets stabbed twice, probably on this kitchen floor. Let's have a look.'

Jairus got down on his knees and crawled to where he

thought Marsland might have lain as he was bleeding out. He got on his back, then stretched himself out, and turned his head to the right. Something caught his eye. He moved closer to the washing machine, then stretched his neck and peered at the wall behind it. He smiled when he saw the bloody fingerprint. 'Hey, there's a fingerprint here in blood. It must be Marsland's.'

He got up as the SOCO fetched her kit and went work on the print.

'Still doesn't help us find Holzman,' Moone said. 'He could be anywhere.'

'Tear this place apart. Look into his financial records, see if he owns any other property. Look for his passport. We need to find something that will tell us where the bloody hell he's gone. Check any CCTV footage in the area to see if we can spot his car. No doubt he would've dumped it by now, but check anyway.'

'OK, I'll get to work.'

His phone was ringing again. Jairus pulled it out and saw the Commander was calling. He walked outside, trying to decide whether to let it go to voicemail or not. He swore, then took the call. 'DCI Jairus.'

'Jairus, I need to talk to you. Come back to the station, will you?'

'I'm rather busy at the moment, sir. Can it wait?'

'From what I hear, you could do with some time out.'

'I'm fine.'

'Just get back here, now.'

The phone went dead. He closed his eyes, sighed, then carried on towards his car.

The Commander was tucking into a takeaway lunch

when Jairus knocked on the office door. Warren beckoned him and indicated to the chair opposite his desk.

Jairus seated himself, put his hands together across his lap and waited for his rebuke. The Commander rearranged his lunch. It smelt like Chinese food. Jairus glimpsed noodles.

'First of all,' the Commander said as he sat back, 'well done for saving that man's life.'

'Thanks.'

'How's Marsland?'

'Hanging on.'

'Gina Colman?'

'Alive, but probably mentally fucked up for a long time to come.'

Warren nodded gloomily. 'I see. What's the deal with Edgar Holzman?'

'I'm not sure at the moment. I think he's how Ashmore and Bryan were getting into the houses. He must've had a connection to the dead businessmen somehow. We're looking into it.'

The Commander nodded, then his face changed. Jairus noticed the thoughtfulness and hesitation in his eyes.

'I know Edgar Holzman,' Warren said, then his index finger came up. 'I should say I know of him.'

'How?' Jairus felt his stomach tighten.

'I saw him at a Freemason's do in central London once. Well, at least I believe it was him. I recognised the name Holzman, took a look at his photograph and put two and two together.'

Jairus nodded. 'What do you know about him?'

'Not a lot. About as much as you, Jairus.'

'So that's it, you met him once?'

The Commander nodded. 'We shook hands. We ate

dinner a few places from one another.'

'Who did he talk to? Who was he friendly with?'

The Commander lost his relaxed expression. 'I don't remember. I'm not one of your witnesses or suspects, DCI. He was at the dinner. I think it may have been him that drove us across town. It was quite a while ago.'

Jairus leaned forward. 'Sir, quite frankly I'm confused. You met him briefly, had a dinner a few seats away from him and may have been in a car he was driving? Why are you telling me this?'

Warren stood up and leaned over the desk. 'Because I thought I should disclose it...well, at least to you.'

'But I take it you want me to keep quiet about it?'

'I'm just concerned in case Holzman tries to say he knows me and drags me into this whole mess.'

Jairus watched the Commander's eyes jump away from him, lowering towards the desk. Ultimately he knew there was something Warren wasn't telling him, something more that he would not communicate. He didn't care, after all it might give him more room to manoeuvre or at least he would have something to bargain with.

'Fine. I'll do my best to keep you out of it. I just hope my investigation doesn't stir up anything else damaging.'

'Just do your job the way you do it best. Get it done. And if you find Holzman, I want to be the first to know.'

The tightness increased in Jairus' stomach. 'Yeah, you'll be the first to know. Can I go now?'

The Commander, looking rather moody, gestured to the door. Jairus got up and made his way through the door and across the incident room. When he heard his phone beep at him, he took it and looked at the text message:

'Meet me in an hour. The White Hart pub, Ponders End. Ian Pritchard.'

The White Hart pub was one of the few London pubs that hadn't changed in nearly thirty years. The decor looked just the same inside, even though the exterior had been given a few licks of paint over the years. Ian Pritchard sipped his pint of real ale, his eyes scoping the fruit machines and the few customers near the bar. Pubs are dying out, he thought to himself and looked towards the door.

The light broke through the gloom along with the tall and broad body of DCI Jairus. He watched the copper scan the room, spot him and stride over. He pulled over a decrepit looking chair and sat in it. Pritchard took the time to examine the detective's rock-like face, and the deep-set eyes that seemed to absorb everything.

'I take it you've been nosing around?' Jairus said, nodding to his notebook on the table.

'How did the stunt go down the other day at the press conference?' Pritchard lifted his drink.

'As well as can be expected.'

'Want a drink?'

'Yeah, but it's a bit early for a pint. What did you find out?'

Pritchard opened his notebook. 'Heard of a character called Aleister Crowley?'

'Yeah, I think so. Wasn't he into black magic, the occult and all that rubbish?'

'Exactly. He was well known for being a Satanist. Even came up with his own religion and had a great deal of followers. There's a lot of celebs who reckon they still follow his philosophies.'

'So what has this got to do with my case?'

Pritchard smiled even wider, taking great pleasure in the detective's ignorance. 'Aleister Crowley also claimed to be a Freemason. Of course, the ranks of the Freemasons have always denied it, but there is a great deal of evidence to suggest it was true. Thing was, Crowley's version of the Freemasons was a little darker than the normal one. Basically, he took the other Freemasons down another route. The Freemasons are all about worshiping something bigger than yourself, like God...'

'Or Satan?'

The journalist nodded. 'Exactly. What Crowley started doing was bringing the rest of the group into disrepute or maybe bringing too much light to their goings on. They had to turn away from him. Even before Crowley there was a group in the Victorian era that also split away from the run of the mill Freemasons and began to worship Satan. Rumours were they also kidnapped young girls from the streets and used them as human sacrifices.'

'Bloody hell. Is any of this true?'

'Maybe. Girls did go missing. But whether or not it was to do with this group is another matter.'

'So what has this got to do with my investigation?'

'You showed me that dress, right? The black and red dress?'

'Yeah.'

Pritchard raised his eyebrows then zipped down to his satchel and fetched out a photocopy of a photograph he'd found online. He felt his heartbeat increase when he pushed it across to the detective and watched his eyes widen.

Jairus stared at him. 'This is genuine?'

'Yes. That girl was found murdered in that dress in

1891. Pretty much the same dress as you showed me. Obviously it's a black and white photograph, but you can just make out the diamonds laid out in the same symbol.'

'Yeah, I see it. Where did you find this photograph?'

'Off a Historical crime site set up by two ex-police officers. It's all about old unsolved crimes. That was one of the early crime scene photographs.'

Jairus smiled. 'Thank you, Ian. You've been a great help once again.'

'And what about my story?'

'You'll have it when this is all done.'

Pritchard fell back into his chair. 'Come on, play the game. I need something to go on. I can't run this because I'll sound crazy. I need to know where this dress came from. Is this to do with Garter?'

'No. Again, if you print anything like that I'll bury you. Literally.'

'So I help you out and get nothing in return?'

The copper sat back for a moment, taking hard breaths, his eyes looking round at his environment. Then he looked at Pritchard again and lowered his voice as he said, 'Again, this did not come from me. You remember the murder of Graham Burgess?'

'Yes, and?'

'There may be a link between him and the disappearance of three girls over the last year. One of them has just been found. If I hear you went anywhere near her, I'll go to work on you.'

'Where was she found? I mean...let me get this right, Burgess and the other murder victims were all Freemasons, and Burgess had something to do with kidnapping young girls? So, this could have something to do with Aleister Crowley and his Satanic cult?'

'Yeah, possibly, but like you said, if you print that

then you'll look like you've gone mad. Worse...I'm sure you'll find some of your bosses are in the Freemasons, and they'd probably end your career.'

Pritchard knew that the owner of his paper was indeed a Freemason. At least that's what the rumour was, and he'd actually been investigated briefly after someone had made allegations he'd been feeding off a high-ranking policeman also in the Freemasons. 'I can still mention the cult. And Burgess.'

'Or you can wait until you've got the whole story, then you won't destroy your career.'

'I can't wait that long. Someone might get the scoop before then. And how can I trust you? You'll probably keep your mouth shut.'

'You have my word that I'll tell you it all. My career's probably finished anyway. I'm the sacrificial lamb. Like you said, why did they let me investigate this? They want someone they can throw to the dogs at the end of it. But I won't go quietly.'

'OK, but what do I do until then?'

'Print a story about a connection between the deaths of the businessmen. Say there might be a dark, sinister link between them. Hint that the police might be after a mysterious ringleader and they're closing in on him.'

'So, you're trying to use me to get to someone?'

'Maybe. I'm not sure at the moment. But when the time comes, you'll get the whole story. You have my word.'

Pritchard sat back, gripped his pint and watched the tall copper rise to his feet. They said no more, just exchanged nods, then the detective walked out the door and vanished.

The journalist looked down at his notebook, realising he had very little to go on. The copper had been right about the Freemason aspect; he had to tread very carefully with it, after all, all he had was unsubstantiated information. And there was the fact that Jairus wanted to use him to send a message to someone, the mysterious person he seemed to think was orchestrating it all.

Pritchard laughed and drank down the rest of his pint, collected his things together and got ready to leave. He was still smiling to himself when he went outside, knowing that Jairus had no idea what was going on either.

CHAPTER 21

Walker had been sent a text message by Jairus telling her to interview Kenneth Shearman, so she grabbed DC Carr to sit in on it with her. They took their time entering the interview room where Kenneth Shearman was already sat, his hands fiddling with each other, his tired eyes almost pleading up at them.

Walker could feel the guilt practically dripping off him as she sat and put a file of photographs on the desk. The man smiled briefly at her, his eyes jumping to the folder under her hand. Carr sat down and crossed her legs, her face remaining blank.

'What's going to happen now?' Shearman asked, his voice low.

'We need to ask you a few questions to get the bottom of the matter,' Walker said and smiled briefly.

'Am I going to be arrested?'

It was Carr who sat forward and said, 'That depends on your answers.'

Kenneth looked worryingly over to her, then to Walker.

'Don't look so worried,' Walker said, 'we're simply trying to build up a picture of events. So, Kenneth... can I call you Ken?'

He nodded.

'Good. So, Ken, you joined the Freemasons roughly a year ago? Is that right?'

He nodded. 'That's correct. It's one of those things you do when you get anywhere in business. They say it helps build contacts, and you're also told that they do charitable work.'

'And the person who introduced you into the world of the Freemasons was Graham Burgess?'

'Yes, I'd done some work for him to do with his property business. A few months on he called me and asked if I would meet up for a business chat, then he brought up the Freemasons. Of course, I was interested. And things seemed to go well, I met the men already high up in the Freemasons. They sort of shook my hand and moved on, but at least I got to show my face.'

Walker nodded. 'And you made your deal with Burgess to hide the items in your house?'

Shearman nodded.

Carr said, 'So where did it go wrong?'

Shearman closed his eyes for a moment, took in a breath and looked at the table. 'I told all this to the other police officer. The detective who came to the house.'

'I know,' Walker said, making her voice soothing. 'But we need you to tell us now. Please, Ken, just tell us what happened.'

He sighed and looked up. 'I'd been going to the meetings and dinners, and charity events the Freemasons had been organising. Everything was fine. Then I get an invite to a special event.'

'Wait, you actually got an invite through the post?'

He nodded. 'Yes, it was very important-looking and it had the Freemasons' sign on it. I just assumed it was genuine. The invite said a car would take me to a special dinner for new members. A car turned up, took me Braxton House. Like I said before, there were a few other dinner guests. Burgess, another man called...I'm sorry I can't remember all their names now.'

'Did you keep the invite?'

'No, I threw it away ages ago.'

Walker opened the folder and took out some photographs. She pushed the photographs of the victims across the table face down, then she turned over Burgess' picture. 'You know this man, right?'

Shearman nodded. 'That's Graham Burgess. How did he die exactly?'

'I can't discuss that. Do you know this man?'

She turned over the photograph of Thomas Henry.

'Yes, he was there at the dinner, but he didn't say very much. Sort of kept himself to himself, which I just wished I'd done. He's dead too, isn't he?'

Carr nodded. 'Yes, they're all dead. You were expecting the same fate, right?'

He shrugged. 'I read about Burgess' death. Then I heard about them all being ex- members of the Freemasons. And of course, I had been waiting to hear from the man who showed me the film of...well, I didn't know what was going on. I just wanted it to go away. I never wanted my family involved in any of it.'

Walker turned over the photograph of Edgar Holzman. 'And do you know this man?'

Shearman tapped the photograph and flashed his eyes between Walker and Carr. 'That's the man who showed me the film.'

'You're sure?' Carr asked.

'I'd never forget his face. The bastard. Who is he? What does he want?'

'We're not exactly sure, but I don't think he'll be bothering you again.'

'I hope not.' He looked down at his hands, then with his eyes a little wet, he looked up. 'What about the girl in the film? What happened to her?'

Walker took out the three photographs of Gina Colman, Kelly Leigh and Ria Saunders. His took in each of them, then he looked up. 'I don't know which one it was. They all look alike.'

Walker nodded. 'OK, Ken. We're going to need you to describe the other men present. How many were there altogether?'

'Six of us. I'll do my best, but the rest of the night was a blur. I'm so sorry. I'm really sorry.'

'I believe you are,' Walker said and packed away the photographs. 'Come on, Ken, we'll take you somewhere more comfortable and you can describe the rest of the guests to our sketcher.'

Walker took him out in the corridor and left Carr to pick up the folders and notes she'd been taking. She put her hand on his back and gently directed him back up towards the incident room and then to the rooms used to seat families in. She watched him walk heavily towards the family room and stop.

'Wait here,' she said and poked her head into the room. Commander Warren was sitting in an armchair opposite another uniformed officer of a high rank.

'Sorry, sir, I'll use another room.'

Warren stood up and came over. 'DI Walker, it's quite all right. How's everything going? Is there any news on the case?'

'Not yet, sir.'

'Where's DCI Jairus?'

'I'm not sure. He's probably out on a follow-up.'

'Good. Good. Carry on, Walker.'

She shut the door and turned to find that Ken had gone to stand across the corridor, his head facing the information boards opposite.

'Come on, there's another room we can use,' she

said and pointed the way to the stairs. 'I'll put you in there and get the sketch artist to come and find you.'

'Thank you,' he said, but she noticed how quiet he had now become.

'Are you OK?'

He nodded, but hardly looked at her. 'Yes. But I don't think I can remember the other men at the meeting. I'm really sorry.'

'But please can you try?'

He smiled a little. 'I'll do my best.'

'That's all you can do,' she said, feeling disheartened and wondering where Jairus had got to.

Jairus walked into the SOCOs' department, or at least the office next to the lab where he never usually goes. A middle-aged man called Geoff Handle looked up at him from across the office, nodded and ambled over, his hands in his lab coat's pockets.

'And what can we do for you?' Geoff said and sat on a swivel chair.

'They dug a bullet out of John Ashmore's head,' Jairus said and leaned his back against the wall. 'Can you tell me anything about it?'

'Ballistics?' Geoff went over to the outgoing files and found a particular one. 'Fired from a nine millimetre. Didn't get a match on any other bullets from any other solved or unsolved crimes. Bring us the firearm and we can match it.'

'That's all?'

Geoff showed his open palms. 'Sorry, but that's the best we can do. Chances are it's been bought illegally like a lot of guns in this country. No registration. You'll have to get hold of the gun. Sorry.'

Jairus nodded. 'Yeah, thanks. Did they get anything useful off the mobile we found with John Ashmore?'

'Just one number, the one that called it. And only Ashmore's prints.'

'Can I have it? I need it.'

Geoff raised his shoulders. 'You know they tried to trace the number, but it was just a pay-as-you-go. It's no longer in action.'

'I know. It might serve another purpose.'

Again, the SOCO frowned and sauntered off into the lab area. He came back with the mobile in an evidence bag and plonked it in front of Jairus. 'You'll have to sign for it.'

'Yeah, I know.' Jairus took the clipboard he was handed and scribbled his signature and snatched up the phone. He nodded to Geoff and strode off.

He hadn't quite made up his mind on his next action, although he had already set it in motion. He'd let his gut overtake his brain as always and had made the call half an hour ago. Warren didn't know anything of the decision he'd made, but that was just as well - he wouldn't like Jairus going it alone. But what did it matter anymore to him? They had tied him to a stake and left him to the wolves.

He carried on his way, the mobile tightly gripped in his hand. He stopped only to pick up a folder from the incident room, avoiding the gaze of any of the staff manning the phones.

He kept walking and found himself out the front of the station, then round the back, heading in the direction of the public swimming pool, and seeing the red buses rumbling along and encircling the revamped shopping city.

The old Town Hall was still standing, looking lonely and out of place against the stylish and post-modern frame of the new Edmonton. If it wasn't listed, its days were definitely numbered.

He saw the squabble of journalists turn when one of their number spotted him. The cameras turned to him, filming his approach.

The voices joined together, all calling questions, asking for his statement, or for him to stand in a particular spot. Without a word, he stepped up on the steps of the old Town Hall and faced them all.

'You better get ready,' he said and gave them a moment. Suddenly the cameras were pointed at him like a firing squad. He breathed in from his diaphragm. 'I'm DCI Jairus from the Special Crime Group. As you know John Ashmore, the Belham Butcher, was shot and killed yesterday. We believed he was helped to escape from prison by a man called Bryan Macintyre. We're asking the public to help us find Bryan. If anyone knows where this man is, please call us on the Edmonton Incident Room number which will be on the bottom of the screen.' Jairus opened the folder and produced Bryan's photograph. 'This is Bryan. He's already attacked one person. Do not approach him. Now I want to talk to Bryan.'

Jairus faced the camera. 'Bryan. You and I talked on the phone. You don't need to do what you're doing. I think you're being used. You're being fed lies. You can call me on the phone we talked on last time. Please call me, Bryan. We can sort all this out. I promise you. Also, we need to find this man, Edgar Holzman.' Jairus lifted up the photograph of Holzman and made sure the cameras could get a clear shot. 'He is armed and extremely dangerous. Please do not approach him, just call the same number with any information you have. Thank you.'

Jairus walked back through the cameras with the folder tucked under his arm. He put his other hand in his pocket and pulled out the mobile phone they found on John Ashmore. It was a gamble. There was very little chance he was sitting watching a television, but maybe he still had hold of his sanity and wanted to know what the police were up to. Suicide was also another possibility, Jairus decided. What if he had felt great remorse for what he had done and couldn't handle the guilt. So far no body had turned up, but that didn't mean anything. They needed him alive.

Jairus stopped and looked up at the tall red brick fortress, took a deep breath, entered, and got ready to face the music.

Edgar Holzman drove the car slowly along the road, looking through the large iron gates, peering in at their exclusive worlds. Occasionally he would spot a swimming pool and shake his head. What kind of idiot builds an open-air swimming pool in England? He slowed the car down when he saw the right house, the one with the ivy covering the bottom part of the front wall. A low glass building stretching out from its belly. An enclosed swimming pool. That's more like it, he thought and removed the newspaper from the passenger seat, revealing his 9mm pistol and the attached silencer. He folded the paper round the gun and then parked the car a little way from the gates.

Before he climbed out, he looked at himself in the rear view mirror, adjusted his tie and made sure he looked suitably presentable. He slipped on his sunglasses and opened the car door.

He monitored the street as he walked calmly to the gate and the CCTV camera that followed his movements. There was no one about, only the occasional passing car.

Holzman slipped his hand into his pocket and brought out a small remote control. He pressed the green button, stepped back and listened as the gates grinded apart. He slipped inside, then hurried towards the main building.

The man and woman of the house would be away at work. The wife would not return until late, the husband would return by 8 p.m. At the latest.

With the gun firmly in his other hand, Holzman used the copied key to open the kitchen door, then moved quickly across the wide kitchen and out into the massive cool hallway. He found the alarm keypad on the wall and entered the code. Everything was still and he smiled.

He looked at his watch, even though time was not the issue, for he had plenty of time until the owner would arrive home. He walked on through the house, testing his memory, seeing how much he recalled from his initial visit. Very little had changed in the few months since he'd looked over the place. Of course, people as always were trusting, and that was their weakness.

He stopped along the long hallway where the framed photographs hung on the wall. There was a mixture of black and white and colour images of the man of the house standing next to other celebrities, sometimes on golf courses, other times in clubs or in some warm-looking foreign location. Holzman stepped closer and took in the tanned, wrinkled face of the man and his obvious silver toupee. He laughed, shook his head and kept walking towards the stairs.

He heard the light tone his phone made and stopped with one shoe on the first step. He took out the phone and read the text that asked him whether everything had gone to plan so far. He replied quickly that it had, then returned the phone to his pocket.

He decided he should fetch the rest of the

equipment from the car. When he returned with the bag, he carried on up into the high-ceilinged upstairs and the marble floors. More photographs were on the walls. He ignored it all and pushed open the doors to the master bedroom. He sat in the brown leather chair near the king size bed, the gun resting on the arm. He waited while the sunlight beamed in through the windows, swirling with the dust, his eyes fixed intently on the landing.

PART TWO
THE CRIME

CHAPTER 22

Jairus trudged up the stairs back towards the incident room, Ashmore's phone in his hand, which was buried deep in his pocket. He took it out and stared at it, willing it to ring, thinking about the bollocking he was probably going to get from Warren when he got upstairs. It would be short-lived though; Bryan would ring and reach out to him. He was alone without his psychopathic partner.

The incident room was alive with calls coming in, people panicking like they do, imagining men coming at them with knifes in their hands. He stopped and listened to the uniforms calming the callers, taking their details.

DI Walker was at her desk, tapping away at her computer, her phone cradled against her neck. Her eyes landed on him and she ended the call at speed.

'Hey, you OK?' she asked as she turned her chair round to him. 'I heard about what you just did. I hope it works.'

'Yeah, so do I. What did Warren say?' His eyes turned to the empty office.

She frowned. 'Nothing. I saw him earlier talking to another top brass, but haven't seen him since. Let's hope he leaves you alone.'

'You talk to Kenneth Shearman?' Jairus rested on a desk.

'Yes I did. He can't remember any names apart from the ones we already know. Typical. Got him with a sketch artist to try and put some images of the other guests together.'

'We need to find them. That's the night it happened, I think. Shearman was drugged, maybe a few of the others were too.'

'Then what? You think Burgess had the girls chained up in his dungeon?'

'Yeah, that's exactly what I think. He drugs them and gets them down there and brings in the men. Films them with the girls. Maybe someone of the businessmen performed willingly, but most were probably drugged.'

'So, he's blackmailing them?'

Jairus shrugged. 'Looks like it. But I don't think it's just that. There's more to it. Have you heard of Aleister Crowley?'

Walker shook her head.

Jairus took out Ashmore's mobile and put it beside him. 'He was a Satanist back years ago. It's said he was into human sacrifice. And before him there were some Victorian Satanists into the same stuff. I've seen photographs of a girl found murdered wearing the same sort of dress as we found at Thomas Henry's place and Garter's.'

'You're telling me that Burgess and the others were Satanists?'

'All I know is that some of the Satanists all those years ago had links to the Freemasons.'

'So perhaps someone's copycatting them for whatever reason?'

'Yeah, but I don't know why yet.'

The incident room door opened and a stocky blond-haired male PC came and stood by Walker. 'DI Walker,

Eve Wallingford is downstairs waiting for you. She's with PC Stiles.'

Walker jumped up and grabbed a few files and shoved them under her arm. 'Thanks, I'll be there in a minute. Someone made her a cuppa?'

The blond-haired PC turned round as he headed to the door. 'Yep, she's got a cuppa in front of her. I'll let her know you're coming.'

Jairus turned to Walker. 'Do you mind if I sit in on this?'

'You're the boss, boss,' Walker said and followed the PC out of the incident room with Jairus on her tail.

'Has Moone talked to Sara Billings yet?'

'I don't think so. In fact, he's been a bit tardy lately. I think he's got problems at home.'

'Bloody hell,' Jairus said. 'We need to talk to her soon. Marsland went to see her just before he was stabbed.'

'We can go over to the prison after we've finished with Eve.'

Walker opened the door to the interview room, causing the young tired-looking woman, who had her hands round a mug of tea, to look up. PC Stiles had pulled her chair round to sit beside Eve.

'You can stay if you want,' Jairus said to Stiles and sat down.

Stiles looked at Eve with questioning eyes and the young woman nodded.

'I'll stay,' Stiles said.

Walker stood with her back against the wall as she said, 'I'm sorry, Eve, that we've had to drag you in like this, but we need to go over things with you. How're you feeling?'

'Better now that I know Hugo's going to be OK.' Eve looked at Jairus. 'You saved his life. Thank you so much.'

Jairus shook his head. 'It's OK. Did Bryan say anything to you? Like why he was after your fiancé?'

Eve sat forward. 'He ordered me to tie up Hugo... but obviously that never happened. And...then he accused Hugo of doing something to some girl, abusing her or something. But I know Hugo wouldn't do something like that. Why would he think Hugo had done something like that?'

'We're not sure,' Jairus said, and tried to smile a little. 'Do you know where Hugo was on July 10th last year?'

Eve's brow creased. 'I don't know. It'll probably be in his work diary. He has an assistant who keeps one. Why do you ask? Do you think Hugo had something to do with abusing some girl? He wouldn't...'

Jairus put up his palm. 'I know. I'm sure it's all been a mistake, Eve. I'm sure he had the wrong person, but we have to ask these questions. Hugo was in the Freemasons, wasn't he?'

'Yes, but he said it wasn't really for him. He found it all very boring. He likes playing rugby and getting drunk with the boys. That's the way he is... He works very hard, and likes to let off steam. I just don't understand why that man came to our house.'

'We're looking into that,' Walker said. 'Did he mention anything else?'

Eve looked over at Walker. 'It's all a blur. I just don't...oh, he said something about worshipping the Devil or something like that. I mean, it's crazy, isn't it? Hugo's not into anything like that. Why would he think he was a Devil worshipper?'

Jairus stood up, looked at Walker and nodded to the door. 'Thank you, Eve. You've been great. We'll have to talk to Hugo when he's conscious. I'm sure it's all been a case of mistaken identity. PC Stiles will take a statement from you. See you later.'

Jairus slipped out into the corridor and faced Walker as she followed him.

'So, it is to do with Satanists,' Walker said.

'Well, Bryan seems to think so,' Jairus said.

Walker folded her arms and leaned against the wall. 'You off to talk to Sara Billings?'

'Yeah. She might actually have some information on Holzman. Someone's got to know where he might be.'

Moone swore when he saw the time, knowing that Jairus would be wondering what had happened to him. Life at home with the baby was getting in the way more than he'd realised. And there was the fact he was missing all the key moments of his development. He would get a text from his wife calling him home and he had little choice but to zip home and help out. He wasn't as young as he once was and the late nights were taking their toll.

It wasn't only the late nights taking their toll; the recent calls from Commander Warren were also crippling his state of mind as much as his wife's constant demands for attention. Most of the calls came late at night or even in the middle of it, and most of the time Warren was drunk. He was reaching out, desperate to know where the case was, complaining that Jairus played his cards far too close to his chest. The word "promotion" was still being bandied about, but so far nothing had been set in motion. Moone was tired, angry, exhausted and worried. Warren was scaring him a little with his heavy drinking, late night calls that made little sense, and his confessions. His wife had long since chucked him out, tired of him hardly coming home. It all sounded hauntingly familiar.

And spookily, he thought, his mobile began to ring in his pocket. He looked in the rear view mirror, making sure he could pull over safely enough, after all it could be Jairus calling him to redirect him or give him an ear-bashing. Except the giant man seemed unlikely to these days, as somehow the horror beyond his eyes had made him more relaxed.

Moone slipped into a parking space along the Hertford Road, on the opposite side to the Black Horse pub. He saw the Commander's number and prayed he wasn't drunk. It was only mid-afternoon. 'Hello, sir.'

'Moone? Where are you?' He sounded a little tipsy.

'On the way back to the station. Why, sir?'

'I need to talk to someone.'

Moone stared at his phone for a moment, grimacing. 'Er...I've got to get back to work. Time is running out. We need to find Bryan...'

'My...life is turning to...shit...Peter. Please, I need to talk to someone.'

'I'm sure you must have plenty of friends you can talk...'

'They don't understand. They don't do what we do, Peter. They'll never understand.'

'I agree with you there, sir.'

'You're a good man, and you have a family. I have a family. We understand each other.'

'I guess we do.' Moone stared at his watch and mouthed an obscenity.

'Life's not always the way we think it's going to be. We make mistakes.'

'Yes, we all do.'

'Where are you?'

'Just arrived at the station. Jairus has just waved at me. Look, sir, what if I meet you later?'

There was a long pause on the other end of the phone. 'Yes, OK, call me when you finish tonight.'

'Will do.' Moone hesitated for a moment. 'Try not to drink any more.'

The line went dead and Moone was left with a distinct feeling of unease. The pressure, Moone understood only too well, was coming hard from above. The City Of London Police's commissioner was on his back too. He'd seen harder men than Warren crumble.

He put the car into gear and pulled out into the road.

On the way to the prison to see Sara Billings, Jairus kept checking Ashmore's mobile, turning his head as he drove. It was sat on the passenger seat, staring up at him. Ring! Ring, you piece of shit.

He could handle this one, do it right and get the job done.

In the prison visitor's car park, he pulled up, grabbed Ashmore's mobile and walked to the main office. He showed his ID and explained the situation, telling them he needed to talk to Sara Billings urgently. The prison officer took him on a journey of cream corridors and iron staircases, his head lifted towards the cells on the levels above him. He imagined the cramped, acrid space, and their small worlds; the lights going out the same time each night. He shivered a little as he followed the guard towards the metal detectors. He came so close to that life. Too close.

He was soon delivered to a private room and sat down at a grimy grey desk. It took them ten minutes to bring Sara to him. She looked a little bewildered as she was palmed into the room and left to face Jairus. He noticed scratch marks on her cheek and a fading bruise under her left eye.

'Sit down, Sara,' Jairus said and pointed to the red plastic chair.

She sat down, still staring at him, then straightened her orange vest. 'Who are you? I don't think I know you.'

'I'm DCI Jairus. I need to ask you a few things.'

'Everyone wants to ask me things,' she said, singing like a girl in a playground.

'How you keeping, Sara?'

She raised her eyebrows, anger shooting to her mouth. 'How do you think? I'm bleeding great, ain't I? Fucking hell.'

'You just need to do your time and concentrate on getting out.'

'Fuck off.' Her eyes were full of tears, her body shaking.

Jairus tried to look kindly as he leaned closer. 'Sara, I can make life easier in here for you. I have that ability. I can get you things.'

'Why the fuck would you do that?'

'Because I need information.'

'And what else? A fucking blow job?'

Jairus leaned back and sighed. 'Look, Sara, I can make life easy or very tough for you in here. By the looks of your face, you've already had some trouble.'

'Can you get me off my face, cause that's what I really fucking need?'

'A man called Terence Marsland came to see you a few days ago. Tell me what you discussed.'

'I can't remember.' She looked up towards the ceiling, her bony fingers scratching at the table.

'Come on, Sara. All I want to know is what you both

talked about and I'll make sure life runs smoother for you.'

'We talked about the weather. How fucking sunny it is.'

Jairus got up and walked quickly round to her side of the desk. Sara jerked round, watching him intently. 'What you going to do? You can't touch me in here.'

'Can't I? Do you think they care? It would be my word against yours.' He stood over her. Then he smiled and crouched down. 'I'm not going to hurt you. I know you're hurting knowing that your little boy is far away from you...'

'That's what he said.'

Jairus rested his backside on the table. 'What else did he say? Did you talk about a vase by any chance?' He watched her hands move nervously, her eyes jump around. 'Come on, just talk to me. The man you talked to, Terence Marsland, is in critical condition. Chances are he might die. Help me find out what happened to him.'

She shrugged. 'Can you get me some kind of deal? Can you arrange for me to see my kid?'

When he walked round back to his seat, Jairus buried the truth deep down, cleared his face and eyes. He looked into her eyes. 'Yes. I can do that.'

'You swear?' Her eyes were bursting with hope. He could see tears.

'I swear. All I need, Sara, is the truth. It'll all come out in the end anyway.'

Her mouth twitched, her eyes fell to the desk. 'I picked her up.'

Jairus looked at her, confused for a moment. 'What do you mean?'

'The girl. The one that went missing. They got me to drive his car and pick her up. She wasn't into men they said, so I had to do it.'

'You're talking about Gina Colman?' Jairus heard his voice break, his fists clenched in his lap.

She nodded and tears started. 'Yeah... They got me to pick her up, and I did.'

'Because they got you drugs?'

She nodded and lowered her head.

'And what about Terence Marsland? The man who came to see you?'

'I told him about Graham Burgess taking me to his house...and the vase he gave to me. That's all I told him. Please. Can you help me?'

'You're telling me that you helped them abduct a young girl just so you could get off your face?'

She sniffled at first, then the full-blown crying began and Jairus watched it all unemotionally. He buried the part of him that wanted to say it was OK. The rest of him was twisted with fury. He stood up and watched the snot and tears joining together. She kept looking up at him, perhaps waiting for a kind word.

'I can't help you,' he said and headed for the door.

'Please...wait!' She was up, wiping her face with her sleeve, her pleading eyes fixed on him.

He watched her from the corner of his eye for a moment.

'Please!'

Then he heard the ringing. Not his phone. Jairus rushed out the door and held Ashmore's mobile phone to his ear, a prison officer now at his side as he walked under the prison walkways.

'Hello,' he said, listening to the hum on the other end. 'Bryan?'

There was breathing on the line, then someone clearing their throat.

'I told you,' Bryan said, shakily, trying to sound

triumphant.

'Yeah, you told me.'

'You...you didn't think I could do it, did you? Did you?'

'I wasn't sure.' Jairus stepped out into the visitor's car park where the sun was trying to break through the clouds. 'There's a problem though, Bryan.'

There was silence on the other end for a while. 'Can you hear me, Bryan?'

'I'm here,' Bryan said, but his voice seemed distant, quieter.

'The man you stabbed, the man you left to bleed to death...' Jairus let the words hang there for a moment. 'He wasn't guilty of the crime you think he's guilty of.'

'He's one of them!'

'No, he's not, Bryan. He was just a young man. Just your average young man. Holzman steered you wrong. He's betrayed you.'

'I'll find him and kill him.'

'So you admit that I'm right? That he's got you doing his dirty work for him? Whatever names he's given you are wrong.'

'I'm going to hang up.'

'Don't, Bryan. Talk to me.'

'You'll trace this call.'

'I'm not tracing this call. I swear to you. Chances are you're in a phone box somewhere and you'll be gone before we can get there. This is just you and me. I want you to trust me.'

There was a sickening laugh on the other end, then a weird moaning sound. 'Trust you? You'd get me in a cell and...'

'Why would I? I understand what you did, Bryan. I know about anger and rage. And I know what it's like to stab someone and watch as the life flows out of them.'

'Fuck...'

'Look me up, Bryan. Look me up online. DCI Jairus...you'll see.'

'You killed someone? Who?'

'A scumbag. An evil bastard. I did just what you and John were doing. We're the same.'

'You're trying to mess with my head.'

'I'm not. I'm trying to help you. You need to trust me. Tell me why you're doing this. You knew one of the girls somehow? That right?'

There was a groan from the other end. 'Kelly. We loved each other.'

'Where did you meet?'

'Do you think I'm stupid? I know you're tracing this.'

The line went dead. Jairus lowered the phone, stormed towards his car, opened the door and then stopped dead. He slammed the door again and let out a shout. A middle-aged man and a young girl stared at him as they got out of a nearby car. He glared back, then opened the car door and climbed in and stared at the phone. He dialled the number for the IT department and waited. When Rich Vincent answered he asked him to identify the number that called the mobile.

'Will do,' Rich said, and there was the sound of keyboard tapping in the background. 'How's the case going?'

'Not good.'

'That bad? Oh well. The number that called that mobile was a phone box situated on the corner of Green Street and Alma Road. Any good?'

'Yeah, thanks.' Jairus ended the call and started the

engine. As he drove he questioned his own decisions, wondering why exactly he wasn't sending officers to get to that phone box as quickly as possible. The reality was that Bryan would be gone. His face was out there and he was a hunted man. Only someone very stupid would hang around the phone box where he'd called the police from. Bryan was many things, among them being naive and angry, but he wasn't stupid. Even so, Jairus put his foot down.

There was also something else troubling him as he drove; he couldn't decide what exactly to do about Bryan, after all, he was out for revenge and justice. Jairus couldn't detect even a little piece of him that found what he had done to the abductors of the three girls as wrong or over the top. What troubled Jairus was the fact that someone was redirecting his rage towards the innocent for some reason. In his gut he knew Hugo was innocent of what Bryan accused him of. As for the other businessmen, he wasn't sure, but some crawling feeling in the back of his skull told him that things weren't as they seemed. He felt a sinister hand moving the pieces like a game of chess. He shook away the thought as paranoia. His distrust of organisations like the Freemasons had made him see conspiracy everywhere. Still, the voice kept on whispering in his ear.

CHAPTER 23

The sound of the front door closing echoed up the stairwell. Holzman sat up straight, his hand grasping the butt of the pistol. He listened out for more sounds. Heels clattered slowly across the tiled kitchen. He stood up, the gun by his side and walked to the doorway, his eyes focused on the banisters. He carefully looked over, still listening to the heels crossing the kitchen then stopping. Then a chatty voice filled the silence. Some kind of Eastern European language was being sung out to someone not physically there. She was on a phone, he decided, and stepped back a little, hiding himself. The young lady had to be his cleaner, but she was not due to clean the house until two days from now. It would be OK if she just stayed downstairs and didn't venture upstairs, but he knew that was unlikely. He retreated further into the bedroom and looked down at his gun, realising that shooting her would not fit into the plan very well. A knife would be a better choice.

He went to his bag of equipment, where he crouched and lifted out a pair of light blue overalls and some surgical gloves. He slipped on the outfit and the gloves and stood in the doorway again, listening out. When he heard her conversation end, he reached into the bag and brought out the large kitchen knife. It was the same make as the one he had provided for

Bryan and John.

He moved lightly but quickly down the stairs and across the hallway, his eyes searching out for the lithe and short frame of the young foreign cleaner. He did not see her at first. Then she appeared from his right. Her eyes sprang open, her body jerking with shock. Then her eyes took him in, and the questioning gaze turned to panic and horror. She fled to towards the back door, but Holzman threw himself at her, moving quicker than her, his gloved hand grasping at her hair. He ripped her backwards, her throat launched a scream. He wrapped his knife hand right around her neck and clamped his free hand over her mouth. The scream was soaked up by his hand and he breathed easier. He took a moment, his arm squeezing her neck tighter, choking her almost to unconsciousness. He pulled his knife hand down when she became limp. Then he thrust the knife backwards, and brought it forwards with force. She sprang up straight, her scream once again buried in his hand. He thrust the knife again, until his hand was soaked and the girl was slipping to the floor. He stood there for a moment, looking down at her and the blood covering his hand and overalls. The situation was now a little more complicated.

Holzman took up the girl's ankles and began dragging her across the kitchen floor.

The phone box was one of those new ugly silver things. Jairus always preferred the old red ones, but those old-fashioned kinds were only ever spotted in quiet English villages. The urban Britain he knew had become faceless, just a grey shapeless creature.

Jairus got out of his car that was parked quite a way up from the phone box, just outside the newsagents and the bathroom showroom. On the other side of the road was a small petrol station and garage. And on the opposite side of the phone box was a new housing development that had replaced some of the factory buildings that had been crumbling away for years. It wasn't the most perfect place to live, not when there was the train station so very near.

He put his hands into his pockets and walked slowly to the phone box, stopping every now and again to look around and watch the houses. He was looking out for twitching curtains. He was building a theory that Bryan would not be far away from this area. His childhood had been lived a few miles away, his junior school was just up the road. Even if Bryan hadn't consciously realised, Jairus knew that Bryan had picked this phone box for a reason.

He took out his mobile and called the incident room and was weirdly glad when Walker answered.

'Hey, where are you?' she said.

'I'm standing near the phone box Bryan called me from.'

'Bloody hell, it actually worked?'

Jairus reached out and touched the door of the phone box and read the graffiti scrawled over it. 'Yeah, but I need to know about Kelly Leigh. That's Bryan's link to all this. He told me he loved her. That's the motive. Love.'

'There's something to be said for it,' she said, but he ignored her.

'Can you tell me where Kelly lived?' he asked.

'Yes, just hang on a moment.' The line went quiet for a couple of minutes then, 'hi, yes, I've got her details up. You're in Green Street right?'

'Yeah.'

'Hmm...Kelly lived in her mum's house which is

almost opposite Brimsdown Junior School. Number 36, Green Street. You're pretty close.'

'I thought so. It wasn't an accident he called from a phone box close to her home.'

'So how does he know her? According to her family and friends' statements, she wasn't seeing anyone.'

'His school was right opposite her home. My theory is he knew her back then, or that's when he first spotted her. Maybe they met, maybe he's always worshipped her from afar.'

'You think he was stalking her?'

'Maybe. I don't know. That sort of psychological mindset can do strange things to people. Stalkers have killed the objects of their obsession for the littlest of reasons, so Bryan orchestrating the deaths of her rapists and murderers isn't surprising.'

'So all you have to do now is find him.'

'Yeah, and I'm pretty sure he's round here somewhere. Do me a favour and get some uniforms down here. We'll go door-to-door.'

'OK, will do.'

'Any word on Holzman?'

'No, his credit cards haven't been used, which means he has cash handy. I looked at his background and he came to England from Germany when he was twenty. Was in the German army before coming over. And looks like he's worked for a horde of companies - administration stuff in offices. Then he took early retirement a few years back. Never been married.'

'So he gets bored easily.'

'Sounds like it.'

'Another thing we know about him is he's a show-off, a narcissist. He pointed Bryan and Ashmore to Henry's house and then offered himself to us as a witness. He could have hidden away, but he didn't.

He wanted to look us right in the eye. He needed to sit across that table from me.'

'Do you think he'll stick around?'

'Yeah, definitely, whatever he's up to, he'll see it through to the end.'

'Then be careful. You're no good to anyone if he turns his sights on you.'

'Don't worry about me. I'll be fine. We need to go over Holzman's property again. We need to find something that will tell us where he is.'

'OK, I'll look into it.'

'Good.' Jairus ended the call and walked, his hands in his pockets, towards where Kelly Leigh had lived. The front door of the narrow terraced house was black. He watched it from across the road, trying to get inside Bryan's mind, picturing Kelly stepping out of the house. Then Jairus looked again at the other almost identical houses that carried on down to the Hertford Road. In the opposite direction there were the new flats. Bryan was there somewhere, watching.

Moone walked down the long hospital corridor, avoiding the domestic assistant mopping half the floor, then walked to the nurses' station. He showed his ID and chatted to them about Marsland's condition. He was stable, they said and passed over some other information, but Moone was hardly listening. He was flicking his eyes down to his mobile, checking to see if Warren had called him for a fifth time. The last time he'd left a drunken voice message. He wasn't quite sure what to do about Warren and his apparently newfound love of booze. He didn't want to be involved. Maybe that's why he was hiding out in the hospital and kidding himself that he was there to visit his ex-colleague and friend. No, that wasn't true -

Moone was there to make sure the old bastard pulled through. It was his selfish idea to palm off some of his workload on Marsland, and therefore it was his fault that he was lying half dead in hospital.

Moone walked into the private room and then flinched a little when he saw a blonde lady sitting by his bed. She looked about fifty-ish and was quite attractive. He couldn't recall Marsland saying he was seeing anyone.

Moone cleared his throat, causing the lady to jump a little, her sad and wet eyes flashing over to him.

'I'm sorry,' Moone apologised and smiled. 'I didn't mean to make you jump.'

She smiled too, but her cheeks were flushed. 'It's alright. Look at the state of me. I must look awful.'

He shook his head. 'You look fine. I'm sorry, I don't know your name.'

'Oh right, sorry I'm Jacqui.'

'I'm Pete. I'm a friend.'

Jacqui looked over at the quiet man lying in the bed. 'Are you one of his old colleagues?'

Moone grabbed a chair and sat down. 'Yes, guilty as charged. I'm a copper.'

Now that he had sat down, Moone gave her a better look, examined her face and looked down at her right hand that she had clenched tightly in her lap. It looked to him as if she was holding something in that hand. When he stared at her profile, a glimmer of memory shone somewhere in the back of his mind. He let his brain flicker for a moment, putting her face next to the records in his head. As always they were a little jumbled so he gave up. 'I'm sorry, but you look familiar.'

She glanced at him, then looked back to the sleeping man. 'You might have seen me about, I suppose. I live in Enfield. Do you live in Enfield?'

'Yes, I do. All my life really.'

'That's probably where you know me from.'

'Probably. So how do you know Terence?'

She smiled over at Marsland. 'I met Terry at the cemetery. He was visiting his daughter's...well, you know.'

'I do. He lets you call him Terry?'

Jacqui looked at him strangely. 'That's his name, isn't it?'

'Well, yes, but he doesn't let anyone call him Terry. It's always been Terence cause that's what he was christened. He must really like you.'

'I suppose.' She looked down at the hand that gripped the mysterious object. 'Do you think he'll be alright?'

Moone stood up and stepped closer to the bed, his eyes falling on Marsland's chest, the soft rise and fall. 'I like to think so. Yes, in fact, I'm positive he'll be OK. He has to be after all the stuff he's been through. And...well, I'm sort of responsible for him lying here, so for my own selfishness he has to get better.'

'Don't blame yourself. You shouldn't let guilt eat away at you.'

'Sometimes it seems impossible not to, and a lot of the time...well, guilt is sort of a comfort, if you know what I mean?'

The lady looked down at her hand and up to Marsland again. 'I know what you mean. I feel awful because of the last thing I said to him.'

'To Terence?'

She nodded, her eyes watering. 'Yes. I wasn't very nice to him. I was rude.'

'Terence isn't the sort to hold a grudge, so I wouldn't worry too much. Anyway, when he wakes up, you can tell him you're sorry.'

'I hope I get the chance.'

'You will.' Moone smiled the brightest he could, pushing away all his doubts. All the time he watched the woman get up and collect her bag and run her hand over her hair, he had the same itch of memory. He'd definitely seen her before somewhere.

'What's your name again?' he asked, still smiling.

'Jacqui.'

He nodded. 'That's right. Jacqui...?'

'Young.' She looked over to the bed, then after hesitating, she walked over and touched his hand. Then she said something, but very quietly so that Moone had trouble hearing. To him it almost sounded like a prayer.

She turned and smiled awkwardly. 'It was nice to meet you.'

'If you give me your number I'll let you know how he is.'

'It's OK, I gave my number to the nurses. Thanks though. Bye.'

Moone watched her slip out the door, then listened to her heels going down the corridor and fading away. Something wasn't right, he decided, then headed along to the nurses' station. Only the young Indian nurse remained at the desk sipping a coffee from a plastic cup. She looked up expectantly as he leaned over the desk.

'The woman who just left...'

'Mrs Marsland?'

Moone felt his eyebrows jump up. 'That's who she said she is?'

The nurse stood up and looked down the corridor. 'Yes. Isn't she?'

Moone showed his ID again. 'Could you call me if

she turns up here again?'

The nurse looked concerned. 'Oh, dear, isn't she Mrs Marsland?'

'To be honest, I'm not sure who she is. Don't worry, I'm sure I'll get to the bottom of it.'

'I don't want to get in trouble.'

'You won't. It's just between you and me. Just let me know if she turns up again. OK?'

The nurse agreed, but looked suitably concerned as Moone headed towards the lifts. He pressed the button for the ground floor, all the time picturing the mystery woman, and trying desperately to recall where he'd seen her before.

Jairus sat on the low wall opposite the line of terraced houses, watching the uniforms walking up garden paths and knocking on front doors. Sometimes the visits were brief and the uniforms were turned away after a couple of minutes, sometimes they went inside. Jairus watched on, seeing them leaving again empty-handed. And so it went on, and he felt more depressed, holding a bottle of water he'd purchased from the nearby newsagents, he almost felt like going into the Golden Hive pub, which he knew the regulars called the Golden Dive. Sinking a few pints might help him wash away the guilt and the memories of Karine.

Carl Murphy, lifeless in his arms. The sirens coming closer.

Jairus shook away the memory and took a swig of water. He was incredibly tired, and his body felt as if it weighed a ton. He pulled himself up and walked towards his car and got in. He sat there for a moment, staring at the uniforms, then started the engine and drove towards home. He pressed play on the CD player and listened to some Billy Bragg for a while, then swapped it for some Bob Dylan. A Simple Twist Of Fate came on. He stopped the song. It was Karine's favourite.

He would soon be home. But he was far too close to resist the gravitational pull of the place where his demons resided. He wondered how much power his guilt would have if it turned into a planet. Then he saw it as a black hole, consuming endlessly until nothing existed, eating time and space. He found a strange kind of calmness and comfort in the thought, of nothing existing at all. He saw himself floating in the emptiness.

Then he thought of all the times when he was a bobby, delivering the bad news to a relative of a loved one's death. One minute there, solid and real, the next gone, sucked into the endless blackness. All that love eaten and destroyed forever.

He came out of his dream and saw he was heading down the back lane towards his lock-up. He parked and sat there for a moment unsure of why exactly he had driven to the place that hid all his secrets.

But he knew why he'd let the pull of it bring him there. Somewhere in his mind over the last few days he'd been thinking of entering the lock-up, grabbing the thing that was in the safe and taking it somewhere where he could destroy it. It needed to be destroyed. Some might ask why he'd kept it anyway. And he'd asked himself the same question, but the only answer that he'd admit to was to remind himself of the darkness he was capable of, of the things he could never allow himself to do again. When the Devil calls, you don't always have to answer, someone once said to him.

He looked at the dark outline of the doorway through the windscreen. Not today. He couldn't face it today, not with all the bad stuff already crashing around his skull.

He put the car into reverse and carefully steered it back to the entrance of the lane. Then he looked at his watch. It was coming up to nearly half seven. He didn't want to be alone, not tonight. He got his phone out and sent a text to Walker asking where she was. It was only a couple of minutes later that she texted back that she was leaving the station and would head over to his place.

He sent back a smiley face, then drove towards home.

CHAPTER 24

Danny Charles watched the gates slowly open, while a few spots of rain landed on the windscreen. He sighed, annoyed that the English summer was once again coming to a very premature end. Like you, his wife might say and laugh. Her sense of humour had always been quite basic. And she would remind him that that was the kind of material he put out when he would perform stand-up routines around the club circuit.

He'd polished his routines since then, he thought, and drove up the driveway and parked before the garage. He pressed the electronic remote and listened to the groan of the door lifting up. The lights flickered on inside the garage and he parked the car at the very end. He heard the door shut behind him, climbed out and walked to the door that would take him into the main house.

He unlocked the door, then quickly moved round to the keypad, still in half darkness, and punched in the code. He relaxed and stretched, then moved his hand over the wall and pressed the light switch. The kitchen was sprinkled with bright lights and his eyes blinked with the brightness of it. Next he walked back through the house and entered the living area and walked round the bar. He poured himself his usual large malt whiskey, then carried on back to the kitchen. He stopped suddenly, the whiskey rocking in the small glass.

He looked down at the floor and saw dirty marks. He tutted. Olga was supposed to have come in early to clean. He shook his head and walked back into the kitchen and then along to the porch area at the back. He opened the large glass doors and turned on the light.

The glass dropped from his hand. It rolled along the floor towards the bare feet of the woman lying there. Her back was covered in blood.

He looked round. His chest ached as he stepped backwards. There was a pounding in his ears. No, this must be a joke. His wife was playing a sick joke on him. He tried to smile, prepared for people to jump out on him and shout surprise. He went closer to the body, crouched down and gripped her. He pulled her over, letting her face slump to one side. He looked into the blank eyes of his cleaning lady.

A yelp escaped his mouth, and he let her go, then scrambled to his feet and began running through the house. The pounding was louder, a pulse jumping in his neck. He ran towards the front doors. A man stood there.

He was stood in the darkness, but he stepped closer, revealing his familiar face. It took Daniel Charles a few moments to recall where he'd seen the man before.

'What're you doing here?'

The man lifted the gun that was in his hand. 'Torturing you. Then killing you.'

Charles spun round, swayed and then launched himself back towards the kitchen. He had to get to the back door, then out to the garage. He could grab something from there, something to use as a weapon. He turned his head, still running, his vision blurring.

The man was holding the gun still, and moving quickly after him. He ran again, dodging the island in the middle of the kitchen, turning towards the door.

Then the man jumped him, sending him sprawling to the floor, sliding a little across the tiles. The man was on his back, astride him. He turned his head, looked up at the dark figure.

He pulled his arm over his head. The blow cracked the back of his head, smashing his forehead onto the tiles. He screamed out. Another blow landed on his back. He kept on screaming.

Then the man got off him slowly and pointed the gun at him. 'Get up. Get up and sit down in the chair.'

Charles pushed himself up, feeling his arms shaking. He swallowed and tried to get to his feet. The man grasped his hair, but it came away in his hand. He threw the wig across the room. Then he yanked him by the arm, pointing the gun to the back of his neck, digging the muzzle deep into his flesh. Charles moved awkwardly, trying not to make any sudden movements. He was panting. He was pushed into the chair, then he looked up at the hawk-like face that stared down at him snarling.

'Keep your hands together,' the man growled. He did as he was told, looking at the unwavering gun, his mind beginning to work. He was trying to remember where he had seen the man before. He had a sense they had talked somewhere. Where?!

The man put a plastic strap round his wrists, and, with the gun nuzzling at his cheek, pulled it tight until it pinched his skin. He let out a moan, but the man only laughed briefly.

After the man had strapped his ankles together and tied him firmly to the chair, he left the kitchen.

Charles tried to form some kind of rational thought,

ignoring the panicked blood pounding in his chest and neck. He started to guess that this was a burglary gone wrong. Obviously he hadn't expected to find Olga and ended up killing her.

He grasped hold of the notion and felt a little more controlled and calm. Then he grimaced and nearly sobbed. The man was not wearing a mask, which meant he could identify him.

Charles began to fight against the ties. The chair legs clattered against the tiled flooring.

The man came back with a bag and put it down, his eyes rising to Charles with a look of quiet mocking. 'It's no good trying to get those off. You won't be able to. Trust me, I've done this sort of thing before.'

'Listen to me...' Charles said, trying to look the man in his dead eyes.

'Yes?'

'I don't know...I don't know what this is about...'

'It's about...it's about nothing in particular. For me, I suppose it's about relieving the boredom.'

'What are you going to do? Are you going to kill me?'

The man smiled and opened the bag at his feet. 'Eventually. But first there are certain things I have to do. I won't enjoy them, but they are necessary. And let's not forget, you have been a very bad man. You've done some terrible, terrible things.'

Charles began to scream. He didn't even know he was screaming. There just seemed to be a howling in the room. The man had stood up and walked slowly towards him with a large pair of shears in his hand. He held a finger to his lips, then returned his gaze to Charles' hand. He grabbed the little finger. His eyes found his victim's. He smiled again as he placed the shears around the finger.

'Number one,' the man said.

Charles bellowed, raising his eyes to the ceiling, his teeth crunching and grinding into each other, sobs gulping from his throat. His feet pushed against the floor. 'Oh, no, no, no, no.'

There was a sharp crack. Charles lifted himself back, almost toppling over, bellowing out the scream.

He caught his breath as he felt the white-hot sting of tears on his cheeks. He was panting, sobbing.

The man stood back and held up his hand. The bloody finger was lying in his palm, a big smile on his face.

Then Charles was screaming again.

With the door already opened, Walker slipped in carrying the customary bottle of vodka into Jairus' flat. Much to her surprise, the tall man was already leant over the kitchen work surface drinking, finishing their last bottle.

She'd never known him to drink on his own before, but it wasn't so much the company he wasn't keeping, but the way he threw the shots contemptuously down his throat. This was a man in the seething midst of self-loathing. She put down her bottle and joined him in finishing off the old one. She looked up into his sore, pain-filled eyes.

'I take it you didn't find any clue to the whereabouts of Bryan Macintyre?'

Jairus shook his head. 'No. We spent a great deal of time stalking the area with no luck. I'm having any CCTV footage looked at, but there's not much coverage round there. I know he's round there somewhere. It's where he feels close to her.'

'Kelly Leigh?'

'Yeah. He could be out there now ready to attack

someone else.'

'But he knows by now that Holzman's been using him. What I don't get is why he would listen to him in the first place.'

Jairus poured another treble and carried it to the sofa where he slumped down. 'Because we now know that Holzman went to see him in prison and must have told him that he knew what had happened to Kelly. Maybe Holzman had some kind of evidence. And they must've struck up a deal. I'll take you to the men who did all those evil things to her. Luckily for Holzman, Ashmore was on hand. Ashmore wants to kill, that's all he lives for. When Bryan told him he was friends with Ashmore, Holzman must have thought Christmas had come early.'

'Then why did Holzman knock him off?' Walker sat by him.

Jairus lifted his heavy shoulders. 'I don't know. Perhaps that was his plan all along. Get Ashmore and Bryan to do his dirty work, then get rid of them both. But Bryan wasn't home, so he got rid of the real killer.'

'But Bryan's still out there trying to finish the job.'

Jairus bent over and put his head in his hands. 'Yeah, and it's my fault. Jesus...'

'You can't keep doing this, blaming yourself for everything. Maybe you should go back to the police...'

'The therapist?' Jairus shook his head. 'There's nothing they can do to help me. Anyway, I'm no good to anyone if I spend my time talking through my problems with a quack. I need to be working.'

'I'm worried that you're going to work yourself into the ground. You look bloody awful. You've got suitcases under your eyes.'

Jairus huffed out a laugh, then picked up the small remote that controlled the stereo. Johnny Cash and

June Carter started singing Jackson.

Walker sighed and sat back. 'I haven't heard this in ages.'

'It's our theme song,' he said and relaxed into the sofa, his head tilted up to the ceiling.

Walker necked her shot and walked deliberately across to the bedroom door. She was tired of all the talk, and work and everything else in her life. She was gambling that the lump on the sofa was feeling the same way and would be happy enough to wipe away the world for a couple of hours.

But it seemed an age before Jairus yawned, stretched and looked over to her and saw the cheeky smile she was wearing. He smiled, but rather tiredly, then ripped himself up from the sofa and went over to her. She thought he looked a little lost for a moment, so she put her hand in his. Then she moved closer, and she found his face lowering to hers. She moved him backwards into the bedroom as they kissed gently. Then his arms wrapped round her, and he half carried her across to the bed.

Kate Roberts had found it hard to shrug off the guilt that had wrapped itself around her since the revelations about her dead boss. She'd cried when she read the papers, and spent two days on the sofa watching crap television, a box of tissues never far away. She couldn't stop imagining the horrors that must have taken place in the dungeon below Braxton House.

She shivered as she parked her car along from Enfield Town, only about five minutes' walk from the town centre. It was Linda's idea to meet and have a drink and something to eat to keep her mind off things. Kate couldn't help think that people must assume she knew all about what had been happening down in that room, although the truth of it made her look inept.

She parked in the small car park opposite the new flash library then walked towards the warren of streets that crisscrossed through the new shopping district of Enfield. She breathed a little easier as she walked, knowing that her best friend didn't suspect the worst of her.

Kate kept walking, but held her handbag closer to her as she spotted a man walking towards her. He wore a hood, had his head down and his hands dug deep into his jacket pockets. He kept his head firmly down, and Kate started to worry that he would bump into her.

He passed by, barely nudging her with his elbow. She felt the movement, the swift flutter of air behind her.

The arms pulled her back and wrapped around her neck. The stubbly hooded face pressed against her neck, his stale heavy breath at her cheek.

She opened her mouth to scream, but his gloved hand clamped tightly over her mouth. Then the gun came into blurry view, pointing between her eyes, wavering all the time.

'Don't struggle, and I won't have to kill you.'

She protested through her fingers, but he started pushing her back the way she had come.

'You parked over there?' he said.

She nodded, and he directed her into the car park. He automatically picked out her car, and pushed her towards the door, then jabbed the gun into her back. 'Get in and drive. Scream and you're dead.'

She opened the door, sucking in the scream that was building, pulsating up through her throat. She wanted to throw up, and her hands shook as she started the engine.

The man had climbed in the back and pressed the gun to her neck. 'Drive us out of here. You got a phone?'

She nodded.

'Give it to me.'

She opened her handbag and took it out and lifted it over her head. The phone was snatched away from her hand, and then she heard the sound of her mobile's keypad beeping. He was calling someone or texting.

There was no dream to escape, or nightmare, just the sweet blackness of sleep, but Jairus peeled back his sticky eyelids and blinked into the dark room. He looked round him, only half taking in the naked sleeping figure of Walker next to him. He pulled the duvet over her lower half and swept his legs out of the bed. It was only 2 a.m., but something had woken him. He climbed out of bed and slipped on his boxer shorts then walked out into the living room. Then he heard it, ringing out somewhere in the room. He knew the ringing wasn't from his mobile, so that meant Ashmore's phone was calling to him. Panicking, he began pulling the place apart, cursing himself for not putting the thing in plain sight. Then he noticed his suit jacket on the armchair. He found the phone and looked at the unidentified number calling. He gritted his teeth, prayed to anyone who might be listening to let it be Bryan calling.

'Bryan?' he said, listening to the nothingness on the other end.

'I want to talk.' Bryan's voice came over the line and there was more pain soaked into his voice than ever before.

Jairus sighed with relief, clenching his fist. 'Listen to me, Bryan, this has gone on long enough. This needs to end. The list of names you've got...the names are useless. They're not the men who did those things...'

'I know.'

'Good. Good. Then we need to talk, we need...'

'You expect me to trust you?'

'Did you look me up?'

Bryan coughed for a moment, then there was the same sickness in his laugh. The desperation oozed over the line. 'Yeah, I did. So you killed that bastard? So what? They said it was self-defence. We're not the same.'

'Yeah? Self-defence is what the papers called it...is what the law called it. It doesn't make it true, Bryan. Let me tell you about Carl Murphy. He was an evil, drug-dealing, sociopath. He'd stomp on anyone who got in his way. There was a kid who the police talked to, just a young ten year old boy who could identify Carl as being the person who stabbed some other drug dealer to death. Carl got wind of it and decided he had to get rid of the kid. So he found out where he lived and grabbed him and took him to a boarded-up house and tortured him for a few days, then cut his throat. Thing was, Bryan, Carl had grabbed the wrong kid. He grabbed Timothy Ayem by mistake. If you saw the things he'd done...'

'So you killed him?'

'Yeah, I killed him. I arranged a meet with him. I pretended I had a deal to cut with him. I told him I could make evidence disappear for money. So I met him and made it look like he attacked me. That's what I did, Bryan. So we're the same, me and you.'

'This is not what I wanted...'

'I know.'

'I just wanted Kelly and me...I just thought...and I tried to get money together, to make a fresh start for us...but that got fucked up.'

'Come and talk to me, Bryan.'

There was silence on the other end for a moment. Then a laugh. 'No. I won't. I need to find them all. I need to put it right.'

'Bryan. Listen to me...'

It was then Walker appeared at the bedroom doorway. She yawned then folded her arms beneath her breasts.

Jairus put his hand over the phone. 'Ally, do me a favour. Call the station and find out who's calling Ashmore's mobile. Now.'

Walker disappeared back into the bedroom, while Jairus put his ear back to the phone. 'Bryan? Bryan!? You there?'

'What's your name?'

'DCI Jairus.'

'No, I mean your first name.'

Jairus sighed out a tired empty breath. 'Does it matter?'

'I've been smart this time. I've given it some thought and I know how to find them.'

'Bryan...?'

The line went dead. 'Bryan? Shit. Shit. Ally?'

Walker returned, wrapped in a bathrobe, her face soaked in disappointment and disbelief. She lowered her phone and looked at him sadly. 'The number that called Ashmore's phone was a mobile belonging to Kate Roberts. Burgess' PA.'

'Oh fuck.' Jairus scrambled about for a moment, picturing it all in his head, imagining the terrified woman frogmarched along, possibly a gun pointed at her head. He never considered her in danger.

Walker stood by, her eyes watching him all the time, a very strange expression on her face. He stopped dead in the midst of his panic, seeing the look in her eyes and knowing. She must have been awake, must have heard their conversation.

'What?' he said.

'I was listening. To what you said to Bryan.'

He didn't look her in the eye, just carried on gathering his stuff together, grabbing his warrant card and clothes. 'I had to tell him something to win him over. I need to gain his trust.'

'So you made up that story?'

He stopped in the bedroom doorway. 'I bent the truth a little.'

'A little? I was hoping, really hoping for a lot. For a massive amount.'

He turned and held her eyes. 'Do you really think that was true? That I could do that?'

'I hope not.'

CHAPTER 25

It was nearly 3 a.m. by the time Jairus and Walker and DS Carr were working the crime scene. A few constables had sealed off the car park and gone off to collect the CCTV footage. Jairus walked across the tarmac square, his eyes scanning the fading white parking spaces, the oil stains and tyre marks. He crouched down looking at the ground. There was little to see, but he just stayed there thinking, wondering how Bryan would handle having a hostage. It was not good by any stretch of the most positive imagination.

Carr had walked off, getting smaller in the corner of his eye. He could only see her as a cream-coloured trench coat standing by a car. He heard her slam her door, then she returned carrying a tablet device.

She turned it round to him so he could see that the CCTV footage of the car park had been sent through. That was the good thing about Enfield Town's revamp, he thought. The system was up to date, the cameras not yet vandalised.

Carr talked to him, but he was far too captivated by the eerie glowing images of the car park on the screen. There was Bryan, pointing what looked like a gun at Roberts' head, frogmarching her to the car. Then they got in. Jairus leaned in further, trying to fix on what was happening in the back. Then he saw Bryan in the back taking the PA's phone.

'We traced her phone yet?'

'It was found on a night bus going towards Seven Sisters,' Carr said. 'He knew we'd track it. He's not too stupid.'

'That's what he's trying to prove. What about her car?'

'We're still trying to locate it. We lost it going out towards Herts. Obviously he's taken the back streets, away from the traffic cameras.'

'But he'll come back to Enfield. He has to.'

'Why are you so certain, sir?'

'Because he needs to be close to her, to her memory. Enfield is where they met or when he first saw her, and the last time he saw her. He's somewhere round there, he has to be.'

Walker began to hurry over after taking her mobile from her ear. 'Jairus, things just took a turn for the worse.'

He looked at her, waiting for her to continue. 'Yeah, go on.'

'A man has just been found cut to pieces, just like the businessmen.'

'I sense a but. What is it?'

Walker nodded. 'He's not a businessman this time. It's a comedian. Danny Charles.'

DS Carr let out a heavy breath and took the tablet back to her car.

'I remember watching him growing up,' Jairus said and ran a hand down his face.

The scene outside Danny Charles' home played like all the other that Jairus had attended, except it was crazier, with the press stalking like wolves. He'd ordered the uniforms to keep them back on pain of death. He looked them all in the eye, while sirens flashed into the night, awaking the neighbours to the terrible thing that had happen.

The SOCOs had already gone in, set up their tent and travelled back and forth from their van. All of the white suits seemed a little more aware of what they were about to do. Someone famous was dead, cut to shreds.

Jairus stood on the edge of it all, watching from beneath an overgrown tree, his hands dug into his pockets. Then he saw Walker leaving her car and ordering more of the uniforms to go on the doors. He saw her turn and take him in, her eyes holding a million questions, but it was only one that was bothering Jairus.

He tucked it all away and strode towards her. 'What we got so far?'

'Dead male and female. Male has yet to be identified, but of course it's Danny Charles. The nation's favourite. The female is Olga Luczynski. She was his cleaning lady.'

'Isn't he married?'

Walker nodded to another large gated house across the road. 'His wife is over the road being looked after by a PC and the neighbours. Mrs Lily Charles found the bodies when she came home in the middle of the night. She's twenty years younger than him. She was out having fun.'

'Yeah? That's nice for her.' He walked on towards the devastation, stopping only to slip under the tape and sign the crime scene log. The SOCOs stopped him in their white tent that spanned most of the driveway, covered him in a forensic outfit and let him into the house. Walker came in behind him, her eyes perceiving everything over a mask. They carefully passed the other white bodies. Camera flashes lit up their faces as they huddled in one corner and took in the man strapped to the chair. His head was missing.

Jairus closed his eyes, tried to clear away all the tiredness and anger, every bad thought he'd ever had. He opened his eyes and looked down at the pale hands that were bound together. Half the fingers were gone. As we're his feet. Blood was sprayed out just about everywhere, covering the floor, his clothes, the wall. Knife wounds littered his chest and stomach. He was killed in a frenzy, or so it was meant to seem.

From around the island in the middle of the kitchen came the green plastic adorned body of Dr Garrett. He removed his mask and nodded to Jairus. 'Your friend struck again.'

'That remains to be seen,' Jairus said, then looked round the floor. 'Where's the girl?'

Garrett stepped over the plates that had been placed along the floor and pointed to the door that led to the porch. Jairus followed him and watched as a SOCO was bagging the girl's hands.

'When did she die?' Jairus asked and leaned over the body, taking in the stab wounds on her back.

'Judging by lividity and lack of rigor mortis, I'd say about eight hours ago. I can ascertain by the blood pooling in her underside, that she was moved shortly after death.'

'What about the male DB?' Jairus pointed at the headless victim.

'He's much fresher. Died about three hours ago. Rigor mortis has set in. Oh and the crime scene manager told me there was a lot of bleach on the floor. Then the blood on top.'

Jairus nodded. 'So he gets in, waits for Charles to get home. The cleaner probably turned up, so he grabs her and stabs her. Cleans up so his intended victim doesn't see it and panics. Same knife as before?'

Garrett nods. 'Looks like it. I'll compare them later. Looks like same cutting tools. Again, I'll be able to tell you more later.'

'And do we know where the head is?'

Walker stepped up. 'They fished it out of the swimming pool shortly before you arrived.'

'I'll email you anything else I find,' Jeremy added and walked back over to the headless body.

'Yeah, thanks.' Jairus turned away and nodded for Walker to follow him back towards the front door. He turned to face her and removed his hood. 'One thing's for sure, this wasn't Bryan.'

She nodded. 'Yes, you're right. The timelines overlap. He was too busy abducting Kate Roberts.'

'Yeah, and the killer got in without breaking in, waited for several hours to kill his victim. He's patient. Bryan is not patient or this organised. So someone wanted us to think he's struck again. My money's on Holzman. Any CCTV footage?'

'It was disabled.'

'Of course it was. Holzman knows the place inside out.'

Walker nodded. 'You want to know what else is sticking in my mind?'

'Yeah, what?'

'Danny Charles was in the papers a while back. He was arrested by Operation Pin.'

'The child abuse investigation?'

She nodded. 'His credit card details turned up in some sting operation. Also, there were rumours from years ago. Things like that never go away.'

Jairus sighed. 'So, what are you thinking?'

'What if the reason Holzman had access to this place was so he could hide any incriminating information?'

'I think you're right. Check his computers. I'm going to talk to his wife.' Jairus walked back through the tent where he took off the plastic suit.

'DCI Jairus?' a voice called out from halfway up the stairs.

Jairus came back in and looked up at the female SOCO stood above him.

'Found this dress on the DB's bed and this DVD.'

Jairus gritted his teeth when he saw the same type of dress as he'd found in Henry's and Garter's homes. 'Good. Get them looked over and send the DVD over to the station.'

The lights were still flashing through the night, still warning of the death that surrounded them. Now people had actually emerged from their warm beds, blinking tiredly at Jairus as he blankly, with hands in his pockets, walked through the uniforms, and across to the gates of the house opposite. He showed his ID and was directed by a female PC into the main part of the house. He hardly took in the wood floors, high ceilings, the chandeliers. He found himself going through a large square archway and standing at the edge of a long room. There wasn't much furniture except a couple of hard-looking 60s style sofas. The curtains were drawn. Three bodies sat on the sofas. There was another female PC, who was bulky with dark brown hair. And a man in trousers and a shirt who was comforting a voluptuous blonde woman in a tight black dress. Lily Charles. He had a faint recollection of seeing her interviewed about something on TV.

He smiled when she looked up through her tears, her eyes a little smudged. He walked over and stood looking down at her. 'Mrs Charles, I'm DCI Jairus. I'm in charge here. I'd like to talk to you if that's OK?'

'She's had an awful fright,' the man comforting her

said.

Jairus looked at him. 'Yeah, I know. I'm sure she'd appreciate a cup of tea. Better make it with lots of sugar.'

The man seemed to realise Jairus meant him to leave, then got up and walked out of the room. Jairus sat down at the far end of the sofa and faced her.

'You been out partying tonight?'

She nodded, seemed to take in her dress, then began to cry again.

'I know it's a terrible, awful thing that's happened, but I need to go over a few things with you. This won't take long. That OK?'

She sniffed. 'Yes...it's fine. I can't believe...he was there...he was...'

'Was this a night when you'd usually stay out late?'

'Yes, this was my night out. It never bothered, Dan. He had work to do anyway.'

'Who had keys to your home and knew the codes to your alarms?'

'Well, just Dan and myself, and his agent, Jeffrey, and his son, Freddie. But you can't think that they would have anything...'

Jairus held up his hand. 'No, I don't think that, but we have to look into these things. Have any of them been recently burgled or pickpocketed?'

She shook her head. 'No, not that I'm aware of. Oh God, I can't stop seeing him.'

'Try not to think about it. I know it's hard, but try and focus on me. By the way, how did you know it was your husband? I mean...'

Mrs Charles swallowed down a sob. 'I know what...what you meant. I saw...oh bloody...I saw his rings. Oh God.'

'I need to ask you about his private life. Did Danny

belong to the Freemasons?'

She looked up. 'Oh God, is this to do with those other murders? He's not a businessman, I don't...'

'Yeah, I know. But please can you tell me if he was in the Freemasons or joined them at some point and left?'

'Yes, he was a Freemason, but he was in a special part of them for actors and show business people. He joined quite a few years ago.'

'Thank you.'

'Why would someone do that to him because he was a Freemason? I don't understand.'

'That's what we're trying to find out. Do you know of anyone else who might have wanted to hurt Danny?'

'No, I can't think of anyone.'

'We're going to need to take a statement from you and there's some dates we need to check with you, to get a picture of your husband's movements.'

'Why?'

He stood up. 'Just procedure. We'll take you to the station in a little while. The constable will stay with you. And make sure his agent gets in touch with us. I'm very sorry for your loss.'

Lilly Charles nodded and put her tissue to her face, so Jairus walked off with all of it going round in his head, trying to fit all the pieces together. Most of all, he kept wondering where Bryan was. He was that one link in the chain that he wanted to grab hold of and pull. There needed to be no more deaths, no more weight on his broad shoulders. Carl Murphy was never far away, hiding in the shadows of every room he entered, whispering in a whimpering voice.

Kate Roberts sat up awkwardly, trying to balance

herself on one elbow. The plastic strap was digging into her wrists. She was lying on a sleeping bag in an empty dusty room. Light brown carpet and bare magnolia walls. She could hear sounds coming from the other room. Sometimes it was pacing, her abductor's boots moving round, while he seemed to mutter to himself. He was mad, insane or whatever they would call it. His eyes were piercing and he hardly made sense.

She wanted to pull the gag from her mouth, but she couldn't quite reach properly. She shuffled herself from the sleeping bag, crawling towards the door. With her head tilted towards the door, she could hear someone talking. Yes, a radio and the news was on.

Outside the windows it was light. It had been that way for a while, so Kate estimated the time as being around 8 a.m.

Then the sound of the heavy boots came across the floor and towards the door. She flipped over, rolled herself back towards the sleeping bag, her heart pounding.

She lay there, half across the sleeping bag.

Like he had previously, the man stood in the doorway looking down at her. And looked about the room, his wild eyes seeming to search for something. She followed his eyes, still breathing hard, her head a little sore from the roll.

In his hand was a steaming cup of something, which he brought closer and put down on the floor by her head, then retreated backwards to the doorway. She looked down at the grimy cup and saw it contained milky tea.

She was thirsty and began moaning about the gag across her mouth. He nodded and came forwards, reaching out his hand. The stale stench of sweat and dirty clothes filled her nostrils as he yanked the gag from her mouth. He put one finger to his lips and pulled a knife from inside his jacket and flashed it at her.

Her kidnapper then crouched down and crossed his legs, sitting as if he was about to meditate. He wrapped his arms around his body as if to warm himself, and kept his eyes mostly on the floor. But his eyes did occasionally jump up to her.

'I don't want to hurt you.'

'Good,' she muttered. 'Then please let me go.'

'I can't. Not until I know everything.' The eyes jumped up at her, making her flinch a little. They dug into her.

'What do you think I know?'

'You were his secretary. You knew all the things he did.'

'Graham Burgess? I didn't know about all that. If I had known what he'd done...I would've gone to the police.'

'Would you? And then you'd have lost your high paid job. How could you have not known what he was up to? You must've have known.'

She struggled to get up, but found herself falling backwards. 'Please...listen to me. I swear I didn't know about what he'd done.'

'He took her to that house and...they destroyed her. They used her and murdered her. Who else was there? You're going to tell me who else was there.'

'When? I don't know what you mean. Please. Let me go. I won't say anything. I won't tell them where you are.'

'Listen to me. Your lord and master had a dinner party where he invited all his Satanist bastard friends, so they all could worship the Devil together. You're going to tell me who else was there.'

'I don't know! I don't know anything about it.' It was the words about Satanism that had pierced her mind with the absolute icy cold truth of the matter. She was trapped in a building with a delusional madman. No amount of denying it would satisfy his appetite for the bizarre. Her only chance was to escape. She looked down at her bound feet and hands. There was little chance of that and it was doubtful anyone was coming for her. She could always scream, but she sensed she would be silenced long before she could gain anyone's attention. She looked up at him. He was talking now, going on about someone called Kelly, saying how they had met, how she had changed his life in those few brief moments. She tried to switch off when he started raving about all the terrible things her boss had done, but still some of it flashed into her mind and she wanted to vomit onto the carpet.

All she could think was that Graham Burgess had a room hidden under Braxton House, where they had found a young girl barely hanging on to life. That much was true. But a Satanist? She didn't know what to believe.

Then her mind sparked to life. 'Maybe we could find something at Braxton House that would tell you who was there at that dinner party?'

The man gave an empty laugh. 'The police are still there. You'd like that, wouldn't you? To deliver me to the police?'

'I didn't know. I didn't think. Let's think. Where else can we look?'

'You must have a list of his friends. His business acquaintances.'

She shook her head and felt tears build up behind her eyes. 'The police have all that. Oh...oh, please, I don't know what I can do or say to you.'

'You can help me find the rest. They all must pay for what they have done.'

Now she found herself blubbing, her nose running with snot, her hands together as if to pray, her mouth pouring out pleading words.

The man shot to his feet and paced about the room manically, rubbing his hands together, or scratching his head. Then he went to the window and leaned against the frame.

'They're out there laughing. They think they've got away with it. Do you know what that feels like? To know they think they've got away with killing the woman you love?'

'No, I don't...please, let me help you.' She looked him in the eyes, tried to hold his stare, to make him trust her.

He turned back towards the window, then pulled the knife from his jacket and walked firmly towards her. She tried to roll away, crying all the time, a gurgling scream building through her. She thought of her friend, Gareth, the man she loved and had never been able to communicate it to. She would tell him. She'd tell him it all if she ever got out of this.

The man was above her, holding the knife as if to bring down the blade hard into her chest. His eyes roared with all the pain ignited inside his mind. The blade shook. Then he lowered it, a tear crawling down his cheek. He blinked and put his free hand out to her face. She started, fearing the knife would make a sudden return. Instead, the man smoothed her face, sighing a little.

'She was so beautiful,' he said, his voice crumbling. 'She...would never admit to...she would never...I loved her so much.'

'I know,' Kate said, her own voice but a whisper. 'I

know you loved her. And it's awful what they did to her. Tell me all about her. Tell me what she was like.'

The man wiped the tears away with his sleeve and sat down opposite her. The knife was on the floor a few inches away as he crossed his legs and began to speak passionately about the young woman who his whole life had become anchored to.

All the time he spoke, Kate Roberts was silently praying to herself, hoping against hopes that someone would save her.

CHAPTER 26

Jairus stopped halfway across the busy incident room when he saw the woman standing in Warren's office. He stood still for a moment, the blurs of bodies moving round him and phones ringing everywhere. He watched the woman, dressed in grey trousers and a light blue shirt. She had light brown hair styled in a messy bob. He walked closer and watched her tidying the files on the desk. When she faced him, he could see her long, thin face and pointed nose. She was in her early forties, he decided, and was in good shape.

He knocked on the door and waited for her to signal him to enter. When she did, he stepped in and put his back to the door. 'Morning.'

She lifted up some files and placed them on a nearby filing cabinet. She looked him up and down for a moment. 'DCI Jairus?'

He nodded. 'Yeah, that's right. And you are?'

'Detective Chief Superintendent Clare Napper. I've been brought in from Poplar to oversee things here for a while.'

'I see. Nice to meet you, ma'am.'

She smiled and rested her backside on the desk and folded her arms. 'Commander Warren has taken some time off. Doesn't sound like he's a well man.'

'News to me,' Jairus said and stepped closer. 'Do you need me to bring you up to speed?'

Napper pointed to the files littered around the office. 'I'm getting myself up to speed, but thanks for the offer. I've heard a lot about you, DCI. There's a lot of charming stories.'

'I doubt they're charming.' He smiled.

'OK, then let's say they are interesting. But, let me tell you, DCI Jairus, I don't want any shit going on while I'm here. I particularly don't want you going off to meet drug dealers in the middle of the night. Got it?'

'Yeah, I understand.'

Napper went round to her desk and sat down. 'You've got quite a handful at the moment. What with all the dead bodies turning up. You think you can handle all this?'

'It's not just me. I've got a good team.'

'Good. Glad you realise that. So go and do what you do. And don't balls it up.'

He opened the door. 'I'll try not to.'

'Oh, and Jairus.'

'Yeah, ma'am?'

'I had a phone call from a government department. They're sending a man over to talk to you.'

Jairus shut the door. 'What government department?'

She shrugged. 'My guess? MI5? So why would they be doing that?'

Jairus gave an empty laugh. 'I don't know. But sounds like I'm about to be told off. I'll catch up with you later, ma'am.'

In an empty interview room, Jairus set up a computer monitor and DVD player. He sat in a chair and sat back, his eyes fixed on the paused image before him. He was waiting. Walker and Moone were in the building, having just got back from making more enquiries. No more leads, they had said to him over the phone. Danny Charles' computer's disc drive had been taken, leaving no evidence of his sordid desires. No, of course not. Holzman wouldn't have let the police find that. After all, the revelation that he was a paedophile would have taken away the focus from the work he had already carried out. And Bryan had disappeared into the night with the PA. There had to be something that would tell him where he would be staying.

Everyone who had known Bryan had been talked to, every relative they could find in the area. They were trying to locate his mother and brother who were somewhere in Spain, but no one seemed to know exactly where.

Bryan was here somewhere. The picture they had of him was of a young lad who liked to lie, to fantasise his life a little. To Jairus it all made sense suddenly. The connection between Bryan and Kelly was a fictional one. He'd seen her, had maybe even talked to her on some occasions, and the bond had been given birth inside his warped mind. His deeply disturbed love of her is what drove him to hunt down the men who had harmed her.

Jairus sat up as the door opened and Walker stepped in, followed by Moone. Both of them looked tired and drawn as they came round either side of him and faced the screen.

Walker put a black coffee down in front of Jairus. 'I thought you might need this.'

Jairus put both his hands round it, feeling the burn on his palms. 'Thanks. You ready?'

Walker pulled out a chair and sat down, but Moone leaned against the wall, his arms folded.

'I'm ready,' Walker said, clearing her throat.
'Ready.' Moone nodded.

Jairus turned back to the screen and pressed play.

Once again they were faced with the dark dungeon underneath Braxton House. The camera took in the writhing young figure on the bed, her hands and feet chained to it. She was screaming through the gag. The camera bounced around, focusing on the walls, the floor, then the man stumbling towards the bed. Hands were pushing him forwards, pushing him towards the girl.

Then the film cut, jumped to the man, Danny Charles, on top of the young woman, pushing himself onto her. Her hair covered her face, but she was moaning through the gag, her pleading words not being heard. The camera moved, revealing the dress she was adorned in; the same black and red dress that was found in Charles' bedroom. Jairus looked down for a moment, put a hand over his face and shook his head. He looked up and watched again, trying to separate himself from what was happening in front of his eyes.

The film jumped again. There was a close up of Danny Charles' face as he forced himself on top of her, his face red and his breath coming faster and faster. His eyes were blank and swirling a little. Drugged, Jairus whispered to himself. He looked at Walker and saw the horrified expression on her face.

He noticed something then. He sat up and moved his head closer to the screen, trying to get a good look at the girl who was being raped. 'There's something not right here.'

'What do you mean?' Moone said. 'The fact that some poor girl is being raped?'

Jairus waved his hand. 'I mean, look at the girl's

hair. It doesn't look right. It looks like a wig.'

Walker leaned in. 'He's right. She's wearing a wig.'

'And...wait.' Jairus rewound the film. 'Look. Look at her arm.'

The image froze on the screen. Jairus leaned forward and tapped the monitor. 'Is that a needle mark?'

Moone came forward. 'Could be. Maybe they kept her high all the time.'

'No, I think there's scars there too. Old needle marks.'

'What're you thinking then?' Walker asked.

'I don't think that's any of the kidnapped girls. I think that's Sara Billings. But they've made it look like one of the girls.'

'Why would they do that?' Moone asked.

'Think about it.' Jairus stood up. 'What if they organised that whole dinner party just so they could film the men with the girls and blackmail them, but some of their victims couldn't make it. What if this is all about making a splash? What better than having film of a celebrity Freemason to get the papers and the media interested. But Danny Charles doesn't make the dinner. So they get him another night, but they can't use the girls, so they have to adapt. They know Sara because she helped them before. They pay her to dress up as one of the girls and film Danny Charles having sex with her. Sara looks quite young. If the rumours are true about him, perhaps they told him she was under age.'

'Oh my God,' Walker said. 'So whoever's been doing all this is trying to destroy their reputations?'

Jairus shook his head. 'Not just their reputations. The Freemasons. The people at the top. That's who they're targeting. The business leaders, the kings of show business. Garter wasn't in England when the girls were taken. I don't think he was involved at all. But they wanted to implicate him. So they send Bryan and Ashmore in his direction. All Holzman has to do is tell Bryan that Garter was involved. They wind him up and let him go. Ashmore doesn't need convincing. He's already thirsty for blood.'

'Makes sense,' Walker said and nodded. 'So, who's orchestrating all this? Holzman?'

Jairus walked round the room for a moment, rubbing his jaw. 'Not just Holzman. He's the fixer, the handyman. He helps out, but think about it, why would all these people fall into their traps? Not for Holzman. No, but if someone with power and influence, someone you thought was trustworthy invited you along…then you're more likely to go, aren't you?'

'Then who you thinking?' Moone asked.

Jairus raised his shoulders. 'I don't know. I'm thinking…maybe a fellow Freemason, but one with a lot of power.'

'So they'd have to be high up in the Masons?' Moone said.

'You're joking right?' Walker looked between them, aghast. 'You think some high up, connected Freemason is knocking off other Freemasons? Why? Why would they?'

'That's the problem,' Jairus said, and ran a hand over his hair. 'Why? Why do you set up your fellow men, make them look like Satanists and get them killed?'

Moone sighed. 'What sort of mind comes up with something like that?'

'A bored one. Someone who's built up their own world, travelled to the top and then wants to destroy that world. A bored, sadistic mind. You ever heard that connection between big business and politics and psychopaths?'

Moone shook his head, looking very confused.

Walker's eyes opened a little. 'I think I heard something. Didn't someone come out with some theory on work place psychopaths?'

Jairus pointed at Walker. 'Yeah, exactly. They reckon if you look round your office you won't be very far away from a psychopath.

Moone laughed. 'Aren't you confusing psychopaths with rats?'

Jairus looked at him blankly. 'No, I'm not. They didn't mean psychopaths as in serial killers or the like, they meant non-aggressive, unfeeling people who only think of their own success and won't think twice about crushing their fellow workers under foot. These people will have a string of failed relationships behind them, but they will be high up in the food chain.'

'Hang on,' Moone said, squinting at Jairus. 'So, there's a nutter businessman knocking off other businessmen? Why? Because of boredom?'

Jairus shook his head. 'No, there's a motive. There's always a motive. We just need to find it. And that's why we need to find Bryan and Holzman. One of them will lead us right to the man at the top.'

'OK, so where do we find Bryan?' Walker asked. 'He could be anywhere.'

'Check over everything we know about him,' Jairus said and headed to the door. 'Really go deep. Every job he had before he got locked up. Leave no stone unturned. Moone, you and I'll go and see Sara and see what we can dig out of her.'

'OK, but I don't think we'll get much,' Moone said and followed him out of the interview room.

When they began their journey down the corridor,

Jairus slowed a little and nudged Moone, bringing his attention to DCS Napper talking to a female uniform officer down the other end of the hallway, right near the stairs.

'What do you know about Napper?'

Moone looked at him. 'Not a lot, apart from she's meant to be a bit of a cow. Hard-working though. She's lent about the various stations when someone needs to be brought into line. So, I guess that's you.'

'Yeah, I suppose it is. What about Warren?'

Moone looked towards Napper. 'I don't know. I think he's had a few problems in his home life, all the usual crap. Thrown out by his wife. Drinking too much. I'm sure he'll get himself sorted eventually. Look out here she comes.'

Napper took her time approaching them. When she reached Moone and Jairus, she looked between them for a moment. 'I can see I'm going to have to separate you two. Go on, Moone, get on with whatever you're doing. Let's hope it goes somewhere.'

Moone raised his eyebrows at Jairus, then sloped off down the corridor.

Jairus leaned against the wall. 'Yes, boss, and what can I do for you?'

'The man has arrived,' she said and nodded towards the end of the corridor. 'He's in my office. Quite frankly, he seems like a self-important wanker. But he's got a job to do.'

Jairus looked along the corridor, his curiosity spiking. 'What did he say?'

'Said he needed a word with you.'

'And who is he?'

'As I surmised, MI5. Basically he's here to tell you off or to stop you poking your nose into something. You must have set off alarm bells somewhere.'

Jairus ran a few things through his head, trying to pries it all apart, spin it around and put it back together again. Nothing stuck. What could he have done to get government agents to come running? The only thing that came to him was the Freemasons. His paranoid mind started to wonder how high the connection stretched. Anger rippled through him.

'Watch it or that vein in your head might burst,' Napper said. 'Just go and see him. Talk to him, hear what he has to say. Then do as he says.'

'What if it goes against our investigation?'

She smiled a little. 'I'm sure you'll be able to negotiate your way round it. Now, run along.'

The thin, suited figure was sat at Napper's desk, his head down, staring at some kind of Tablet device. He looked up when Jairus knocked on the door, his face clear of emotion, and nodded for him to come in. The man wore a dark blue suit, red tie. He looked in his forties, with tidy short brown hair with scatterings of silver at the temples. He was lean, hollow in the cheeks. Grey, serious eyes.

'You're DCI Jairus?' the man said, and put his device on the desk and clasped his hands together.

'Yeah, that's right. And you are?'

'Why don't you take a seat? This won't take long.' The man's eyes jumped to the seat opposite.

Jairus hesitated, feeling the burn of anger already clawing its way through him. He sat, trying to calm himself, preparing for more anger to arrive. 'You didn't answer my question. Who are you?'

'Stephen Hopkins,' the man said. 'I've come from MI5.'

'So what's this all about?'

'Edgar Holzman. You tried to match some of his

fingerprints a couple of days ago.'

'Yeah, that's right. So, his prints flagged something up? What?'

'I can't discuss that,' Hopkins said and sat back. 'You understand that, surely?'

'No, I don't. We're on the same side, right? I need to know who he is.'

Hopkins smiled. 'He's Edgar Holzman. He was born in Germany, went to school there, joined the Army, then moved here with his father when he was nineteen. He's led a pretty uneventful life.'

Jairus rubbed his face, pushing the anger down further. 'So why're your lot so interested in him?'

'That's classified. I'm just here to tell you to leave him alone. Walk away.'

'Ha. We believe Holzman has been helping two men kill people. He's also shot one man. And possibly tortured and beheaded another man.'

'Can you prove all this?' Hopkins raised his eyebrows.

'Not right now. But I will.'

'Well, when you can, let me know and we'll talk.'

'And what about now? He's out there. What if he kills again?'

'That's our problem.'

Jairus leapt to his feet. 'No, it's my problem. How am I supposed to sit back and forget about him? How do I live with it?'

Hopkins shook his head. 'That's just what you have to do. There's no room for discussion. It's done and dusted. You just keep your lot out of our way.'

'So that's it?' Jairus leaned over the desk. 'Your investigation is more important than ours? Three girls went missing. Two of them are more than likely dead. One is seriously messed up from all the horrific things they did to her. Holzman is involved. I need to find him.'

Hopkins sighed. 'I'm really sorry about that. I really am, but it all comes down to priorities. What we're looking into is a national security issue. National. I have to think about the bigger picture. A lot more people could get hurt.'

Jairus stood up and looked towards the windows. 'So, you think...what? Holzman is planning on blowing up somewhere? Something like that?'

'I cannot discuss it.'

As Jairus stood silently for a moment, in his mind he saw his hands clamping on the agent's lapels, ripping him from the desk, shaking him. In reality, he felt his jaw grinding. 'If you help us find him, then we can get him off the streets. Job done.'

'You know it doesn't work like that. We have to keep an eye on him.'

'So you have him under surveillance? You have people watching his house?'

Hopkins put his hands behind his head. 'That would probably be a waste of resources at the moment. Like you, we're spread pretty thin these days. We tend to use more technical assistance. Mobile phone, bank accounts, etc.'

'Jesus.' Jairus clasped his face and took in a deep breath. 'Just tell me if he has any other properties.'

'Again, I can't do that.'

'But you have that information?'

Hopkins stood up and tidied his tie and suit. 'Yes, but again I can't tell you. Well, this has been a fascinating chat and everything, but I need to get back to work.'

Jairus watched him flash a smile in his direction, then walk around the desk and head for the door. He quickly stepped in his way, cutting off Hopkins' exit.

The agent raised his eyebrows. 'Yes? And what do you think you're going to do?'

'Whatever I have to.'

'Really? I read up on you before I came down here, DCI Jairus. You've an interesting background. You managed to get away with killing a suspect. That was pretty impressive. Now what, you're going to try and get away with trying to shake some information out of me? Let me speak plainly. I don't care about your case. I have my own caseload to think about. I need Holzman out there. And I'm not going to let you imbeciles mess that up. So you might want to step out of my way, because I can make life very difficult for you, DCI Jairus. Your career could end very suddenly.'

Jairus stared down at him for a few seconds, then let Hopkins pass by. He turned and watched the agent walk across the incident room and followed. He stopped at the whiteboard, stared at all the photographs for a while, absorbing it all. Then he looked through the files and found the photographs taken of Gina Colman's injuries. He closed the file again, breathing hard, trying to decide what to do next. A course of action had been given birth in his darkest imaginings, but he shut it off, sealed it away. He shook his head, telling himself that he could not tread that dark path again.

CHAPTER 27

Moone was sitting in one of the prison's interview rooms, his phone clamped to his ear. For the sixth time that day, Commander Warren's phone had gone straight to voicemail. He left another message, pretty much pleading with his boss to get in touch.

He was feeling guilty. He hadn't bothered to meet up with the Commander the other night, even though he was aware that the old man had been reaching out to him. The aggravation of looking after a drunk who was on the edge of a nervous breakdown was all he needed, what with his own crumbling marriage to deal with. He wanted to tell Jairus about what was going on, but suspected Warren wouldn't like that at all.

The door opened and Sara Billings came in, her hands in her pockets. She sighed, pulled out a chair and sat down. She didn't look him in the eyes, just raised her eyebrows and said, 'Yeah? What is it now?'

Moone put away his phone and rested his arms on the desk. 'We haven't met before, Sara. I'm DS Peter Moone.'

'You all look the same to me.'

'That's funny, because skinny blonde junkies all look the same to me. They're a dime a dozen. Actually, no that's wrong, because you are pretty special, aren't you?'

'Am I?'

'Oh yes. You see, it takes a real special type of person to drive a sex offender's car and pick up some poor girl so they can have their way with her.'

'You can say all you like. I've heard it.' Sara tapped her temple. 'It's in here all the time going round and round. I'm fucked, I know it. I'm fucked up in my head. I know.'

'You know they're going to have you back in front of a judge some time soon?'

Sara put her face in her hands. 'Shit. Shit. Shit. What am I supposed to fucking do about it?'

'There's not much you can do, except tell us everything.'

Her hands fell away. 'I have! I don't know what else to say. What do you want me to say?'

Moone leaned across the desk, waited for her scared eyes to meet his. 'What about the fact that you starred in one of the films? How about that? Talk to me about that, Sara.'

Her eyes flickered away. 'What films?'

'Come on, we're not stupid, Sara. We know you were in one of the films. All we have to do is match the train lines on your arm with the girl's in the film.'

Sara's hand crawled over to her left arm and began scratching at it. 'So I was in one of the films? You going to do me for that?'

'Do me a favour, Sara,' Moone began. 'Think about someone other than yourself for a change. Can you do that? Why did they put you in the film?'

Her eyes tightly shut, she shrugged and then looked at him. 'I don't know. All I know is he turned up at my house. He gave me money. Got me where I wanted to be, fucking high, off my fucking nut. All I had to do was pose in one of their films. What did it matter to me? So I did it. Do you think it was nice for me? Going down into that fucking awful place? I was shitting myself.'

'All this time you've known it was there?' Moone slammed his fist on the desk. The prison officer appeared at the small window in the door, but Moone shook his head and he went away again.

'That bastard they brought down there...that bald ugly filthy bastard...do you know what he made me do?'

'I don't have to imagine, Sara. I've seen it. And do you know what? I'm going to find out why it all happened. Why you and those girls went through what you did. We think there's someone else putting this all together. Do you have any idea who that may be?'

She shook her head. 'I don't know. But you might be right. He was worried that day. Really scared.'

'Who was?'

'Burgess. He was panicking. It was important the bald guy should be at their dinner party, but he wasn't there. He was getting in a state about it. So they got him there later. That's all I know. They thought I was too out of it to know what was going on, but I was listening.'

Moone sat back and nodded. 'You better be telling us everything this time, Sara. For everyone's sake. And for your boy's sake. Because if I find out you're lying again or holding something back, I'll wait til he's older and I'll tell him all about his mum.'

Sara lurched out and grasped his arm, her eyes wet with tears. 'I am. Please, please. You've got to believe me. That's all I know. I'm sorry for what I've done. I really am. I can't sleep, do you know that? It's all going on in my head...like...like ants crawling over my brain.'

Moone took her hand away and stood up. 'I'm going to send someone over so you can take a look at some photos. Please see if you can ID anyone.'

She just kept looking up at him. He turned and headed for the door, unable to turn and look back at her.

Jairus was sitting at a desk in the corner of the incident room, his eyes scanning the files in front of him, the scattering of photographs of victims and killers. The faces of the young girls stared up at him, smiling a little. He only saw the pleading in their eyes, the acts that they would have had to perform. He grasped his head with both hands, grinding his jaw. He blocked it all out, tried to focus on the plain facts again.

Everything in the missing girls' lives had been thoroughly sifted through. One of the key factors that connected two of the girls was Sara who was now locked up. The other factor was Graham Burgess who was lying in bits in the morgue. Jairus looked at the photographs of the dresses. All made by one young designer who had killed herself, although nothing about her suicide stood out as unusual. But it wasn't difficult to make a murder look self-inflicted, especially when the victim had a history of mental illness, which Winter had.

He sighed and leaned back in his chair. There were missing pieces. Holzman and Bryan were those missing parts of the puzzle. He needed to find them, to put several questions to them, but the only person who had information on Holzman was a self-important government agent. A plan kept formulating in Jairus' mind, but he kept pushing it aside.

Walker entered the incident room, her notebook in

her hand. 'Just talked to Danny Charles' agent. On the day of Burgess' infamous dinner party, Charles was visiting his brother in hospital in Cambridge. He'd had a heart attack. But he was invited.'

Jairus nodded. 'So, Danny Charles was meant to be there but couldn't make it. Moone called me a little while ago after his visit to Sara. She backs up the story. She posed as a victim so they could film him in action later on. Apparently she reckons Burgess was panicking because the guest of honour hadn't shown up.'

'Interesting. So, sounds like he was scared of someone.'

'Yeah. Has Mrs Charles been shown photographs of the other victims yet?'

'I haven't, but I don't think it was one of my jobs.'

Jairus sighed walked over and picked up the action list. He looked through the all the jobs listed. He sighed again. 'It was Moone's job. What the bloody hell's going on with him?'

'He's one of those rare coppers who manage to hold down a marriage...well, barely.' Walker shrugged.

Jairus closed the action list and pointed to the door. 'Yeah, I know, so let's go and do his job for him.'

Walker grabbed the file of photographs and followed him out of the incident room.

Lily Charles was staying at a friend's place, which was a luxurious flat in a 1930s art deco apartment block just a few streets away from Camden High Street. Walker parked the car, and Jairus climbed out and followed her towards the building that sat back behind a tall metal gate. There were buzzers on the gate, so Jairus pressed them all until a woman's voice spoke to him, asking who was there.

'Lily Charles?' Jairus asked. 'It's DCI Jairus. We need to ask you a few questions.'

'Can you face the camera, please?' Lily Charles croaked from the intercom.

Jairus huffed and turned towards the camera that sat on top of the gate like a buzzard.

The gates made a buzzing sound and opened. Jairus dug his hands into his pockets and strode up to the main building and pushed open the main door with Walker on his heels. They hurried up the white stone steps that wound all the way up to the fifth floor where they found Lily Charles waiting in an open doorway.

She let them into an open-plan apartment with real wood floors and windows that stretched the whole length of the room. Jairus stood with his back to the window, while Walker sat down on the sofa.

'I'm sorry about all that fuss, but the press have been sniffing about.' Lily snatched a couple of tissues from the coffee table and sat down on the other end of the sofa.

'Yeah, I bet they have,' Jairus said. 'I'm sorry to have to keep going over things, Mrs Charles, but you can understand how important it is we get it all right.'

'I know,' she said and wrapped the tissue round her finger. 'Go ahead.'

Jairus cleared his throat. 'I have some photographs to show you. We want to see if you recognise anyone.'

'OK,' Lily said and sat up straighter, seeming to prepare herself.

Walker opened the folder and handed her a picture of Thomas Henry, then his daughter, Marie. Lily took the photographs and studied them for a moment. She looked up. 'These two were in the papers, weren't they?'

Jairus nodded. 'Yeah. Have you met them before?'

She shook her head slightly. 'No. Definitely not.'

Walker passed her the photograph of Graham Burgess. Again, Lily studied the image for a few seconds, then looked up empty.

'I don't know this man either.'

Jairus nodded to Walker and she handed Lily the photograph of Sir Robert Garter. This time her eyes widened and looked confusingly at Jairus. 'Oh my God. Was he killed by the same people?'

Jairus stepped forward. 'Do you know him?'

'Well, yes. I've only met him a couple of times, but he and Danny were good friends.'

'Really?' Walker asked. 'Do you know how they met?'

She frowned. 'I can't quite remember, but I'm sure it was at some charity do. Something to do with raising money for children. It was a few years back. I don't think Danny had seen him for quite a while. I remembering him mentioning that he'd died. But I didn't pay much attention. Oh my God, who's doing this?'

'Don't worry, Mrs Charles, we're close to finding out,' Walker said.

Jairus came over and sat in an armchair. 'Have you ever spent any time in his home?'

'Only his apartment, the one overlooking the Thames.'

'How recently?'

She frowned again. 'Maybe a year ago. I'm not sure. He let us stay there a couple of times while he was away.'

Jairus felt a smile breaking his face, but pushed it down. The hairs were standing up on his neck. 'And he gave you a key?'

'It was a card. Kind of like the ones you get in hotels.'

'Have you still got it?' Jairus got up, feeling the nervousness creeping through him. He felt wired.

'We might have. It should be at the house, but to be honest I haven't seen it for a long time.'

Jairus rubbed his hands together. 'But you never gave it back?'

'I'm pretty sure we didn't. Why are you asking...?'

Jairus held up a finger when he heard the phone ringing in his pocket. Again, not his own phone. He ripped the phone out of his jacket and stared at the unrecognised number calling. Bryan. 'I'm sorry, but I have to take this. DI Walker will carry on asking the questions.'

With Walker's eyes burning questioningly at him, Jairus rushed from the apartment and hammered down the stone stairs. 'Bryan? Talk to me, Bryan.'

There's a huff of breath on the other end. There's a laugh too, lightly in the voice. 'I'm talking to you, aren't I?'

Jairus stepped outside, feeling light spots of rain. 'Yeah, I suppose you are, Bryan. Taking Kate Roberts like that. I know what you were doing.'

'Oh yeah, what was I doing?'

'Sticking your fingers up at me. I know you're upset and angry...'

'You don't understand how angry I am.'

'Yeah, I do. I told you before. I understand perfectly. So let me help you. Together we can catch the rest of the bastards.'

'I'm not going to catch them so you can lock them up for a few years! I'm going to cut them up! Make them suffer!'

'That's what you want to do, Bryan. I know that.

But it's a big leap from desire to actually going through with it.'

'I can do it.'

'Can you? I don't think so.'

'How about his secretary? Why don't I start with her?'

Jairus laughed. He pushed it out, made himself laugh loud and clear, even though he was burning inside and out. He didn't want to gamble with a woman's life, but there was little choice. 'You won't hurt her. You'll look at her and you'll see Kelly, Bryan. Look into her eyes...'

'Fuck off! I know what I'm doing. I've got it figured out this time. You know I was in prison a long time and I know some pretty nasty people. Maybe I wouldn't be able to hurt her, but they would.'

The twist in Jairus stomach tightened. 'You wouldn't do that, Bryan. That would make you just as bad as...'

'Listen to me! Listen to me!'

Jairus breathed hard. 'Yeah, I'm listening, Bryan.'

'You're going to do as I say. Got it? You're going to listen to me, and do as I ask.'

Jairus gripped his face with his free hand. 'Go on.'

'You're going to bring me the names of the others. You're going to investigate and then bring me the next names on the list.'

'I can't do that, Bryan.'

'Yes you can. And you will. Or she gets terrible things done to her.'

'Let me talk to her...'

The line went dead. Jairus stared at the phone, his heart pounding. He called the number. It rang for a second then went to nothing. He called again but was told the number was out of use.

He let out a shout that lasted a few seconds, swung round and punched the wall. He looked down at his battered knuckles, then put away the phone.

Walker came down the stairs, her face full of questions.

'Who was that on the phone?'

'Warren.' Jairus began heading towards Walker's car.

'What did he want? Is he OK?'

'Not really. He's got problems.'

Jairus stood by her car waiting for her to unlock it.

'So, what do you think about what Mrs Charles said?'

'I think whoever put all this in motion knew that Danny Charles sometimes stayed at Garter's. That's the reason they were desperate to get Charles to that dinner party. My betting is that not only did they want to frame him, they wanted to get the keycard off him and copy it to get into Garter's. Otherwise how were they going to get close to him?'

'Makes sense,' Walker said and climbed in.

Jairus got in too. 'I think Garter is the focus of all this. For whatever reason, he's the real target. All the others don't mean anything without Garter as the icing on the cake.'

'If that's true...well, he's dead. Why go and kill Danny Charles?'

Jairus rubbed his eyes. 'Because he was a loose end. We might've got hold of him and got him to spill the beans. We need to search for that key card at Charles' house.'

'OK.'

Walker drove them away from the building, but Jairus kept noticing her glancing at him. 'What?'

She took in a heavy breath and kept her eyes on the

road. 'I was just wondering if you were OK. I know I've said it before, but I'm worried about you.'

'You don't need to be.'

'Well, I am. I think all the stuff you've been through is getting to you. Why don't you go back and see that therapist?'

'It doesn't help. It stills comes back to me. Still plays over and over in my head.'

'You relive it?'

He nodded, regretting admitting to his weakness. 'Yeah, pretty much.'

'I mean, you have flashbacks and all that?'

'I suppose.' He looked away at the passing traffic, wishing he could jump out of the car.

'You're describing post-traumatic stress disorder.'

He looked at her and saw the concern dripping off her. 'Maybe. Look, can we stop talking about this?'

She rolled her eyes. 'Fine.'

'Stop the car.'

'I said I'd stop talking about it.'

He shook his head. 'I know. Just pull over.'

Walker slowed down and pulled over to the kerb. Jairus got out and took out his mobile. He dialled the IT department and heard Rich's distracted voice come onto the line.

'And what can I do for you, DCI Jairus?'

'I just got another call on Ashmore's mobile. I need to know where the call came from.'

'I'll do my best. Hang on.'

The line went quiet for a while and Jairus walked away from the car, dodging the pedestrians coming towards him. He turned round and saw that Walker had got out and was heading towards him.

Rich's breathing came back on the line. 'Sorry, Jairus, but the call came from a disposable. Out of use now. I can try my best and find out where the phone was when the call was made, but might take me a while.'

'Yeah, do that. By the way, you had a chance to look into Holzman's financial dealings?'

'I've dug around a bit. He seems to have retired a while back and closed his bank accounts. Looks like he's been dealing in cash ever since as the paper trail ends.'

'Great. Can you start digging round the other victims' financial records? Look for anything unusual.'

'OK. What you got in mind?'

'Not sure, but I got this itch in the back of my skull.'

'I hate when that happens.'

'Me too. Talk to you later.'

Jairus hung up and walked back to Walker.

'Who did you call?' she asked.

'Rich Vincent. I asked him to dig around the victims' financial records.'

'What you hoping to find?'

Jairus opened the car door. 'I'm not sure. I'm making this up as I go along.'

She smiled at him. 'I doubt that.'

They both climbed in. After Walker started the engine, Jairus turned to her and said, 'I was reading a Graham Greene novel a while back...'

'Hang on, you were reading Graham Greene?'

'He's a great writer. Anyway, he said that when a writer begins the first word of a novel, his brain, or his subconscious, has written the rest already.'

'So?'

He shrugged. 'I think it's the same with crime. As soon as a detective sees the first victim, their brain has already put the pieces together. I just need to get it out of my subconscious.'

Walker shook her head and steered the car into the road.

CHAPTER 28

Marsland was dreaming about his wife. But it didn't seem like a dream at all. He was standing in her hospital room, her lying on the bed, pale and skeletal. Except her legs were badly swollen, bloated. They were using IV drips but the fluid was just collecting in her legs.

'Is this it?' she asked him, fear glowing in her eyes.

He grasped her hand. 'No, darling, it's not.'

But it didn't take long after that. All the time she slipped away and he held her stick-thin hand, he pushed her confession to the back of his mind. She had not mentioned it again, because her mind had been scrambled from all the drugs. Her last moments were in between sleep, her eyes only opening momentarily to gaze around the room blankly.

Then she was gone.

Marsland opened his eyes and coughed. His throat was burning. His blurry vision cleared and he focused on the hunched figure with the newspaper in front of him. The paper came down and the weary eyes of Peter Moone took him in with a big grin.

'Welcome back to the land of the living,' Moone said and came to the bedside.

'Thanks,' Marsland said, his voice a croaky whisper. 'You been here long?'

'Ever since they brought you in.'

'Yeah, right.'

Moone put two fingers to his temple. 'Scout's honour. You had us bloody worried, Terence.'

'I seem to spend too much time in hospital these days.'

'You're right about that.'

Marsland fought to sit up. 'Edgar Holzman! He stabbed me.'

Moone nodded and patted his shoulder. 'Yes, we know. It's all in hand.'

'You got him banged up?'

'Not yet, but won't be long.'

'So he was involved with Burgess?'

'Yes. But we're not sure how. Or why. But we're putting the pieces together. Sara Billings is up to her neck in shit.'

'Yes. She's a messed up young lady.'

'Well, let's not talk about that, old friend. Let's look forward to better times.'

'I'm done.'

Moone raised his eyebrows. 'Does that mean what I think it means?'

Marsland nodded. 'Yes, it does. I'm finished poking my nose in where it doesn't belong.'

'Really? Jesus.'

'I'm serious.'

'I can see.' Moone laughed a little.

'I'm going to go home and spend the rest of my retirement listening to jazz, collecting stamps and minding my own bloody business.'

'Bollocks.'

'Yes, OK, but I'm done with helping people out.'

Moone slapped his hands together for a few seconds. 'Well done. About time you saw sense. I know I dragged you into all this mess, and I feel bloody awful about that, but maybe it was the kick in the arse you needed. Go and enjoy the rest of your life. I see you've already got yourself a girlfriend.'

Marsland shook his head. 'No.'

'Come on. Older lady, blonde? Not bad looking.'

Marsland smiled. 'Oh, Jacqui? No, she's some woman I bumped into. How do you know her? I take it she was here?'

'Yes, sitting by your bedside. I tell you what, she's really familiar. Where do I know her from?'

'No idea. But I need to find her and apologise. I was very rude the last time I saw her.'

'Well, I'm sure she'll forgive you.'

'I hope so,' Marsland said and looked a little sadly around the room. 'So, this is the start of my boring life.'

Moone nodded and squeezed Marsland's shoulder. 'Yep. This is it. And it's much better for you. High in fibre and all that rubbish.'

Marsland smiled.

'Well, I better be off. Got killers to catch.' Moone walked to the door.

'Hey, I don't suppose you've seen my son recently?'

Moone lost his smile. 'No, mate. I haven't.'

Marsland nodded and watched Moone leave.

Jairus didn't bother pushing down the plan anymore. He let it rise to the surface like a bubble. A dark, oily bubble.

He got Walker to drop him off at the Holmwood estate and ignored her questions. He couldn't bear to utter a word as he got out. He felt that anything he said to her would be coated in betrayal and tainted by lies. And so he stood on the edge of the estate and saw the anger in her eyes as she pulled away.

Then he turned with his hands in his pockets and strode into the Holmwood estate with its beige-coloured houses and grey concrete flats. There was very little colour apart from the various doors to the houses opposite the blocks of flats. Jairus entered the archway that led up to the six floors above him, and took the stairs two at a time. He could hear the boom of base coming from one of the flats above him. On Adrian Wells' floor, he found that the heavy sound of music was coming from his place. He hit the door with his fist, then rattled the letterbox, but there was no reply. Jairus sighed and hammered his fist again, then heard the music quieten a little. He knocked again and waited.

The chain went on, then the door opened a crack and Wells' lean, and wired face looked through the gap at him.

'Oh, fuck me,' Wells spat and tried to shut the door.

Jairus pushed the door open. 'It's OK, Adrian, I come in peace.'

'Yeah, fucking right. Last time you were here you broke my fucking nose.'

'Yeah, and I'm truly sorry about that. Sometimes us coppers get a bit overexcited.'

'You're a psychopath.'

He nodded. 'Probably more of a sociopath, but I'll give you that. Come on, Adrian, let me in. It's worth your while. I'm not a policeman today. Look, I don't want to stand out here much longer.'

Adrian stared at him for a moment, then nodded. Jairus moved his hand away and let him close the door and remove the chain. The door came open and Jairus saw Wells walking away across the grimy carpet, flip flops slapping at his feet. He was in long brown shorts and a dark red T-shirt. He went and collapsed on the sofa, his feet hanging off the end.

Jairus walked to the cluttered kitchen and started opening cupboards. 'You got tea here somewhere?'

'Middle cupboard above the sink.'

Jairus found a small box of teabags, then turned to a giant pile of washing up. He managed to pull two mugs from the wreckage and washed them up and made them both a milky tea. He sat Adrian Wells' tea down on the coffee table in front of him, then sat down on a tatty armchair. The base from the jungle music was travelling right through Jairus.

'Turn that rubbish off,' Jairus said.

Wells glared at him. 'Fuck off. I fucking mixed that.'

'I don't care. Turn it off.'

Wells swung his legs off the sofa and grabbed the remote. 'You the music police now?'

'Yeah.'

Wells turned the music off, and looked sideways at Jairus. 'Why do you want the music down? You wired for sound? Someone listening to us?'

Jairus laughed. 'No, Adrian. No one's listening. Now, I need your help...'

Adrian took out some tobacco and skins and began rolling a cigarette. 'You need my help? Fuck me. I feel like fainting. And tell me why I should help you when you broke my fucking nose last time I saw you?'

Jairus leaned forward. 'Do you care about anything apart from smoking dope, mixing shit music and wanking?'

Wells poked the rolled up cigarette between his lips, then shrugged. 'What else is there to care about?'

'What about your sister? Carly? How old is she?'

His face stiffened as he lit the roll-up and narrowed his eyes at Jairus. 'Fourteen, maybe fifteen. Why the fuck are you asking about her?'

'What if you found out that some evil wanker had... well...done something pretty awful to her?'

Wells pointed an angry finger at Jairus. 'Don't fucking...just don't.'

'Then help me. Help me get back at the bastards who did some evil things to some young women, then killed them.'

Wells took a deep lungful from his roll-up, then blew out the smoke. 'And what do I get out of it? A nice warm feeling inside?'

Jairus stood up and dug his hands into his pockets. 'You get a copper who owes you a massive favour. You'll have something to hold over me.'

There seemed to be a lot of thoughts going through Wells' mind as he smoked, his eyes looking off towards the window. Eventually he looked up at Jairus. 'So, what would I have to do?'

Jairus pulled his wallet from his jacket and took out a hundred quid and put it on the coffee table. 'First of all, go and buy five of those cheap pay-as-you-go phones. And a couple of masks.'

'Masks? Fuck sake, what're we going to do? Rob a bank?'

'Not if I can help it. Oh and while you're out shopping, find me one of these.' Jairus wrote something on his notebook, ripped out the page and handed it to Wells.

After stubbing out his roll-up, Wells looked at the note, then at Jairus with his eyebrows raised. 'Fuck me. Is this still to do with the job we're doing or your own personal sick taste?'

Jairus grinned and pointed to the piece of paper. 'Just get them. And the phones, and keep your mouth shut.'

'Well, I'm not about to go shooting my mouth off about this, am I?'

Jairus ignored him and opened the front door. 'I'll meet you here at 11 a.m. tomorrow and I'll tell you what we're going to do.'

Jairus stepped outside the flat, and shut the door behind him. He looked down on the grey estate, his conscience screaming at him.

Back at the red-brick fortress, Jairus headed up the steps, his hands in his pockets, still the voices battling in his head. If he were a cartoon character, he decided, there'd be an angel and devil sitting on his shoulders. In reality, it was called cognitive dissonance. Either way, the devil was shouting louder.

Jairus reached the incident room and faced the whiteboard, staring at the images of the businessmen victims. He wanted be able to see the truth of it all, the aspect of the case he couldn't quite see yet. There would be something there to link them all together and point them towards the evil brain behind it all. Whoever it was, wanted them to be focused on the Freemasons, to make it look as if some sinister satanic cult was operating, abducting and sacrificing young girls. And so far they had fooled him, manipulating him into feeding the story to the press. He made a note to get in contact with Ian Pritchard and make him quit his investigation.

Then Jairus tapped the photograph of Sir Robert Garter and had the overwhelming feeling that he was the epicentre of it all, the real focus of the orchestrator's plot. Why else would they go to all the trouble to get hold of Garter's key card? Unlike the other businessmen, who Jairus felt were simply cannon fodder to Holzman and his mysterious accomplices,

Garter was almost untouchable. He represented something very powerful.

Jairus heard the glass door behind him open and the sound of heels coming towards him. He turned to see DCS Napper. She stood next to him and looked over the board.

'This board gives me brain-ache,' she said. 'I'm hoping it makes sense to you.'

'It's starting to,' he said and tapped Garter's photograph. 'He's the key. He symbolises power, money, influence. That's what this is all about.'

'And what startling and concrete piece of evidence suggests that?' She raised her eyebrows.

'Something in the back of my head. Garter's killers, and the people giving them their orders, went to great lengths to get into his building. And one of the dresses the girls were tortured and killed in was placed at the scene. But Garter wasn't in the country when the girls went missing. Something's telling me he had nothing to do with their abduction or their murders.'

'We still don't know what happened to the other two girls. Although, I'm inclined to think they're gone.'

Jairus nodded. 'Yeah. We need to find the connection. The thing that really bonds them all together, something that the orchestrators of all this don't want us to see.'

'You mean Holzman? From what I read, looks like him and Henry and Burgess were in it together.'

'I disagree. I don't think Henry was a willing participant in any of this. I think Holzman and Burgess drugged him and filmed him with the girls. Like the rest of the businessmen they filmed, I think they used the film to keep them quiet, threatening to make it public if they talked about what had happened. But the films were also to be used to make it look like they were involved in a secret satanic part of the Freemasons.'

Napper crossed her arms. 'Why would anyone go to all that trouble? Maybe you've got it wrong, did you think of that? Maybe the victims were in some kind of sex ring.'

'I don't think so. I've also got a theory that Marie Henry found out what was going on, probably from nosing round her father's house. He probably convinced her not to go to the police and to leave the country.'

'OK, but you've yet to convince me of any of this... and you'll have to convince the CPS too. And what's happening about the PA? Bryan's got her, hasn't he? What are you doing about getting her back?'

'We've got uniforms canvassing the area. Bryan's mugshot is out there. It's about all we can do.'

'Have you heard anything more from him?'

Jairus shook his head. 'No, ma'am. He's gone quiet.'

'I find that very strange. Why has he taken her? Surely she's a bargaining tool?'

'No, I think he thinks that she might know something about the other businessmen involved. He's clutching at straws.'

'Then what happens when he realises that she serves no purpose to him? She gets a knife in her?'

'I'm not going to let that happen.'

Napper stared at him for a moment. 'See that it doesn't. Oh, and by the way, Kenneth Shearman is waiting for you in interview room 3. Specifically asked for you.'

Jairus nodded. 'Yeah? OK, I'll go and have a word with him.'

Jairus walked towards the interview rooms, then

stopped dead for a moment, breathed in deeply. There was a dizziness wrapped around his head. It was tiredness mixed with too much caffeine. He wondered about his blood pressure, then pushed the thought from his mind, took another deep breath and pushed open the door to interview room 3.

Kenneth Shearman was sitting at the desk, dressed in a smart dark grey suit. A cup of coffee was on the desk in front of him. He looked worried, nervous. He sat up when Jairus entered the room.

Jairus sat down, leaned back, smiled. 'So, Mr Shearman, what can I do for you?'

Shearman hesitated for a moment, his hand tapping at the desk. 'I...I was wondering how things were progressing...and...well, I was wondering if I was going to be charged.'

'At this moment in time, we have no concrete evidence that you've done anything wrong. We have only your statement. I doubt very much we will be charging you with anything.'

Shearman nodded, but his nervousness didn't seem to leave him.

'Is there anything else, because I'm afraid I need to get on?'

There was more than just nervousness in Shearman's eyes, he decided. There was a little fear too. He leaned forward and said, 'Is there something you want to say to me? Has something happened?'

Shearman sighed. 'I don't know if I should say anything or not. I feel like I'm a bit wedged in.'

Jairus ran a hand over his head. 'Mr Shearman, you can talk to me. Whatever has happened, you can tell me.'

Shearman nodded. 'I don't want to start any trouble...'

'Trust me. Just say what you want to say.'

'Very well...do you remember when I was last here? I was interviewed by one of your colleagues? A female detective?'

'Yeah.'

'Well, she took me through the station, and we ended up at an office, but when she went in, there were two policemen in uniforms talking in the room. Well...you see, this is difficult.'

Jairus rubbed his eyes. 'Just tell me. It's OK.'

'I recognised one of the policemen. The one sitting on the right.'

Jairus had a sinking feeling, quicksand soaking his skin with its coolness. 'In what way did you recognise this policeman? I don't understand what you mean.'

'I mean...I believe that the policeman I saw that day was one of the men at the dinner I attended at Braxton House.'

Jairus was silent for a while, allowing Shearman's statement to settle. 'You believe? That's quite an accusation.'

'I know. I know it is. I've been going over it in my mind ever since.'

Jairus leaned forward. 'So, think for a moment, be sure...did you see him at the dinner?'

Shearman sighed, looked away for a moment, then nodded. 'I'm sure.'

Jairus got to his feet. 'I'll be back in a minute.'

Once outside the interview room, Jairus leaned his back against the wall and put his face in his hands and let out a pained breath. He lowered his hands and made sure no one was watching, then strode off down the hall and up the stairs. On the way he pinched a couple of framed photographs of other high ranking officers. Then he slipped into Napper's office and found the holiday snap Warren had previously kept on his desk. Luckily for him, Napper had put it to one side. With the framed photographs tucked under his right arm, he slipped the family snapshot of Warren and family into his jacket pocket.

Jairus returned to the interview room and put the two framed photographs on the desk, making sure Shearman had a good view of them both. 'The man you recognised should be one of these men,' Jairus said and tapped both photographs.

The businessman looked between the two pictures, frowned and looked up at Jairus. 'No, it's not either of those men. I'm sorry, I was sure it was him...'

'Did he have thick dark hair?'

Shearman shook his head. 'No...he's got light brown hair...a bit thin on top, I think.'

Jairus rubbed his jaw and closed his eyes for a moment. A knot had formed in his stomach. He took a long deep breath and pulled out the photograph of Warren and his family and pushed it across the table. 'Mr Shearman, is this the man?'

Immediately he saw the photograph, Shearman looked up to Jairus, his eyes wide. 'That's him. That's the man. He was at Burgess' house...'

Jairus held up a hand. 'Listen, Mr Shearman...I need you to do me a favour...I need you to forget about this for a while.'

'Forget about it?'

'I promise you I'm going to look into this matter and I won't rest until I've found out exactly what's going on.'

'You understand I'm not saying he's done anything wrong...just that he was there.'

Jairus stood up. 'Yeah, I understand. Trust me, I'm going to get to the bottom of this.'

CHAPTER 29

Ten minutes after he saw Kenneth Shearman off, and reassuring him again, then splashing water in his tired eyes, Jairus stormed through the building looking for DS Moone. He'd called him a couple of times, but there had been no answer.

Jairus was wired. He sat in the incident room for a few minutes, trying to think, to put some kind of plan of action together, but nothing came to him. He looked down at his right leg and saw it was vibrating, jittering up and down manically. He tried to calm himself. Where the bloody hell was Moone?

Then a few seconds later his mobile was ringing. It was Moone, so he walked back along the corridor, answered it and asked him to hang on while he went down to the car park.

'Where have you been?' Jairus asked, holding the phone tight to his ear.

'Doing follow-ups. Why?'

'What's been going on with Warren lately?'

There was a pause on the other end. 'I'm not sure. Trouble at home, I think.'

'You sure you don't know anything more than that?'

'Scout's honour.'

'You weren't even in the bloody scouts.'

'Look, what's going on?'

Jairus walked down the ramp, away from a couple of uniforms who had stepped out of the station. 'I've just been talking to Kenneth Shearman. He's managed to identify one of the men at the dinner with him at Burgess' place.'

'Go on.'

Jairus lowered his voice. 'Commander Warren.'

'Bollocks.'

'He's sure. After chatting to him, I'm sure. It makes sense. The Commander has been acting very strange lately. I mean, you think about it...he put me on this, fought for me to be put on this. Why?'

There came a groan from Moone on the other end of the phone.

'What is it, Pete?' Jairus asked.

'Shortly after all this started, Warren came to me and tried to buy me. Wanted me to keep a close eye on you. Wanted me to feed him info in exchange for a change in rank.'

'Why the bloody hell didn't you tell me?'

'I don't know. I'm sorry I didn't. I just assumed he was worried about his decision, worried you were going to do something reckless again.'

Jairus felt the knot tighten, but now it was followed by a surge of anger. 'We need to talk to Warren. Where's he living?'

'Er...not sure. I'll try and call him.'

'Call his wife too. Then call me back when you locate him.'

Kate Roberts was sat up with her back against the wall, watching the man with the knife pacing the floor, looking at his watch every now and again, his eyes even more crazy than before. His mumbling and mania seemed to have increased since he went out and came back again. She was scared. Terrified. The little hope she had that the police would suddenly be knocking on the door was almost gone. He stared at her when she began to whimper and cry, but she couldn't help it. The only food she'd had in the last few hours was a takeaway burger, and she had found it hard to consume, the sickness having long since gripped her throat and stomach. He brought her bottles of water and that's about all she could keep down. Her eyes were puffy and her head hurt from all the crying.

'He's not leaving much choice!' the man groaned and turned to her, his eyes burning. 'Does he want me to do it? That's it! He wants me to do it, then they'll have an excuse to shoot me. They'll come in here and blast me away. They're all in it. The fucking bastards. They're all Masons, all worshipping the Devil. The fuckers are after me.'

Then he rushed to her and she flinched as he squatted beside her, his eyes pleading with her to understand. 'I don't want to have to do it. You know that, don't you? I mean, you'll be giving yourself to something higher than yourself if it...if I have to. You understand that, don't you?'

She nodded, frightened of questioning his mad words.

He smiled a little, patted her shoulder. 'They have to be stopped. If they think they can help Satan take over, then they've got a big fucking surprise coming.'

She mumbled into her gag, trying one last desperate attempt to communicate with him. He looked at her, stared at her for a few moments, examining her like she was a puppy. Eventually his hand dragged the gag from her mouth and she gasped.

'What were you saying?' he asked, waiting, his eyes growing darker.

'I was…I was trying to ask you about Satan.'

He frowned. 'What about Satan?'

She kept herself in check, managed to stop herself from whimpering. 'Do you really believe they all believed…or worshipped Satan?'

'Yes. Yes, of course they did. That's what it was all about! I thought you understood now.'

She nodded. 'I do. I mean…it all makes sense now.'

'They were taking the girls to use them as sacrifices to Satan. That's what they did to…' He winced, looked down and nodded for a moment. When he looked up, there were tears in his eyes. 'That's what they did to Kelly. We were going to be so happy together.'

She smiled sadly. 'How long had you two been together?'

'Nearly…well, for as long as I can remember. I used to see her every day. Through my window.'

'You must have loved her so much.'

He coughed, more tears trickled from his eyes. He wiped his eyes with his sleeve. 'I did. I still do.'

'So…' She took a deep breath. 'How do we find them? These men? The ones that killed Kelly?'

He looked at her for a moment, blankly. Then a smile stretched his stubble-covered face. 'I've got that under control. The police are doing it for me. I've got them in the palm of my hand, you see? They have to do what I say.'

'Why?'

'If they don't, then you…' He stopped speaking and stood up quickly. He looked angry, then sad and wiped his face again. 'I can't talk to you. Not about this.'

'Please don't kill me.' She put all the pleading she could in her voice. 'Don't sacrifice me like they did to Kelly.'

He stared at her. From the corner of her eye she could see the knife trembling in his hand. She thought of what the pain would be like, and was about to beg for her life when he left the room without another word and slammed the door behind him.

It was well into the afternoon when Moone swung his car by the front of the station and picked up Jairus. He climbed in and Moone roared them up Hertford Road, neither of them saying anything for a while. Jairus was watching the world rip past, life flashing briefly before him, bodies on the street doing their thing. He thought about Kate Roberts for a moment, wondering what she was going through. Then he turned to look at Moone. His eyes were fixed on the road, his face looking drawn, his teeth biting at the side of his mouth. Always a telltale sign that Moone was worried.

'You're really worried,' Jairus said.

Moone flashed his eyes at Jairus. 'He's been drinking heavily. Phoning me lots. Jesus…he's been at the end of his tether.'

'Yeah, but it's not your job to look after him.'

'His wife doesn't even know where he is. That's not right, is it?'

Jairus saw the questions, the worry, hanging on Moone's tongue. 'No, I suppose not. She didn't know anything?'

Moone shook his head. 'Nothing. She'd kicked him out ages ago. Said he was drinking, losing his temper a lot. She couldn't put up with it anymore.'

'Yeah, the stress of the job will do that.'

'But it's not just that, is it?'

Jairus shrugged. Then he looked down at his mobile that was ringing. It was Rich Vincent calling him back.

'Yeah, Rich?'

'I've located the phone you wanted. Most of the calls were made from the address that the mobile's registered to. Number 15, Belmont Rise. Of course, I noticed who the mobile's registered to.'

'Yeah? Well, keep it to yourself, will you? Where's Belmont Rise exactly?'

'It's one of those new developments in the East End. Near the Olympic Park. Lot of money poured into those places.'

'Thanks, Rich.' Jairus hung up. 'Head for the Olympic Park.'

Jairus climbed out of the car and looked towards the row of sharp steel and glass boxes that lined the new development. It was like something out of Miami. A path snaked its way through the centre, cutting through a tree-lined park. People walked dogs, sunbathed or sat on park benches. It was an idyllic scene crammed into the centre of London's greyness.

Moone climbed out and rubbed his head. 'Which building is his?'

Jairus pointed to the enormous billboards announcing that the buildings were yet to be lived in. 'They've yet to be sold. It must be on this side.'

They jogged along the tree-lined street, their eyes climbing up the floors, trying to see into the glass of each apartment. Jairus found the right street, then they ran round the back where the entrances were located. Each solid block of steel and white stone had a massive set of glass doors. They slid open, letting Jairus and Moone into a large airy foyer.

The pressed all the buttons on a keypad on the wall next to the mail boxes. Jairus saw one button had no name next to it and kept pressing it.

'I'm feeling very uneasy about this,' Moone said, his eyes burning out to Jairus.

Jairus patted his back as a female voice croaked from the intercom, asking who was there.

Jairus held up his ID to a camera that was positioned high above them. 'We're policemen. We need to get inside.'

After a few seconds, another set of glass doors clicked open, and they walked quickly towards the lifts. All the way up in the lift, Moone was fiddling with his finger, tapping his leg, breathing hard. Like Jairus, he had a bad feeling crawling over him. Jairus kept seeing cut up bodies, heads on poles.

The lift doors opened, revealing a long narrow hallway, metal doors on either side. Jairus stormed forward, his head turning to take in the numbers, seeing the comical doormats, the worn trainers left outside.

He found the right door and banged on it, looking over at Moone who was doing everything but bite on his nails. All the late nights, all the stress appeared over him like a blanket. The light greyness of his eyes had turned to coal black.

Jairus bashed the door again, then leaned his face close to it. 'Commander Warren? Are you there?'

There was no response from inside the apartment. Suddenly the sound of a small snapping bark came from halfway up the hallway and a young man and woman, who had a tiny puff of white fur running round their feet, stared at them.

'You seen the man who lives here recently?' Jairus asked, raising his ID.

They both shook their heads, looked at each other blankly. The young man said, 'No, don't think I've ever seen him. Is something wrong?'

'No, you can take your dog for a walk.' Jairus watched them hesitate, then pull their ball of fluff back to the exit. He looked at Moone. 'Call him.'

Moone took out his phone and dialled Warren's number. Jairus pressed his ear to the door.

'I think I can hear ringing.'

Moone dragged a hand down his face. 'Shit. They've killed him, haven't they?'

Jairus turned away from him and lifted his leg and punched his shoe at the door. Moone joined him and they both battered the door for a few minutes until the lock seemed to give. Jairus turned sideways and shunted the door until it swung inwards and they found themselves looking into an open-plan flat. Wood floors stretched on towards a white and chrome kitchen that spread across one corner. The living area sat in front of it, just a little way from the large glass windows that looked down on the park beneath.

Jairus walked across the floor, hearing his steps, and Moone's, echo around the ceiling. He walked round the kitchen and stopped dead. He was looking along a narrow hallway. There was a skylight halfway along it. Jairus began jogging towards the shape hanging from the skylight. He stopped a foot from the figure, which was hanging limply and pale in front of him. He reached out a hand, then stopped himself.

'Oh...fuck...shit.'

Jairus swung round to see Moone at the far end of the room, just a silhouette against the sun. 'Yeah, I know, it's bad.'

Moone took a couple of steps closer. 'Why the fuck...I was meant...oh shit.'

Jairus watched Moone back up against the wall, then slip down it. He looked at his watch, then up at the lifeless body of Commander Warren. 'I'm going to look for a note.'

Jairus ducked and went further down the hall where he saw the master bedroom, a second smaller bedroom, and then a large plush bathroom. He looked around for a while, but found no note, but did find a laptop. He stared at it for a moment, trying to decide on the best course of action. The Commander was cold. Nothing was going to help him now. But people knew they were in the building, there was a timeline to think of. They needed to make the call soon, but as soon as they did they would have the force crawling over everything. He didn't know how much power the person orchestrating it all had; were they in fact a high-up Freemason and police officer?

Jairus snapped on some gloves and carefully picked up the laptop and began walking down the hallway towards Moone who looked up from his hands on hearing Jairus' steps. 'I was meant to meet him the other night...he sounded pretty fucked-up... but I didn't...'

Jairus crouched down and patted his shoulder. 'It's not your fault, Pete. He was obviously up to his neck in all this shit. It was going to end badly for him either way.'

Moone spied the laptop under his arm. 'What're you doing with that?'

'Warren's laptop. I'm going to take it to Rich.' Jairus stood up and started walking.

'Hang on, watch about protocol? We've got to call this in.'

Jairus turned to him. 'Think about it. Chances are whoever has been pulling the strings here has had Commander Warren in their pocket. That means they've got quite a bit of power and influence. They obviously put pressure on Warren to get me to head this investigation.'

Moone shrugged. 'Why would they do that?'

'They're playing games, amusing themselves. Whoever they are, they're wealthy, quite powerful, and bored, mentally disturbed, and have an absolute hatred for the Freemasons.'

Moone followed Jairus back to the front door. 'But we've still got to call it in.'

'Give me ten minutes, then call it in. This is a suicide, not a murder. Either way, they'll neatly file it away. I need to see his laptop. I'll get it back here as quick as I can.'

Moone turned and looked into the apartment, then back at Jairus. 'OK. You've got ten minutes.'

'I know,' Jairus said and left the apartment.

CHAPTER 30

He'd called ahead and talked to a tired-sounding Rich Vincent. There were piles of work building up the IT specialist said, and sounded even more stressed that Jairus had something urgent for him. Jairus promised him that he would owe him a big favour. Rich had sighed and told him to hurry the fuck up.

Jairus headed into the IT cave and put the laptop on Rich's desk. Vincent adjusted his ponytail and wheeled himself towards the laptop.

'Gloves,' Jairus said and watched Vincent raise his eyebrows, then snap a pair of latex gloves on.

'Why do I get a feeling this isn't exactly kosher?'

Jairus put a finger to his nose, then pointed to the laptop. 'Can you download all the history on there? I need to get it back where it belongs.'

Rich frowned, then opened the laptop and turned it on. 'Yeah, I can do that.'

'What about the password?'

Rich laughed. 'Not a problem.'

Within a couple of minutes, Rich swore and pushed himself back from his desk. He pointed at the laptop. 'You're having me on, right? Philip Warren? That's another Philip Warren, right? It's not your man, Warren?'

'No, it's another Philip Warren.'

Rich looked at him for a moment. 'Oh shit. Shit,

shit.'

'We haven't got much time.' Jairus checked his watch and realised that the force would be crawling all over his apartment by now. He'd had a text from Moone telling him he was calling it in. That was twenty minutes ago. It would take him another twenty minutes to get back there with the laptop.

After a few minutes, Rich slapped his hands together. 'I've got it all. You better go. And I never saw it.'

'Deny everything,' Jairus said, stuffed the laptop under his arm and stormed out.

Jairus arrived back at the scene behind an incident response car that he'd ordered to clear the way for him. The laptop was in an evidence bag beside him. As soon as Jairus had parked he spotted Moone standing outside the building smoking a cigarette. It was a long time since he'd seen Moone puffing away. That meant things were bleak in his head. He saw his colleague nod to him and crouch down and pick up an evidence bag with something silver and square inside that looked very much like a laptop to Jairus.

'Here,' Moone said and came close to the passenger window. He slipped the evidence bag inside.

Jairus grabbed it. 'What's this?'

'I thought fast and borrowed a laptop from the neighbours. Swapped it with the real one.'

Jairus gave him Warren's laptop, which Moone slipped inside the bag. 'Did you find anything on it?'

'Won't know until Rich takes a look at the files. Find a note?' Jairus nodded to the building.

'No, but that's not unusual. I better get this to the crime scene manager.'

'How's everything going in there?'

Moone shrugged. 'Not good. It's never good having to deal with one of your own.'

Jairus nodded. 'Yeah, I know. I'm going to get back to the station.'

'Fine.' Moone sloped off towards the scene, and Jairus watched for a moment, before reversing and driving off. Even though his mind kept replaying the image of Warren hanging from the skylight, he decided it was no good focusing on it too much. There was no note left by Warren, which told Jairus that he was ashamed by his recent actions- something else Jairus didn't want to focus too much on. He decided to let the laptop tell him the whole story.

He was confident that the truth was hidden somewhere in the history of the men who had died so far. It had to be there somewhere or he had nothing at all. Then his mind turned to the plan he had put in motion. The only way he knew how to find Holzman, was to poke at the only person who could divulge exactly what it was all about. But he had one more part of his plan to put in place, and it was something that would need all of his persuasive skills. But he was tired, running on empty and not totally sure he could even raise a smile.

Back in the station, the mood was dark everywhere he went, with uniforms nodding to him, reflecting the sullen atmosphere. He stepped back into the incident room just in time to see that DCS Napper had gathered the team together. He slipped in and rested his back against the wall, listening to his boss begin a difficult speech. An investigation into why he had taken his own life would be started, she said, and added that no one was to make any comment to the press until a formal statement was made tomorrow.

Napper talked on for a while, occasionally looking towards Jairus.

She finished up by saying, 'OK, well, we still have work to do, and I'm sure Commander Warren would want to us to carry on doing what we've got to do. Let's get back to work.'

Napper came over to him, so Jairus remained with his back against the wall, arms folded across his chest. 'You and Moone found him, yeah?' she asked, her eyes burrowing into him.

'Yeah, that's right.'

'Why did you go over there?'

Jairus wondered if she had talked to Moone yet. Chances are she hadn't, he decided. 'Moone was trying to get in contact with him, worried about his state of mind. Moone couldn't get hold of him, so we went to his wife. She hadn't heard from him either. They'd gone their separate ways a while back, but the kids wanted to see him. We managed to trace his phone to his apartment and that's all there is to tell.'

She nodded and looked round the room at the rest of the team that had begun to chat, half in shock. 'And there wasn't any note?'

He shook his head.

'Maybe it was stress. Depression...whatever...it happens to coppers all the time.'

'Yeah, I know. Can I get on, boss?'

She held up a hand. 'Hang on. I hear you weren't at the scene when the back-up arrived. What's the story there?'

'Nothing. There was urgent stuff to deal with.'

'Like what?'

'Bryan's family,' Walker interrupted. She stood behind Napper. 'DCI Jairus was helping me locate them.'

'Really?' Napper looked between them. 'And have you found them?'

'Yes, ma'am,' Walker continued. 'I've got them in the family room. Bryan's mother and brother have been living in Spain for the last five years. It's taken a while to get hold of them.'

'Let's go and talk to them,' Jairus said and pulled open the door, allowing Walker to go through first.

'I've got my eye on you, Jairus,' Napper said to his back.

Out in the corridor, not far from the family suite, Jairus turned to Walker. 'Thanks for that. You saved my skin.'

She nodded, but looked kind of sad. 'You looked like you were being backed into a corner.'

'You OK?'

She looked him straight in the eyes. 'No, can't say I am. I can't believe Warren is gone. Why did he do it?'

Jairus didn't have time for questions and answers. 'I don't know. Maybe we'll never know.'

'And how comes you left Moone to deal with it?'

He sighed. 'Don't get like Napper, Walker. I just had other stuff to deal with. Like several murders.'

She nodded. 'OK. Let's go and talk to Bryan's family.'

As Walker was about to open the door to the family room, Jairus touched her arm. 'Listen, Ally, I'm going to need you to do me a big favour.'

'I thought I just did you a big favour.'

'Yeah, but I'm talking a massive favour.'

She rolled her eyes. 'What?'

'I'll tell you after we talked to these two,' Jairus said and pulled open the door.

Sitting at the desk was a plump curly-haired blonde in a light blue dress and a younger man in a blue linen shirt. The woman was deeply tanned and the room smelt of coconut oil.

'Mrs Macintyre?' Jairus said.

'Hello, yes, that's me,' the woman said, looking rather concerned.

Jairus nodded to the young man and sat near him. 'I appreciate you coming in. It took us a while to find you.'

'Yeah, it was my old neighbour, June, who got hold of me and said you were looking for me. You're trying to find Bryan, that right?'

Jairus smiled. 'I'm afraid so.'

'What's he done now?' the young man said.

'You're Bryan's brother, Duncan?' Jairus asked.

'That's right. Look, we don't have much to do with Bryan anymore. Last time I saw him was when I went to Devon to visit him in prison. He's been getting into more and more trouble. We've done all we can to help him, but he just throws it back into our faces.'

Jairus nodded. 'I understand this is tough on you all, but I still need to ask you some questions. Was Bryan religious at all?'

Duncan gave a strange sort of laugh. 'Our dad was the religious one and tried to brainwash us all with it.'

'He was always going on about God,' Mrs Macintyre said, frowning.

Duncan sat forward and touched his mum on the hand. 'Why don't you go and get a drink, Mum. I can handle this.'

Jairus turned to Walker. 'Yeah, my colleague will get you a drink, Mrs Macintyre. Can you, DI Walker?'

Walker flashed him a stern look, then went over to Mrs Macintyre and escorted her out of the room.

Once Jairus was alone with Duncan, he said, 'Your brother, with the help of an accomplice, has been torturing and killing businessmen.'

Duncan closed his eyes for a second. 'Jesus... Bryan...' Then he looked at Jairus. 'I knew he was wired a bit wrong, but... I mean, why's he doing it?'

'We believe he was after revenge...still is.'

'Revenge for what?'

'Have you heard of a young woman called Kelly Leigh?'

Duncan's brow creased up. 'Kelly Leigh? Yes, of course I've heard of her. She went missing a while ago. What's this got to do with Bryan?'

'Did your brother ever talk about Kelly?'

'Talk about her? Yes, nonstop sometimes. But that was way back. Years ago. We lived up the road from her for years. He'd watch her out the window. So... do you think Bryan had something to do with her vanishing like that?'

Jairus stood up. 'No, but I'm trying to get inside your brother's head, to understand why he's doing the things he's doing.'

'I'd say you were onto a loser. Bryan's mind has never worked like everyone else's. He's lived in a fantasy world most of his life.'

Jairus stared at Duncan. 'Do you think he could have formed some kind of connection with Kelly?'

'I don't know if he ever talked to her.'

'No.' Jairus turned round and leaned his back against the window. 'I mean, in his head. All those years ago. Could she be like a linchpin in his mind?'

Duncan nodded. 'I suppose. He used to stand at the window and watch her walking by. It's funny, but our father being the religious nut that he was, used to join him at the window and say that she was an angel. That Bryan could never touch a girl like that, that she'd never want to be with him because he was a little sinner.'

Jairus stared at Duncan for a moment, then closed his eyes, picturing it all, almost seeing Kelly Leigh walking by. He wondered how long his obsession had been carried with him, and then it all clicked into place. Kelly had become an intricate part of his mindset, the one solid concept he carried with him. The taboo. The forbidden fruit he couldn't have.

Jairus put out his hand so that Duncan could shake it, which he did, although he looked confused.

'Thank you,' he said. 'You've been a great help.'

Jairus walked out of the family room and along the corridor and stopped when he heard Walker talking in an office a little way along. He looked in and knocked on the door frame. Walker looked around, and so did Mrs Macintyre who was sitting in a chair with a tea in her hands.

'Can I borrow my colleague, Mrs Macintyre?' Jairus asked.

The woman smiled at him. Walker followed him along the corridor where he stopped her at the staircase.

'Did you find anything out?' Walker asked.

'Kelly Leigh is a figment of his imagination.' Jairus rubbed his hands together.

'But she's real.'

'Yeah, but not the version in his head. The Kelly Leigh in his head is an angel, something to be worshipped. He idolised her, loved her. Imagine what that's done to his mind now that he knows all those terrible things were done to her.'

'What are we looking at?'

'I think Bryan's a lot more dangerous than I first thought. His mind is splitting open. I think Holzman must have spotted that in him. Somehow Holzman recognised that side of him and used him. All he had to do was to tell him what had happened to her. He wound him up and let him go.'

'Bloody hell. What now then? Where is he? We need to get him away from Kate Roberts.'

Jairus nodded. 'Yeah, but first I need you to do me that favour.'

Walker gave him that look he hated, and the unimpressed sigh. 'What do you want me to do?'

He lowered his voice, got closer to her ear. 'I need you to go into Napper's office and call this number.'

She looked down at the card he was putting in her hand.

'Hopkins? MI5? You're taking the piss.'

'I wish I was,' he said and looked about the corridor. 'I need you to call him and say you're Napper's PA or whatever, and get him to come over tomorrow. Give him some bullshit about needing a meeting with him about Holzman. Try and get him here around lunchtime.'

She looked down at the card. 'I can't do this, Jay. I can't phone a bloody MI5 wanker. What the bloody hell are you planning to do?'

'It won't come back on you,' he said. 'I promise. We need to find Holzman. It's either this or he's a ghost. Do you want him to get away?'

Walker shook her head. 'Bloody hell...no, but...'

'Come on, she'll probably be off in a meeting right now.' Jairus led the way back up to the incident room, where they both slipped inside and hung about the whiteboard for a while.

Napper was in her office talking on the phone, writing something down. Jairus opened a file and watched her.

'What if she stays there for ages?' Walker said,

pretending to look over the whiteboard.

'She'll go in a minute.'

As soon as Napper put down the phone, she collected together some files and grabbed her bag, then awkwardly made her way out the office. She looked over at Jairus for a moment as she opened the incident room door. He nodded to her, then she was gone.

'Right,' Jairus said, nodding to the door.

'What about this lot?'

Jairus looked round the room at the bodies sitting at the computers, or on their phones. He rubbed his face and nodded for Walker to head to Napper's office. Walker moved towards the door, while Jairus slapped his hands loudly together, bringing all the attention to him. The team looked round at him expectantly, so he pointed to Bryan's photograph on the whiteboard. 'Right, Bryan Macintyre...how are we on him, people?'

DC Carr said, 'Still got uniforms doing door-to-door. We've spread the area wider, but still no luck. He could be anywhere.'

Jairus shook his head. 'No, he's still in Enfield. He needs to be near the memory of Kelly Leigh, the places he used to see her. Someone's got to spot him sooner or later.'

From the corner of his eye, Jairus could see Walker in Napper's office, picking up the receiver and dialling the number. 'What about the Danny Charles' crime scene? Anything there?'

'Nothing useful,' Carr said. 'Whoever killed him, and the cleaner, were careful. Cleaned up after killing the girl, then waited until Charles came home. Garrett confirmed that the same type of tools were used, but were not an exact match.

'I did find something interesting in his diary that

his agent sent over,' Carr added. 'It's a diary from last year, but on the 5th of August Danny Charles has written *security* and underlined it.'

Jairus smiled. 'Could be something.'

'I was thinking, what if that's how they found out about his security systems? He gets worried about the security of the place. Then gets someone in to look it over and that person gives the information to our killers.'

'Yeah, but that means Danny Charles would have to be particularly worried about his security. Maybe Holzman and Burgess arranged for the place to be broken into at some point in the past. Check it out.'

He heard the door of Napper's office click and saw Walker slipping out. She gave him the thumbs-up, so he turned back to the team.

'OK, right, get back to those phones, people. Call me with any developments.' Jairus followed Walker out of the room and stopped her in the corridor. 'So, what happened?'

'He's coming here at twelve tomorrow. I had to say that she was taking him out for lunch to discuss the whole Holzman business.'

Jairus squeezed her shoulder and grinned. 'Nice one, Walker.'

'So what happens when Hopkins turns up here expecting to see Napper?'

'Let me worry about that.'

CHAPTER 31

WPC Karen Small Parked up from the shops on the Hertford Road. She took out a wet-wipe from the glove box and wiped the sweat from her brow. Someone had turned up the heat considerably. She felt far too stifled in her stab vest as she climbed out of the incident response car and walked to the newsagents. She needed a large bottle of water, her mouth was so dry. She was only a couple of feet from the shop when she spotted the man. He was coming out of the fried chicken place carrying a bag of food, his mouth moving, muttering to himself. He looked grotty, with greasy hair and a face covered in brown stubble. Then his eyes fell on her, then darted away. She noticed him walking faster. What really bothered her was the thick army style jacket he was wearing in the blistering summer heat.

She watched him pass, a flicker of recognition biting at her as she hurried back to the incident car. She slipped inside and the heat swamped her as she looked through the information she had been given a couple days ago. Faces to look out for. She picked out the black and white image of Bryan Macintyre. If it was him, she decided, he looked very different. In the photograph there was no stubble and the hair was shorter, but even so she had an inkling it could be him. She started the car, a little disappointed to be heading away from her bottle of water, and broke her way through the traffic. She crawled along towards Green Street on the left, keeping an eye open for him, praying she hadn't scared him off. She was about to pull away when she spotted the army coat hurrying off halfway down Green Street. She drove slowly after him and saw him cross the park, going diagonally over the grass football pitch and past the cemetery. She parked and began jogging after him. She got on her radio and called it in, describing the suspect and asking for back-up.

Then she slowed down as she saw the man come to a stop. He turned his head and took her in, staring, seeming to look questioningly at her. She looked into the staring eyes as he put down the bag of food. He kept looking at her, waiting.

She decided to step closer, her hand gripping her baton. 'Excuse me, sir, can I ask your name and where you're going?'

He stayed still, staring blankly at her.

'Sir, did you hear me?'

He nodded, or at least she thought he did. 'Where do you live?'

The man moved his hand and pushed it inside his jacket. Karen Small took out her baton when she saw the knife come out, shaking in his hand.

'Now, don't be stupid. You don't want to use that. Put it down and we can talk properly.' She shook the baton and released it to its full length. The man kept staring at her.

Then he spoke in a broken voice.

She asked him to repeat what he'd said, praying for back-up to appear.

'I said, are you one of them?'

'One of who?'

The man kept looking at her, staring, seeming to weigh up the situation. Then he put the knife back into his jacket, spun round and ran. He headed for the fence surrounding the park, and leapt for it. He pulled himself up and over and into the cemetery, and WPC Small ran after him.

He was standing on the grass on the other side of the wall, glaring at her, with the knife back in his hand. She elected to stay put. No way to get over that wall without him stabbing her in the leg in the process. She was about to say something, to keep him talking, but he heard the approaching sirens, backed away and ran into a wooded part of the park.

There had been little on the TV to keep his mind off things, so Marsland had turned it off and just lain there. He was still weak, and he was not allowed to move because of the stitches. His guts felt as if they might spew from his body if he turned the wrong way.

A dark-haired nurse had come to take his blood pressure and temperature, and so he watched her for a moment, going about her business, paying no real attention apart from an occasional smile. They were rushed off their feet, and it was understandable that he didn't get much conversation time. It was strange, he thought, how after all this, he wanted to talk to somebody.

He looked down at his hands as the nurse left the room.

It was a few seconds before he noticed that somebody was standing in the doorway. He looked into the man's eyes and smiled. For the longest time he hadn't felt himself properly smile. It burnt his cheeks, but felt good.

Dylan, his son, stood in the doorway, a slight smile

coming onto his face. He came further into the room. He was dressed in a check shirt and jeans. He looked much older to Marsland, sort of world weary.

'Come in, Dylan,' Marsland said, pointing to the chair by the bed.

Dylan nodded and sat in the chair and looked about the room. 'I take it they're looking after you all right?'

'Yes, of course,' Marsland said, trying to sit up. 'How've you been?'

'Not bad.'

'Good. How's Erin?'

Dylan smiled a little, and Marsland saw a sudden awkwardness fill his eyes.

'We got married, actually.'

'When? Why...'

'It was just Erin and me. We ran off to Vegas.'

Marsland nodded, feeling more lonelier than ever. Dylan wasn't even looking at him really, not for any length of time. 'I can't say I blame you. I wish me and your mother had done that.'

Dylan lowered his head a little, fiddling with his hands. 'So, you're all right then?'

'Yes, I'm fine. You don't have to worry about me.'

Dylan's head shot up. 'Oh yeah, you're fine aren't you? You only got yourself stabbed. When are you going to stop poking your nose into other peoples' business?'

'I was just trying to help...'

'Help? It didn't help...' Dylan stopped talking, then stood up and blew out a breath.

'I'm really sorry, Dylan.' Marsland watched his son walk over to the door, his eyes seeming to look towards the window.

'Yeah? But she's still gone.'

'I know. And there's not a day that goes by that I

don't think about it. I know I'm to blame.'

'Yes, you are.' Dylan huffed then looked briefly at his dad. 'Sorry. I shouldn't have said that.'

'But you're right. Listen, where are you staying?'

'A hotel.'

'Why don't you stay at my house?'

Dylan shrugged. 'I'm Ok. When do you get out of here?'

'A few days. Maybe two, I don't know really.'

'Maybe we can do something when you get out?'

'That'd be great, Dylan.' Marsland felt his smile burning into his cheeks again.

'Good.'

'There's just a couple of things I need to sort out when I'm on my feet again.'

Dylan swung round to him. 'And what's that then? Poking your nose in again?'

'I've just got someone I need to go and talk to...'

'Yeah, whatever. Call me when you've woken up to real life.' Dylan stormed out of the room, leaving Marsland to call out to him in vain.

Jairus stopped his car across from the park and walked towards the huddle of police officers that had gathered round the bench near the entrance. He showed his ID and watched the uniforms move back, leaving a young and blonde female constable sitting alone on the bench. She looked up from the cup of takeaway tea she was sipping.

Jairus turned to the uniforms. 'Go on, people, get knocking on doors.'

Then he sat next to her, smiled a little. 'What's your name?'

'Karen.' She sat back a little.

'DCI Jairus.'

'Yes, I know. I'm sorry, sir, but I lost him.'

He patted her shoulder. 'Yeah, but don't worry. He probably had a knife.'

'He did.'

'Then better you lost him than get stabbed. Where did you see him first?'

She gestured up the road. 'Along Hertford Road. He was coming out of the fried chicken shop.'

'And he had just bought some food?'

'Yes, he had a carrier bag of food.'

Jairus stood up and looked towards the Hertford Road, shading his hand from the sun. 'So, chances are he was heading home.'

'I would think so.' She sipped her tea. 'But God knows where he lives.'

'Do you remember which way he was going when he left the chicken shop? Was he heading straight ahead, to his left, or what?'

'Straight ahead I suppose.'

'So, towards Brick Lane?'

'Yes, I reckon.' She stood up.

'Come on,' he said and nodded for her to follow him.

'Where do you think he's gone?' Karen asked when they eventually reached the junction of Green Street and the Hertford Road.

Jairus looked towards the chicken shop, blocking out the grind of traffic and the young group of girls in skimpy clothing chattering past. Then he looked over to the road leading into the Brick Lane Estate. 'Now, when people are lost, they usually go left...and similarly we know that if someone wants to shake someone off their tail, they'll go in the completely opposite direction.'

'So you think he was originally headed over the hill

there into the Brick Lane Estate?'

'Yeah, maybe. You got your notebook handy?'

'Sure.' Karen handed him her notebook and a pen.

Jairus scribbled something down, then ripped out the page and handed it to her, along with the pen and notebook. 'There's a shop called Keith's back there, next to the continental supermarket. I need you to go and get the stuff on that list.'

She looked at the piece of paper. 'Really?'

'Yeah, really.'

She nodded, then hurried off towards the shops. Jairus was left alone, staring over the hill, able to see the roofs of the houses over the crest. He knew there were a warren of roads and council houses, most of which the occupants had bought at a cheap price back in the late eighties. And there was a new block of flats. Bryan could be hiding anywhere and going to door-to-door would take too long and would give him time to run.

Jairus took out his mobile and rang Walker's desk.

'DI Ally Walker.'

'Hi, it's me. What have you got on Bryan Macintyre? Any connection to the Brick Lane Estate?'

'Hang on.' He heard Walker tapping away at her keyboard before her voice came back on the line.

'Only thing I can find is that he worked as a labourer on the houses they built right at the end of Brick Lane, right on the site of the old school, Suffolk's School.'

'Thanks.'

'Any good?'

'Not sure. I'll tell you later.' Jairus ended the call and put away his phone in time to see PC Small coming towards him with a carrier bag. She looked a little concerned by the contents of the bag, but passed it to him anyway.

'What exactly are you planning to do with all that stuff?' She nodded to the bag he was looking inside of.

'I don't think I should tell you,' he said and put on a smile. 'You stay here. If you don't hear from me in twenty minutes, then you better send some uniforms after me.'

'Hang on...'

Jairus ignored her and carried on up Brick Lane, his eyes taking in the jewellery shop on his left, and the grocers that used to be the first video shop in the area. Happy days, he thought to himself and walked up the hill, looking down at the grimy train tracks and the houses next to them. A jumble of houses sat to his right, and the small and compact Brick Lane estate, made up of several dilapidated low-rise tower blocks. He kept on moving, travelling the length of Brick Lane, focusing on the distant yellow brick three-storey town houses.

Jairus gripped the carrier bag tightly in his hand, ignoring a group of kids in school uniform kicking a football across the street. Then he entered the small area of townhouses. A big sign told him that some were still available to buy.

He went up to the first door and hammered on it, then the next one, and the one after that. Soon people were coming out of the houses, complaining.

Jairus hammered on the last door, but no one came to see what all the fuss was all about.

Kate Roberts had heard the sound of Bryan's boots thudding across the floor and around the flat, had heard him swearing, muttering. Several times he had pushed open the door and stared at her, then shut it again. A few minutes later he had come in again and stared through a chink in the curtains at the street, still muttering.

She mumbled through her gag, but he didn't even look at her. He had said that he was going out for food, but now he was acting even crazier than before. She could not help but weep.

Then there was the hammering at the front door. She thought she also heard a voice calling Bryan's name.

The door opened, Bryan was standing there sweating, red-faced, the knife in his hand. He was crying. He wiped his face with the back of his hand then rushed her, yanked her up, dragged her into the next room and threw her to the floor.

'Oh God, please help me now,' Bryan sobbed and fell to his knees.

Then came pounding from downstairs, followed by a smashing sound. More footsteps rose up through the house and a man appeared at the top of the stairs, a carrier bag gripped in his hand.

Bryan got up quickly and pulled the gun from his jacket, pointing it at the man. Then the barrel swung round and Kate closed her eyes. She opened them again, unable to control her tears as the black hole was inches from her head.

'Let her go, Bryan,' the man said, that's when Kate realised it was the detective.

'How can I? She's the only thing I've got.'

The detective stepped forward, looking into Kate's eyes, nodding to her, then holding up the carrier bag. 'I've got what you wanted here, Bryan. You told me to find out who the other men are and I did. I managed to uncover a massive cult, a ring of Satanists that kidnapped girls and sacrificed them.'

'You're lying.'

The tall detective gestured to the bag, lifted up and

opened it. 'It's all in here, Bryan. All the information on the bastards that did those terrible things to Kelly and the other girls. Like I said before, I'm just trying to help you.'

Kate saw the gun wavering, Bryan shaking and staring at the bag.

'Show me,' Bryan said, his voice rising higher.

The detective reached in and took out an envelope bulging with paper and put it by his foot. 'Here it is, Bryan. All the information you need.'

There came a laugh from Bryan, a sickening empty laugh. 'Kick it to me.'

'Hang on,' the detective said and grabbed something from the bag, pulled it out. Kate watched on, hoping and praying that she would soon be free.

She was confused, watching the detective sprinkling something onto the envelope. Then she realised he had a can of lighter fluid. His hand delved into his jacket pocket and brought out a box of matches. He quickly struck one.

'Don't!' Bryan screamed, then his eyes flashed down at Kate. 'I'll shoot her!'

'Yeah, and I'll burn all this information.' The copper raised his eyebrows, the flame retreating back towards his fingers.

'You do that and I'll shoot her!'

The detective dropped the match onto the envelope. Nothing happened straight away and Bryan watched, mesmerised. Then the flames started up, small at first, then larger, hungrily eating away at the envelope.

'Stop it! Stop it!' Bryan kept moving towards the envelope, then back again, jittering all the time, doing a manic dance.

'Then let her go, Bryan! You can have me as a hostage.' The detective raised his hands as if to surrender.

Bryan looked down her, looked at her bound ankles. He took out his knife and cut the ties.

Kate Roberts stumbled to her feet and rushed towards the detective, crying again, trying to gulp breaths. The detective pulled the gag from her mouth and took the ties from her hands and squeezed her shoulder. Then she ran for the stairs, her vision blurred by her tears, wanting to look back, but too scared to.

Jairus stamped down on the flames for a few seconds until smoke wafted up from the charred manilla envelope. He looked at the gun now being pointed at him, and the wide staring eyes jumping from his face to the envelope.

'Give it to me!' Bryan shook the gun.

'Careful, Bryan.' Jairus crouched down and carefully picked up the envelope.

'Here, give it to me.'

'First, tell me about Edgar Holzman.'

The gun lowered a little, while Bryan seemed ready to spit. 'He's a liar.'

'Where did you meet him?'

'He came to visit me in prison. Told me he was an uncle of one of the girls and had found out what had happened to Kelly, and the bastard said he could prove that the Freemasons had taken her. Said they controlled the police, and that the only way for them to pay was for us to kill them.'

Jairus stepped closer to him. 'Who's Holzman working for? He's taking his orders from someone.'

'I don't know. I don't know...all I know is they killed her. And they have to pay.'

'Do you know where Holzman might be?'

'No. I don't know...but I'll find him.'

Jairus threw the envelope at Bryan's feet, then watched him crouch down, his hand crawling out to grab it.

He looked in the envelope and ripped out the white pages, each one blank. He looked up at Jairus, shaking the sheets at him. 'What's this? Where's the info? The names?'

'There are no names, Bryan. There is no satanic cult. Holzman used you to kill those businessmen. He set you up. For some reason they wanted to make it look like the girls were used as human sacrifices in a satanic Freemason's ceremony. Whoever is giving Holzman his orders is trying to bring the Freemasons into disrepute.'

'That's not true!'

'It is, Bryan. You killed the men that took Kelly. They're dead. It's over.'

'No, it's not!' The gun was shaking in his hand, the tears pouring down his face.

'You know it's true, Bryan. Think about it. I need to find Holzman, Bryan. Help me.'

Bryan let out a deep painful breath, then jerked the gun round to his jaw, pushing the barrel into his skin.

'Don't do that, Bryan.' Jairus stuck out his hand.

Bryan gritted his teeth. 'What else have I got? I'll go to prison for the rest of my life. Or they'll lock me up in some institute.'

Jairus lowered his hand. Bryan was right, they would stick him in a small, suffocating hole for the rest of his life. Jairus had faced that, and had realised there was no perceivable way he could have survived.

'Don't put the gun there, Bryan. You could end up blowing out only part of your brain and end up breathing through a tube for the rest of your life. The best way is by sticking the gun just behind your ear.'

Jairus mimed it for him.

Bryan took the gun from his jaw, his hand shaking. He pushed it behind his ear, his teeth gritting together, tears streaming down his face, a groan coming from his clenched teeth. Harsh breaths were bursting from his lips. Fingers tightening. Breath. Breath.

A loud howl.

The blast boomed towards Jairus. He flinched. Felt a spit of blood hit his forehead. He watched Bryan slump to the floor, the gun dropping beside him.

He stood there staring for what seemed forever, the ground beneath him seeming to shift, then fall away. He was suddenly looking at himself and then down at the body on the floor.

What had he done?

Even when the armed response officers poured into the house, Jairus remained staring, simply watching them clearing the weapon from Bryan's body. One of the team was shouting, his mouth stretching wide, but Jairus heard nothing from his lips. The gun blast was still ringing in his ears.

It was half an hour later that Jairus found himself in a light blue forensic outfit. They'd bagged up his clothes and took them away, leaving him sitting in the back of a squad car.

The other door opened and DCS Napper joined him, staring at him, looking him up and down. 'You're in one piece, I guess that's something.'

He looked down at himself and then up at her. 'Yeah…I suppose.'

'What the bloody hell happened in there?'

'I was doing my job.'

Napper gave a burst of angry laughter. 'Your job? If you had been doing your job, you would've called for the Armed Response Unit, or anyone for that matter.'

'By then he could've killed her,' Jairus said and looked forward, trying to control the shakes that had begun to ripple through him.

'This'll be looked into,' she said, her voice cooling. 'Did you get a chance to talk to him? Did he tell you anything useful? Please tell me he gave you something?'

Jairus shook his head.

'Oh…that's bloody wonderful. Right, you are going home. You're going to get some sleep.'

He looked at her and saw that she meant it. 'And then what?'

'Like I said, this'll be looked into. Take some leave while I sort this mess out.'

'But I need…'

She pointed a finger at his face. 'You're going home. You're taking some bloody time off. Look at you. You're shaking. Go home. Get drunk. Drink tea, whatever you want to do. But do not turn up for work tomorrow. You got that?'

He nodded and looked down at his hands.

'Right,' she said, grabbed the handle, but stared at him for a moment before she climbed out and left him alone.

CHAPTER 32

With a change of clothes on his back, a mug of coffee in his hand, Jairus felt better. The shaking had ceased a while ago, and now he could think straight.

He sat on his sofa for a few minutes, playing back everything, pushing past the flashes of Bryan with the gun pressed against his skull. He blinked. Sipped some coffee.

He still had Holzman to track down, a task now made harder because Napper had taken him off active duty. Walker was his best bet. He'd have to feed off her, stick close and let her do the official stuff.

Jairus heard his mobile squeal out to him, then pulled his phone from his pocket and looked at it. He frowned as he saw he'd had a text from Ian Pritchard. He opened it and read it, then read it again: 'I need to talk to you. Urgently!'

There was an address under the text, somewhere in deepest, poshest, Islington.

Jairus parked outside the Victorian house in Noel Road, and sat for a moment looking over to number 64. They were much sought-after Victorian houses, each going for a couple of million, at least. He got out and strolled, hands in his pockets, over the road, watching three pigeons pecking at the pavement. He went down the steps that led to the basement and knocked on the shiny blue door, then rang the bell.

It took a couple of minutes for the door to be opened, and for Ian Pritchard to be looking at him through the gap. Jairus huffed when he looked at Pritchard's face; it had obviously been punched and kicked by someone. His eyes were filled with blood, his face bulging, his top lip split open.

'Bloody hell,' Jairus said and entered when Pritchard opened the door wider.

Pritchard, dressed in a thin blue dressing gown over his still bloody shirt, shut the door and slumped onto his dark grey sofa.

Jairus stood in the middle of the open-plan flat. He looked down the end of room and saw the white kitchen and steps leading up to a large garden.

'So, what happened to your face?' Jairus asked and sat at the other end of the sofa.

'You knew this would happen,' Pritchard said and winced. 'Don't pretend you didn't. You were using me to needle someone.'

Jairus showed his open palms. 'Honestly, Ian, I have no idea what's happened. Just tell me what's going on.'

Pritchard turned off his TV and sat back on the sofa. 'I was coming back from having a few drinks last night, early hours of the morning actually. I crossed the park, then got a street away from here and next thing I know someone's grabbing me and shoving me against a wall. Then I'm punched several times in the face, stomach, and I end up on the ground and they start kicking me in the head. They did a lovely job, as you can see.'

'Yeah, but I'm sure you'll get your good looks back. So who did it?'

'Don't know. They were wearing a balaclava. But as

I lay there they whispered in my ear. They said, "Make sure your editor gets your story on the Freemasons and the satanic cult by the end of the week, or else", then he shows me a photograph of my nephew! Fucking hell, what the bloody hell have you got me involved in?'

'You checked in with your nephew?'

'Yes,' Pritchard said and got up and headed down to the kitchen. 'Called my sister this morning. He's fine. They were just making sure I behaved by scaring me.'

Jairus joined him. 'What you going to do?'

'What choice do I have? I'll have to hand it in?'

'And will your editor publish it?'

'I've already had two missed calls from him asking where the story is. I didn't even tell him I was looking into it. So I wonder how he knows?'

Jairus rubbed his face, watching the journalist take the kettle to the sink and fill it up. 'He's getting his own fair share of pressure from someone.'

Pritchard turned round, resting against the sink. 'So who the bloody hell can exert that much pressure? What are we talking about?'

'What are you thinking?' Jairus was building his own picture, but he was curious what conclusion the journalist would make.

'Well, obviously the Freemason aspect keeps coming back to me, and I know that some of the people above my editor are Freemasons.'

'But everything about this whole mess suggests someone is trying to destroy their reputation. Why would they want to publicise the whole satanic worshipping part of it? Someone deep inside the organisation is trying to destroy things, break everything apart. Being one of the Freemasons is how they're orchestrating things. That's how they glean the information they use to blackmail other members into doing what they want.'

'So they've managed to get themselves in a very powerful position.' Pritchard took out a couple of mugs. 'Want a coffee?'

Jairus hardly heard what he said, his eyes were fixed through the glass doors at the far end, and the lawn across from them. He was trying to put a face to the mysterious person who seemed to be pulling all the strings. 'They've managed to get themselves into a powerful position, but I don't think they'll be that high up in the pecking order.'

'OK. How do we find out who they are?'

'There will be a signature.'

'What does that mean?'

'I mean, whoever is orchestrating all this will be there in the details, even the holes, the bits we can only see the outline of. They won't be able to resist leaving their mark. I've probably even met them already.'

'So what do we do now?'

'You do nothing, just stall your editor, tell him you're finishing it all off. I'm in the process of tracking down a very important lead. The one person who might actually lead me to the organiser of all this massacre.'

'Did you want coffee or not?'

Jairus shook his head. He heard his phone but decided to ignore it for the moment. 'No, I've got to go.'

Pritchard saw him to the door, and Jairus could not help but take one more look at his bulging and battered face. He strode back to his car, slipping his mobile from his pocket. He looked at the name coming up. Mr Colora who lived off the back lane where Jairus had his lock-up. Jairus had given him his number in case of an emergency. He didn't bother ringing him back, just started the engine and raced towards Ponders End.

It was early evening by the time he crawled the car down the lane and stopped outside the lock-up. He pushed open the car and looked out at the door, then swore. It was slightly open and the padlock had been cut off. He climbed out and opened up the lock-up. He pulled the light on, and stared round at the furniture, ornaments and books. Nothing seemed out of place.

Then he heard the garden gate behind him squeaking open and turned to see Mr Colora coming towards him. He was a skinny Italian man with a round belly and pockmarked skin.

'It's terrible,' Colora said and threw his hands in the air. 'Did they take anything?'

Jairus hadn't turned his head yet, had not dared look towards the old battered safe. He could see it out the corner of his eye, the big metal box. 'Doesn't look like it. Thanks for calling.'

'That's good news.' Colora smiled.

'Yeah. Did you hear or see anything?'

'No, I'm very sorry. I came out here to clean my car and saw it was open and called you. It's terrible.'

'Yeah, it is,' Jairus said, praying the man would piss off. 'Well, thanks anyway for calling. I'll sort this out.'

'You going to call the police?'

'No, there's no point. Nothing valuable has been taken.'

'Why would they break in?'

'Yeah, that's the question.' Jairus, finding his only course of action now was rudeness, turned and pulled down the door to the lock-up, closing off Mr Colora's view. Jairus listened as he heard Mr Colora shout out a farewell and walk away. Jairus breathed in a couple of times, still seeing the blurry shape of the safe in the corner. Then he walked round the room for a moment, rubbing his jaw and his eyes, bringing himself back round to face the safe, preparing himself for the worst.

The door was open a little. There was no signs of the door being forced. He looked closer, focusing inside, even though by that point he knew that the thieves had succeeded in getting what they had come for. He put his hand in as if he might touch the object that had been secured there for the last year. He stood up and blew out a breath.

Someone had followed him one night, had seen him slip into the lock-up, and decided to investigate. Whoever it was they now had possession of his darkest secret, the one thing that could destroy his career and life.

Jairus stepped back, burning with rage, anger at himself for keeping the object.

He swung round and grabbed the first thing he saw. He snatched up the office chair and hurled it at the wall. It caught and smashed one of Karine's prized ornaments. Jairus bent over, his teeth gritted, breathing fast and heavy. Then he took deeper breaths and calmed himself, focusing in on the task in hand. He had other things to worry about, and would let whoever had taken the contents of the safe contact him.

Tomorrow would be a tough and exhausting day and he would need sleep before he travelled back into the dark once more.

Marsland wanted to get out of bed, even though the wooziness kept wrapping itself round his head. The stabbing had damaged his lower intestines he'd been told, and that meant danger of infection. An IV drip of antibiotics was standing by his bed slowly passing the drugs into his system. The nurses came and went, clocking off to be exchanged with another nurse who was always the complete opposite of the one before. His last nurse had been rotund and had fiery red hair, the next was Indian and short and skinny. They all treated him well and did their jobs professionally. They looked tired though, and so did the doctors who came by and told him about the surgery he had had and the damage and danger the wound had caused. He had hardly been listening, as his mind was fixed on Dylan and the fact that he had stormed out hours ago. Now he was trapped in the sterile room, only a small window to look through that presented him with the cold grey shape of another building. He could only see smoke or steam escaping from a chimney. He listened to the squeak of trolleys and sensible shoes that travelled up and down the corridor. He could hear the nurses talking, swapping stories, or barking orders.

It was a while after trying to read a newspaper, but finding his vision going a little blurry and his eyes trying to shut, that he looked up and thought he saw a woman standing in the doorway. The shape moved away quickly. He sat up a little, then had a sudden thought.

'Jacqui!' he shouted. 'Jacqui?'

He waited for a moment, then heard the tap of shoes coming towards the doorway. He saw her face first of all, her cheeks a little scarlet, her mouth and jaw sullen. She had dolled herself up, and had a light and short grey trench coat wrapped around her. There were spots of rain on her shoulders. He looked round and saw the streaks of rain on the window.

'I'm sorry, I just thought I'd pop in and see you,' she said, her eyes jumping round the room. She seemed to hesitate on the threshold, a slight smile trying to form.

'Come in, sit down.' He pointed at the chair next to the bed.

She came over to the chair and stood for a moment, looking him up and down. 'It's good to see you're alright. I was so worried.'

'Yes, I managed to survive,' he said and laughed or at least tried to. It came out as a huff.

She sat down. 'I can't believe someone stabbed you. Did they catch him?'

'Not yet, but I'm sure they will.'

She rolled her eyes, then lifted her sight to the water jug at his bedside. 'Do you want some water?'

'No, I'm fine. Do you want some?'

She shook her head. 'No. I'm sorry I was so rude to you the last time I saw you.'

'No, don't be silly. I was poking my nose in. I always do that. Look where it gets me. I'm sorry, Jacqui, I shouldn't have been poking my nose in. You're just a person, not someone who's committed a crime and I shouldn't have been nosing about.'

Her face changed. 'I haven't been completely honest with you.'

'You haven't? What do you mean?'

'There's a big part of my life that I hadn't mentioned.'

He nodded. 'You're still married?'

She laughed. 'No, no. There's a part of my life…a huge part of my life that some people seem to have a problem dealing with. Not everyone, but some people.'

'Go on. I'm listening.'

Jacqui opened her trench coat a little and reached

her hand into the thin jumper she wore beneath it. She lifted out a gold cross necklace and let it hang there.

Marsland focused on it, examining the crucifix. 'Oh, right. God.'

She laughed, then nodded. 'God. Yes. I found God a few years ago. Before that I was an awful, judgemental person. I was full of hate. So, so full of…anger…'

'It's OK. I understand.'

She looked up at him, sort of staring. 'I don't think you do. I was so horrible. I think of myself then and the things I thought about doing. Then I went to church one day…I don't know why I went. I hadn't been since a family wedding when I was a teenager. I always hated churches. Then I just saw this church and I thought…why not go in there. So I just sat at the back and I kept staring up at the statue of Jesus on the cross. The blood coming out of his hands. And I talked to God. I asked him what I should do. I wanted him to get rid of all the hate I had in me. I didn't want it anymore. And I got up and left. I felt kind of peaceful then, but it wasn't long before I was full of hate again. But, you know what, days after it was…well, it was as if the hate was fading away. You know what I mean?'

Marsland nodded, unsure of what else to do or say.

She smiled. 'I realised the hate was going. I started going to church all the time and soon…well, I am like I am now.'

Marsland held back his surprise. 'That's good. It's good you found something to believe in, something to help you.'

'Then I met you. At the cemetery. And I learnt about all the terrible things you'd been through. And I knew then.'

'You knew what?'

'I'm sorry. I'm waffling on.' She stood up, tucked

the chair under the bed. 'I've got to go, Terry.'

'Wait...'

'I won't be seeing you again, Terry. Please don't come and find me. I know you know how, but please don't.'

He called out to her, but she kept on walking out the door and he listened to the tap of her shoes fading down the corridor.

Not expecting a message from Napper on his phone, Jairus raised his eyebrows when he saw it. Then he grimaced, thinking about the pile of shit he'd left behind yesterday. He checked the news and saw that the press office were keeping tight-lipped when it came to the suicide. Bryan Macintyre was dead, gunshot wound. That was pretty much all that the press had. Neighbours commented, saying that a tall man had gone into the building before Bryan was found dead. And they mentioned the hysterical woman too.

Jairus ate some toast and headed for the station, mentally preparing himself as he drove, and all the time trying to think about the scumbag who now had his life and career in his hands. It wouldn't be long before they showed their hand, but he wanted to be able to walk up and hammer on their door and grin.

Jairus headed up to Napper's office, ignoring the faces of the team, the ones that congratulated him and the ones that simply nodded.

He knocked and opened the door and sat before her, waiting for her sharp, fox-like eyes to take him in.

'Right bloody mess you left yesterday,' she said and put down her pen.

'Yeah, I know. And I'm sorry to hell that he's dead.'

She raised her eyebrows. 'Are you? Are you really? Because I have a report here from the pathologist. It makes for very interesting reading.'

'Yeah? Why's that?'

She looked briefly down at the report, then up again. 'Dr Garrett said that Bryan Macintyre must have put the barrel of the gun directly behind his ear. I won't go into the technical detail that he has, about the gun residue and all that, but I will concentrate on the placement of the gun. Right behind the ear.'

'I'm not following you.'

'Really? Because I heard you were clever, despite your ape-like appearance. You see, putting a gun right behind your ear and pulling the trigger is a sure fire way to get the job done. Pardon the pun. No cock-ups. No risk of surviving with brain damage. Most people put the gun in their mouth or to their temple. But Bryan puts it behind his ear. That's how professional killers do it. That's how I knew Barry George didn't murder Jill Dando. Her killer put the gun right behind her ear. And that's what the pathologist said when he examined Bryan.'

'Are you trying to make out that I shot Bryan and tried to make it look like suicide?'

'No, I'm stating that it seems a bit weird that he knew to do that.'

'Maybe he read it somewhere? I think you're jumping to conclusions.'

'Maybe I am. Either way, all the facts and forensic evidence says Bryan killed himself.'

Jairus relaxed a little, his clenched fists unfolding. 'I know. I watched him.'

'We've notified his family.'

'Good. Was that all you wanted to see me about?'

She sat back a little. 'They say you're clever, but you act bloody stupid sometimes. You could have got you and Kate Roberts killed. But you wanted to be a hero.'

'No, I wanted to get her away from him and I needed to know where Holzman was. I thought I could get the info out of him.'

'But he didn't know.'

'No, he didn't.'

She sighed. 'Well, we've got an eye out for Holzman at the ports and airports.'

'He's getting help from someone so he may have even skipped the country by now. Probably got a new passport.'

'We'll find him.'

Jairus pulled himself up from the chair. 'Well, let me know if you do.'

'Go and get some rest and think about your future.'

He didn't look back at her, just headed back out the office and across the incident room.

CHAPTER 33

Stephen Hopkins was listening to LBC, barely taking in the debate that the host was having with a caller about the freedom of the press. When he did listen, he just laughed and shook his head, aware that what the press were allowed to know was what he and other agencies allowed them to know. If anything was deemed too disturbing for public consumption, then his bosses put a D-notice on the information and that was that. With the implementation of the new terrorism laws, came a few satisfactory new political positions that warranted them a new hand-hold on public knowledge. What they now deemed too shocking for the public was immediately eradicated without political debate. After all, there was no politician high enough or trustworthy enough to be allowed to have any real power. These days, the prime ministers were kept on a very short leash, to prevent them believing they actually ran the country, a trap they had fallen into in the past.

Briefly, Hopkins' mind turned to the woman he was about to have lunch with, the DCS of the Special Crime Group. Even though she was at least fifteen years older than him, he had to admit to a certain amount of attraction towards her. She had that quiet, but stern allure. She dressed well and looked in good shape, plus he was sure there was some kind of chemistry between them, even when she barked at him about the inappropriateness of their agencies crossing swords. Part of him had been imagining getting up, walking over to her and kissing and undressing her.

And now she wanted to meet again and have lunch.

Hopkins smiled to himself as he pulled up at some traffic lights. He was now approaching the North Circular. To his right was a barren piece of wasteland that was halfway through being prepared for development. Above him was a concrete bridge, and the rumble of traffic filled his ears.

A figure in baggy jeans and a hoody came quickly across the road carrying a bucket and a wiper. Hopkins leaned out the window and said, 'Don't even think about it. I'm not paying you to clean my windscreen. Get a proper job.'

Then the back door opened and Hopkins tried to turn round to see what was happening. Something dug into his neck and he froze.

'Don't look round,' the deep grumble of a voice said. 'Or I might have to take your head off.'

The skinny man with the wiper ran round the car and jumped into the passenger seat. Now in his hand there appeared a small knife.

'Is this a carjacking?' Hopkins kept looking at the knife pointed at his waist.

'No,' the voice said behind him. 'The light's green. Keep driving. I'll give you directions.'

'I work for the government,' Hopkins said, shaking his head. 'If you get out now I might forget about this. Otherwise you'll find yourself locked up for a very long time.'

'Yeah? I'm terrified. See that car parked over there, on the right between the van and the Nissan?'

Hopkins looked. 'Yes.'

'Park up the road a bit from there, maybe round the corner.'

Hopkins did as they said and pulled on the handbrake.

Hopkins felt the object being dug into the back of his neck again, and the breath of the man by his ear.

'Get out, and I suggest you don't try to make a run for it.'

Hopkins nodded, and pushed open the door. He was thinking, summing things up, trying to decide what exactly these men wanted. He heard the back door shut and the footsteps behind him, scraping the road. Out of the corner of his eye he saw the skinny figure coming round the car, his head turning quickly.

Then something left the skinny man's hand, hurtling and clattering onto the other side of road.

'What are you doing?' the other man said, sounding annoyed.

'What?' the skinny man said.

'You can't leave that there.'

'You want me to pick the fucking thing up?'

'Yeah, because it's evidence. Go and pick it up.'

The skinny man stood still for a moment.

'Go on, pick it up. What sort of fucking criminal are you?'

The skinny man let out a burst of expletives as he trudged over to the object like a moody teenager and picked it up.

Hopkins suddenly felt the other man behind him. From the corner of his eye he could see he was tall, wide too. His head was a dark shape, probably a mask covering his face.

'Your car will be tracked, right?' the tall man said and pushed him on. He pointed to the car next to the van and ordered him to get in the back.

Skinny man slipped in behind the wheel and took them all into the traffic, heading off somewhere east. The big man pulled out a balaclava and told Hopkins to put it on backwards, then pushed his head down, and got him to sit on his own hands.

'You're going to be in so much shit,' Hopkins said through the material.

'Yeah, and if I could hear you I might give a shit.'

Jairus walked along the grey, water-stained concrete balcony, eyeing the door numbers. He stopped, knocked on the door and looked down at the small piece of greenery below the block of flats. He could smell spicy food drifting up from one of the other flats and immediately his stomach rumbled. He could hear music inside, the heavy boom, boom, boom of one of Wells' mixes.

The door opened and Wells stood there holding a bag of chips. 'Where did you bugger off to?'

'I didn't want to have sit through the whole performance,' Jairus said, pushed past him and walked through the hallway with its peeling lime green wallpaper, and entered a shabby narrow kitchen. Jairus found an old mug, washed it out and poured some water into it. He gulped it down and looked over at Wells who was still munching his chips. 'How can you eat at a time like this?'

'There's always time for chips.'

'Yeah, and do you realise exactly who we've got in there?'

Wells shrugged and put the last chip in his mouth. 'Yeah, cause he said he was MI5. For a minute I thought he said MFI, but that hasn't been round for donkey's years.'

'Yeah, right.' Jairus put down his mug and faced

the door to the living room, then put his hand on the doorknob.

'Hang on,' Wells said. 'You not going to put a mask on?'

'No point.'

Jairus opened the door and immediately the stale odour of sweat and cigarettes wrapped themselves round his face. He gagged a little, ignoring the thin shape sitting smoking in the corner of the bare room. There was only a little light green carpet in each corner. The wallpaper wasn't too bad in the living room, except somebody had written something very poetic and vulgar near the window. The dirty blue curtains were drawn and a cheap-looking desk lamp resting on the floor illuminated the mattress.

Jairus let his eyes fall onto the figure lying on the mattress. All the time he stood there the naked figure writhed and mumbled into his gag. His eyes were now bulging.

Jairus saw a dusty kitchen chair and sat down on it. He smiled a little at Hopkins, who was still fighting with the ties on his hands and feet.

'Looks like you've found yourself in a compromising situation,' Jairus said and sat back.

There came more blaspheming through the gag.

Jairus held up a hand. 'Yeah, I know, I know. You're really pissed off, but you didn't leave me much choice, did you? Anyway, let's face facts, you really shouldn't be shocked by this...I mean, your people, and especially MI6, have been doing this sort of stuff for years. You know, blackmail and all that. At one time the British government would only recruit men and women as spies who they could blackmail, just so they knew they would have to carry out the most horrific and morally grey missions that they were ordered to complete. So think of it as a return to the old days.'

Tired of watching Hopkins stare and mumble at him, Jairus turned to the skinny figure on the chair. He smiled a little when he saw the sinewy man dressed in a bra and knickers that did little hide his assets. The funniest thing about him, Jairus decided, was his beard.

'What's your name?' Jairus asked the transvestite.

'I like to be called Diana,' he said, in a surprisingly high voice, then stubbed his cigarette out on the window ledge.

'Then Diana it is. Diana, could you remove his gag?'

'As long as he doesn't bite me. I don't think he's too pleased with me, darling.'

'He won't bite,' Jairus said and watched Diana cross the room and remove the gag from Hopkins' mouth.

They all sat still for a moment, frowning, waiting for Hopkins' spitting and snarling mouth to cease. Soon he was bent over, heaving, as if he might vomit.

'You nearly made yourself sick,' Jairus said.

'You're dead. I know you. I know your face. You're done. You've had it. All of you! The skinny fucker eating chips out there, and this freak! And you, you stupid fucking copper. You're first on the list.'

Jairus leaned forward. 'Yeah, I know...or maybe you'll be finished when we make public the photographs and film my friends made of you. How about that?'

'That's it? That's your threat? Plain old blackmail?'

'Yeah, because I need to know where Holzman is.'

Hopkins let out a burst of angry laughter. 'You can't touch him. He's ours.'

'Yeah? He's yours is he?' Jairus looked round to see Wells standing behind him, a big smile stretching his bony face. 'Where's the camera?'

'It's around here somewhere,' Wells said, his head spinning to look round the flat.

'You better not have pinched and sold it,' Jairus called out as Wells walked into the hallway.

'Look at you,' Hopkins groaned through gritted teeth. 'You're a bunch of fuck-ups. Don't you feel even a little pity for your two associates? After all, you're leading them into hell. You can't blame them, they're just freaks. An obvious junkie and...well I don't know what the other one is...but they're fucked like you now. I take it they know you're a sociopath? Do they know how the death of your girlfriend loosened something in your cranium? Sent you into some kind of self-destructive spiral? But I guess it's the psychology of it, isn't it? You like to control everything and everyone around you, but she got away.'

Jairus stood up, the wave of molten hate flowing up through him. 'I'd shut up if I was you.'

'Yes, she's probably better off dying like that...'

Jairus roared forward, snarling, clasping Hopkins by his throat. 'You say another word about her and I'll break your neck. You know I'm capable of it.'

There was something in Hopkins' eyes then, a slow recognition that maybe he had pushed things far enough.

'Let me go and maybe I'll forget this whole thing.'

Jairus turned round when Wells tapped him on the shoulder. He took the digital camera from him. 'Let's have a look.' Jairus flicked through the images, smiling to himself, slowly dampening the embers inside. He saw a particularly sickening image and turned the viewer round to show Hopkins. He laughed when the agent began to rage again.

Jairus nodded. 'Yeah, these will look good on the net.'

'You wouldn't dare.'

Jairus lowered the camera, and moved his head close to Hopkins', widening his eyes. 'Look into my eyes. You know I will. I've got nothing left to lose. Don't dare me, mate. So what's it to be?'

'Doesn't look like you've left me much choice.'

Jairus shook his head. 'No, I haven't, have I? All I want to know is where he is. Nobody needs to know the info came from you.'

Hopkins stared at Jairus for a few seconds, then looked down at the mattress. 'He spends a lot of time at a flat in Wood Green. It was owned by a pensioner called Michael Farraday, but he died a few years ago. Somehow Holzman got hold of the keys.'

'What's the address?'

'252 Wilson Road. It's the top flat. Now are you going to let me go?'

'Now, tell me, how did you get onto Holzman?'

'Oh my God, you want the whole bloody story?'

'Yeah.'

'We got a tip-off.'

'From who?'

'I have no idea. I just get told to keep an eye on him because he's been posting things online, anti-government stuff, anti-establishment stuff. Basically he fits the profile of someone planning on doing something drastic. He'd spent years doing the same old job, getting nowhere. He'd even dabbled in right wing politics. Everything suggested he was an angry man planning to get back at the government. We see it all the time. Except it all stopped. Nothing. He retires and goes back to a normal life.'

'So why're you still interested in him?'

'We found payments into his bank accounts from companies that didn't seem to exist. Someone had gone to great trouble to hide his financial dealings. Usually we follow the money to the source and end up face to face with some kind of terrorist organisation, like an extreme right wing group.'

'But you came up empty?' Jairus' mind whirred. There was something jabbing at his brain, but he couldn't quite grasp it.

'Yes, we came up blank, but we were hoping that keeping an eye on him might eventually lead somewhere, then you lot poked your noses in. Now, are you going let me go?'

Jairus leaned over and rustled Hopkins' hair. 'Soon. My friends will let you go once I check out this flat.'

'You better fucking hurry up.'

'Yeah, I'll be as quick as I can.' Jairus nodded to Wells as he took out his mobile and walked out the flat and back along the balcony. By the time he was hurrying down the concrete stairs that reeked of urine, Walker had answered her phone.

'Hey, boss, where the hell have you been?' she said lightly, but he heard the deep curiosity in her voice.

'Napper made me take some leave.'

'I know, but I thought I might...'

'Listen, I've got a possible address for Holzman in Wood Green.'

'Where did you get that information?'

'You don't want to know,' he said and walked into the small car park below the building.

'Bloody hell, Jay,' she said, huffing out a breath.

'Yeah, I know. Look, an anonymous tip-off will come through soon. Best thing would be for you to keep an eye on his house. I'll meet you there. Better wear something more casual.'

'Napper's just come into the incident room. I've got to go. Text me the address and I'll meet you there as soon as the call comes in.'

'Good,' Jairus said and ended the call.

CHAPTER 34

Jairus text Walker and arranged to meet her in the middle of the estate behind Shopping City in Wood Green high street. Jairus was sitting on a wall in among the dying flowers and bushes that had been planted to make the estate look less urban. No amount of flowers were going to disguise the squalor, he thought, and looked round at the windows of the flats all around him. Windows were open, fans sat on the ledges, the occupants desperately trying to circulate the air in their rooms. The smell of marijuana drifted from one of the windows, probably the same one where more peaceful, but loud tunes were being played from. He recalled his early days when he was in uniform, part of a team that spent most dawns hammering down doors and raiding the local dealers. He'd lost count of how many times he'd found himself presenting a search warrant on the very estate he was now sitting waiting in.

Walker pushed open the glass doors and walked up to him, now dressed in jeans and a black low cut T-shirt. 'So, which scumbag did you get to call in?' she asked.

'Does it matter? As long as we get hold of Holzman.'

'You're not even supposed to be here.'

Jairus stood up and walked back through the doors with Walker following him. 'I know. I'll camp somewhere out of the way. Just make sure you tell me when he turns up.'

'So, you're convinced that Holzman has a conspirator? Someone he's planning all this with?'

'Yeah, I do.' Jairus stuffed his hands into his pockets as they crossed Wood Green high street and then headed down a side street.

'For what reason?'

'To muddy the name of the Freemasons. You've heard of the journalist, Ian Pritchard?'

'The name's familiar. Why?'

'He was attacked the other day, and told that he either published the story that he'd been putting together on the recent Freemason murders and a possible link to a satanic cult, or something bad would happen to his nephew.'

Walker swung round and clutched his arm. 'What? Has this been reported?'

Jairus stopped, but kept looking up the street. 'He reported it to me. Whoever's putting pressure on Pritchard, is also pressurising his editor. The story will get published.'

'And because the story involves a business giant and TV star then it'll get plenty of media attention.'

Jairus nodded. 'Yeah, exactly.'

'So, who's putting on the pressure?'

'Not sure yet. But undoubtedly we've met them or interviewed them. They would have wormed their way into the Freemasons at some point to gain trust, but they obviously have a burning desire to destroy them.'

'So they probably are a Freemason?' Walker asked.

'I'd say so.'

'That's going to be a long list of names.'

'Yeah, it will be. But hopefully if we can get hold of

Holzman then we can cut all the hard work out. Any luck finding Garter's key card?'

'No sign of it.'

'I didn't think so.'

Walker turned on the next street and Jairus followed her, seeing she was heading for the centre of a square with a small children's playground at the centre of it. All the houses that lined the roads surrounding them were big Victorian red-brick buildings. The cars were parked on the road, all tightly crammed in. When they reached the playground, they sat on one of the walls, where it was possible for them to get a view of Holzman's street.

'Where are the team camped?' Jairus asked, folding his arms.

'They've got the major routes in and out of here covered. They'll radio when they see him coming in.'

'If they see him coming in.'

She looked at him and shook her head. 'He'll turn up. I've got a good feeling.'

'I'm glad you have.'

'Napper grabbed me on the way out. Made me bring some armed response officers, so they're dug in up the road.'

Jairus nodded. 'Yeah, he could be armed.'

'How you feeling after what happened with Bryan Macintyre?'

Jairus hunched himself over and rubbed his face. 'I'm fine. He killed himself. There wasn't much I could do.'

'Doesn't sound like there was,' she said and squeezed his shoulder. 'We should go for a drink after we've got Holzman locked up.'

He looked at her. 'Yeah, we should.'

She narrowed her eyes. 'You're agreeing to that

because you don't think we'll get our hands on him.'

Jairus laughed. 'No, I'm really not. We will, we'll go for that drink.'

She turned away and looked about the streets, but he examined her for a moment, once again realising that she did indeed resemble Karine, and that perhaps he was guilty of haunting the memory of his ex-girlfriend. He could not help it and knew the gravitational pull of the desire to feel again what he had back then was far too strong to resist. And of course, the distraction was all important too, as it helped to smother the whimpering that filled his ears at night and the quiet parts of his day.

'I'm sure Napper will pull you back in sooner or later,' Walker suddenly said, turning to him with a smile.

'Let's bloody well hope so, or I'll go insane twiddling my thumbs at home.'

Jairus had volunteered to fetch them some coffees from the little Italian coffee house near the tube station in Wood Green. He wanted to walk for a while and was quite happy to leave Walker and the rest of the team to stalk Holzman's new stomping ground. Part of the problem, and his desire to get away from the stakeout, was that he had suddenly decided that Holzman had flown the coop.

He knew, if he was right in his theory, that Holzman was getting financial assistance from an as yet unseen player in the game, which meant the probability that he had received new documentation to help him leave the country was high. Although another thought had started to burrow away at his brain; he was wondering exactly who had tipped off MI5 about Holzman in the first place, and was forming a very shaky theory that perhaps his fellow conspirator had done it in a move to get rid of him now the time was right. Jairus sighed as he carried back the coffees, knowing that all his hunches and theories amounted to nothing. Even if he did find out who had orchestrated the whole game, chances are he'd be far too careful to leave a trail to his own doorstep.

Jairus felt the vibration in his pocket, put down the coffees on a nearby bench and took out his phone. Walker was calling him.

'Yeah, what happened?' Jairus asked.

'A car's turned up and parked up the road. Looks like a grey-haired man sitting in it. No one can get a good enough look to see if it's Holzman.'

'Shit,' Jairus said and began jogging towards Walker's position. 'We need to get someone closer.'

'He's sitting in the car, just waiting for something.'

'Waiting to see if the coast is clear.' Jairus gripped the phone to his ear as he jogged down the side street, the playground now in sight.

Jairus reached Walker and saw that she had been joined by another plain clothed male officer, DC Jack Lees.

'They've run the car and it's registered to a taxi driver, Derek Garden,' Walker said, standing up and looking down the road. 'DS Carr just called me and said he's got out the car and just entered Holzman's building.'

Jairus rubbed his head. 'Find the taxi firm he works for.'

'Carr's working on it,' Walker said. Her phone rang again and she walked away for a moment, asking questions and nodding. She put her phone away and faced Jairus. 'He works for Green Lane Cabs. They said they got a call out to a pub in Hertfordshire, then the driver was paid to pick up some personal items from the top floor flat.'

'That's Holzman's flat,' Jairus said, then started walking in the direction of the flat.

'Where do you think you're going?' Walker called out to him.

Jairus turned round. 'Get them to grab him when he's on his way back. Maybe he can tell us where Holzman is. And get some officers over to the pub in Hertfordshire.'

'You're not going to walk up there are you?'

'Why not? Holzman isn't coming. He sent the taxi driver to pick up his stuff.' Jairus walked on, feeling his heart sinking, seeing the dusk edging its way into view. The longer shadows were stretching out and he could feel their chances of catching Holzman fading with the light. They'd been there a few hours for nothing and now it would all come down to going through all the names that would be thrown up by their investigation into the Freemason membership. And he knew that chances were he'd come up against a wall of hostile faces, all telling him to be quiet and go back to doing his job.

Jairus walked towards the building, his eyes fixing on the cars parked up the street. Then he saw one indicate, and pull out into the road and begin travelling further away. He walked faster, watching the brake lights come on towards the turning.

The squad car lurched out of the next street and cut off his escape. Soon his team were around the car, lifting the taxi driver out. As Jairus approached, the middle-aged man looked confused as he took in all the people staring at him and the serious shape of DS Carr who was right in his face.

He grasped the taxi driver by the back of his shirt

and pushed him away from the swarm of officers. He just caught the gasps and protests of Carr and the rest as he directed the man round the corner.

He stopped and faced the man, looking into his worried eyes.

'Derek, yeah?' Jairus asked.

'Yes, but what's going on? What have I done?'

'Who paid you to come here?'

'Some old bloke. I got sent down to Cheshunt and he was waiting for me.'

'And what did he say to you?'

'Asked me if I could pick some stuff up from his flat. He took out a wad of cash and gave me two hundred quid. I wasn't going to turn it down.'

'That must have made you suspicious.' Jairus paced up and down for a moment.

'Yes, but it was two hundred quid and all he wanted was some glasses, a book, and a watch.'

Jairus laughed a little. 'That's all? No passport or anything else?'

'No. Just the things I said. Am I in trouble?'

Jairus shook his head. 'No, you're not. But we've been had.'

Jairus turned and walked off, hands in pockets, back the way he had come. He saw the figure of Walker coming towards him, her face full of questions.

'Holzman knew we were coming,' Jairus said as he got close to her, 'or at least he was trying to find out if we had the place under surveillance.'

'Shit.'

'Yeah, exactly. Let's keep walking back towards Wood Green.'

'What are you expecting to find there?'

'A pub. He's gone. It's blown. He now knows we were watching the flat. Better start searching the place, see what turns up.'

He kept going, hearing faintly in the background Walker telling the team to search the house. Then she was behind him, trying to catch up.

'That's it?' she said, getting level with him. 'Now we give up?'

'Even if we do catch Holzman, I doubt he'll tell us anything. He'll go to prison and keep his mouth shut.'

'Then we find a way to make a deal through his lawyer, that's the way it usually works.'

'Yeah, I know,' Jairus said, but he kept on moving with Walker behind. She remained quiet as they went, the sky darkening little by little.

He couldn't bring himself to talk- not to her or anyone and he could feel himself looking blankly at the passers-by, a large part of him wishing he was living their lives. Anything now than to be himself, carrying the guilt that seemed heavier than ever. He'd failed before but this somehow stung even more, perhaps because it was his first case since the horror of the year before.

'So, we're getting drunk?' Walker said and he could feel the way she had artificially lightened her mood for his sake.

He said nothing, just looked towards the end of the street and the high street that cut through it. There were a couple of bars on the other side, set back a little, nearer the tube station. Just in front of him stood another plain clothed officer who nodded to him, but Jairus kept walking.

A black car came along the high street and turned towards him and Walker. It nearly came to a halt then sped up and pulled up alongside. The window was open, allowing the man's voice to drift out to him.

'Good evening, DCI Jairus.'

Jairus saw the short black hair and sunglasses first. Then the hawk nose. Holzman's smile stretched under the glasses as he lifted his arm and pointed the gun at Jairus' stomach.

'Step back a couple of feet,' Holzman said. 'And you.'

Jairus had momentarily forgotten that Walker had been behind him and he turned to see her stood frozen to the spot.

'Go,' Jairus said to her. 'Leave, now.'

'Don't you go anywhere, darling,' Holzman said and turned his dark glasses to her.

'Run, just go!' Jairus shouted, but she remained still and said, 'I'm not going anywhere.'

'See, Jairus, she's a good woman.' Holzman turned the gun back towards Jairus. 'Now, put your hands in your pockets.'

Jairus was trying to judge the situation, trying to calculate how fast he could get to Holzman. But he kept seeing Walker out of the corner of his eye, knowing that he might be able to get a couple of shots off.

'Hands in your pockets, Jairus. Then on your knees.'

'You can get fucked,' Jairus growled.

Then Holzman turned the gun slightly towards Walker. 'Really? I think I could make a nasty hole in your partner's stomach from here.'

Jairus knew he had little choice. He gradually lowered himself to his knees and dug his hands into his pockets. 'Now I'm on my knees, why don't you tell me who put you up to this?'

Holzman's smile beamed. 'I'm sure you'd love that, Jairus, but I'm not one of your average lowlife criminals that rolls over the moment they come face to face with authority.'

'Get behind me, Ally.' Jairus gestured to Walker.

'Don't, Ally or I'll kill your boss.'

'Holzman, keep your eye on me,' Jairus said, hearing his own voice shaking. 'Keep your gun trained on me.'

'You sound scared, Jairus,' he said, swinging the gun a little. 'Just like Marie Henry that night. Yes, I was watching. I wanted make sure the boys did what we wanted them to do.'

'You've got nowhere to run to now,' Walker said, and he could hear the fear thick in her voice. 'Just lower the gun.'

'Who said I was going to run?' Holzman pointed the gun firmly at Jairus. Jairus took in a breath, his hands lifting from his pockets. He saw his own reflection in Holzman's sunglasses, and Walker's too.

'Go! Run!' Jairus shouted at Walker.

Holzman twisted the gun, lifted it a little, pulled the trigger.

The sound blasted out, echoing round the walls. Jairus fell back, Walker cried out, and Holzman's car roared off down the street.

Jairus got to his feet, his ears ringing, and swung round to see Walker huddled up against the wall, her face pale. Her hands were grasped to her chest where blood was oozing through her fingers. He knelt beside her and pushed her hands away. He put pressure on the wound that was close to her heart. Her eyes were fluttering, and she seemed to look everywhere but at him.

'Ally!' he shouted. There were bodies around him now.

Her head moved, but only a strange hollow breath escaped her mouth.

He turned and saw faces all around him. 'Has anyone called an ambulance?' He looked back at her and noticed there was no longer any sound or movement coming from her. 'Ally! Ally!'

'She's gone,' another voice said.

'No...she's fucking not,' Jairus said, and pulled her closer to him.

'She's gone, boss,' the voice said again, and a younger officer came from the crowd and helped Jairus to his feet, while a uniformed officer took charge of Walker.

Jairus looked around the street for a moment, trying to take it all in but failing. He moved away, looked far up the street, thinking of Holzman, then looked towards Walker, her head turned limply to the left. He began to walk forwards, even though the same young officer was now talking to him. Then he was being called, but Jairus had begun to jog in the direction Holzman had driven. He found himself running through the streets, his vision jumping round to the buildings surrounding him, his chest pounding. He could see now a line of officers sealing off the street ahead. An armed response officer was there, his submachine gun gripped in his hands. Jairus walked fast towards the scene, producing his ID as he approached the uniforms. Up ahead he could now see a black car had driven up the pavement and collided with a wall at the end of a garden. The vehicle was steaming and had been cordoned off.

Jairus showed his ID to the uniforms and slipped under the cordon. 'What happened to the driver?'

'He headed off down there on foot,' a female officer said, pointing to a narrow alleyway. 'Armed response has him pinned down in one of the houses.'

Jairus headed down the alleyway and towards the

shouting voices. There was a back gate that led to a garden of a house. The shouting was coming from over the fence. Another uniform was guarding the gate, his hands resting on his stab vest.

'Where are you going?' the uniform asked.

Jairus held up his ID. 'In there.'

'You can't go in there, sir, it's not safe right now.'

'I need to talk to him, our suspect.'

'Sorry, sir, but the Armed Response Unit are trying to get him to release his weapon.'

'Put the gun down on the ground and put your hands on your head,' a voice said calmly from inside the garden.

Whatever was said in return, Jairus couldn't hear.

'Put your fucking weapon down now or we'll be forced to open fire!'

There was a pause, then a call, a word called out that Jairus couldn't understand. Then came the boom of shots pounding out. The uniform turned and opened the gate as the word 'clear' was shouted after a few seconds.

Jairus followed the uniform into a long garden with a set of child's swings halfway down and a pond to the right. French doors at the rear of the house were open and the white curtains fluttered in the breeze. One of the Armed Response Unit appeared through the curtains as he slipped his gun over his shoulder. He took off his helmet and nodded to the uniform. 'He's all yours now, boss.'

'Is he alive?' the uniform asked.

'No, he's full of holes. You can try CPR if you want.'

Jairus stopped in the middle of the garden and looked around him, staring at the flowers in the beds, the pond, the fence surrounding the whole area. He tried to make sense of the objects around him, tried to form a reality from everything going on, but all he saw was meaningless shapes. Then his mind spun backwards, replaying the gunshot, the high-pitched ringing in his ears, the smell in the air. He saw Walker crumpled by the wall, her hands trying to hold in the blood.

He turned round and faced the thin triangular shape that should've been the carefree and playful shape of a kid's swing. He went to it and rested his hand on it, the image of Walker playing over and over in his head. He couldn't stop it, could not put another image in its place. He closed his eyes and heard the sob burst from his own lips. The tears tore down his face, burning his skin, rattling out of his body. The image of Walker was mixing with the bloodied shape of Carl Murphy.

CHAPTER 35

Back at the station, Jairus went straight up to the incident room, and was glad to see Napper was not in her office. He pulled up a chair in front of the whiteboard after he called Rich Vincent and told him to come upstairs. He sat for a few minutes staring at the photographs of the businessmen and the girls, sometimes getting up and rearranging them and sitting back down. His mind flashed bloody images to him, but he sunk them back down, fighting for clarity. He bent over and gripped his face, letting out a moan. When he took his hands away, he looked round at the rest of the room that seemed quiet. The other officers had turned to look at him. He thought he saw some sympathy, but mostly accusations.

'What?' he bellowed. 'What're you looking at?' He turned back to the whiteboard.

The incident room door opened and Moone came through. 'What the bloody hell are you doing here?'

'Don't start.'

Moone looked around the room for a moment, then stepped closer to Jairus. 'I heard what happened...I still can't believe...'

'And what do you think I feel like?'

Moone nodded and ran a hand down his face. 'I should tell you that Napper is on the warpath. She heard you ran off from the crime scene.'

'I went after Holzman, what did she expect?' Jairus stood up and grabbed Garter's photograph and put it at the top of the board.

'It's not looking too good, mate,' Moone said, his voice weak, distant.

'What doesn't look good?' Jairus was hardly listening. He could hear the whimpering, and the image of Walker lying crumpled by the wall was all he could see.

'Everything. All of it. Walker's...gone...I still can't get my head...and you run off...and what happened with Bryan.'

Jairus spun round to him, now taking in what Moone was saying. 'I know. I'm finished. I'm fucked up in here...completely fucked up, but I need to get to the bottom of all this. You need to help me.'

'Maybe you need to let us...'

Jairus moved forward, pressing his face closer to Moone's. 'You need to help me. The person who orchestrated all this, they're destroying everything... my life, Walker's life...they've taken that...'

Moone stepped away. 'You need to calm down. You're not thinking straight.'

The door opened again and Rich Vincent came in carrying a laptop. 'Hey, you wanted my help?'

Jairus pointed to a nearby desk. 'Yeah, thanks, Rich. Set yourself up over there.'

Rich nodded to Moone, then pulled up a chair at Walker's desk. 'I heard what happened...'

Jairus held up a hand. 'Yeah, but I need to know what you found on Warren's laptop. Did you manage to dig around his financial dealings?'

'I did,' Rich said and tapped away at the laptop. I found that Warren had been in a lot of debt. Like a lot of us, the cost of his living was far outweighing his income.'

'So maybe that's why he killed himself?' Moone said, pulling up a chair.

Rich shook his head. 'No, you see, over the last year or so, his finances took a slow change. He went from being in the red, to being far into the black.'

Jairus went over and stood behind Rich. 'How come?'

'Well, first of all small but regular amounts of money began appearing in his accounts. He had a few of them with different banks. I looked into where the money was coming from and it seemed, on the surface, that it was coming from various companies. The sort he could be advising, like the way a security expert might advise a private company. But then I tried to find these companies, and I ran a blank. Whoever set these companies up covered their tracks very well. Now they don't seem to exist.'

Jairus rubbed his face. 'What about Holzman?'

'Like I said before, his accounts appeared to be closed, and he was probably dealing in cash.'

Moone nodded. 'Yeah, we found a great deal of cash hidden at his house.'

'Chances are we'll find more at the flat,' Jairus said. 'So, Rich, any other similarities in the finances of the other businessmen?'

'Well, not really,' Rich said and tapped away at the keyboard again. 'In the case of Graham Burgess, the house he owned...Braxton House, he bought that for a large amount of money, but he didn't really have that amount of money available to him.'

'That doesn't mean anything,' Moone interrupted. 'Businessmen find money, borrow, strike deals or whatever...'

Rich nodded. 'That would make sense, but he

didn't borrow any money. There's no sign of any such financial dealings. All I can find is large amounts of money coming in from properties he apparently sold. Thing is, I don't think these properties ever existed. I can't find any trace of them.'

'So what have they got in common?' Jairus said.

Rich shrugged. 'They've all come into a lot of money, and in very mysterious ways. But their tax affairs are all in order, which means the Inland Revenue would not be knocking on their doors.'

'Never try and fool the tax man,' Moone said, sighing. 'That's what my old man told me.'

Jairus nodded and pointed at Moone. 'Yeah, that's right. That's the way to keep your money deals quiet, make sure the tax man isn't on your back.'

Rich shrugged. 'So, what does that mean? There must be loads of businessmen who do dodgy deals and manage to keep the tax man at bay.'

'But what have they all got in common?' Jairus asked again. 'It's the absence.'

'What?' Moone asked, exchanging confused looks with Rich.

'It's the mysterious invisible hand that's giving them money. There's a hole in all this. A man-shaped hole. A man-shaped hole and he has the ability to make money appear from nowhere.'

'And who could that be?'

Jairus strode quickly towards the door, pulled it open and disappeared from the room.

Moone had taken a quick look in on Gina Colman, but quickly retreated when he saw she was being visited by her mother and father. He watched them sitting there quietly, both staring at the bed where their daughter lay, her vacant eyes staring at the wall. He saw the father wipe a tear from his eye.

Moone slopped off, nodding only to the police constable guarding the room, and headed to see Terence Marsland.

He expected to see the old man lying in bed looking bored and anxious, so he got a big shock when he turned into the room and was met with Marsland putting on his shirt and tie.

'What the bloody hell do you think you're doing?' Moone asked, looking him up and down.

Marsland turned to him awkwardly, obviously still unsteady on his feet. 'Going home.'

'You can't, Terence, you've only just recovered from two stab wounds. You need to lay on your back for a while.'

Marsland did up his tie. 'Then I'll lay on my back at home. I can't lie in here anymore.'

Moone caught sight of a nurse going past the door. 'Hey, excuse me, nurse, can you tell my friend he can't leave?'

The nurse, who was slim with dark hair, stepped into the room for a moment. 'Terence has discharged himself against our advice. If he feels unwell, he should come back immediately.'

Moone watched the nurse turn and hurry away. 'I don't believe it. How can they just let you walk out like that?'

'Because I'm mentally sound. There's nothing they can do to keep me here.' Marsland turned round too quickly. He put his hand on the bed and steadied himself for a moment before putting on his jacket.

'You're crazy,' Moone said and pulled up a chair and sat in it.

'You look exhausted.'

Moone nodded. 'It's been a mad few days.

Commander Warren hanged himself.'

Marsland turned to Moone. 'What?'

'It's all fucked up. I don't want to go into it now. Oh, but the good news is that the man who stabbed you, Edgar Holzman, is dead.'

'Don't suppose he spilled the beans before he died?'

'Unfortunately not,' Moone said, then hung his head as the more disturbing events came back to him. 'And you remember DI Ally Walker?'

Marsland nodded. 'Yes I do.'

'Holzman shot and killed her.'

'Bloody hell. I'm sorry. I never got to work with her, but I heard she was good.'

Moone stood up. 'Yes, she was. You sure you want to leave here?'

'I have to, otherwise I'll go mad.'

Moone sighed. 'OK. I'll drive you home.'

'It's OK, I'll get a taxi.'

'No way. I'm driving you home. Come on.'

Marsland smiled, but only briefly. He walked carefully to the doorway, while Moone stepped to one side. The once tall and wiry policeman Moone had known had been replaced by a lanky, worn-in-the-face man. There was something beyond Marsland's eyes now, a trace of the terror and guilt that now haunted him. Moone couldn't even imagine what it would be like to find your daughter murdered, and to know that you were partly to blame. He shuddered at the thought, and closed it all off.

It seemed to take them ages to reach the car park, and when Moone looked round at his ex-colleague, he saw the sweat gathering on his brow and top lip.

They got into the car and drove in silence for a moment, Moone turning his head to take in the profile of his friend every now and again.

'Did you remember where you'd met her before?'

'Sorry?' Moone said, flickering out of his dream.

'Jacqui? The woman who visited me in hospital. You said you recognised her.'

'No, I can't say I remember. Could be anywhere. My mind's a bit all over the place at the moment, to be honest. What you up to?'

'I just want to...actually I don't know what I want to do. I feel I need to find her and talk to her.'

'Why? You like her? Want to take her out for dinner?'

Marsland shrugged. 'I don't know. I don't think so. I just feel like...like she needs help.'

'Maybe she's a bunny boiler.'

'I don't think so. She came to see me the other day and told me she was a born again Christian.'

'Oh...' Moone grimaced. 'You could do without that...unless you've found God too. It wouldn't surprise me, what with all the shit you've been through lately.'

'No, I haven't. I just need to find her.'

'So what do you know about her?'

'I know she goes to a club every Thursday night.'

'So let's find out who runs it and find out where she lives. How about that?'

Marsland nodded.

Moone drove on while watching Marsland hug his belongings in a carrier bag, all the time trying to recall where he knew Jacqui from.

CHAPTER 36

Jairus stuffed his hands into his pockets as the lift took him up far into the building, counting the numbers above his head. He felt a little dizzy, perhaps because he hadn't slept for quite a while. Sickness too seemed to be rising through him, and then a sudden burst of adrenalin. He clenched his fists in his pockets as the doors opened, revealing the busy floor of Crow and Co Bank.

His stomach tightened as he reached the main desk and showed his ID. 'I need to see Raymond Crow.'

A young woman, possibly the same one they talked to last time, looked up at him. 'I'm sorry?'

'Don't be sorry. Just get on the phone and tell Raymond Crow I need to talk to him. It's urgent.'

'I'll see if he's free,' she said, looking a little annoyed.

'Yeah, you do that.' Jairus walked away from the desk.

Ally Walker lying crumpled by the wall, the blood oozing through her fingers.

Jairus took in a deep breath and turned to see the London skyline through the expanse of windows.

'Mr Crow said you can go through to his office.'

Jairus stared blankly at the young woman before he interpreted her words, nodded and strode along the thin strip of carpet.

He opened the glass office door without knocking

and stood over the large desk at the centre of the enormous room. Crow looked round from his computer screen 'How can I help you, DCI Jairus?'

Jairus smiled. 'I need your advice on a matter. A sort of financial matter.'

Crow sat back a little. 'So basically you're after some free financial advice?'

'Yeah, kind of.'

'Why don't you sit down then?'

Jairus nodded and sat down.

'So,' Crow said, 'what exactly can I help you with? Investments? Securities? Pensions?'

'Vengeance.' Jairus sat back and waited.

Crow frowned. 'I'm sorry, I don't understand. Is this some kind of police joke that I don't get?'

'No, I'm just trying to put it all together, and I'm wondering what could drive a successful man, who runs a big financial company like this one, to plot such an intricate scheme to try and bring the Freemasons into disrepute.'

'I don't get you,' Crow said. 'Are you accusing me of something? I thought you needed my advice.'

'Yeah, like I said...I need to get into the brain of someone who would destroy the lives of three girls and a few businessmen to get back at an organisation like the Masons.'

'And I'm not sure what you're going on about. I have a meeting in twenty minutes, so if you're accusing me of something...?'

'You see, I realised when looking at the financial dealings of all the businessmen involved, and my former boss, that someone with a lot of financial know-how must be pulling the strings. They had neatly tied up the loose ends, and made sure the Inland Revenue wasn't left wanting, therefore avoiding any chance of investigation.'

'Look, I don't know what's going on...'

Jairus slammed his fist down on the desk, making Crow flinch. 'Come on, stop playing games. You know there's nothing I can do, I can't arrest you because I've got nothing tying you to the girls' murders or the murders of the businessmen. You're home free.'

Crow sat back, his brow flattening and a slow smile appearing. 'OK, Jairus, I was just seeing how far I could take it. You got me. So, basically all that brought you to my door was just a hunch?'

'Yeah.'

Crow smiled even more. 'That's brilliant.'

'Holzman's dead.'

Crow sat up. 'It was only a matter of time. I knew he would either end up getting killed or I'd have to deal with him.'

'He killed my friend.'

'I'm so sorry,' Crow said, putting on mock sympathy.

'No, you're not. You don't feel sympathy or empathy. Chances are you were brought up in a materialistic world where people didn't seem very important but things did. I suppose your family cared about money more than they did their child. You were probably palmed off to the nanny.'

There came a burst of laughter from Crow. 'Nice. Try and dig into my psychology. It won't work.'

'Then why the Freemasons? Tell me that.'

Crow shrugged. 'Boredom. It gets pretty boring when you've got everything you've wanted. I'm a collector, you see. Antiques. Paintings. Companies. But most of all I like to collect people. You see I have many irons in my fire, both legal and illegal. I've advised a lot of criminal organisations in my time, shown them how to launder their money, but I've always advised them to make sure the Inland Revenue get their cut. You have to keep a legitimate face on things. That's the important thing. That's why I've always made sure I've kept distance between me and the criminals I've dealt with. But I also make sure that I have enough on those fraudsters and gangsters to keep them in my pocket. That's the way I like it. Make sure you work with people that have a weakness. You can either offer them something they greatly desire, or if that doesn't work, you get something on them. It doesn't matter to me in the end, as long as I collect another asset. I even tried to collect you, but you weren't interested.'

'So you just decided to collect some of the members of the Freemasons too?'

'Yes.'

'And I take it you had already drawn Burgess into your collection?'

'I stumbled upon him while searching through the ranks of the Freemasons. The more people you meet, the more psychologically damaged people you find. I soon realised he was a sadistic sociopath. He had a rather interesting upbringing. I made him successful, pushed him towards a few deals and then got Holzman to bring him into the fold. Knowing Burgess was a sociopath and had a inconsolable desire for young women, made him very valuable to me.'

Fighting back the desire to grasp Crow around the throat, Jairus said, 'And what about Holzman? Where did you dig him up?'

Crow leaned back and put his hands behind his head. 'Do you believe in synchronicity?'

'Carl Jung's idea that two seemingly unrelated events can be meaningfully related in some way?'

'I'm impressed. Well, you see Holzman was a

very anti-establishment character. For whatever reason, he had this deep hatred of authority or any kind of government. I came across him by accident. He worked for one of my smaller companies in an administrative role, and it was brought to my attention that he was using one of the computers to look at rather controversial Internet sites. I told my IT guys to keep an eye on what he looked at and to keep me in the loop. Once I had enough material I had a quiet chat with him and soon he was part of my collection. All it really took to buy his loyalty was to offer that one thing he desired. And that was destruction of the establishment. And of course, the Freemasons are full of establishment figures. That's how they get their little secret deals done.'

'Yeah,' Jairus said and looked down to see his leg jittering, his hands shaking. 'So why the hatred of the Freemasons? There must be some reason.'

Crow stood up. 'I think I've talked enough. Let me show you something that you'll find very interesting.'

Jairus got to his feet, taking special notice in the change of expression that had taken place on Crow's face. He'd gone from casual boredom, to a quiet excitement. The businessman straightened his suit and walked to the far wall, stopping beside one of the large paintings. He pressed the wall and there was an electronic buzz. Crow pulled open a hidden door in the wall, revealing a metal door with a keypad next to it. His hand fluttered over the numbers for a moment, then the metal door clicked open, revealing another room. On the walls were more paintings, but these were valuable. Jairus spotted a Van Gogh that he knew had been stolen a couple of years ago, and next to it was a Picasso. Delicate vases and sculptures sat on plinths in the far corners of the room.

Crow ushered Jairus to a plinth at the centre of the room. A cloth covered the square object that sat there. Jairus felt his stomach twist.

Crow lifted the cloth, revealing the knife rack and the kitchen knives that were resting inside it. He faced Jairus with a smile. 'You may recognise this object. This was taken from a lock-up in North London that you own. Now, as you can see this is a rack of kitchen knives. Just an ordinary set, the sort any couple might buy.'

'Yeah, just get to your point.'

Crow smiled. 'There's one knife missing. See the empty slot in the block? Where could that knife be? Could it be the knife used to kill Carl Murphy?'

'You can't prove that.'

'But isn't it interesting. That means you went home, grabbed that knife and took it with you when you went to meet Mr Murphy. You planned it. You knew what you were going to do. But then you must have come to your senses and put his prints on the knife and claimed he had brought it himself. Luckily they believed you and you were let off. So, the question is, Jairus, why did you keep the evidence? No, don't answer...let me guess. I think you kept it as a souvenir...like a lot of killers do.'

'I'm not about to discuss my workings with you. Anyway, there's nothing linking me to that set of knives.' Jairus walked over and leaned against the plinth.

'Hello, Ivan,' Crow said and turned towards the open door.

Jairus turned and saw the thick-bodied suited man standing in the doorway. He recognised him from his last meeting with Crow. He was the man sitting by the door in the restaurant.

'Ivan is my right hand man,' Crow said, smiling again. 'He brought me the knives. And also he found this.' The businessman put a hand into his inside pocket and produced a photograph which he held out to Jairus. 'I've got copies, so don't worry. You can have that one.'

Jairus took the photograph, looked at it and tried to keep the surprise from his face. The photograph had been snapped in the kitchen of their old house, perhaps even the day they had moved in. Jairus and Karine were standing in the middle of the kitchen next to the cooker. Beside them, just to Jairus' left, was a set of knives identical to the one on the plinth. Jairus looked up. 'It must have taken him a while to dig this out.'

'It did,' Crow said. 'He was there a few hours. So, to cut a long story short, I have something on you.'

Jairus grinned. 'You can't buy me like you bought my boss.'

'Now, Commander Warren was incredibly easy to buy. All I had to do was offer him a financial helping hand and he rolled over. Then I collected him together with the others at the dinner party, and with the help of Ivan here and Burgess and Edgar, we filmed them with the girl. I'm afraid Burgess took things a bit far and abducted a few other girls and had his way with them. That's why I had to make sure my two angels of death disposed of him pretty quickly.'

'Yeah, and they were certainly efficient.'

'Come on, Jairus, you surely can't be upset that Burgess is dead? He got what he deserved.'

'You helped him rape and murder.' Jairus moved forward, allowing Crow a glimmer of the violence in his eyes. Out of the corner of his eye he noticed Ivan flinch.

'A necessary manoeuvre, I'm afraid. I needed them involved in something that would shock the public, and with the help of your journalist friend and his boss, who owes my bank a great deal of money, they will be disgusted and shocked by the satanic worship of the Freemasons.'

'Do you think people have long memories?' Jairus laughed. 'They don't. But tell me about Sir Robert Garter. He's the one you were really targeting, the one you went to real trouble to frame. What does he symbolise to you? Don't tell me...he's part of an elite world that you'll never be part of. He's old money and they've always looked down on your kind.'

Crow was blank for a moment, then smiled. 'You've got me all wrong, I'm afraid. Garter and Danny Charles were just means to an end, public figures that everyone would be shocked to discover were involved in satanic rituals.'

'No, there's more to it than that.'

'Think what you like, Jairus, but one point remains. You belong to me now.'

Jairus looked round at the emotionless face of Ivan, wondering how quickly he could move, considering whether he had enough time to throttle Crow. 'Hand it into the police. I'm finished anyway.'

There came another brief laugh from Crow before he said, 'I thought you might say that. That's why I did something else a little underhand. Your colleague, Detective Sergeant Moone, is a family man, isn't he? Two kids now, am I right?'

'You better be careful what you say next.'

'What if some disturbing images of children were found on his computer? That would destroy his career and his life, wouldn't it?'

'Don't even think about it.'

'And if you try and do anything about it, then another of your colleagues will have the same thing happen to them. And don't doubt that I can make it happen.'

'It wouldn't stick.'

Crow reached out and patted Jairus' arm. 'You keep telling yourself that, but by the time it gets resolved, if it ever does, their lives would be in tatters, wouldn't it? And of course there would be rumours, wouldn't there?'

Jairus turned away, pretending to look at the paintings and sculptures for a moment, all the time trying to figure a way out of the mess. He found nothing he could do.

'And,' Crow suddenly said, interrupting his thoughts, 'if you decide to try and do something desperate, then let me tell you that I won't like it, but I'll make sure something terrible happens to DS Moone's family. Ivan here would take care of it.'

Jairus turned round and stared at the solid man in the suit who gave a single nod.

'What do you expect me to do?'

Crow pointed to the door, and Ivan stepped aside, allowing Jairus to step back into the office. Crow locked the vault again and sat back down at his desk. 'There is one little loose end that needs tying up. Gina Colman. I'm afraid I can't have her talking to anyone. It's too risky. I need her brought to me. That'll be your job.'

'You're fucking joking.' Jairus leaned over the desk, glaring at Crow.

'No I'm not. I'm deadly serious. And you don't have any choice. I'll give you until tomorrow at midnight. Bring her to Braxton House. I'll meet you there. And Ivan will meet us there too just in case you try anything.'

'I'M A FUCKING POLICEMAN!'

Crow nodded. 'And you were a policeman when you murdered Carl Murphy.'

'There's a guard on her door. And there are CCTV cameras.'

'You'll think of something. You're very resourceful. Now, if you wouldn't mind leaving.'

Jairus stood up straight and stared at Crow for a moment, watching him turn back to his computer screen, then pick up his phone.

He turned round swiftly and headed back to the door.

CHAPTER 37

With his hand grasping the wall, Marsland rested for a moment. He caught his breath, trying to shake away the fog from his brain. He stood up and straightened his jacket and walked as straight as he could to the front door and rang the bell.

He leaned against the wall, listening for the tell-tale sounds of someone coming to the door. He was sorry that Moone had had to go back to his duties. He could have done with someone to keep him steady. Maybe leaving hospital so soon wasn't such a good idea, but then he wanted to get things neatly sorted out before he could return to his fatherly duties.

The door opened and a short man, around seventy years old with only a tuft of white hair at the centre of his scalp, appeared.

'Percy Johns?'

'Yes, that's right. What can I do for you?'

'Is your wife home?' Marsland rested against the wall again.

'Well, yes, she is, but what's...' The man looked deeply at Marsland. 'Are you alright? You look white as a sheet.'

'I don't feel great.'

'Come in,' the man said, helping Marsland down the hall and into a flowery living room.

Marsland found himself sitting in a very large and

flowery armchair. 'Thanks.'

'I'll call Bren and tell her you're here. How about a cup of tea?'

'Thanks, that'd be great.'

Mr Johns walked out into the hall and Marsland heard him travel halfway up the stairs and call out his wife's name. A few words were exchanged, then Brenda Johns came into the room. She was a small but round old lady with grey permed hair.

'Hello, love,' she said. 'Can we help you?'

'I'm Terence Marsland. I'm sorry to disturb you, but I wondered if you know a woman called Jacqui. I heard you run the Thursday night club and that she goes regularly.'

'That's right. But I haven't seen Jacqui for ages. I organise it, but I spend most of my time at home these days, love. Percy can hardly walk when his sciatica kicks in.'

'I see. Do you know much about her?'

She was about to answer when Percy came wobbling in with a tray of mugs.

'Here we go, a nice cup of tea will sort you out,' Percy said and put down the tray on the coffee table. 'The colour's returned to your face a bit now.'

Marsland took his tea, and looked expectantly at Mrs Johns.

'Where was I?' she said, scratching her neck.

'Jacqui?' Marsland prompted.

'Oh yes, I haven't seen her in a while. Don't know much about her really. Keeps herself to herself. My mate Margaret said she's seen her going to church on Sundays. She's a nice lady really. What's this all about then? You're not her husband, are you?'

'No, I'm not. I'm an old friend and I thought I'd look her up, but all I knew was that she went to the club on Thursdays. Don't suppose you've got an address for her?'

'Well, yes, I have. Percy, you've given her a lift before, haven't you? You must know where Jacqui lives.'

Percy sipped his tea. 'Jacqui? Yes, I dropped her off about a month ago. Lives off Carterhatch Road. Why's he want to know about Jacqui?'

'Why don't you ask him yourself? He's sitting right there.'

'I'm an old friend,' Marsland repeated.

'Well, if you want to go, I'll drop you off there. I want to pop to the shops anyway.'

Marsland shook his head. 'It's OK. I can make my own way there. I can get the bus.'

'You're not getting on the bus,' Mr Johns laughed. 'You look bloody terrible. I'll drive you. Finish your tea and I'll take you.'

'Thanks. That's really kind of you. By the way, do you know anything about her sons?'

It was Bren who rolled her eyes as she took up her tea. 'Well, as far as I can gather, one son is in prison and the other...well, he's no longer with us...God rest his pour soul.'

'Do you know what happened to him?'

'I think...and I could be wrong but another friend of mine told me he killed himself. And apparently he was only young.'

'I see.'

'I think that's when she found God. Anyway that's all I know.'

Marsland sipped his tea. The woman he was building a picture of was a sad and lonely lady that life had been very brutal to. He was now even more determined to find her and help her in some way. But once again he promised himself, and Daisy, that it would be the last time he'd poke his nose in.

As soon as Moone received the text, he jumped in his car. He had a strange feeling as he drove over to North Middlesex Hospital, a kind of prophetic insight into things; everything had changed in the last couple of weeks, and he'd realised a few days ago that nothing would be the same again. How exactly right he would be, he hadn't known. Now he was heading to the morgue, realising with an eerie tightness in spine and shoulders, and a few black-winged moths in his gut, that he was about to lay eyes on his colleague for the last time.

He still couldn't register that she was gone, that he would no longer see her sitting at her desk in the corner of the incident room. Her face came to mind, but it was blurry, fading already. He told himself he'd find a photograph and put it up in the incident room.

Moone took the lift down to the morgue, then walked the long lime corridor and through the double doors. He stopped before the viewing room, leaned his back against the wall and took in a few deep breaths. He nodded to himself, hearing the distant sound of a trolley rolling across a floor somewhere. He pushed open the door that led to the narrow corridor. It was painted white, and near the end was the window that allowed the mourner to view their departed.

Jairus was hunched over on one of the leather chairs opposite the mirror, his face buried in his hands. Moone made his approach as loud as possible. Jairus took his face from his hands and wiped his eyes.

'Sit down, mate.'

Moone sat down and looked up at the window, feeling his heart drop a little. 'How're you doing?'

Jairus gave an empty laugh. 'Yeah, I'm great. Managed to get one of my colleagues killed...'

'That wasn't your fault.'

'Wasn't it? Feels like it. I've made quite a few mistakes lately, and people seem to be dying all round me.'

Moone stood up, but looked away from the window. 'That's just the way it is. Bad things happen.' Then he looked round and fixed his eyes on the purple sheet that was lying over the body in the centre of the tiny room. He looked at her blank, expressionless face. He couldn't quite connect the body to the one that had moved so gracefully round the station, had smiled at him on so many occasions, always taking the piss out of him.

'Pete...' Jairus said, his voice seeming very distant.

Moone sat down beside him again.

'If you found yourself in a situation where you ended up with your back against the wall...and the only way out meant doing something that was wrong... but by doing it you saved one of your friends...would you do it?'

Moone stared at his friend and his eyes looked back at him with pleading. He saw a man at the end of his world, everything spinning out of control around him. 'If it meant saving someone? How bad is the bad thing?'

'Pretty bad.'

Moone looked at the wall opposite. 'I'd have to weigh it up, but I guess if I had no choice...'

'Then you'd do anything you could to save that person?'

Moone nodded, even though he could see the answer to the question might be the wrong one. Part of him wanted to run to Napper and spill his concerns in front of her, to tell her exactly what Jairus had just said to him, and all the doubtful, dark things he suspected he had done in the last fortnight. Then he watched Jairus' expression change, the light come on again in his eyes, his fists clenched at his side as he got to his feet.

'Thanks, Pete.' Jairus rubbed his eyes.

'You've made up your mind?'

'Yeah, I have.' Then Jairus turned to him. 'But I'm going to need you to do something for me.'

'Go on.' Moone's stomach knotted.

'Nothing bad. There's going to be an anonymous tip-off coming into the station about a dodgy character. He might be a bit dangerous. I'm going to need you to lead the search of his house. Better take a couple of armed officers with you. Can you do that?'

Moone breathed in. 'If an anonymous tip-off comes in...then I guess I have to follow it up.'

Jairus squeezed his shoulder, took out his phone, dialled a number and put it to his ear as he walked along the corridor. 'Thanks, Pete.'

Mr Johns stopped the car and pulled on the handbrake. The house had a red-brick wall all round it and some large black gates.

'That's where I dropped her off last time,' Johns said.

'Does she live alone?'

Johns shrugged. 'I don't know. She seems pretty lonely, so I reckon she might.'

Marsland opened the car door. 'Thanks for the lift. I really appreciate it.'

'I'll wait for you, if you like.'

'No, you don't need to do that. I'll get a taxi home. In fact I might head back to the hospital.'

'You do look a bit green.'

Marsland smiled and pulled himself out.

He opened the gate that squeaked and then pressed the door bell. He pressed it a couple of times before he heard the lock being opened.

Jacqui's face appeared and immediately went from surprise to shock horror. The door began to shut again, but Marsland pressed his hand against it.

'Hey, it's me, Terry. I thought I'd come and see how you are.'

'Please leave me alone.' Jacqui tried to push the door closed, forcing Marsland to put all his weakening his strength into holding it open.

'What's wrong? I just feel like I owe you an apology.'

'You don't. Just go! Please. Please leave.'

The door shut in his face, and he stepped back, the dizziness invading his brain once more. He felt very much like retreating, to go off and have time to think of another battle plan, but anger suddenly rose through him.

He took a moment to calm himself, then rang the bell, hammered his hand on the door and flapped the letterbox. Jacqui opened the door again, her cheeks red and her eyes wide. 'Please, Terry. Please go away. Please. This isn't a good time.'

'Let me in and we can talk about it,' Marsland said and quickly pushed the door open, forcing her to get back against the wall. He jerked back as she gripped his arm, her voice now just a shallow sound in his ear.

'Terry...listen, I'll meet you in...' She stopped, a word caught her throat, her eyes rising upwards.

Marsland looked up when he heard the creak of floorboards above them. 'Who's that?'

'No one. Look, Terry...'

'Mum!' a young man's voice called out impatiently.

'Who was at the door?'

'No one, love.' Jacqui's eyes jumped to Marsland and he saw the absolute horror in them in.

Then the footsteps came down the stairs, and he could see she flinched with every one.

The young man, who was wearing a light blue vest, his arms covered in tattoos, stopped halfway down the stairs and took in Marsland for a second, then his eyes jumped to his mother. 'Who the fuck is this?'

'You can talk to me if you really want to know,' Marsland said, feeling Jacqui's nails bite into his arm.

The young man came down the stairs and stood a little taller than Marsland. 'Alright, who the fuck're you?'

Marsland was about to introduce himself, when Jacqui said, 'This is my friend, Terry.'

'Your friend?'

Jacqui nodded. 'Terry, this is my eldest boy, Nathan.'

'Nice to meet you, Nathan.' Marsland watched the boy take him in and nod, then walk back towards the kitchen. He stopped and took a pack of cigarettes from his jogging bottoms. He put one between his lips. 'Why don't we all sit down and have a cuppa like a normal bunch of people. Not that there's anything normal about this fucking family, Terry.'

'Don't talk like that, love.' Jacqui left Marsland and hurried towards the kitchen. 'I'll put the kettle on.'

Nathan took out a lighter and lit his cigarette. 'What's your story, Terry?'

'My story? It's not very interesting.'

'I've just got out of nick. Your story's got to be more riveting than mine. Every fucker inside has got the same fucking story. They got fucking caught.'

'Mind your language, Nathan,' Jacqui said, her voice trembling. She filled the kettle and put out some mugs.

Marsland watched the young man take in a deep draw of his cigarette, then turn and walk into the kitchen. He suddenly wanted to be anywhere but in the house with these two. He was getting a strange sensation as he walked towards the kitchen. He wasn't sure if it was Jacqui's extraordinary fear of her son, or something else, but he was now on edge. Something bad had happened in their lives, and Marsland thought of the youngest son, now departed. He'd committed suicide, the Johns had informed him, or at least that's what they had been told.

Marsland stood in the kitchen and made eye contact with Jacqui. Her eyes were wide, a little wet and she was shaking. Then he noticed something gripped in her hand that she had taken from her pocket. He moved to the side of her as Nathan sat down and continued smoking at the kitchen table. Marsland subtlety reached down and clasped her hand and lifted it a little. She opened her hand, revealing the small gold crucifix that she had gripped so tightly it had left red angry marks in her palm. He looked up and saw the tears pouring from her face. Now she openly sobbed.

Nathan jerked his head round to her, then his eyes, dark and filled with suspicion, jumped to Marsland. 'What the fuck have you said to her?'

'Nothing,' Marsland said and faced the young man. 'But I'm starting to wonder why your mother seems so terrified of you.'

Nathan took the cigarette from his mouth and let out a laugh. 'Terrified of me? Fuck's sake. Mum, are you scared of me?'

Jacqui shook her head and grabbed some kitchen towels to wipe her eyes. 'No, course not, love. I'm just a bit out of sorts today.'

'Who is this fucker?' Nathan pointed his cigarette at Marsland.

'He's my friend. I already told you.'

'No, you haven't told me anything.' Nathan stood up and stubbed out his cigarette, and moved towards Marsland. 'You tell me. Who the fuck are you?'

'Nathan, please don't be like this,' Jacqui pleaded.

'Shut up.' Nathan turned his eyes back to Marsland. 'So?'

Marsland could hardly think straight. The strength was leaking out of him and the dizziness was now tightly wrapped round his skull. 'My name is Terence Marsland.'

Nathan seemed to chew on this for a moment, then looked at his mother. 'Why do I know that name?'

She looked down.

'Mum?' Nathan gripped her chin and jerked her head up. 'Why do I know that name?'

Marsland found his hand grasping Nathan's wrist and tearing him away from Jacqui. Then suddenly he was being choked, a large hand digging into his neck. Marsland focused on the wild eyes burning into his.

'Who the fuck are you?'

'He's a frie...' Jacqui begun, but was shoved sideways and she crumpled to the floor.

'My name is Terence Marsland...and I used to be a policeman.'

Nathan let go of his neck and stood back a little. His eyes focused, then came a sudden darkness being pulled over his thoughts. He pointed a finger at Marsland. 'You're fucking him, aren't you? Is that fucking him, Mum?'

Jacqui pulled herself to her feet. 'Yes, it is, but it's not like that now. I found him Nathan. I found him and got to know him so I could tell you that's he's a good man.'

The realisation swept over Marsland and he wanted to throw up. 'Jacqui? What was your younger son called?'

Nathan ripped forward, his lips curled back, his face an inch from Marsland's. 'Shaun! He was called Shaun! Shaun Clarke! Do you remember that name? Do you remember him?!'

The name and face came back to him. The young man who had been in trouble with the police for several minor offences. Then the major one, trying to rob a local petrol station. It had escalated to violence because of the older lad he was with. Shaun Clarke got a year in prison. When Marsland talked to him across the interview room, he had the feeling that he was doing it all to impress his older brother, the hard man and habitual criminal of the area.

He looked up and saw the guilt and fury in the eyes of Nathan. The fist bolted Marsland sideways, buckling his legs and nearly dropping him to the kitchen floor.

Jacqui pulled Marsland up and turned to face her son. 'Nathan, listen to me. I've asked for God's forgiveness. I've prayed for us all...'

'Oh shut up! Shut up with all that bollocks! I told you! I told you what I would do when I got out! Didn't I?'

'That's why I found him. I wanted you to know that he's a good man. He wasn't to know what Shaun would do.'

'I don't fucking want to hear it!' Nathan swept round, bellowed out a pained shout, then turned round to Marsland, jabbing his finger at him. 'You fucking killed him! You might as well have tied the fucking sheet round his neck!'

'I had to do my job,' Marsland said. 'I really wish things had worked out differently, I really do.'

'He's telling the truth!' Jacqui said, touching her son's arm.

He shrugged her away. 'Stop sticking up for him. How can you forgive him for what he did? Shaun's not here because of him! Can you live with that? Cause I can't.'

Marsland saw something then. He recognised the look in the boy's eye. A complete blanket of hatred covered him and now there was little chance of it lifting again. His best chance was to get out of the house.

'I think I better go.' Marsland began to walk to the kitchen door, but Nathan knocked him out of the way and filled the doorway.

'You're staying right fucking here.'

'I know you're angry, Nathan,' Marsland said, 'but you have to try and calm down. You don't want to do something that'll land you in prison again.'

'I don't care. Do you think I fucking care?' Nathan went quickly up the hall and pounded up the stairs.

Jacqui grabbed Marsland's sleeve and began pulling him towards the door. 'You better go. Give him a chance to cool down.'

'OK, but maybe you should...'

'Where the fuck do you think you're going?'

Marsland turned round and saw Nathan standing halfway up the stairs. Then he saw the gun in his hand. 'Nathan. Don't do it. Whatever you're thinking, you would regret it.'

Nathan came down the last few steps, the gun now pointing at Marsland. 'Get back in the kitchen. Go on, and you, Mum.'

'Nathan, put that down.' Jacqui walked towards the kitchen, her head twisting to stare at her son, the horror stealing the colour from her face. 'Please, Nathan. Think of your brother.'

'I am thinking of Shaun. I've done nothing but think of Shaun.'

Marsland placed his hand against the wall, keeping himself steady, staring at the gun. 'Why don't you let your mum leave, Nathan, and me and you can talk about all this?'

'I want her to see this. I want her to see you on your knees.'

Marsland backed his way into the kitchen, finding himself hitting the kitchen table. Now the gun was lifted, shaking a little not far from his face. The eyes behind the gun were fixed on him, the mouth under them opening and shutting. But a high-pitched noise seemed to be filling Marsland's head, and his heartbeat was in his skull. He felt like he was falling and the earth was no longer under his feet.

Then Jacqui was in front of him, grabbing her son. Nathan put his arm round her, trying to push her away. Marsland rushed forward, but Jacqui slammed backwards into him. Then the gun was lifted to him again. The eyes staring out to him.

Marsland saw him squeezing the trigger.

The blast filled the room, and the shudder and wave of it passed through Marsland. He saw Jacqui slump to the floor and fall to one side. A circle of deep red blood blossomed from her chest as Nathan let out a howl. He fell to his knees, his eye momentarily taking in Marsland, as if he was pleading with him for a moment. Marsland crouched down and pressed down on the wound, then felt her neck with his other hand. There seemed to be no pulse. His eyes flickered when he saw the gun lift, expecting it to point towards him.

Nathan turned the gun and put it into his mouth.

With his bloody hand reaching for the gun, the boom bellowed out once again and punched into his ears. Marsland collapsed onto his backside. Somewhere during his time staring at the people sitting quietly around him, a siren began to scream distantly, growing louder and louder.

CHAPTER 38

Jairus pulled up across the street from the Victorian town house. It was painted white and black and had two pillars on either side of the front door. He watched DS Moone and a few constables go up the stone steps to present the search warrant. He lowered his head and watched for signs of life upstairs. Someone panicked. The blinds opened then quickly shut.

Jairus looked at his watch and saw that it was nearly nine p.m. His head shot up when he heard the thud of the battering ram slam into the door. The officers poured into the house and for the next few minutes shouting came out of the front door. Four constables came out with their arms wrapped round Ivan Kaverin, forcing him forwards, all ignoring the angry and abusive protests coming from his mouth. Once the Russian was escorted to an awaiting van, Jairus climbed out and headed for the house, his hands deep into his pockets.

DS Moone walked along the real wood floors and took in the expanse of the building. There was little furniture. The Russian liked to live a minimalist life it seemed. Maybe it was all the time he'd spent behind bars, Moone decided, knowing that like the army, it sometimes leaves inmates with a dislike for clutter and disorder.

Moone started up the stairs as no one had begun the search in the top floor of the house. As Jairus had suspiciously predicted, an anonymous tip-off had been supplied over the telephone claiming that a man called Ivan could be found at that particular address and he was in possession of illegal firearms.

Moone was too tired to even think about the ramifications of Jairus' actions over the last week, and supposed that forthcoming investigations into his actions would bring about their own conclusions. The man was his friend, but he could defend him only so far. His other friend, Marsland was now back in the hospital. The doctors were treating him for shock, but said he would make a full recovery. Moone just felt terrible that he hadn't recognised Jacqui as the mother of Shaun Clarke.

Moone stopped and turned round when he heard heavy footsteps behind him on the wooden steps. Jairus was now coming up the stairs with his hands buried in his pockets.

'Hey, Pete,' Jairus said and overtook him. 'I see you got Ivan banged up outside.'

'Yes, but what the bloody hell are you doing here?'

Jairus stopped at the top of the stairs. 'Thought I'd help you search the place. You done his bedroom yet?'

'No. What the bloody hell's going on?'

Jairus smiled. 'Nothing, just giving you a helping hand.'

When Moone entered the bedroom a few seconds after Jairus he found him with his back to the large window looking down at the bed that was in disarray. Jairus nodded to Moone. 'He's a messy bastard, this Russian.'

Moone looked around the room and then back to Jairus who was now wearing blue latex gloves. 'Did you find anything?'

'Yeah, a machine gun and a few grenades.' Jairus laughed, but Moone saw no signs of humour in his eyes.

'Hey, Jay,' Moone said and walked round the bed. 'You OK? You're really starting to worry me, mate.'

'Yeah, I'm fine. Got a few things to sort out, but it'll all be sorted soon.'

Jairus headed for the door. 'Oh, and can you do me a favour and keep our Russian friend busy for a few hours?'

'Any chance you going to tell me why?'

'No.'

Moone sighed, feeling the tension twisting his shoulders and neck again. 'I'll do my best, but I haven't got much to hold him on. He could easily walk out of the station in an hour.'

'Just do your best.'

'And we can't find his car,' Moone called out, but Jairus' heavy footsteps pounded down the wood stairs.

Jairus kept walking along the lime green corridor, striding as fast as he could, keeping his head down, desperately trying not to bring any attention to himself. He looked at his watch. It was just gone 11 p.m. It was tight, but he could make the meeting. All he had to do was keep up his end of the bargain and all would be done. What choice did he have now but to go through with it?

He hesitated at the end of the corridor, looking up at the sign opposite telling him to turn right for the Camberra ward. He took a deep breath and buried all the doubts and his moral convictions and swung right and headed for the police constable who was sat reading a magazine outside Gina Colman's room. The whole ward was quiet and Jairus could only see one nurse sitting at the nurses' station right at the far end.

The constable stood up sharply when Jairus showed his ID.

'Anything to report?' Jairus asked and looked into the window and saw the silent figure of Gina Colman.

'Nothing, sir. I've had a family in again tonight and counsellors have been in to see her all the time. She isn't really responding to anything.'

Jairus looked the PC in the eyes. 'You must be thirsty or hungry.'

'I'm OK. Had a tea about...well, a while ago.'

'Yeah? Well, go to the canteen and get a coffee or something. I'll stay here.'

The PC looked pleasantly surprised as he grabbed his stuff together. 'You sure that's OK, sir?'

'Yeah, I'd like to keep an eye on her.'

'Thanks,' the constable said and headed towards the bank of lifts.

Once he was sure the PC had gone, Jairus opened the door to the room and stepped inside. The girl was curled up on her left side, facing the window. He walked round and saw that her eyes were closed and fluttering. He stood there for a moment, clenching and unclenching his fists, trying to come to terms with what he was about to do. When he heard a squeak along the corridor, he headed out the door and found Adrian Wells, with his hood pulled up over his head, pushing a wheelchair towards him.

'I've just seen a fucking copper,' Wells said nervously, his eyes jumping round the corridor.

'Yeah, I know, but he's gone for a break. We don't have much time.'

'You really doing this?' Wells stopped as he was

about to push the chair into the room.

'I have to. I don't have any other choice.'

'And why the fuck am I helping?'

'Because you don't have any choice. And I'll owe you.'

Wells gently pushed the chair into Gina Colman's room and steered it carefully round the bed. 'Bloody right you will.'

'Shut up and help me.'

Together they gently lifted the girl from the bed and sat her upright, then got the wheelchair in the right position. The girl's eyes seemed to open for a moment, but did not seem to see either of them at all. Jairus looked down at her and paused, frozen to the spot.

Wells was staring at him. 'What is it?'

'I wonder if she's aware of what's happening.'

'Does it matter?'

Jairus watched the girl for a moment, feeling his stomach sink down to the floor. He nodded. 'It's just the thought of taking her back there...'

'Make up your mind.'

Jairus scooped her up in his arms, feeling the nothingness of her, and put her in the wheelchair. He took a blanket from a nearby chair and put it over her. He stood back as Wells pushed her out of the room. Then he followed, feeling the anger and sickness mixing together and spreading through him, contaminating his thoughts as he walked towards his darkest moment.

A pool of moonlight illuminated the floor of his hospital room keeping Marsland awake. He pulled himself up and stared across at the window and the cool shimmer of silver light that radiated through the glass, forming the square of perfect light. He wondered for a moment on the perfectness of it and the total imperfectness of people. How could nature be so formulated and efficient and divisive in its ruthlessness, when humans were the complete opposite? But there were humans who lacked the emotional weaknesses and delights of others, and they were those who seemed to act on immoral instinct. Killing. Causing suffering for the sheer pleasure of it, or, like Nathan Clarke, in pure hatred.

Marsland pushed the image of the dead mother and son from his mind as he shivered and wrapped his arms round himself. He was empty now, and felt as if he had been set adrift. He imagined going back to his lonely existence inside the quiet walls of his new home. For so long he had found solace there in the absence of others, alone with his own thoughts. He was loathed to enter his home, seeing it more now as a prison than a home. Perhaps, he decided, it was some kind of punishment for the pain and destruction he had brought in his wake.

It was a few seconds before he realised there was a figure in the doorway, and when he did he assumed it was one of the nurses. He turned his head and saw Dylan staring at him. A smile came to Marsland's face.

'Dylan? What're you doing here?'

Dylan stepped into the room. 'Your friend, Peter Moone, he called me and told me what happened.'

Marsland nodded. 'Did he? Well, look at me, you were right…I poked my nose in again and look what happened.'

'Yes, I told you what would happen. I keep telling you.' Dylan came closer.

'I just wanted to help her. I thought…well, I thought I could help. I suppose that's why I keep trying to help people, because I feel bad for all the stuff…'

'The way you just turned your back on us when Mum died?'

Marsland looked down at his hand, unable to look up and see the anger and disappointment that he knew would be in his son's eyes. 'Yes. I just…I couldn't… and Daisy…if I hadn't… oh God, if I just hadn't got involved…'

'I want to tell you something,' Dylan said, walking along the bed and stopping by his father.

'Yes?'

'I've always been proud of you. I always have been. You've always put other people first, tried to help them, even at your own cost. And I know that Daisy was proud of you too. She told me not long before she came to stay with you. I know she must be proud of you now.'

Dylan put his arms round his father and squeezed. Marsland sat there for a moment, his hands still resting on his lap, his mouth opening to say something, feeling the myriad of emotions beating about his brain. He lifted his arms and hugged his son back.

'I'm proud of you too,' Marsland said and could not stop the sobbing.

CHAPTER 39

Jairus parked round the side of Braxton House, then his eyes fixed on the figure on the back seat, a skeletal shape under the blanket. She murmured, and an invisible piece of ice stabbed into his spine. He leaned forward and buried his head into his chest, then pressed his face against the steering wheel. His body shook as he let out the tears that had been building up. He no longer listened to the whimpering as it had grown quieter since he'd made the worst decision of his life, perhaps giving satisfaction to his demons.

He looked up suddenly when he heard the sound of another car engine crawling along towards him. He could barely see a figure at the wheel of the sleek black Mercedes. It had to be Raymond Crow.

The car door opened and a man stepped out and stood looking towards his car for a minute or so. Jairus climbed out and showed himself, put his hands out to show they were empty. He turned and looked at the girl on the back seat and said a silent sorry to her and walked slowly towards Crow.

'It's a nice peaceful night and the moon is shining,' Crow said, but his eyes jumped to Jairus' car. 'Is she in there?'

Jairus nodded. 'Yeah, she is. What are you planning on doing to her?'

Crow smiled. 'I just need to make sure she doesn't

tell anyone about all the things she's seen.'

'See, that's what I don't get,' Jairus said, watching Crow stepping over to his car. 'You gave the impression that you didn't like having the girls treated in such a way, but I think you're afraid of her identifying you. Why is that?'

Crow removed his smile. 'Stop asking questions and get her out of there.'

Crow was taking some keys out of his pocket when a silver BMW appeared at the far end of driveway they were standing on. Jairus looked towards the car, but it was impossible to see who was sitting at the wheel. The BMW's lights flashed, and Crow, now with his hand shielding his eyes, nodded and turned to Jairus. 'That's Ivan. You better get her out and hurry up about it. You don't want Ivan upset with you.'

Jairus looked towards the silver car for a moment, then heavily walked to his own car and opened the passenger door. The girl looked peaceful and he felt his heart being torn at, clawed by his own morality. He closed his eyes, breathed deeply and carried her from the car.

Crow had rushed towards the house and opened the front door and waited there looking about him, his hand tapping at his side. When Jairus approached him he caught a glimpse of his face in the moonlight and saw his eyes were wild. He had transformed from the smart, resourceful banker into something much more animalistic.

'Downstairs,' Crow barked. 'And hurry up, you stupid fucker.'

Jairus carried Gina Colman back down the stone steps where they had rescued her from, where he himself had lifted her back into the light. Now he was delivering her back to Hell, back into the arms of

Satan himself.

Crow hurried down the stairs and pulled open the secret door that led into the dungeon. The stench gripped Jairus' face and for a moment the girl seemed to stir. He prayed she would not awake from her peaceful sleep now. Not now, please not now.

'Put her on the bed.' Crow pulled open the door to the small dirty room with the metal bed.

'Why?' Jairus stood still.

'You know why.' Crow pulled off his tie in two quick moments, his eyes now wide and staring.

'You raped her too, didn't you?'

'Does it really matter? Get her on the bed. Now. Remember, Jairus, that you work for me now. I can make you rich and successful, or I can break you to pieces. Your choice.'

'I do not work for you.'

Jairus flinched a little, when Crow almost leapt forward, his fist waving in the air, his eyes even crazier.

'YOU WORK FOR ME! YOU DO WHAT I SAY!'

Jairus crouched down and put the girl on the floor and stood up. He moved his arm round to his back and pulled out the gun he had taken from Ivan's house. Crow's eyes jumped to it with more confusion than horror or shock.

'What do you think you're doing?'

'You're going to tell me why you did all this. Or I'm going to shoot you in the head.'

'Fuck you. You wouldn't.'

'I've already killed one suspect.'

'Put her on the bed.'

Jairus lifted the gun. He pulled the trigger.

Crow let out a scream and collapsed to the floor, grasping for his knee, that was now a volcano of blood. He writhed around, hurling abuse. Then he looked up, breathing hard and laughing a little. 'My grandfather, a very successful owner of a haulage company, joined the Freemasons so he could get further ahead in life. They promised him so much success, even though he was working class. They said that God did not worry about such things as class, and God is what they all believed in. Fuck. You shot me. You fucking…'

'Keep talking.'

'He got throat cancer. He was dying. Did they come and see him, did they make him more comfortable, or try and help? No, they stood by and waited for him to die. And do you know what they did? You'll love this. They gave my grandmother a coffin to bury him in with the Freemasons' symbol on it. That's it. That's all they did.'

The fury lifted, spread out above him like a cloud, pulling in and reining the darkness that seemed to engulf him. He nodded to himself, as an explosion of blood in his chest seemed to pump the fury to every part of him. 'That's all? That's why you put this girl through hell?'

But Crow only laughed, and kept clutching at the hole in his leg.

Jairus picked up the girl and carried her out of the dungeon and back up the stairs and out of the house. He passed his own car and headed for the silver BMW.

Adrian Wells climbed out and helped him put the girl in the back of the car. He placed the blanket carefully over her and shut the door again.

'Now what?' Wells asked.

Jairus did not reply, just went to his own car and opened the boot. He closed off his mind as he opened the bag he had put in the back. He took out the forensic outfit and slipped it on. He put on some rubber boots too, then carried the bag towards the house, only

stopping to face Wells. 'Take her back to the hospital.'
Wells nodded.

But Wells did not go back to the hospital straight away. He followed Jairus into Braxton House and down the stone steps, watching the tall and broad shape of the man dressed in the shiny white suit. Jairus stopped in the doorway to the dungeon, where the sound of Crow shouting and moaning was drifting from.

Jairus turned round as he opened the door and stepped inside. Wells looked at the bag that was open. He saw some knives and what he thought was an electric saw. He stepped back, and looked up into the dark, blank eyes that exchanged glances with him.

Then Jairus closed the door behind him.

Printed in Great Britain
by Amazon